KU-599-370

MICHAEL JECKS

The Tournament of Blood

**SIMON &
SCHUSTER**

London · New York · Sydney · Toronto · New Delhi

A CBS COMPANY

First published in 2001 by Headline Book Publishing

This edition published in Great Britain in 2013 by Simon & Schuster UK Ltd
A CBS COMPANY

1 3 5 7 9 10 8 6 4 2

Simon & Schuster UK Ltd
1st Floor
222 Gray's Inn Road
London
WC1X 8HB

www.simonandschuster.co.uk

Simon & Schuster Australia, Sydney

Simon & Schuster India, New Delhi

A CIP catalogue copy for this book is available
from the British Library.

ISBN: 978-1-47112-627-7
eBook ISBN: 978-1-47112-628-4

Typeset by Hewer Text UK Ltd, Edinburgh
Illustrations © Jill Tytherleigh
Printed and bound in Great Britain by CPI Group (UK) Ltd, Croydon, CR0 4YY

For
Katie Marjorie Bond Jecks,
with all a father's love.

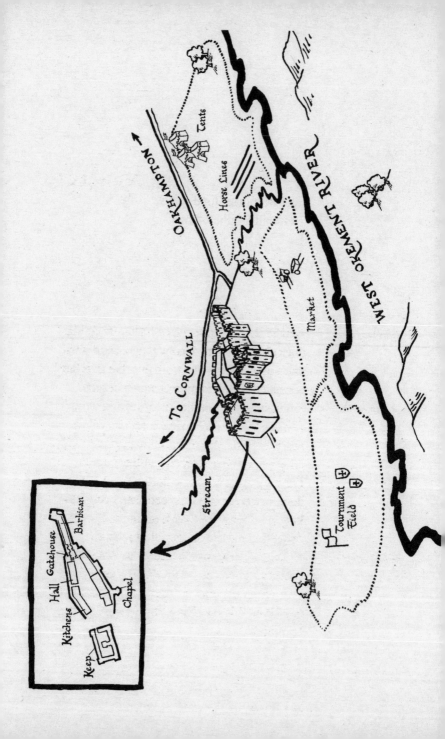

GLOSSARY

Aketon　A long-sleeved garment, of fustian or similar thick cloth, often padded with wool and sewn like a quilt, which was worn over the shirt but beneath the mail to protect a man-at-arms.

À outrance　Fighting under conditions of war. In a tournament this meant using weapons of war: sharp sword, sharp lance, dagger and all other equipment including full armour.

À plaisance　Fighting for show or entertainment. When demonstrating their speed and prowess, knights often used bated, or blunted, weapons to reduce the danger of bloodshed.

Banneret　A knight who was entitled to command other knights and men-at-arms under his own banner; also a title of knighthood conferred by the King for valour on the battlefield.

1

Béhourd

This was a limited *hastilude* between squires or training knights, occasionally an impromptu response to a celebration. Sometimes events had the knights wearing *cuir bouilli* and fighting with whalebone swords, such as at the 'Joust of Peace' at Windsor in 1278.

Ber frois

The grandstands built to accommodate ladies, nobles and the wealthier classes. They would have surrounded the main fighting area, forming an oblong so that knights could run *courses* against each other directly in front of the spectators.

Coat armour

Over the *pair of plates* a knight would wear a decorative tunic upon which he would have his heraldic symbols, his 'arms'. From this the tunic came to be called *coat armour*. It didn't offer protection from attack, it only emphasised the nobility of the wearer. Also called *gypon*.

Collée

This was the term given to the light blow from the hand, according to the *Ordène de Chevalerie* and other contemporary books dealing with knighthood. The *collée* was given by the man who had girded the new knight with his sword, and commonly it was given by the fellow's lord. It was only rarely given by the King himself except after a battle or tournament, at which times it was worthwhile making knights to reward them. The Church tried to take over the dubbing of knights, just as they took on the responsibility of crowning kings, in an attempt to demonstrate that priests were superior to warriors, but they did not succeed.

Commencailles The initial stage of a *mêlée* or medley in which a few knights selected for their skill would display their abilities in preliminary skirmishes before the main fight.

Course One run through the *lists*, so one attempt to hit an opposing knight.

Cuir bouilli Leather boiled, shaped and hardened to form a solid, but light covering, used to protect both men and horses.

Diseur Just as with any sport, rules were invented and must be monitored by professional judges. These referees were called *diseurs*.

À l'estoc Literally 'at the point' of a sword. *Estoc* was sometimes used to mean a vicious thrust into the chest cavity, under the ribs and leading upwards into heart and lungs: a killing blow.

Gypon See *Coat armour* above.

Harbinger The members of a household sent on before the Lord's arrival in a new location to prepare the way for him, ensuring that rooms were available at inns en route and finally making the destination ready. Often a rich man like Lord Hugh would have *harbingers* for his servants as well.

Hastilude Literally 'spear-play' from the Latin *hastiludium*: this word was the common term for a *joust* in the 1300s. I've used 'tournament' and 'joust' in the story because they are better understood by readers in the twenty-first century.

Hauberk   The name given to the coat of mail worn over the *aketon* but beneath the *pair of plates*.

Heralds   *Heralds* grew to importance largely through tournaments, because it was they, the experts in reading heraldic insignia, who must confirm a man's lineage to ensure he was entitled to participate, and call out his name as the knight rode into the lists to *joust*. Afterwards it was the heralds who proclaimed the honour and prowess of the winners.

Heraldry   As warfare and the *mêlée* required ever stronger armour and men's faces became concealed, knights resorted to symbols painted upon shields, pennons and banners so that their footsoldiers and friends could recognise them. This was the basis of *heraldry*, which developed into a systematic means of displaying a man's heredity.

Joust   Generally this meant single combat on horse or on foot. Commonly in this period, a *joust* consisted of: three *courses* run with the lance, three with swords and three more (if both competitors could still stand!) with axes. More recently, of course, a *joust* has come to mean *hastilude*.

Lists
Once the *mêlée* gave way to the rather safer idea of individual knights running *courses* against each other, it was desirable that the clash should take place before the spectators. There was, after all, little point in a knight displaying brilliant prowess in a field half a mile away where no one could see him. Thus *lists* were created: an enclosed space in which the fighting took place.

Mêlée
Also called a *medley*, this was a free-for-all: in essence a battle. All weapons were genuine and there were few rules. The thrill for the participants came from booty: seizing another knight's weapons, horse and armour, as well as taking the man hostage and demanding a ransom. Those who held the field at the end of the day were victors, while the losers must run to the money-lenders.

Misericorde
Literally 'compassion' or 'mercy', this name applied to small shelves for monks to rest on and save their legs during long services, as well as rest homes for monks to recover their health. However, it was also the name of a knight's dagger used to deliver the *coup de grâce* to a wounded comrade.

Pair of plates
The name given to the stout armour worn over the *hauberk*. It comprised a heavy-duty cloth or leather garment which had, on

the inner surface, a series of plates stitched or riveted in place. Often the rivet-heads could be seen, shaped like flowers for decoration. Inside, the plates overlapped to give greater protection. The *pair of plates* was replaced by large individual plates of armour.

Tenant

Occasionally a knight wishing to prove his prowess and strength would issue a challenge to all-comers, promising to fight whomsoever took up his challenge. He was the *tenant*.

Tilt

To prevent horses running into each other while charging, a rope was sometimes slung between two posts, a cloth draped over it, and the horses were supposed to run their courses on the right, with the knights holding their lances to threaten the man approaching on their left. In later years (from about 1420) the rope was replaced by a more substantial, low wooden fence.

Venant

A man who answered a *tenant*'s challenge.

Vespers

Although this commonly meant the sixth canonical service (now called Evensong), *vespers* also meant the eve of a festival. As such it came to mean the vigil day before a tournament and was later used as the technical term for practice runs by knights at each other.

CAST OF CHARACTERS

Sir Baldwin de Furnshill   Once a Knight Templar, Sir Baldwin has returned to his old home in Devon and is Keeper of the King's Peace. He's known to be an astute investigator of violent crime.

Lady Jeanne   His wife, to whom he has been married only a year. Jeanne is a widow whose first husband treated her cruelly, and now she is learning to enjoy married life for the first time.

Edgar   Baldwin's servant and trusted steward. Edgar was Baldwin's Sergeant when he was a Knight Templar and is, like his master, a highly experienced fighter, trained with all weapons.

Simon Puttock   The Bailiff of Lydford is the Stannary Bailiff, responsible for law and order on

	Dartmoor under Abbot Champeaux, the Warden of the Stannaries.
Sir Roger de Gidleigh	Exeter's Coroner and for some months a friend of Sir Baldwin.
Margaret Puttock (Meg)	Simon's wife, daughter of a local farmer, whom he married many years before.
Edith	Simon and Margaret's daughter, nearly fourteen years old.
Hugh	Hugh has been Simon and Margaret's servant for many years. Although the previous year he left them to marry, he has now rejoined them.
Lady Alice	The teenaged daughter of a neighbour of Sir John's, orphaned when she was a small child and subsequently taken by Sir John as his ward.
Squire Andrew	Sir Edmund's squire is a battle-hardened older man with the quick reflexes of a professional man-at-arms.
Sir Peregrine of Barnstaple	Lord Hugh's loyal servant. This banneret is as keen as his lord to see how skilled Lord Hugh's host, his army, is.
Sir Walter Basset	Known for his violence in tournaments, Sir Walter of Cornwall is quick to anger and never forgets an insult. In great debt to money-lenders, he is keen to earn money from a tournament.
Lady Helen	Sir Walter's beautiful and loyal wife.
Wymond Carpenter	Master-builder and craftsman, Wymond has worked alongside Hal for several years. Morose, and truculent with it,

	Wymond is disliked by his workers and others.
Lord Hugh de Courtenay	This nobleman has decided to patronise a tournament, in order to assess the skills and loyalty of his vassals in the wake of the Battle of Boroughbridge, in which Earl Thomas and his men were killed.
Sir John de Crukerne	A knight from West Dorset who is attending the tournament with his son. He is Lady Alice's legal guardian.
Squire William	Sir John's son, whom Sir John would like to see engaged to Alice and who is expecting to be knighted at the tournament.
Benjamin Dudenay	A usurer, Benjamin has often helped knights who need to raise money, either to pay ransoms or to buy arms and armour. He also helps men like Lord Hugh to fund the tournament itself.
Squire Geoffrey	Alice's lover who, like William, anticipates being knighted at the tournament.
Sir Edmund of Gloucester	This wandering knight is without a lord since Boroughbridge and wishes to impress Lord Hugh with his prowess in the lists.
Helewisia	Alice's maid, a servant from Sir John's household.
Herald Odo	A herald who has returned to England after some years in France and Germany learning new songs and a little about the Continental approach to heraldry and tournaments.

Sir Richard Prouse   Grievously wounded many years before in another tournament, Sir Richard is bitter about his hideous scars and disabilities.

Hal Sachevyll   A renowned architect of the buildings involved in a tournament, Hal also considers himself an expert on the pageantry associated with these events. Filled with magnificent ideas which would challenge the purse of a king, he often has to scale down his initial concepts to meet the needs of his clients.

Mark Tyler   Lord Hugh has one herald who remains with him and who bears the title 'King Herald' of his household. Mark is a middle-aged man, sour-natured and jealous of others who might try to take his post.

AUTHOR'S NOTE

When one considers the medieval period, one automatically thinks of damsels in distress and knights in armour. The era is filled with tales of knightly chivalry, of errantry, of honourable fights and pageantry. And one of the most potent symbols of that era of glorious chivalry is the joust. One man against another; both keen to show their prowess and courage.

Hollywood would have us believe that tournaments involved two men riding against each other, both behaving thoroughly courteously, both equal in rank and honour, each one trying to knock his opponent from his horse in as polite a manner as possible. Naturally when one fell, the other would wait until he was on his feet again, and then the two would go at it again, probably stopping for a nice cup of tea to refresh themselves.

But Hollywood hasn't quite got it right. In the early days, tournaments were far from civilised, which is why the Church banned them from the year 1130 at the Council of Clermont.

Tournaments altered over time. There were several different

forms, but all developed from one aim: to teach men to fight in war. The earliest version shows this most clearly, because it was a straightforward battle. Called a *mêlée*, it involved two groups of armed men meeting between two villages or towns (in other words not in a small field but in a non-specific and large battlefield); they charged and fought just as if they were in a real battle, no holds barred. Participants went at each other hammer and tongs, with three or four against one, while others hid behind trees hoping to ambush the unwary. The most unscrupulous might even wait at a nearby tavern until all the contenders were exhausted, then ride in to take as many prisoners as possible. Competitors wanted to win not because of some abstruse concept such as *chivalry* – but for hard cash.

When a knight knocked merry hell out of a competitor in the fight, he could capture the fellow, drag him off the field, and then ransom him. This was how our betters used to behave and was presumably the foundation of the fortunes of several of our leading families. Not only could the knight take a ransom, he could keep his victim's armour and horse. This at a time when a good warhorse could cost as much as £150. To put this into perspective, the salary of a skilled worker was 3d per day, an unskilled worker 1½d per day; thus the horse was worth 12,000 man-days – well over thirty years – for a *skilled* worker. It's no wonder people have estimated the expense of a warhorse to have been roughly the equivalent of a modern battle-tank.

Naturally, capable knights could make themselves large fortunes. One prime example was William the Marshall, who tended to win rather regularly. He and another enterprising young knight formed an alliance in 1177, travelling across Europe from one tournament to another for ten months, sharing their profits equally. They successfully ransomed over 100 knights in that time. Of course such men didn't only win short-term money, either. Often they would catch the eye of a wealthy patron, someone who could give them a more secure future.

This form of limited warfare was conducted under the rules of battle then in force – which more or less suggested it was bad form to execute a prisoner because he was worth more alive – and combatants used real weapons of war. No weapon was banned. Swords and axes were sharpened; maces and clubs, lances and bills were all wielded. Not surprisingly, this resulted in severe injuries and, commonly, death. One of the better-known tournaments was between the British and French at Châlons-sur-Saône in 1273, during which the Count of Châlons caught Edward I about the neck in an attempt to pull him from his horse. Edward apparently deprecated such treatment and lost his temper. So did others. Before long the competitors were joined by their foot-soldiers, and a pitched fight was carried on in earnest. As a result of the deaths and injuries that ensued, this has gone down in history as 'The Little Battle of Châlons'.

Bloodshed was no doubt one of the reasons why the Church set its face against all forms of tournament, but other objections weighed heavily too. The Church disliked the fact that tournaments encouraged dangerous knightly passions: lust and greed. Still, the idea of condoning deaths in the field was not a happy one for bishops or popes. They banned tournaments.

The ban was extensive: no participant could be buried in consecrated ground if he died in the lists. However, this prohibition cannot have succeeded because the Church had to keep repeating the message regularly. We know that knights who died in tournaments *were* routinely buried within churches, cathedrals, graveyards and elsewhere – with supportive churchmen holding the services. Eventually the Church had to give up and permit tournaments once more.

There were, in fact, good reasons why the Church rescinded the ban in 1316. Acre had fallen, meaning that the Kingdom of Jerusalem was lost. It was essential, in the minds of many of the Christians of this time, that a strong force of knights and men-at-arms should be trained for war in order that they could participate in a new Crusade.

The same opinion did not strike so much of a chord with kings throughout Europe. When great lords declared themselves keen to hold tournaments, gathering together all their adherents and peers, trouble could soon follow. For instance, after he had signed Magna Carta, King John's nobles got together and began plotting against him during a tournament.

It is noticeable that strong kings supported tournaments, no doubt seeing in them a means of keeping warlike lords occupied and training up youngsters, while weaker monarchs tended to ban them, fearing, like King John, that the motivation for holding them was more to hatch plots and treason than for the delight of getting beaten about the head by an axe-wielding lunatic on a heavy horse.

British kings, in turn disliking and then promoting tournaments, were far too worldly to think that the Church's prohibition could succeed, so monarchs from Richard I onwards began a tradition followed by successive governments: *when in doubt, tax it.* A fee was charged to hold a tournament, and all those attending must also pay on a scale according to rank.

There were attempts to prevent injuries; Richard I's ordinance was itself partly intended to reduce the butcher's bill. Edward I improved on the safety aspect by requiring participants to swear to keep the peace – and pay for their licence up front! He also restricted the number of followers that men could bring with them, insisting that grooms and footmen should be unarmed, that squires alone should be allowed to join their lords for feasts, and that all weapons should be bated, or blunt. This was known as fighting with arms *à plaisance*, rather than weapons of war, which was called *à outrance*. *Béhourds*, in which men fought with padded leather armour and non-metallic weapons, were popular with the knights; the garments, one imagines, being a great deal lighter and cooler than full armour.

It was at this time that the social aspect of tournaments developed: they became pageants, with market stalls, feasting, dancing and acting on offer for the elite. Expectations of the sports altered and new methods of running tournaments had to be thought up.

Just as today people turn up in their thousands to watch a boxing match or motor race, in the medieval period people wanted to go and watch their heroes battle it out. When the course could be anything up to some ten miles long *and* wide, when all the fighting could take place anywhere within those hundred square miles, it was hard for spectators to see the action – and possibly hazardous too. Far better that the action should be contained in a smaller area, that fighters should be roped off, or stands built for fans, with all the business being presented before them.

To do this, the old system of *mêlée* had to change. Fights started being contained within a 'ring' of sorts, with stands all about. But this was not all. Now, with the growth of chivalrous stories such as those of King Arthur, men wanted to have an opportunity of showing their personal courage and skill. That was impossible in a seething mass of fighting bodies, so the individual tilts began to develop – and as they developed, so rules were designed for them. There was a gradual move away from the massed battle towards the more civilised joust. Only gradually, of course, because in this bloodthirsty age people wanted to see death and mayhem, but there was a move to have tournaments over several days, with jousting acting as a warm-up for two, three or four days, leading to the grand finale of the *mêlée*. One assumes it would have been impractical to reverse this: the knights would all have been sore and probably deaf after the *mêlée*.

King Edward II was always very keen on tournaments: his favourite, Piers Gaveston, was a talented fighter, by all accounts. However, Edward was soon persuaded that tournaments were inherently dangerous and he should not allow them to continue. This was because 289 knights met at Dunstable for a tournament during which they co-ordinated their grievances against Gaveston, which were then related at the following Parliament in the April of 1309. Again, in 1312, a tournament was used as the excuse for a gathering which allowed rebels against Gaveston to raise an army. After this, Edward set himself against any tournaments until 1323 when he submitted to the wishes of his brothers and permitted one.

This being the case, the reader may be surprised that I have decided to set my tournament in 1322. It is even more surprising when one realises that under Richard I's law, only some five specific fields up and down the country were to be used: they were near Salisbury, Stamford, Warwick, Brackly and Blyth. None was near Okehampton.

However, if there is one thing which is clear about history, it is the fact that *nothing is clear*. Even if one hears that hard and fast rules were imposed, one soon learns that the opposite is recorded. When I began to conceive this story, I read of Edward

II's ban on tournaments and was going to try to make the story fit his brothers' event of 1323, but then I heard of a knight who had been forced to flee from a joust and beg for a pardon because he accidentally killed his opponent *in 1318*. This clearly happened during Edward's ban, and equally clearly the location (Luton) wasn't a site selected for licensed tournaments.

I believe that the evidence shows that the kings never intended to stop *all* training for knights. The intention of the royal prohibition was to prevent great multitudes of grandees gathering and plotting the current monarch's downfall. Thus Edward would not have wanted Earl Thomas of Lancaster and the Earl of Pembroke to meet with all their men because the two were powerful and could unite against him – but a lesser baron like Hugh de Courtenay was not in the same league, and if Edward wanted Hugh's men to help in the King's host, should Earl Thomas rebel (as he did), obviously the King would want Hugh's men to be capable of serving him. Therefore I believe that limited 'training' tournaments went on all the time; they were marginally less expensive for participants and were probably looked upon as handy for keeping rural knights and squires in training. England certainly had need of trained fighters – as she has all through history. It is only in the last fifty years that the British Government has become so fearful of its own subjects that successive Parliaments have banned target pistols, shotguns, target rifles, and even pea-shooters.

For those who wish to find out more about knights and tournaments, there are remarkably few good books. One I would recommend is *Chaucer's Knight* by Terry Jones, because although it tells of a time a few decades after this, it is so readable and informative that it is invaluable. I would also recommend *Chivalry* by Maurice Keen, an excellent, scholarly work that explains much about the motivations of knights, squires and heralds. I can also highly recommend *The History of the Tournament in England and France* by F. H. Cripps-Day – but I fear that few will be able to find it, since it was published in 1918.

The main setting for this story is in and about Okehampton Castle. I have always been very keen to pick locations which readers can visit and ideally imagine how things might have been, and Okehampton gives a better impression than many other places.

Tournaments would often have been held in market squares – for the simple reason that contestants and spectators needed access to food, drink, clothing and weaponry. Pictures and wood-cuts show townsfolk looking on as a pair of knights charge each other, or as a small army battered at each other with axes, swords or maces. All about can be seen shops and hucksters, clearly showing that the market continued while the knights fought.

However, I think it's likely that a warlord like Hugh II would have wanted to be closer to the comforts of his castle than in a small town like Okehampton. He would, I think, have wanted to stage a tournament in a more magnificent setting, some-where with the potential for processions, for drama and display. The castle is perfect from this perspective.

I have described the whole setting in the story itself, but perhaps a brief outline of the lands beneath the castle walls would be helpful. In effect it is a series of meadows. The first, at the eastern end, is a tapering area which is not quite so large as the others, bounded on one side by the river and the other by the castle. The next is a kind of rough oval, again with the river on the southern side, but following the contour of the castle's ridge on the other. Finally there is a third area, which this time is less long and thin and is instead broader, if a little shorter. There is one ford up near the castle's front gate, and a second in the third meadow.

The castle has been imaginatively protected from collapse by English Heritage without detracting from its character. The meadowland beneath the castle, lying within the sweep of the river, is flat and broad. Walking over it, it's easy to imagine the small fair set up, trestles all over with pots and jugs of ale or wine, barrels broached and tapped, pies and poultry cooking over smoking fires, bread being offered by maids with baskets, the odd hawker, a beggar or two at the gate, while further on would be the merchants with their bolts of silk and velvet, trying to tempt the knights into buying presents for their wives, their lady loves, or more likely for themselves, to make them appear still more gaudily marvellous.

Okehampton Castle has suffered dreadfully over the centuries. It was built soon after Hastings, by Baldwin Fitz Gilbert, Sheriff of Devon under William the Bastard, and was mentioned in Domesday. It became a de Courtenay property when Robert de Courtenay married Baldwin's great-great-granddaughter in 1172. The earls of Devon were the de Redvers family, but the male line died out in the 1200s. Hugh de Courtenay married one of the de Redvers women, and subsequently became Earl in her right in 1335.

There are enormous cracks in the walls, and the outer curtain wall to the north has all but disappeared, but this little castle has a wonderful feel to it, especially if one makes the laborious ascent to the old tower on top of the steep spur. From there you can peer down at the yard before you, or gaze down the steep hill toward the meadows, up at Dartmoor, or at the line of the old roadway. It may have been a small fort, but lying as it did on the main road from Cornwall, it had a tremendous strategic importance. It is well worth a visit.

After the foregoing, the more vigilant readers will have noticed that I spelled the town's name as 'Okehampton' and not 'Oakhampton'.

When I wrote the first of the *Templar* series, I wanted to use old spellings of place names. I thought they were more interesting, but to my surprise a number of people have complained or have accused me of not knowing the area because I can't spell the town's name properly. For them, all I can say is that I wanted to use the names as they would have been spelled in the past. In the same way I have stuck in the main to old-fashioned spelling of people's names.

For those who dislike the 'Oak' spelling, I hope that seeing the more modern spelling here in the Author's Note will satisfy them. After all, the Author's Note is written in and about the twenty-first century – it's only right that Okehampton should be given its contemporary spelling!

With a work of this type the writer has to study many aspects of history, from methods of fighting to the clothing worn, to how Okehampton Castle would have looked in the 1320s. I am hugely grateful as always for the help of the Exeter University Library staff and the staff of the Devon and Exeter Institution, and any errors are entirely my own.

I've found it enormously enjoyable getting to grips with tournaments and I only hope you find the story as interesting to read as it was for me to write.

Michael Jecks
North Dartmoor
April 2000

CHAPTER ONE

Benjamin Dudenay, known to most people as 'Ben the money-lender', was not popular, so his murder caused no distress except to his three outstanding creditors, whose demands for compensation were stolidly rejected by his widow, Maud. She was content to live on the proceeds of his wealth, feeling no need to maintain his business, and steadfastly claimed impoverishment whenever bailiff or beadle asked that she settle the dead man's debts.

Fortunately Benjamin's death was much easier to arrange than his murderer had anticipated. And it was equally fortunate that the killer was unknown, that he had been away from the city of Exeter for so long that his victim could not anticipate an attack.

It had been such a shock to see the banker after so many years, that Philip Tyrel dropped his cudgel.

His life had altered so much. Even his name had been changed now, though he still thought of himself as Philip, but to see Benjamin again made the years fall away.

Somehow Philip had expected the fellow to be dead. Benjamin wasn't a young man when he'd killed his victims and Philip had momentarily thought he must be mistaken – it must be a trick of the light that made this fellow look like Benjamin. Yet he followed him all the same, wondering if his memory was playing games with him after so many years. Then, when the money-lender entered a hall, Philip heard him accosted by name – *Benjamin Dudenay* – and he had to lean against a wall to prevent his falling. This was the devil who had ruined Philip's life in the pursuit of his own profit. This was the fiend who made money from the deaths of men, women and children.

Philip could have walked away from Exeter and put the place from his mind if he had not seen Benjamin, but now he felt revulsion fill his soul.

He had never before harmed a man, let alone killed one, yet when he saw Benjamin later, strutting down the street and smiling suavely at other leading citizens, saw him arrogantly dropping coins into the alms bowls which the beggars thrust towards him, Philip felt his anger rising. As he stood staring at the rich building that proclaimed Benjamin's importance, his blood called out for vengeance.

That night, Benjamin haunted his dreams, alongside the faces of Benjamin's victims, who cried out for justice – as they had every night in the years since they had perished. Philip shot awake, sweating as they called to him, searing his soul with their pitiful pleadings. Each time he dozed they returned to him, tortured, shrieking faces, until another traveller at the inn grew so irritable at his restlessness that he heaved a boot at Philip's head and demanded tersely why he didn't go and seek his mother among the whores at the river and let other people sleep.

Philip went out. Before light he found himself outside Benjamin's hall again as if his feet had themselves instinctively made the decision to take him there. The usurer left his house as the sky was changing from violet to gold and the sun was beginning to lift above the horizon. As if in a trance, Philip set off after him.

The streets were quiet at this time of day. A few people scuffed to church, an apprentice ran to his work after spending the night with his girl, a cat arched its back and spat at a lean and expectant-looking terrier.

Benjamin strolled past them all, ignoring both people and animals. Philip was torn between excitement and terror. Walking swiftly, he overtook the man and then stopped at the entrance to an alley, bending to retie his hose. The light from the waxing sun caught Benjamin's face and Philip felt his anxiety slip away. There could be no mistake: it was definitely him. The money-lender still wore that same supercilious smile of yore. He glanced down his nose at Philip and in that moment his fate was decided.

The cudgel dangled from his belt. Ben took one last, fateful step and Philip snatched it up, cracking Benjamin over the head. The banker fell like an axed hog, flat on his belly. Working speedily, Philip dragged him into the alley. A short way in he found a low doorway leading to a tiny cell-like room, a storehouse, and he hauled the dead man inside. Then Benjamin moaned.

Philip nearly dropped him and bolted, he was that close to panic. He'd hoped the blow had slain Benjamin, yet now the man was feebly moving, grunting to himself. Swallowing hard, Philip gripped his cudgel. He lifted it again even as Benjamin's hand began to move towards his battered skull. Then Ben's eyes opened and he squinted up.

'Take my purse, you whoreson, if that's what you want,' he croaked.

'Money? You killed my family for *money*! Do you think a few coins can save you?'

'I killed *who*? You're raving, man. I've never seen you before in my life.'

'I am Philip Tyrel!'

'Philip? Philip Tyrel? Oh, my God!'

Gritting his teeth, Philip brought his cudgel down, not once but five, six, seven times. He felt a spatter strike his cheek and his belly rebelled as he saw the result of his actions, but he couldn't stop. At first he knew the fear of a man who dare not leave a witness to his crime, but then it was overtaken by anger in the memory of the people this banker had slaughtered. Their broken, ruined bodies, their gaping mouths begged for retribution.

Then it was over. Philip looked down, panting. The ghastly sight gave him a spasm of horror, and he went out to the alley and threw up. Reluctantly going back inside, he could see that there was no possibility of Benjamin ever being able to accuse him.

Philip squatted at the side of the body, tears welling. He had become what the banker had been, a murderer. He had himself broken one of God's Ten Commandments and taken life. If he was discovered, he would hang.

Yet soon his despondency began to fade. Even if he was discovered he had done his duty. Justice had been visited upon the banker. Benjamin Dudenay was dead, and that was an end to the matter.

In the main road at the top of the alley was a stream and Philip went to it and dropped his cudgel in, watching the blood as it was washed away by the flow, creating a stain like a massive red feather in the water. He dipped his hands in and wiped his face, then rinsed out his mouth.

Standing, he felt as if he had been freshly baptised, free of sin or any guilt. Benjamin had deserved his end. Even the manner of his death had been somehow suitable, his head smashed and destroyed. His own wife would find it hard to recognise him now, just as Philip and the others had struggled to identify their own loved ones.

There was a tavern nearby and Philip made his way to it. At last, he thought, the terrible dreams could end. He had done his part and the deaths were avenged.

Of course, that was before he met the other men responsible for the deaths.

One day later, when Benjamin's body was already chill on the earthen floor, in a field not far from Crukerne, Alice Lavandar walked with her lover, holding his hand as they passed through the long grasses up the hill. When they reached the top, the land before them was smothered in a light covering of frost, making all look grey in the shadows, although where the sun touched the grass and woods there was a salmon tinge as if the land itself was heated from within by its own health and fecundity.

Alice could see that Geoffrey was proud but tongue-tied. She squeezed his hand, smiling at him, and he returned the pressure. If he agreed, this would be a huge step for both of

25

them – dangerous, even – not that he would believe her warnings, she thought.

'Are you well?' she asked when he winced.

'Oh, yes.' His return from the Battle of Boroughbridge, where his master had been killed, had accorded him high honour in her eyes. It was fortunate, he thought, that she would never know the truth of his campaign.

'See that?' she said, pointing at the fields ahead of them. 'It's all mine; my dowry.'

'With *my* eyes, I am lucky to be able to see you here at my side,' Geoffrey smiled thinly. 'Anyway, it's only yours if Sir John allows you to have it.'

'He has to; he can't stop me.'

'I think he'd rather it remained under his control. You're not old enough to look after it as far as he's concerned, are you?'

'I am old enough to marry.'

'Yes, but he can keep your dowry for as long as he wishes.'

'I am sixteen. He has no right.'

'He has every right, Alice, you know that.'

She was silent. Alice knew she was old enough, according to the Church, to contract her own marriage now she was over sixteen, but that didn't matter in legal terms. She was still the chattel of whichever man controlled her life: her guardian – or her husband. 'He wouldn't keep all my dowry for no reason,' she said.

'Sounds like you're trying to convince yourself,' he said with a grin.

She shrugged. 'I hate him. I hate his son as well. Why should I reward him for murdering my father?'

Geoffrey was a solid youth and well-muscled, with thick arms and legs made sturdy by exercise. A sandy-coloured thatch of hair lay thickly over his brow, almost as far as his clear grey eyes, reminding her of a sleepy puppy peering out from beneath a blanket. She knew he wanted her to hold him – but they still had too much to discuss.

'He will try to marry me,' she said.

'That is what I am most scared of,' he agreed.

'He wants me to marry his son.'

Geoffrey shot her a quick look. 'Then there's only one way to prevent him.'

'Yes.'

He stopped. A cloud had passed before the sun as the two spoke, but now it was gone, and Alice could feel the sunshine on her face as she turned to him. He put his hand on her shoulder, surveying her seriously. 'Alice, will you marry me?'

Her heart lurched. She had expected it, had tried to tease him into this for weeks, but it was a thrill to hear his words. All of a sudden her legs felt a little weak, but her heart fluttered as if it was about to break free from her breast. It was impossible to stop the smile that pulled at her lips. 'Yes.'

'Even a clandestine marriage?'

In answer she took his hands and stared into his face. 'I will be your wife. I swear to be yours for all my life and no other man's.'

'Then I will be your husband,' he smiled, and pulled her to him. The ceremony was now complete – and binding. 'Who needs a church door? We'll tell the priest when we have time.'

She responded eagerly to his kiss, pulling him down to the grass beside her, and there, with the cool spring air washing over them, the two made love, sealing their wedding contract. They had given their oaths; they were married before God and Alice knew only relief, even if they must keep their promises secret for a short while.

Sir Roger of Gidleigh, a thickset man with heavy shoulders and shrewd dark eyes, approached the alley with a scowling visage, regretting the merry gathering he had been forced to leave in order to perform his legal duties. As Coroner in the busy and prosperous city of Exeter, he must often desert his friends during their drinking parties, but he had been looking forward to this session, and learning that a corpse had been found was a source of grave irritation. Why did people choose such damnably inconvenient times to be killed?

'In here, Sir Roger.'

Following the watchman, he ducked beneath the lintel into the small chamber. It was lighted by a smoking tallow candle that gave off a thick and noisome stench, as if a pig was being slowly burned in the room. At least it provided enough light for him to see the body.

The corpse was lying face uppermost, his hands at his side, and the head appeared to be lying on a shining halo. In the candlelight it looked like a sheet of bronze, and Sir Roger grimaced. 'Bloody hell!'

'A right evil bastard did this, sir,' the watchman wheezed. He was an old man, much older than Sir Roger, and he had to lean upon his staff as he surveyed the body. 'Stabbed?'

'No. Beaten till his head was a pulp.'

'Jesus save us!' Sir Roger squatted. 'Any weapon?'

'Nothing. I suppose the killer took it with him.'

Sir Roger reached out and prodded at the skull, thickly crusted with blood. 'Christ, what a mess.' Standing, he eyed the corpse thoughtfully. There was something about the brutality of this murder that gave him pause.

Then he shrugged. He'd think about that later. 'Gather the neighbours and we'll hold the inquest immediately.' The people who lived nearest to this place had to be fined to guarantee that they would appear at the next session of the court and present their evidence. He shook his head as the old man limped outside to begin gathering the jury and muttered to the corpse: 'So who the hell killed you, Dudenay? And *why*, in God's name?'

CHAPTER TWO

Walking up the road towards his home, Bailiff Simon Puttock cocked an ear, listening intently. As soon as he heard the dismal wailing scream, he sighed happily and his stern features relaxed.

From here, the road which led up from Lydford cleave, the cleft at the bottom of which the fast-flowing river hissed and swore, he could often hear the bellowing of prisoners in the stannary gaol declaring their innocence and demanding release, but today all was silent, the gaol empty for once, and there were no screams from the great square blockhouse. Instead it was the shriller cries issuing from his own house that made him smile because Simon, after many long years of trying, was once more a father. In January his wife Margaret had given birth to a son whom they had christened Peterkin after their dead firstborn boy.

Only two and a half months old, yet the boy had disrupted their home. Simon paused at his door, hearing the howls of desolation, confident that the boy was even now being cradled by his wife and rocked in an attempt to lull his tiny, indignant frame to sleep. 'Some hope!' his father muttered wryly after too many broken nights.

His house was less than half a mile from Lydford Castle. Limewashed walls and thatch made for a warm and pleasant dwelling. From the rear he could see the peasants working in the fields. Each field consisted of a narrow strip of land, and Simon could look along his own from the yard behind his house to see how the young crops were faring. In and among them men and women wandered, tending the plants to ensure that there would be plenty to eat over the coming summer and winter.

It was hard for farmers. They never saw the end to their labours, not until they died. Each year was simply a fresh round of back-breaking jobs. At least his own villeins wouldn't have the extra worry of the poor devils around Oakhampton, he reflected. The planned tournament up there would have them running around like blue-arsed flies.

He entered his house and peered in at his hall. There was no one there, so he walked through to the garden, cocking an ear upstairs. His son's complaints had died away, and he could hear nothing from the small chamber which he proudly thought of as his solar. Instead he heard calling from his yard, and walked out to seek his wife.

As soon as he left the hall, he was struck in the midriff by a short figure pelting along at full speed. Sitting abruptly, winded, Simon struggled for air while his assailant plonked down in front of him, laughing.

'Father, what were you doing there?'

'You stupid, clumsy, misbeg—'

'Simon!'

As his eyes regained their focus and he could take in his surroundings, he recognised his wife. 'Meg, can't you keep the child under control?'

'Child?' Edith demanded, her smile instantly replaced by a black frown. 'I'm nearly fourteen.'

Simon ignored his daughter, clambering to his feet and rubbing his belly ruefully. He was a tall man, with thick, dark brown hair frosted at the temples. With his face ruddy from the wind and rain, he scarcely looked his age, almost thirty-six.

His wife, Margaret, a tall, slender woman whose blonde hair was turning grey, smiled serenely. Over the years since their marriage she had seen him change considerably, but now she was delighted to see that he was losing the thinness about his cheeks and at the edges of his mouth. They had been caused, she knew, by her failure. It was easy to remind herself that many women couldn't give their husbands the sons that they craved, but in Margaret's case there was an intense guilt because she had regularly conceived but then miscarried since poor Peterkin died. She felt as though her womb had shrivelled inside her, was incapable of supporting another child.

After Peterkin's death, Margaret had blamed herself for the way that her man shrank in upon himself. He withdrew, his hair greying and his complexion growing sallow. Each time she conceived she was aware of his solicitousness, which only served to make her feel still more wretched as each time she failed to give him another son.

Not now. Simon could hold his head high once more, and the light of contentment filled his eyes, making them gleam with an inner fire. Right now he was eyeing his daughter with orbs that appeared to shoot fire – and Margaret was convinced that their incendiary impact would soon make itself felt.

'Well, Dad? You could have hurt me!' Edith declared, hands on her hips. 'You should have looked where you were going.'

'You dare try to blame me?' Simon thundered.

'Edith, fetch wine! Go!' Margaret ordered and, hearing the sharp tone of her voice, Edith shot her a glance, giggled, and sprang away. 'You appeared in the doorway so swiftly you made me jump,' she said reprovingly. 'I could have dropped Peterkin.'

She saw his gaze flit down to the bundle in her arms and his fury cooled immediately.

'I thought he was upstairs. Is he all right?' Simon asked.

'I think so, yes, but really, husband, in future, please be more careful.'

'*Careful?*' he repeated with a sarcastic lifting of his brows. 'And pray how should one be careful about a daughter running into one's stomach? She was like a whirlwind at full-pelt, the little heathen.'

'Please don't swear about your daughter,' Margaret said distantly. 'She is upset enough as it is. She has a brother – not something she had expected – and her nose is out of joint.'

'Ah, you think so?' Simon asked. 'Jealous, is she?'

'Just a little. And confused.' Margaret looked down as Peterkin gave a short gasp and snuffle. 'She is at an age when she will notice boys – and some have noticed her, too.'

'Dirty little sods, the lot of them! Let me catch them sniffing about *my* daughter and—'

'It's only natural, my love.'

'Many things are natural, but that doesn't mean I have to condone them,' he grunted. 'The thought of some idle whoreson mounting my girl . . .'

'It will happen. Edith is a young woman,' Margaret said softly. 'She will be thinking of a husband soon.'

'Humph.' Simon knew she was right, but the idea that his little Edith was almost an adult, ready to breed and raise her own family, was hurtful – as if the girl had acted treacherously towards him and his wife.

'Shush!'

He looked over his shoulder to see his daughter appear carrying a jug and mazer for him, walking slowly and carefully with a small towel over her left arm and shoulder like a steward. 'Thank you, Edith.'

She passed him the cup and wine, watching with her head set to one side as he drank and replenished his cup. 'That's better!' he sighed appreciatively.

Edith walked to her mother's side and both women stood eyeing him narrowly.

Aha! he thought. This is it. 'Is something the matter?'

'We both saw him,' Edith said accusingly. 'Who was it?'

Simon gave her a serious look. 'When a messenger is sent to me, little girls shouldn't worry themselves about the messages. After all, they might be secret.'

'Will you have to travel away?' Margaret asked, frowning. 'He wasn't wearing the insignia of the Abbot.'

'No, it wasn't one of the good Abbot's men,' Simon confirmed. As Bailiff, he reported to the Warden of the Stannaries, who was presently Abbot Champeaux of Tavistock. 'Although he came from the Abbot.'

'Well?' Edith demanded impatiently. 'What did he want? He was in too much of a hurry to have been here to pass the day in chat with you.'

'What if I was to say that he carried private and secret news for me alone?' Simon asked aloofly.

'I'd say you were lying,' Edith said confidently.

Simon gave her a stern look.

'I asked the stableboy after the messenger had gone in to see you,' she explained with delight, her dimples flashing momentarily.

'And what did he say?'

'That the messenger was called Odo, that he's a Herald for Lord Hugh, and that you have been asked to help organise a tournament. Oh, Daddy, is it true? Are we going to have one here?' she begged, her pose of disinterest falling away like tresses under the scissors.

'No, we are not,' he said severely. And then his face broke into a smile. 'It'll be in Oakhampton.'

Sir Roger stood at the door to Benjamin's hall and allowed his gaze to rise from the door to the jettied upper stories and windows – properly glazed with real glass, too – which looked out over the street.

His expression was grumpy. It often was, but today, standing here and staring at this magnificent house, he felt bitter. Never a man who had appreciated usurers and bankers, he found this place with its extensive undercroft, wide shopfront and large hall with solars and other chambers, an insult. 'More rooms here than five houses,' he muttered. Such conspicuous flaunting of a man's wealth was obscene.

The door was opened by a maid. 'Your mistress here?' he grunted.

'In the hall, sir.'

'Show me to her.'

Mistress Dudenay didn't rise. Her hall was a long, broad room, its timbers darkened from the fumes of the fire which crackled in the hearth in the middle of the floor, and the high windows illuminated the space with a meagre light, the dirty glass letting in little compared with Sir Roger's own unglazed holes.

The atmosphere suited the situation; it was dim and gloomy.

'Madam, I'm sorry to be forced to ask you these questions.'

'Then don't. I'm in mourning, Coroner.'

'I have a duty, as you know. I must discover, if I may, who killed your husband and where the murder weapon is.'

She was a short, dumpy woman and now she lifted a hand as if in surrender, not meeting his eyes. 'What do you want?'

'Did your husband have any enemies?'

'None that I know of. He was a banker, but no one appeared to want his death.'

'What of the men who owed him money?'

She turned her face and called over her shoulder. A white-haired clerk appeared in the doorway. She sent him away to fetch her husband's papers and soon he was back, arms filled.

Mistress Dudenay gave a fluttering gesture with her hand. 'My late husband's accounts. If there is anything, it will be in there.'

She lapsed into silence as Sir Roger followed the clerk to a table at the wall. The Coroner was grateful for her composure. He was all too used to having to deal with the screaming bereaved, but somehow this woman's quiet desperation was more unsettling. The clerk carefully laid the sheets down, apparently in some logical order, although Sir Roger could make no sense of it. He had never learned to read. Waving a hand at them, he asked, 'What does all this mean?'

The clerk sighed. 'These are my master's accounts. They show all his income.'

'He loaned money in return for interest?'

'There are always some men who need money. If they require it, why shouldn't a man with money charge them for the use of it?'

'If that's so, some of those to whom he had lent money would benefit from his death.'

'They might consider so,' the clerk acknowledged. 'Although I think Mistress Dudenay is capable of securing the return of any funds my master loaned.'

'With interest, no doubt,' Sir Roger grunted.

'As you say,' the clerk agreed imperturbably. He was used to people complaining about his master's methods of earning a living. The Church taught that it was wrong to make money from money – that men should create things and sell them on was natural, but to demand interest from wealth which they themselves had no need of was profiteering from God's plenty. If a man had so much money he could lend it, he should do so without asking for more.

'As it happens, my master owed money himself,' the clerk said, and pointed to the names of three prominent citizens of Exeter.

He read them out to Sir Roger, who responded, 'None of

these are murderers! Now, what of the names of those who owed *him* money? Who are they – and how much did they owe?'

'There are many names. From farmers to knights, although smaller debts surely don't matter.'

'You think so? A villein owing a shilling might feel it worthwhile to remove the debt by removing the man to whom it was owed. In the same way a squire who owed a pound might feel the debt to be insupportable,' Sir Roger said. He had seen enough murders committed for a penny. 'You have such men?'

The clerk gave him a sad smile. 'Whenever there is a battle or *hastilude* men will need money to pay ransoms or replace their equipment. Squire William of Crukerne was at Boroughbridge and only recently borrowed two pounds for a new axe and mace. Squire Geoffrey here owes another pound and a few shillings.'

'More than a pound for a squire must be a heavy debt.'

'Yes. And then there are the knights. They have expensive tastes. A good warhorse will cost over a hundred pounds. Here we have Sir Richard Prouse. He owes a matter of forty pounds, two shillings and fourpence.'

Sir Roger whistled. 'So much?'

'He had need of it. His villeins are poor, working on scrubby lands, and his cattle have suffered a murrain. He lost half his herds last year.'

'Who else?'

'This is the amount owed by Sir Walter Basset. Seventy-three pounds and—'

'God's mercy!' Sir Roger expostulated. He didn't hear the remainder. 'You're telling me that a knight owes him . . . By the Virgin!'

'He has only recently come back from Bordeaux. He came here and asked for money as soon as he returned. And then we have Sir John of Crukerne.'

'How much?'

'One hundred and thirty pounds, less fifteen pennies.'

Sir Roger gaped.

'He had to buy a new warhorse.'

'You see?' Mistress Dudenay had been silent but now she stood and fastened a black cloak at her throat. 'You see which men had a reason to kill my man? One of them sought to avoid repaying his debts.'

'Are you sure of that?'

'Sure?' she sneered. 'They have all been in the city recently. My husband saw them.'

The clerk bobbed his head. 'They were here for the court.'

Sir Roger could remember seeing them. All the knights had appeared to sit as a jury or watch justice take its course when the King's Justices arrived. 'Did any of them threaten your husband?'

'Not that he told me,' she admitted grudgingly, 'but he was asking for his money back from all of them.'

'Why?'

'Lord Hugh de Courtenay is to hold a *hastilude* at Oakhampton and Benjamin was funding the building works. He needed all his debts to be repaid.'

Sir Roger cocked an eye at her. 'If Lord Hugh is to hold the show, why did your husband need to get involved?'

She gave him a blank look. 'Lord Hugh doesn't carry vast fortunes with him in his purse, Coroner! How would the timber be bought, the cloth and decorations purchased, unless someone was to pay? And who better than a man of business? When Lord Hugh's men arrive, they will reimburse those like my husband who have used their own funds to make sure that the tournament has gone forward successfully. If Lord Hugh needs more, he will pawn his plate.'

Sir Roger nodded and cast an eye over the incomprehensible papers. Still, 'Over a hundred pounds,' he breathed. Even he could be tempted to kill a man to escape that sort of debt.

It was almost a month later, in late April 1322, that Sir John of Crukerne himself heard of the coming festivities. Slapping his thigh, he gave a grunt of pleasure at the news. At last he could complete his son's education.

Sir John had a large manor high in the hills, a green place with many woods and good pastures, a place which kept him in good funds. His villeins were a miserable, froward group, but with a little effort he ensured that they produced enough for him. It was a tough calling, that of knighthood: a man had duties and responsibilities, most of which were expensive, and he must depend upon *this* bunch of dim-witted serfs! Whoresons, most of 'em.

Leaving the messenger swigging from a jug of ale, he strode out and shouted for his horse. It was time for some exercise – for man and horse. Standing and inhaling the air, he waited for the great destrier to be saddled.

The grooms were terrified of the stallion, as well they might be. Pomers could be vicious for no reason. Only a few weeks ago he had kicked out at a peasant girl and it had been necessary to pay the child's father a shilling to compensate for the scar where the horseshoe had slashed like a sword, but that was what a destrier was for; it was trained to bite and kick, and Pomers was *very* well trained. Sir John had paid twenty-two pounds just to have the horse properly broken, and the money was well spent.

With a discordant clatter of metal on cobbles, the great dappled creature appeared, two grooms holding his bridle.

Sir John took the reins and climbed into the saddle while Pomers side-stepped furiously, then turned and tried to bite his thigh. 'Get off, you bastard!' he spat and yanked at the reins, jerking Pomers's head away. He raked his spurs up the horse's flanks and the destrier took the hint, tossing his head angrily once, as if to register a resentful protest, but then darting forward.

The horse was wilful, but Sir John was an experienced rider and refused to give the beast his head. Pomers needed a careful hand and swift retribution. Sir John was capable of both. He kicked Pomers into a sharp gallop as he approached a straight lane, only checking his headlong rush when he saw a wagon in the distance. Yes, the destrier was perfect – quick, easy to instruct once you had his measure, and strong. With his size and stamina, he would easily carry Sir John with all his armour. The knight was ready for a tournament, especially since he might win a good ransom or two. He certainly needed it.

It was annoying that he would have to find a new money-lender now that Benjamin had died. Sir John had need of funds to pay for a new suit of armour for his son, William – and he still owed the usurer's widow a fortune. The thought of the vast sum brought a shudder to his frame. He had needed to buy Pomers because his last mount had died, but the debt was crushing. Especially when that bastard Dudenay had suddenly asked for his money back. In full. Well, his bitch of a wife could whistle for it.

He rode back to his courtyard and bellowed for his grooms. Carefully climbing down – he knew too many people who'd been caught by a temperamental toss of the horse's head as they dismounted – he passed the reins to the groom and strode indoors, finding his son talking to the messenger.

'Father! A tournament!' The boy was obviously excited.

'I know, I know. Yes, you'll be coming too.'

'Thank you, Father. I won't let you down.'

'You'd better not,' Sir John said curtly. Squire William, his son, was seventeen years old. Strong of limb, fair-haired and with the blue eyes of a Saxon, his boy had grown into a handsome man who was ready to take the last honour of manhood now he was of an age.

The trouble was, his head was filled with trumpets and glory now he had returned from his first battle at Boroughbridge, where the King's men destroyed the forces of his rebellious uncle, Thomas of Lancaster. William had served well in combat, and had taken his own prisoners, making some money, but not enough to replace the horse he had ridden and which had died. The nag he had taken from those captured was on its last legs, too.

More expense, Sir John groaned inwardly. For now his son could make do, borrowing Pomers. Squire William had no idea what risks Sir John ran on his behalf!

CHAPTER THREE

Sir Baldwin de Furnshill, Simon Puttock's friend of the past six years, was interested to see that the good Bailiff had sent him a note. He took the wafer of paper from the herald and walked to the window to examine the seal before opening it. Puttock's mark was easy to recognise – a buzzard's head impressed into the wax – and Baldwin smiled before he pulled the seal from the paper.

'I am grateful for this,' he said. 'Are you hungry or thirsty? I have some good ale ready and there is always a pie in my kitchen for a man who has travelled far and fast.'

Odo the herald smiled weakly and motioned to a stool. 'For now, my Lord, I would be grateful merely for a seat that doesn't rock beneath me. It is many years since I have been a messenger. It doesn't suit me so well as heraldry.'

Baldwin grinned understandingly. Heralds were the eyes and ears of their masters, pointing out which men had displayed the greater prowess or courtesy in the tournament, or espying the insignia of the enemy in battle, and guiding their masters away from dangerous opponents; in peacetime they were musicians and entertainers. Prolonged journeys were not sought by men who enjoyed a more contemplative lifestyle, and although this Odo had a certain wiriness about him, he was bent, like a man who has travelled too much in his time.

'Where do you go after this?' Baldwin asked.

'Back to Tiverton, where I can pick up my flute and practise again. With fortune, I may win the heart of a woman visiting the tournament. I've always found that a ready wit, a tune, a rehashing of another man's poetry and a purse full of golden coins will win companionship.'

'Many would say that showing prowess with a sword would be a better way to win the heart of a lady.'

'So they might, my Lord, but they would be fools. What sort of woman wishes to see her man risking his life on a field of battle? No, give me a buxom wench with a sparkle in her eye and a ready laugh, one who will keep your bed warm, but who will still mull your ale and cook your breakfast in the morning. You can keep all the tarts who hanker after a man's hose because he's knocked five or six others on the head!' Odo said sagely, adding, 'On the other hand, I have learned some new stories from France which should please – although no doubt Lord Hugh's fellows would prefer tales of their own valour. I'd better study his knights. It wouldn't be sensible to forget the deeds of men who might decide to cut my hair with a battle-axe!'

Baldwin chuckled. He found the herald highly entertaining. 'I'm sure you'd be safe from any number of axes, Odo.'

'Perhaps. A fellow learns to duck, doesn't he?' Odo agreed. 'But I prefer an easy life. Let me escape from danger and I'll be happy.'

He was a slender man in his forties, with an intelligent ruddy-coloured face and mild grey eyes. In some ways he reminded Baldwin of a slimmer, shorter version of his friend Simon Puttock. Near-white hair framed a gleaming pate, and his head was thrust forward, giving him a permanent stoop. He wasn't a true hunchback, but somehow gave the impression that he carried a weight upon his shoulders, a suggestion which was given the lie by his cheerful visage.

'Have you often been in danger?' Baldwin asked.

A serious set came to Odo's face. 'I have avoided it wherever I could, Sir Baldwin, but I have committed my sins like all us poor folk.'

'I am sure you could find a Pardoner willing to forgive them in exchange for money,' Baldwin said lightly.

'I have no doubt. There are always thieves prepared to gull the gormless,' Odo said. 'But for my part, I doubt whether God would be impressed. No, I'll make my own peace with God, if He wills it, without the intervention of a conman.'

'How did you come to be in Devonshire?'

Odo shrugged. 'I have no home. I've wandered widely all my life, about the continent, travelling from Guyenne to Paris, for a herald must learn new songs – what is he without his songs of chivalry? – but I grew to miss my own language.'

'I suppose a herald can travel easily. He will be welcomed in any great household.'

'Oh, yes,' Odo smiled. 'Although sometimes I wonder whether lords should enquire more carefully about some of their newer staff. Even I have committed my sins.'

'So you said,' Baldwin nodded, glancing at him. 'But you wouldn't hurt my lord Hugh?'

'Ah no! My most heinous crime I still feel was venial. I found a man who was hiding from justice, a man with fear stamped upon his face. I have no idea what made me do it, probably mere sympathy, but I gave him food and helped him escape.'

'Was he a felon, then?'

'He was a renegade, Sir Baldwin – a sergeant from the Knights Templar.'

'How did you find him?' Baldwin asked sharply.

'I was at a town with my master when we heard the Hue and Cry and were told that a fugitive had been seen, a fellow who had been born in the town but who had joined the Templars. You know what happened to them. All the knights were imprisoned and tortured. Many were executed. A terrible injustice, I always felt. Well, we set off with hounds and men-at-arms to seek this fellow and a short way from the town, I twisted my ankle and had to return. And when I got there, I saw a fellow with stubble, a filthy tunic with a faded mark like a Templar cross on his breast, and a pronounced limp. He didn't even deny it; he told me he was so tired I could kill him on the spot as far as he was concerned.'

'What did you do?'

Odo gratefully took the large pot of ale proffered by Baldwin's grim-faced servant Edgar and said with quiet conviction, 'Do? Nothing! He seemed to me to be a fair, reasonable man, a fellow of integrity and honour, who had been betrayed or lied about. And I don't believe all this bollocks about the Templars being evil. They were the Pope's own army, and protected pilgrims all over the world. How could they be evil? No, I think they were destroyed for other reasons. Anyway, I wouldn't willingly see him killed, so I gave him food and showed him a path which should avoid the men seeking him.'

'Did you learn his name?'

Odo grinned. 'If I had learned it, I ensured that I speedily forgot it, Sir Baldwin. The man was a renegade. It could do me no good to remember him.'

Baldwin eased his grip on his cup. He had tensed to hear the name Knight Templar, for although this Odo obviously had no idea, Baldwin had been a 'Poor Fellow Soldier of Christ and the Temple of Solomon', a Templar, and he too had survived only because of the help of others, although survival had been hard. It had left him with deep tracks raked into his forehead and at either side of his mouth, and while his melancholy had left him since his marriage, and crows' feet at his eyes proved that his nature now tended to be more cheerful, there was a steady intensity in his eyes that many distrusted. Beyond the curious fixity of his stare, the only visible proof of his past lay in the scar at his cheek which twisted the line of the neat beard growing along the edge of his jaw.

'Anyway,' Odo continued, moving uneasily in his seat as he felt the force of Baldwin's gaze, 'not long afterwards I met an English lord who accepted me into his retinue, for he missed English songs and tunes. With my flute-playing and my experiences on the battlefield, it was easy to win a post as herald. Who better could a lord gain than someone like me?'

'Who was that?'

'Hugh Despenser the Elder,' Odo said, and then chuckled at Baldwin's startled expression. 'I know – many don't like the man, but I found him a good master.'

'Perhaps, but he is no friend of Lord de Courtenay.'

'No. That is why I told Lord de Courtenay right away about my service to Lord Despenser,' Odo grinned. 'I came clean about it – yet there is no trouble. Lord de Courtenay is now my lord.' He paused. 'A herald must tread a difficult path sometimes. When my lord Hugh returned to England this year, I came with him. I had witnessed enough death and fighting abroad. It seemed like a good time to return and share my knowledge.'

Baldwin was curious. 'And what sort of knowledge would that be?'

'Ah well, have you seen the new craze for weapons in Europe? And mercenaries from Germany now wear plate armour.'

'Like an English coat of plates?'

'No. Where we use interlocking plates to cover our chests, the Germans use one plate alone. I have heard that in Benevento some years ago the Germans charged a stronger force of Provençals and were winning the day because their armour was so strong it was proof against all their weapons. It was only when some sharper-eyed Provençal saw a gap beneath the armpit of these knights that the Provençals could turn their enemies aside. There was a great cry of "À l'estoc!", "At the point!", and they began to sweep through the enemy.'

'A hole under the arms?' Baldwin enquired doubtfully.

'Yes. Where the breast- and back-plates met there was a gap, and there a man might stab a sword. Bear it in mind, should a heavily armoured German ever attack you!'

'Interesting. Still, it will make you a much sought-after herald. A man with knowledge of foreign customs and weapons is always attractive. You are happy to be home?'

Odo pulled a face. 'Well, you know, I sat upon my horse on the way here today and stared about me at the country-side, and do you know what I saw?'

Baldwin shook his head.

'Green. Everywhere I looked, the land was green. Verdant, healthful, with glorious and riotous plantlife on every side. Where there weren't trees, there was grass – all over the place. And do you know what struck me?'

'No.'

'For all this grass to have grown, for all these trees, for all the flowers, there must have been plenty of sodding rain! Yes, it pisses down all the time here!'

The planning for the tournament at Oakhampton had been set in train weeks before the event was due to start. Messengers had to reach all the wide domains of Lord de Courtenay: knights from Cornwall to Carlisle received invitations and either groaned because of the journey they must undertake or crowed with delight at the thought of the money and renown they could win.

At his castle in Gidleigh, Sir Richard Prouse took the note and gave it to his priest, listening with a set face to the cleric's slow reading. When he had finished, the priest gave him a sympathetic glance over the top of the sheet, but Sir Richard ignored him, turning his back while he considered. He had no desire to take the man into his confidence. He didn't trust the feeble, weak-minded fool enough to enlighten him about his own innermost feelings. Dismissing the messenger and curtly telling his priest to seek out food and ale for the fellow, Sir Richard limped slowly to his upstairs chamber.

A tournament; another *damned* tournament, and he was invited to witness the 'festivities'.

It was because of tournaments that the castle was built upon debts and mortgages. That was his father's legacy: a place without the finance to support it. All he could have used was bound up under other people's control, like that whore's cub Benjamin, the money-lender who had fleeced his estates after his father died. If it wasn't for him, Sir Richard could have come into his estates with some dignity, but no! Benjamin had been determined to take all he could. He had an English name, but in terms of his business dealings he was as much a thief as a Venetian!

That was the trouble with jousting. If a man became hooked on the thrill he could gamble away his entire inheritance. Many a man depended upon his wife's financial acumen to protect lands and property. A knight was no use if his sword and charger were in pawn to a usurer. And Sir Richard's father had been completely hooked on the sports.

Whereas Sir Richard perpetually wore a strained, anxious expression and with his deepset eyes under his dark hair looked older than his almost thirty years, his father had appeared much younger than his thirty-four years merited when he died; he was a cheery, pleasant, open-faced man who accepted the blows fate dealt him with a calm resignation or charming self-effacement but, like any gambler, believed that the next joust would recoup his losses. In part it was his very assurance and easy manner that had attracted so many women to him. Sir Richard knew all too well how other men's wives would look to Sir Godwin and invite him to their beds. Especially at tournaments when they could be bowled over by the handsome knight's easy flattery. *Courtesy*,

Sir Richard sneered to himself. That was what they called it, those self-righteous arses in the nobility; if not they called it *chivalry*, as if that excused a man who persuaded a woman to ignore her marriage vows and lie with him. Sir Richard himself could exercise all the courtesy in the world and never win a woman's heart. Not with his disabilities.

If his father hadn't died, maybe he could have grown to respect him. He often wondered about that – whether if he had come to know Sir Godwin a little better he could have learned even to *love* him. Instead all he could see was the gross foolishness of his rumbustious lifestyle, the drinking and whoring, the madness of a man who lost so much money he couldn't afford the best arms to protect himself, and who died for the lack.

Sir Richard had witnessed his father's death at Exeter. It was an unfortunate mace blow – misaimed, it didn't strike Sir Godwin a ringing buffet on the centre of his helmet as intended, but glanced down the side until it caught his shoulder. It was the kind of blow that all knights were used to, one which would bruise but shouldn't incapacitate a man with full armour, yet all could see at once that Sir Godwin was badly wounded. He fell back as if stunned, then stumbled. The spectators saw him put down his sword as if he wished to surrender, then let his blade fall to the ground, grabbing for his helm. He tripped, still desperately clawing at the steel of the helmet, and then there was a shout from the crowds as someone saw the blood seeping from beneath his helm.

Soon everyone could see that the fallen knight was dying. Squires and heralds ran to him from all over the field while Sir Godwin's opponent let his mace fall and lifted off his own helmet, gazing at the dying man with bemusement, wiping his hair from his brow. Then someone managed to remove Sir Godwin's helmet and all could see the bright blood pumping.

Afterwards they pieced together what had happened. The spiked mace had caught the junction of helmet and mail tippet, and a rivet had sheared inside the helmet. It was bad luck, everyone said, nothing more: the rivet had shot away and the flap of steel it held in place had been exposed, slicing through Sir Godwin's neck like a dagger and opening his jugular.

He could still see his father's body lying in a lake of blood, limbs moving lazily, mouth opening and closing, the blood dribbling now, while his mother gripped his shoulder with fingers of steel. All about them men clamoured noisily, some sombrely making the sign of the cross, others baying for the blood of the victor. It was clear that his opponent, the other knight, was in danger, and a small group of squires surrounded him and hastened him from the field when the crowd turned nasty, folks pressing forward to the barriers. Sir Godwin was popular, known to all the watchers in the stands, and his killer was not.

Sir Richard had been a youthful squire of only some fourteen summers then, back in 1306, and in the years that followed, he had been forced to attend several other tournaments in order to win his spurs as a knight, but that had all ended in 1316 at the tournament in Crukerne when he was twenty-four. Since then he hadn't been able to participate, of course, and he tended to try to avoid them. He saw them as the frivolous pursuits of the foolish and indolent. His time was too taken up with building up the profits of his estates.

It was fortunate that Sir Richard's mother, of blessed memory, had been a talented woman and skilled with finance.

She had scrimped and saved, juggling the profits of the estates in an attempt to keep the place afloat. His mother was no fool, thank God, and she was, like so many women, a good manager of money, but even so the place soaked up his treasure like a sponge. Matters were beginning to improve and Sir Richard had managed to qualify for knighthood when he was nineteen, but then came the disastrous famine of 1316, and he had been forced to borrow money again. Another visit to Benjamin; another crippling debt. And if 1317 was little better, 1318 was a disaster, and not only personally. There simply were not enough villeins to support the place and all their efforts were needed to keep Sir Richard solvent.

Gidleigh was only a tiny castle, little more than a tower with a wooden fortification encircling it for protection from wild animals, but he wouldn't see it taken from him. It was all his father had left him. Sir Richard had no need of a great household. Only those who aped great lords needed the hangers-on, and Sir Richard was happy to live the life of a quiet rural knight. He had enough money now, just, to support himself if he lived frugally, and that was why he objected to attending tournaments. If he was to attend, surely he would have to display those qualities expected of knights, and that would mean he must pawn his belongings again, perhaps even his best pewter.

There was little enough left now, since Benjamin the Usurer had taken all he could. Sir Richard spat a curse at the 'foul offspring of a leprous whore' but it didn't ease his loathing for the banker.

At least the poxed bastard couldn't do the same to anyone else now. Not that Benjamin alone deserved Sir Richard's detestation. Others had helped destroy him. Others deserved his revenge. Especially Hal Sachevyll and his foul lover Wymond Carpenter. And Sir John, of course. Sir John of Crukerne, who had killed Sir Richard's father with that mace-blow and then helped destroy Sir Richard himself when he was crippled.

He bunched a fist and brought it down on a table, trying in vain to vent his rage – but it was no good. It never was. His frustration was caused by his body's limitations and all he knew now was a sense of impotence at the injustice of it all. Sir John, Wymond and Hal had done this to him. And now he must go to another *hastilude* to witness their so-called skills. He glanced with hatred at the paper in his hand. Much though he'd like to ignore it, he couldn't. He would have to go all the way to Oakhampton. Well, it could have been worse. Lord de Courtenay could have asked everyone to visit him in one of his castles farther north. At least Oakhampton wasn't too far.

Although with his ruined body it would take him long enough to travel even that distance in his coach.

CHAPTER FOUR

'Who is it from, Baldwin?' asked his wife Jeanne when she entered the room a few minutes later. Edgar had taken the soggy Odo from the hall to the kitchen to eat his fill, and she found Baldwin still contemplating the paper with a dubious expression.

'Simon,' he said. Jeanne crossed the room and sat near the window so that the light shone clearly upon her needlework. Baldwin smiled at her, but then his face hardened as he read the note. 'He's organising a tournament.'

Jeanne caught his tone of voice and sighed, pinning her needle into the cloth and leaving it there. 'And?'

'Hmm?'

'I said, "And?". You have a face that would curdle cream, Baldwin. What is it he is suggesting? Oh, I understand! He invites you to go along and help! That means travelling miles to some wind-swept and chilly field.'

'Yes, he has asked me to join him,' her husband admitted,

55

'and to help with the tournament. Thank God I don't need to participate at my age.'

'Wouldn't you secretly like to?'

'A *hastilude* is dangerous enough when you are young and fit.' He patted his growing belly. 'It would be lunacy for me to tempt God by pitting myself against men half my age.' More seriously he added, 'And I want to see our child growing.'

She touched the silver crucifix at her neck. 'Let's just pray it is born safe and healthy,' she said. 'When is the jousting to be?'

'Not for a while. Late June.'

'You should see to your armour, then. There will be events or feasts where you will be expected to wear it.'

'Jeanne, I'm sure I won't need to worry about that! Lord Hugh would hardly expect a man of my age to take up arms and tilt before him.'

'It would be better to be safe than be forced into a course and find that your armour doesn't fit you any more,' she said firmly and rose to her feet. Usually an elegant, slender woman with the pale complexion and red-gold hair of the north, she had to puff and blow as she levered herself upwards. As was his wont recently, Baldwin went to her side and helped her with a hand under her armpit.

'Thank you,' she gasped. 'It is hard work to get up now. Oh! And it aches so much! I shall tell Edgar to see to your arms and armour. I would worry else that you could be in danger.'

He watched her rubbing at her groin with a worried frown. This was his first child, and the tournament held little terror for him compared to the thought of what his wife must soon endure. It was hideous, all the more so since one of his villeins had recently died in childbirth. Jeanne was his first wife and he had only been married a year; the thought that he might lose her was appalling. 'You'll be all right,' he said gruffly.

Hearing the note of alarm in his voice, his dog walked over to him and thrust his nose into Baldwin's hand. 'Good boy, Aylmer,' he said absent-mindedly, watching his wife go to the door which led to the privyhouse. She had lost her cheerful smile and now all he ever saw in her features was a stolid fortitude, as if all she could concentrate on was giving birth and ridding her body of this extra weight.

She disappeared and he patted the dog's head. 'What do you think, Aylmer? She'll be all right, won't she?'

It was hard for him to come to terms with his impending change in status. Other men he knew accepted fatherhood as easily as buying a new horse or dog, but Baldwin had mixed feelings. Although he was desperately keen to have his own children, when he had been a Knight Templar he had taken the threefold oaths of obedience, poverty and *chastity*. His wife's present shape was all too obvious proof of his failure and Baldwin still found that his vow haunted him, reminding him whenever he thought of it that he had broken an oath sworn before God. It was futile to try to exorcise the demon. He knew that he would die with the weight of his failure dragging at his soul, no matter how much he hoped and prayed he might find peace before death.

There was another facet to the destruction of his Order, and that was that he had a deep and abiding loathing for any form of injustice. His Order had been destroyed as a matter of politics and greed, the King and Pope taking all they could from the Templar treasuries while burning any Templars who could not be forced to confess to sins which any reasonable man would have known to be false. It was this which had fired his determination to prevent injustices and led to his position as Keeper of the King's Peace in Crediton. Wherever possible he tried to save men from conviction and punishment for crimes of which they were innocent; it was a novel approach in an age when most Coroners and Sheriffs were happy to imprison those people whom the local jury accused, but Baldwin preferred to investigate methodically. When possible he tried to free the innocent and only convict the guilty – a trait which had led him and his friend Simon to some surprising discoveries in the last six years; occasionally to horrific ones.

He was learning to relax somewhat at home now he was married. Since first meeting Jeanne, he had become aware of a sense of ease, a general relaxation of spirit. He was less driven, he told himself with more than a hint of smugness; less bitter, more tranquil generally.

'What are you smirking about?'

He started at his wife's voice but laughed when he saw how her head was tilted, her eyebrow lifted in sardonic enquiry. 'Considering fate and marriage, my Lady.'

'I suppose I should be glad, then, to see you wearing that hound-like expression of devotion,' she said, returning to her chair.

'And I should be glad too, to see how such a magnificent lady could bear to tolerate such a mean and disreputable fellow as me,' he responded with a bow.

'That's all very well,' she said, sitting slowly with a hand on her belly. 'Ooh! That's better.'

'About this tournament. I hardly think it is necessary for me to attend,' Baldwin said. 'And I have no desire to go and display myself in shining robes at ridiculous expense just to prove my vanity.'

'I am delighted to hear it – I wouldn't wish to see you wasting good money in a frivolous manner. You must have taken part in many *hastiludes*, my love, but from what you said, you are glad to be able to avoid this one?'

'I certainly have a dislike for being beaten about the head and body by ape-like drunks who occasionally lose their tempers and flail about them with a mace or axe. I should have thought that you would be nervous about seeing me enter the fray.'

'As for that, I expect you would be a match for competitors half your age.'

'Perhaps, except this would not involve only one or two single combats,' Baldwin said, slapping the message with the back of his hand. 'Simon says that the events will take place over three days: the first for the opening and some early jousts, the second with more individual challenges, and then a finish with a grand *mêlée* in which two opposing teams will try their fortune.' He winced. 'Think of it: two teams of knights at it hammer and tongs. Entering the ring on horseback until they are brought to the ground, then stumbling about, many of them blinded by dust and dirt and stunned by the blows raining down on them from all sides. Those who are captured will lose their horse, armour, weapons – and have to pay a ransom besides for their freedom. My God! It's such a waste! And you want me to enter this?'

'It always looks so spectacular,' she told him honestly. Like many women, she enjoyed watching knights practising.

'You want to be a widow so soon?' he growled but then he remembered and could have kicked himself. 'My darling, I am sorry. I wasn't thinking.'

Jeanne was not upset. 'I lost my first husband when he died young, Baldwin, but you know I do not regret it. I cannot lie: I hated him. It was a relief when he became ill and succumbed. You mustn't treat everything so seriously. And I wasn't pulling a face because I was hurt by your words; I had a twinge, that's all.'

Baldwin felt as if the world had suddenly jolted beneath him. 'A "twinge"? What do you mean, a "twinge"? What sort of a "twinge"?' he gabbled.

She eyed him with amusement. 'Baldwin, you have seen plenty of hounds give birth to their whelps, and mares deliver themselves of foals. You know what sort of twinge.'

Baldwin threw a glance over his shoulder at the door. 'I . . .'

'Shall sit and amuse me. You don't expect me to explode in a moment, do you? How long does a birth usually take? Sit here, hold my hand, and keep talking.'

'You're sure you won't, um . . .'

'It's the beginning, but that may mean I have another thirty hours. It doesn't feel very urgent yet,' she assured him. '*Sit!*'

Reluctantly he obeyed her, still gripping the message. His dog, hearing the sharp command, simultaneously squatted behind him.

'Stop staring at my belly like that! Now, tell me what Simon plans. Why is he organising this tournament, anyway? What has it got to do with the tin miners, with the Stannaries?'

'It is not his responsibility to arrange such events,' Baldwin admitted, 'but Lord de Courtenay has asked him to help. He wrote to Abbot Champeaux to enquire whether Simon could be released from his duties for a while. You may recall that Simon's father used to be a steward in the pay of Lord de Courtenay's father until old Lord Hugh's death in 1292. Apparently Simon's father was most adept at setting out the grounds and siting the *ber frois*, the stands. So our Lord Hugh asked that the former steward's son should be allowed to help with *his* latest tournament. It is a matter of tradition – and an honour for Simon.'

'But surely the Pope has only recently removed his ban upon all tournaments?'

'And the King has imposed his own,' Baldwin agreed.

'May the Sheriff prevent it?'

Baldwin laughed aloud. 'The good Sheriff is one of Lord Hugh's men. If I know him at all, he'll be chafing at the bit to be there himself! No, there is no likelihood that the King would stop it.'

'Are you sure?'

'If the good Lord Hugh de Courtenay considers that he can arrange to hold a spectacle, I see no reason to think he is wrong,' Baldwin said. 'Perhaps he has a dispensation from the King. In any case, Lord Hugh has requested and the good Abbot has enthusiastically agreed. Even now Simon is travelling to Oakhampton, I expect.'

'Why is the Lord de Courtenay so keen to hold a tournament, I wonder?'

'It's probably something to do with that primping coxcomb Sir Peregrine of Barnstaple, Lord Hugh's banneret. He is always scheming and playing political games. It is just the sort of vain, pointless affair he would think diverting.'

'You still do not like Sir Peregrine?' Jeanne said lightly,

her hand moving back to her belly. It felt as if her pelvis was preparing to explode.

Baldwin had not noticed her wince. 'I do not. Give me a plain enemy with a sword in his hand any day in preference to a subtle, devious courtier like Sir Peregrine.'

'He was always polite and courteous to me.'

'He would be,' Baldwin grunted.

She continued musingly, 'And I felt very sorry for him over that woman of his.'

'Yes, he was plainly upset when she died,' Baldwin said, and then his attention flew back to his wife as he recalled that Sir Peregrine's woman had died in childbirth. 'I am sorry,' he added wretchedly. 'I didn't mean to remind you that—'

'Stop blathering, Baldwin,' she snorted. 'I am not going to die. I'm going to have a perfectly normal delivery – unless, of course, you unbalance my humours by interrupting me every few minutes with apologies for what you may or may not have done!'

He saw that she had gone pale, and now both her hands were at her belly. 'Are you all right?'

'It's like cramps, but it's not coming fast enough yet,' she murmured half to herself. 'Still . . . Oh, wipe that look off your face, Baldwin, and pour me some more wine!'

Later that same day Sir Peregrine of Barnstaple was seated in the small hall over the gatehouse warming his hands about a pot of spiced wine.

'Did it take long to get here from Sir Baldwin's house, Odo?'

'No, Sir Peregrine. Only the afternoon. It's downhill from Furnshill to Tiverton,' the herald replied, sipping at his wine.

'How was the good knight? Did he seem reluctant?'

Odo laughed. 'Sir Peregrine, he's much more concerned about his wife's pregnancy. It's his first child.'

Sir Peregrine grunted. Over the last year his woman and their child had died in childbirth. 'What of the others?'

While Odo spoke about the people he had visited, Sir Peregrine's mind wandered. It was hard to concentrate on so many different matters at once. The main thing, he knew, was that the tournament must go to plan, without embarrassment and without alarming the King. For the King would have his spies there to see that there was no risk of treason among his subjects.

Sir Peregrine knew he was fortunate to have professional heralds. Lord de Courtenay's own man, his 'King Herald' Mark Tyler, was incompetent and lazy. It was fortunate that they had found Odo, a man who had served in other large households. He had experience of continental jousting, and was a much better musician than Tyler.

'What do you think of Mark Tyler?' he asked abruptly.

Odo hesitated. 'You want me to slander him?'

'Your answer already does!'

'His playing can be good, but he does have a problem.'

'What's that?'

'Why do you value me?'

Sir Peregrine was ready to snap that he had his reasons, but then he caught sight of Odo's expression. Odo was no fool, and Sir Peregrine did value his opinion. 'Because you have travelled. You can tell us of the honourable customs which exist in foreign lands and relate highly prized deeds of valour.'

'That's right. I have seen the world and I have officiated at tournaments from Bordeaux to Paris. It's the first duty of a herald to find new tales of courage – but Tyler has no idea. He has once, I hear, been to Guyenne with his lord and that was many years ago.'

'If he is so provincial and dull, why are you here?' Sir Peregrine asked sharply.

'He is so provincial and dull that I should soon be able to take his position,' Odo said frankly.

Peregrine had to grin and shake his head. Ambition was no sin. 'Well, if this tournament goes smoothly, I might help you,' he said at last. He didn't need to explain why. Tyler was one of the least popular members of the household, universally disliked for his rudeness and overbearing manner.

'I thank you. I shall not let you down.'

'Do not,' said Sir Peregrine, but then his attention flew outside: he could hear horses' hooves. It was so late the gates would shortly be locked for the night, and the arrival of a traveller at this time of day was so unusual that he cocked his head to listen. Sure enough there was the sound of running feet and a sharp call of enquiry as a man-at-arms demanded the stranger's business.

Sir Peregrine motioned to Odo to remain where he was – the poor fellow had ridden twenty miles or more that day – and pulled on a thick cloak. No matter how often you tried to drum these things into the heads of the dim-witted bastards at the gates, they would still treat all visitors as enemies. That was the problem with hired guards, they had no idea of courtesy or hospitality.

As he left the hall and stood at the stairs leading down to the yard, he reflected that it probably wasn't surprising, since many of the mercenaries who were employed in the castle had in fact been disinherited or deprived of their livings by men such as this visitor. Many of the fighters who protected the place had once been squires or men-at-arms, but had lost their masters in battle and were now forced to eke out a living by offering their services to others. They were not tied to Lord Hugh de Courtenay by feudal loyalty, only by necessity.

Lord Hugh had little need of additional vassals: they were an expensive resource, after all. Men whom he accepted into his ranks cost him their food and lodging, their spending money, their arms, their mounts, their clothing – everything. Whereas a mercenary was cheap; he expected a wage, supplemented with bread and ale, but would clothe and arm himself.

This visitor looked just the sort of man who could have caused mayhem to many. That he was a knight was obvious from his golden spurs and enamelled belt. Long in the body, with square, heavy shoulders, he had the build of an athlete. He sat on his horse like a man born to the saddle, moving easily with the animal as it skipped and pranced, blowing loudly through its nostrils. The man wore a brimmed felt hat against the chill, a heavy red riding-cloak and a warm-looking tunic of green wool over a greying linen shirt while his boots looked like best Cordova leather.

'Good evening, sir,' Sir Peregrine called.

At once the horse whirled so the visitor could face him. Sir Peregrine found himself being studied intently, the traveller's eyes flitting over his worn and slightly faded tunic before fixing upon his face.

The stranger had thick brown hair worn shorter than was fashionable, and intense grey eyes that were curiously disturbing because not only did he not blink, the irises were small, making him look as if he was holding them wide in challenge. His face was square and large, the jaw jutting a little. His nose was broken, and there was a scar beneath his left eye from a raking stab wound. Sir Peregrine decided that he did not like the look of him one little bit.

'Godspeed,' the stranger called. 'Are you the Keeper of this castle?'

'I am,' Sir Peregrine answered. 'Your name, sir?'

'You may call me Sir Edmund of Gloucester. I have heard that there is to be a tournament in your lord's demesne. Is that correct?'

'We're holding a festival in our castle at Oakhampton,' Sir Peregrine confirmed.

'I should like to participate.'

'You would be very welcome, Sir Edmund.' Sir Peregrine bowed, but truth be told, he was reluctant to accept strangers to the tournament. Men who were unknown could prove dangerous. They might lose their tempers and kill combatants, or by dropping a sly word into the ear of a bitter loser, cause a feud which could lead to bloodshed.

The knight smiled as if he could read Sir Peregrine's mind. 'May I ask leave to stay here the night? There is an inn, but a traveller can often be waylaid in a new town.'

'Of course, Sir Edmund. The stables will look to your horse, and if you have servants, they would be welcome to join you in the hall.'

'I have only a squire and an archer,' the knight said. He shouted through the gateway and soon a man with a nut-brown face and rough dark hair appeared on a heavy pony. He wore green like a forester, and had a long knife hanging from his belt while a rein held in his hand led a second horse, which was laden with sacks and provisions, as well as what looked like a pair of longbows well-wrapped in waxed cloth. A thick bundle of arrows was securely strapped alongside. Behind him came a blue-clad man, who trotted quickly under the castle's entrance leading his own sumpter horse. It was heavily laden, rattling and clanking, apparently with armour, and lances projected forwards and backwards.

Although he didn't look above medium height, the squire gave Sir Peregrine the impression of wary power restrained only with conscious effort, just like his knight. His eyes moved over the whole yard, taking in the hogs in the corner, chickens scrabbling among the dirt and twigs, the lounging guards. Sir Peregrine thought a smile of disdain twisted his face at the sight, as if he was amused by the quaintness of the place.

If anything, he felt that the squire deserved more careful watching than the knight. The squire was older; he looked a formidable fellow and Sir Peregrine's attention remained upon him as he rode to a stable and sprang down as agile as a cat, and gave the reins to a young boy.

As the three visitors were welcomed into the castle, Sir Peregrine experienced a feeling of unease. This fighting trio looked like a good team – possibly one of the best, and he wasn't used to feeling outclassed.

CHAPTER FIVE

A week had passed since Jeanne's false labour, which had subsided as suddenly as it began. A good night's sleep, and the pains had been put down to a bad bout of wind. Now, however, there could be no mistake and Baldwin watched his wife with rising anxiety. Jeanne knelt on a cushion on the floor and gripped her maid Petronilla's arm, eyes squeezed tight shut as the contractions ground into her belly.

He knew perfectly well that women were built for this, that their bodies had been given to them by God to produce children. He also knew that Jeanne was being supported by a woman who had experience herself of childbirth – and yet the knowledge was no help. Watching his wife, he knew only panic that she might not endure.

Poor Jeanne looked so tired as she waited for the next clenching; her eyes scarcely noticed him or the room, but instead were turned in upon herself. Baldwin wished he could comprehend what she was going through – but he couldn't.

He had appealed to Simon Puttock many months ago now, asking how the Bailiff coped with *his* wife's childbirth, and Simon had merely laughed, saying, 'It's a woman's thing. You don't go and help your shepherds in lambing, do you? No – so why on earth sit in with your wife? You can't help because you don't know how – all you can do is unsettle her. Women know what to expect and all that, so I leave them to it and find someone to share a glass of wine or ale with me. So will you, if you have any sense!'

'Let them get on with it,' Baldwin repeated to himself, watching as Jeanne's maid gently wiped her brow with a cloth dipped in rose-water. It was definitely a tempting thought, running outside to escape, but he felt his departure would be pure cowardice in the face of his wife's suffering.

'Could you fetch some wine?' Jeanne gasped after a moment.

Petronilla nodded and rose, walking quickly from the room.

'Water, too!' Jeanne called after her.

'How are you?' Baldwin enquired tentatively.

She looked up at him. The dampness on her forehead made her look pale and ill in the candlelight, as though she was perspiring from a fever. 'I'm not in pain, Baldwin, it's not like that, it's just that it's so *relentless*! I know it won't end until the baby is ready, but I wish it would hurry!' She stopped suddenly, closing her eyes, her head falling forwards, a hand resting on her belly. 'Here it is again – come here. Quick!'

He went and crouched at her side as she stiffened, her arm gripping his, eyes tight shut, a sighing gasp breaking from her as the ripples cramped through her womb. It lasted but a few moments, but to Baldwin it was an age. 'That's it. It's finished for now,' she sighed.

Baldwin was relieved to see Petronilla return and watched the maid mix wine with warmed water, holding the cup to Jeanne's mouth. She sipped and swallowed, then leaned back. For once Baldwin poured himself a cup of wine and drank it neat. He glanced at the water, but then tipped more wine into his bowl, drinking deeply. Turning, he was in time to see his wife moan and reach for the bucket at her side. Before he could speak, she was sick, vomiting and spitting. Shivering, she sat back.

'More wine?' Petronilla asked.

'No.' Jeanne shook her head, eyes closed. 'It'll only make me sick again.'

Petronilla nodded and wiped her brow.

'It's very cold in here,' Jeanne said accusingly. 'Baldwin, can't you make the fire hotter?'

'Of course,' he said enthusiastically, glad to be able to help in even so minor a way. He threw logs onto the hearth and turned to find that Petronilla had left the room to fetch more rose-water. 'Are you well?' he asked with the return of his nervousness.

'It's . . . coming again. *Come here!*'

He hurried to her and she grabbed at his arm, her fingers digging in while he stared down at her. It was an appalling sensation this, knowing that there was nothing he could do to ease her anguish, but he was reassured by her apparent resilience and fortitude.

'It just keeps on, again and again,' she whispered.

'Don't worry, it'll soon be over,' he said heartily.

Her eyes flashed at him. 'Don't you bloody *dare* say that again! And why's it so fucking hot in here?'

The next morning, in his castle at Penhallam, Sir Walter Basset slapped his thigh when the message was delivered and read out to him. 'A tournament? With all Lord de Courtenay's knights? Wonderful! I can feel a treasury of money coming my way! Darling? My Lady?'

His wife Helen left their steward to decide on his own which barrels should be taken up to the castle's buttery, and walked to her man's side. 'What is it?'

Sir Walter told her of the summons. 'It's excellent! Just think of the men who'll be there – old fools, many of them. There're bound to be loads of easy targets. Think of it! Ransoms, horses, armour – and even a handout of cash as a reward for my prowess from Lord Hugh!'

Helen listened, and in truth she could smile with him. His joy was ever-infectious. He was large, strong, and entirely masculine, his whole body covered with a light curling down of black hair. His odour was to her the finest perfume; his leathery skin was rough against her own, which she found intensely erotic. His scars were proof of his chivalry; his hands large and powerful. He was not tall, but huge. Barrel-chested, his frame rested on short but solid legs. His constant practice with sword and lance had given him the massive shoulders of a wrestler, while his neck was almost non-existent.

But he wasn't ugly. He moved heavily, as befitted some-one with so substantial a frame, but above it all, he had calm eyes of a deep blue, which were commonly crinkled at the edges with pleasure. His mouth was a little too wide, above

71

the pointed chin, but his features were regular and pleasing, especially when he smiled. When he grinned, Helen would swear that he could tempt an angel. Now his sheer delight and conviction meant that the news of the tournament was in every way as pleasing to her.

'So long as you don't fall and damage your new armour,' she teased.

'For you I would tilt without armour,' he said gruffly. 'For my Lady's honour, my hide would be enough.'

'I prefer jousting with you when you're naked,' she giggled.

'Come to the chamber now. Prove it.'

'I don't have time,' she protested.

'I order it,' he said simply.

'My Lord,' she said, surrendering happily.

Their solar was at the other side of the hall, and they walked through it to their private chambers. There a man was sweeping away old rushes.

'Out!' Sir Walter snapped and the man fled while the knight untied his hose and pulled off his shirt.

Helen watched him while she slowly removed her skirts and tunic. In every way he was a good husband to her, kindly and generous, and a master in the tournament. They had been married three years now, and she had never yet seen him bested.

'Hurry, woman! I'll burn with lust else!' he grumbled. He was already on their bed, the blankets pulled back, and now he took hold of her and pulled her towards him.

It was a wonderful body, he thought, holding her at arm's length a moment while he felt his ardour mount. Long in the leg, slim in the waist, she had a flowing mane of red-gold hair framing a finely sculpted face with small nose, high cheekbones and slanted green eyes.

Sensing his impatience, she quickly climbed atop of him, kissing and stroking to ensure his pleasure. It was her duty. She knew that he would suspect her of adultery if she ever rejected his demands, and his response would be swift and uncompromising. She made love with a silent passion until he spent, and then worked a little longer, more slowly, until she gasped and fell onto his chest, her breathing gradually calming.

His chest was damp with their sweat. She kissed it, then rested her cheek on his shoulder, twining her fingers in the thick hair of his breast. 'You're confident of winning?'

Glancing down at her, his voice registered his surprise. 'Do you have any doubt?'

'I have never seen you lose.'

'Yes, I will win. I have the horse, I have the equipment, and I know I have the most virtuous Lady to egg me on.'

'After that display? You can still think me virtuous?'

'For a woman, yes. Yes, I would say you are honourable enough,' he said. 'You wouldn't dare to be otherwise, would you?' He gave a low chuckle as he rolled her onto her back and climbed between her thighs.

Only when he had exhausted himself and could lie back with his hand on her belly did his mind return to the tournament. Sighing contentedly, he allowed himself to consider the thrill of riding once more against another man.

It was rather like this taking of a woman, he thought. There was a similar tingle to the blood, a similar clutch at the belly, a heightened awareness of life. And the delight as an opponent fell was similar to the pleasure when a woman surrendered herself. Both were exquisite, wonderful experiences. Different, but similar in some way.

He had never lost in the lists. He couldn't. He would take on any odds to win because within him he knew he harboured a strain of explosive cruel violence that exceeded the fabled madness of a *berserker*. When his blood was up, his rage was like a red mist which encompassed his entire being, and he could throw himself into combat without a thought for his own safety, beating at his opponent with a wholehearted ferocity that terrified any who stood before him.

It even shocked *him* sometimes. Like when he had almost killed Sir Richard Prouse six years ago at Crukerne. Not that it was his fault. Anyone could fly off the handle in a *mêlée*; he wasn't the first. It was nothing to be ashamed of. Especially in a battle. The ransom had been paid in full, which was what mattered. More business for that usurer Benjamin, no doubt.

The memory of Dudenay brought a scowl to his features. Tight fisted bastard son of a Parisian peasant's poxed dog! His charges for the armour had been extortionate. It was all Sir Walter could manage not to put his hands about the money-man's throat when he had demanded his interest. Never again, thank God! Not now the creature was dead.

Baldwin felt his wife's grip tighten as the contractions returned, her breathing changing until she was almost panting while her fingers dug into his forearm, making him wince. Gradually her breathing recovered and Baldwin blew out his cheeks in relief as her fingers released him.

She looked up at him, her hair clinging damply to her forehead, her face pale and weakly. 'I feel so cold now. As the contractions get me, I burn, but as soon as they pass I freeze.'

Wary after her earlier outburst, Baldwin ventured nervously, 'Um . . . should I put a log on the fire?'

'My winter cloak would be easier. Then I can throw it off when I'm hot again.'

He went to the chest and pulled out a heavy woollen cloak lined with warm squirrel fur, draping it about her.

She touched his hand. 'Thank you.'

'How much longer will this go on?' he asked quietly.

She looked up at his wretched expression, and rested her hand on his, smiling up at him. This was a new experience for her, a strange, overwhelming experience, but it felt oddly natural. There was no fear for her, no terror, although she was aware of the risks: she had seen other women die in childbirth, especially when the delivery took too long. That was something that didn't worry her. At a fresh sensation her attention turned inwards again.

'I can feel the baby,' she said softly. 'It's moving . . . dropping downwards.'

His face relaxed slightly, but she could still see his anguish. In his eyes she could see his concern, his fear for her. She reached up and pulled his head down to her, kissing him. As the next wave of pain mounted she let him loose. 'You can't do anything here, Baldwin. Go! Leave Petronilla with me and we will call you when all is done.'

He was tempted to argue, but then he saw the cramping begin to distort her features again, and he rose quickly, calling for Petronilla.

CHAPTER SIX

The man called Philip Tyrel was in a lousy mood when he walked into the field. Later than he had intended, tired from his long journey from Exeter to Oakhampton, all he really wanted was a comfortable bed and pot of cool ale to soothe his exhausted limbs, but he must first put up his small tent, see to his horse and prepare for the jousting.

It took less time than he had feared. Soon he repaired to the market and once he had a quart of ale inside him with a beef pie to keep it company, he began to feel more human, but his feeling of glumness remained.

His tiredness wasn't caused solely by the journey to get here. This lassitude was a manifestation of his decay. All creatures died sooner or later, their bodies rotting until only the bones remained, but for his part he knew he had begun to die on the day he had seen his wife crushed to death. He craved the peace of the grave. It was so long since he had known comfort or true rest, and his spirit was flagging.

After killing Benjamin he had felt so good it was as though a rush of fresh vigour had sunk into his very marrow, as if he had found himself, miraculously, ten years younger. He could almost think that some form of energy had been absorbed by him from the man whom he had killed. An alchemist he had once spoken to in Rome had hinted of an emanation given off by living beings, something that only occultists and the trained knew of, and it was from this, he had said, that the secret of eternal life could be determined – but the fellow had been drunk, and his discourse soon sank into incoherent rambling.

Perhaps it was not so fanciful a concept. He had heard that a man who took the life of another gained a little of the dead man's power, and that was certainly his own experience. His sight had never been so clear, his limbs so strong, his hearing so acute as after Benjamin's execution. His very soul felt invigorated.

Could it be that when a man ended another's life, this was always the result? he wondered. If so, any killer must kill again, for no one would be able to resist the addictive temptation to repeat the experience. If a man enjoyed such a sense of revitalisation after killing and subsequently found himself like this, enfeebled once more as his body continued its journey to the grave, there must be a constant urge to kill afresh and renew oneself.

But no power on earth could renew his life. Since the terrible day sixteen long years ago, when his wife and two young children had been taken from him, he had travelled regularly. Battles, tournaments, quests, he had thrown himself into them all hoping to win some ease, and if not, death. Except he had failed. He had gained a certain renown, but it had not helped. His grief was too deeply ingrained in him. He knew that only death could excise the pain.

As his thoughts grew gloomy, the crowds made him claustrophobic. He turned away from the people and walked quietly to the river, standing near a great oak and gazing at the rippling waters. A lick of sunlight caught the back of his neck like a soft kiss, and he smiled sadly, recalling that last kiss on that last day. If only he had remained with them. It would have been good to have died at the same time.

He sighed and threw a stone into the waters.

Benjamin's death was not the same. The man had broken God's laws: committing usury and causing deaths. If he was any other man, if he was a peasant and had been responsible for so many deaths, he would have been executed. But no, his crimes were ignored because he was wealthy. At least he had finally paid the price of his unbearable greed. Perhaps that was the reason for the sudden burst of dynamism that flooded Philip after the event – it was God's way of rewarding him, to show that Benjamin had deserved his fate. Revenge was justifiable.

If the banker had only been guilty of usury, Philip would have been able to forgive him, but that wasn't his sole crime. In his insatiable hunger for money, he had maximised his profits with his accomplices by skimping on the wood they had acquired to build the *ber frois*, the grandstands, at the tournament at Exeter in 1306. Benjamin had been a member of a trio consisting of a builder, an architect and himself as financier, who helped set out tournament fields, to construct the stands, the barriers, weapon rests and so on. Benjamin paid suppliers for the materials, working to a budget which the tournament organiser agreed with him, and if he and his friends scrimped and saved on materials, they could pocket the difference.

That was why Benjamin's stands had collapsed, why Benjamin had to die. Because he had charged for the best timbers but had used the cheapest, and when people filled the stand, the stand fell.

Now Benjamin too was dead, punished for his greed.

Not that it would bring back those who had died; nor could it renew the ruined lives of the survivors. Philip wiped away the tear that smeared his sight, and with an effort smothered his emotions before they could overwhelm him. He had work to do.

Walking back the way he had come, he continued beyond the armourers towards the field. There, he cast a professional eye over the stands, nodding at the size and siting. All looked well enough at first glance, but then he caught sight of a rotten board panelling a side-wall.

He walked over and touched it; the wood felt damp, as though rot was eating into it. Such timber should never have been used. He only hoped that the boards which formed the flooring were of better quality. Putting out his hand, he touched the wood again to prove to himself that this was no figment of imagination, that his mind was not deteriorating. His every sense was heightened, and before his fingers encountered the chilly wetness he could *smell* the disease in the planks.

A shiver rattled its way through his body and he was struck with a sensation of freezing, as if he had been instantaneously transferred to winter and left naked, standing in snow. Then a bird called out a shrill tune and he felt the sudden warmth thrill him as if God had chosen that moment to bestow a smile upon him.

He couldn't be sure, but how many carpenters were there who specialised in tournaments? Perhaps he could soon have his revenge on a second man. One who was even more directly culpable than the money-lender.

There was one way to verify his impression. He walked to the ale-sellers and gazed upon the drinkers, but his target wasn't there, so he returned to the battlefield and stared about him. Then he saw the carpenter. Up near a rack of lances, Philip spotted him, bent at his task and he knew he had found his second victim.

Strolling towards the castle, Sir Baldwin felt the holiday atmosphere that pervaded the place. For a while, enjoying the sight of flowers at the hedges, the cheery cries of traders and hucksters, the teasing and ribald comments passed by men to women and returned, he could forget that the purpose of this festive occasion was a series of fights, many of which would inevitably be bloody, possibly even fatal.

He had left his servant Edgar in charge of his cavalcade. Horses, carts and men were everywhere fighting to keep together in the crowd. Now Baldwin was in the midst of a stream of wagons and carts, with only the protection of his small riding sword. It was almost new, but he was delighted by it. The blade was a fabulous peacock blue, and inscribed upon one side was *BOAC*, standing for *Beati Omnipotensque Angeli Christi*, meaning 'blessed and omnipotent are the angels of Christ', while on the reverse was the small cross of the Knights Templar. The two, he felt, were charms as powerful as any prayer or scrap of paper sold by a pardoner.

Many folk were drinking freely from skins and one man was so drunk he fell to the roadside and rolled into the river with a loud hiccup. Baldwin was concerned that he might drown, but two other travellers reached down and rescued him, one amused, the other loudly proclaiming his fury at being forced to get his best velvet coat wet to 'save a drunken sot who'll probably be dead in a few days anyway, and it'll be a good thing for all of us when he does bleeding well die and stops being such a nuisance to his fellows'.

The castle lay a half-mile or so further upriver from the town, and Baldwin studied it as he approached, eyeing the improvements.

This was Lord Hugh's main post on the road that led from Exeter to Cornwall, and the last time Sir Baldwin had been here, many years before, its dilapidation had been all too evident. During Lord Hugh's minority, from 1292 to 1297, it had been maintained by the King, and although Lord Hugh had been saddened by its condition when he saw how badly it had fallen into disrepair, there had been little he could do until he came into his inheritance.

As soon as Lord Hugh was twenty-one, he took over his estates, determined that the castle should be renovated and made fully habitable again. From what Baldwin could see, he had achieved a great deal. The timber bridge over the stream that bounded the northern walls was new, replacing the old one. That had been so rotten that many travellers had bypassed it, preferring to ford the stream farther up than put their faith in the decaying wood. Once over the stream, the road curved under the northern side of the castle, beneath the soaring new curtain wall.

Baldwin stood at the side of the road and let other travellers pass by while he ran his eyes over the place. It had a curious design, but that was only because it was so strongly placed. Baldwin was sure that he had seen a place built to a similar design before: long and narrow, sited upon the long spur of a hill. He smiled when he pinpointed his memory: it was like Richard Coeur de Lion's Château Gaillard, albeit on a smaller scale. Both lay on top of ridges, taking advantage of the lie of the land.

At the south-west point of Oakhampton was a keep set atop a solid mound. This had been a part of the spur, but beyond the keep the land had been dug away and used to raise the keep's mound still higher, creating a deep and unbridgeable crevasse and making attack along the line of the spur itself all but impossible.

In front of the keep was an almost triangular bailey, holding the hall, kitchens and chapel and main accommodation for Sir Hugh's men. A square barbican faced the bridge, and it was connected to the main gatehouse some 100 feet behind it by a high-walled corridor which extended like a long finger of moorstone pointing at the bridge. Any attacker who succeeded in breaking down the door to the barbican would run the gauntlet of concentrated fire from above all the way along that length before he could attempt to storm the gatehouse – a suicidal mission if ever there was one, Baldwin acknowledged.

Above the roadway the ground rose steeply to the curtain walls bounding the castle itself, and when Baldwin continued with the flow of people to the southern side of the place, he saw that the walls here were set as high above the meadow. The castle loomed above the people meandering from tents to stalls as they surveyed the goods on display.

Usually Oakhampton was a tranquil castle. Far enough from the town, which was itself remote at the best of times, the castle saw only occasional travellers passing along the road. From the dung that lay about so liberally, this field was normally pasture for sheep, horses and cattle. With the river flowing around in a great loop, the soil must have produced good grass for the animals even in the driest summer, and this would commonly be a pleasant, out-of-the-way place where a man could sit on a stone at the water's edge and contemplate his life while the sunlight danced over the waters. Or so Baldwin assumed, for today it was a scene of lunatic mayhem.

Men milled about and bellowed at each other. Here, at the foot of the barbican, nearer the river, there was a set of horse-lines, but the main part of the field was now a tended area with gaily coloured pavilions, flags fluttering in the breeze. Squires and heralds set out the carefully painted shields of their masters so that others could challenge them, while spectators strolled idly by, confirming who was present. The sight made Baldwin want to groan. He knew that his own tent would soon be erected, a damp and chill home for a week.

Eventually he came to a second field which was dedicated to a market. It was filled with small sheds and wagons where local folk had set up stalls. Food, ale and wine were in plentiful supply, but so were bolts of cloth, jewels and trinkets, because wherever knights met to tourney, their women would be close at hand to egg them on, and even if they weren't, knights were among the vainest of men, forever seeking fashionable or expensive cloth to proclaim their richness. It was natural for merchants to try to sell gold, silver and silks at a tournament, just as it was natural that the usurers and money-lenders would also be on hand. They too had their place.

Beyond this was a third field, and it was here that Baldwin saw his friend.

'Simon!'

On hearing his name called, Simon Puttock turned, wearing a scowl which only faded when he recognised Baldwin. He was standing by a lance-rack at the side of a *ber frois*, talking to a sandy-haired man with a sallow, pinched face. At the lance-rack itself leaned a short, squat, truculent Celt with near-black hair and blue eyes, who wore a leather apron. From the adze thrust into the apron string, Baldwin assumed he was a carpenter.

'Baldwin – thank God! I thought it was more problems! How are you, old friend? I was beginning to wonder whether you'd plead fatherhood to avoid the event. How are they?'

Baldwin noticed that the other two men appeared irritable, but he saw no sign that Simon wanted to return to his discussion with them. 'Jeanne is fine, but very tired,' he replied. 'Our daughter Richalda is keeping her and Petronilla awake through the night.'

'Not you?'

'Yes, she keeps me up as well,' Baldwin admitted. There was no surprise to it. His manor house was a good size, but the solar block was not vast and Baldwin was learning that one baby girl could make more noise than any animal of the same size when desiring attention.

'Is Jeanne coping?'

'She fluctuates between weeping from sheer frustration and tiredness, and laughing with delight when she sees what she calls a smile on the baby's face.'

'You don't see it?' Simon asked.

'There is nothing *to* see,' Baldwin said severely. 'The child is a mass of bawling noise, nothing more.'

Simon made no comment, there was no need. Baldwin's words might have been harsh but his tone, when he spoke of his daughter, was gentle and proud.

'And how are Margaret and Peterkin?'

'They are fine. Meg's perfectly used to podding. I left her to it,' Simon said absently, then he appeared to recall the man at his side. 'Oh, Sir Baldwin, this is Hal Sachevyll, who is designing the *ber frois* and setting out the space for fighting.'

Baldwin gazed at him blankly. 'The *ber frois* aren't ready?'

'No,' Sachevyll snapped. 'It's ridiculous. We've got the main frames up in place, but we need fresh timber for the flooring. The stuff we've been given is useless. Soggy, rotten and feeble.'

'The wood's shite,' the carpenter asserted. '*I* wouldn't stand on those planks. They're rotten.'

'It's an outrage, Bailiff,' Hal Sachevyll declared passionately. 'All the timbers are of poor quality and there's scarcely enough, in any case. I demand that the town provides more.'

'We've been through this already, Hal,' Simon said shortly. 'If you want more timber, you'll have to pay for it.'

'I *have* paid! The stuff delivered is just not good enough, is it, Wymond?' He appealed to the carpenter, who spat at Simon's feet.

Simon looked at him coldly. 'Then buy more. You have been given a good sum of money to make the tournament work, haven't you? Use it.'

'What, waste more of Lord Hugh's money? It may be loaned by a money-lender, but Lord Hugh will have to pay it all back sooner or la—'

'You have enough to build,' Simon said impatiently. 'You suggested a budget, I daresay. Stick to it.'

Hal sighed. 'Look, Lord Hugh told me how much he wanted to pay. He agreed a budget with my banker, and Lord Hugh will settle up later. But that doesn't mean I can go willy-nilly ordering fresh wood and—'

'I repeat: you have enough funds. Use them!'

'Our banker is dead, Bailiff. Murdered some weeks ago. I would pawn my own few belongings, but since you have plenty of wood here, why not give me some? It's all Lord Hugh's. And it's his own villeins who shortchanged me, supplying rotten timbers when I ordered the best. You should command them to give us more for their lord's honour.'

'For the last time, I'm not going to steal from the towns-folk,' Simon said sharply. 'Why don't you make the stands smaller, or have lower rails at the front? I can't believe you really need so much wood.'

'You've never built stands, have you, Bailiff?' Wymond the carpenter interrupted. 'Maybe you'd like to take my fucking hammer and show me how to do it?'

Simon's patience was frayed. Unused to such rudeness, he was close to losing his own temper. His features hardened, but after a moment's effort he composed himself. 'Well, perhaps you can show me what I fail to comprehend, Wymond.'

'Yes, I too should like to see these *bers frois*,' Baldwin said.

With Wymond following, swearing, Sachevyll led them to the high walls of the stands enclosing the lists.

Baldwin left Simon and the other two as they argued, the carpenter pointing to weaknesses and the dearth of wood while Simon shook his head and declared himself satisfied with the preparations. Instead Baldwin went to look at the layout. He was grateful that a small team of workmen were sawing and hammering because their row smothered the noise of the bickering between Simon and Sachevyll.

The area was large. There would be space for at least fifty knights to contest within its fencing, first with horses, then on foot. Baldwin had seen many tournaments, and this seemed to have been set out with skill. The space between the *ber frois* was adequate, there was plentiful land for the horses to build up their speed, and the stands were a good size for all the men and women who would want to come and watch the spectacle.

It would be interesting to see a tournament again, he thought. He had practised regularly while a Knight Templar and had fought in the lists, both in individual clashes with lance on shields, and in the *mêlée* where everyone wielded their favourite weapon after the initial brutal, thundering collision, but now he was approaching fifty years of age he was happy that younger bones and muscles should have their turn.

He heard the voices behind him as the others approached. Hal was talking. 'And just look at this! I've never *seen* such shoddy lumber! My heavens, I shudder to think what Lord Hugh will think when *he* sees it. It's an embarrassment, that's what it is.'

'If it's the best—'

'Don't fucking tell *me* it's the best they can do,' Wymond rasped. When Baldwin turned to glance at them, he saw that the carpenter was right before Simon and pointing with a furious finger.

The Bailiff's voice was curt but controlled. 'Perhaps it would be better if you could get on with the *ber frois.*'

'I don't want to be associated with—'

'You already are, Master Carpenter, so I suggest you get on with it.'

'*Not without better wood.*'

'Christ Jesus, give me strength!' Simon cried heavenwards. 'Wymond, get back to your work, and if you need more, petition your friend Hal here.'

'You'll have a disaster. It's happened before, a long time ago, at Exeter,' Sachevyll said, panicking. 'You'll have a collapse and then where will we all be?'

'In the shit,' Wymond spat.

'What happened at Exeter?' Baldwin asked.

'A knight was killed and the crowd was angry. He was a well-liked fellow and the mob wanted the blood of his killer. They all moved forward, and the barrier gave way before the press, letting people tumble out. Women were smothered beneath the bodies, Sir Baldwin. Women and children, all crushed. It'll happen here if the Bailiff remains obdurate. I warn you now: if you don't get me new wood, I won't be responsible.'

'Lord Hugh advanced you sufficient funds to buy decent wood. If you skimped in order to line your own pockets, you'll have to buy more. No matter what, the safety aspect is entirely *your responsibility*!'

'If anything goes wrong, I'll blame you,' the carpenter stated. 'It's not my fault if the thing's unsafe.'

'Yes, it is,' Simon insisted. 'It's the responsibility of you both to make the stands safe.'

'I don't see what I'm supposed to do with this crap. If there was some decent timber it'd be different, but—'

Simon cut through the carpenter's grumbling monotone. 'God's teeth! Just get back to your work, you lazy, whining whoreson, or I'll have the Lord Hugh's Bailiff arrest you as soon as he arrives.'

'You can't do that without a reason,' the carpenter sneered and was about to add something to his words when Simon took a short step forward. Immediately Wymond drew his hammer and hefted it menacingly. 'You want to attack me, eh? You want some of this?'

'Put that thing down, you misbegotten shit of a Plymouth alewife!' Simon roared.

'Make me!'

Baldwin stepped between the two. 'Simon, there is no point in fighting. He's beneath you.'

'Oh, yes?' the carpenter screeched, enraged. 'I'll have his fucking head off, and we'll see who's beneath who, then, eh?'

Baldwin said nothing, but his hand went to his sword.

Hal put a hand on the carpenter's arm. 'Come on, dear,' he soothed. 'He's not worth it.'

'Try anything and you will be arrested,' Baldwin said flatly.

'Come now, Bailiff – squabbling with the hired help?'

Hearing the amused, laconic tone, Simon tensed. While they had been arguing, the King Herald, Mark Tyler, had lounged over. He stood watching their argument with ill-concealed distaste, like a nobleman who was above any such grubby disputes. Two heralds stood with him, both looking on with frank interest. Baldwin recognised one as Odo, the messenger who had given him his invitation. Odo was wincing as though pained by the King Herald's tone.

Simon privately considered Lord Hugh's King Herald to be a fat, obnoxious fool. Tyler had an easy time of it; he took over when all the hard work was done. And what then? Maybe he'd adjudicate occasionally, sing a few songs, praise some knights for their courage, and then retire to a tavern or Lord Hugh's bar with some cronies while other men did all the serious work.

The dark-haired man, with the double chin and expanding paunch beneath his multi-coloured tabard covered with Lord Hugh's insignia, wore an expression of resignation, as if he had expected no better of Simon than that he should quarrel publicly with a carpenter. It made Simon realise what a spectacle he was making of himself and the thought that he had done so before the King Herald made him recover his poise instantly.

'Touch me, and you'll be arrested or dead in a moment,' he said to the carpenter. 'Get back to your work or I shall demand the King Herald arrests you in Lord Hugh's name.'

Seeing a mutinous light in the carpenter's eyes, Baldwin pulled an inch or two of his sword blade from the scabbard, but Wymond had stood his ground long enough. He hawked and spat and lumbered away.

Sachevyll threw his hands in the air.

'This is wonderful! *Quite* astonishing! You realise you're going to ruin the whole show? Now you've upset my friend, what's next? I ask you, can we possibly get things completed if you molest my people? What Lord Hugh will have to say when he sees all this mess, I shudder to think. You need to find more wood, Bailiff, because otherwise I refuse to accept any responsibility. I'll tell Lord Hugh whose fault it was when he comes storming over the place. And I'll tell him I warned you the stands are dangerous, that they might collapse. The *ber frois* could be filled with his friends and their women – you want to see Lord Hugh's friends falling and breaking their legs and arms, even dying?'

'Master Sachevyll,' Simon said with an icy calmness, 'you are quite right to be concerned. *You* are Lord Hugh's servant, while I, a humble bailiff, am a servant of Abbot Champeaux. I have nothing to answer to Lord Hugh about. I owe him no homage, I seek no patronage.'

'You are as much Lord Hugh's man as I am, myself. We both take his money to make this tournament work.'

'No, I do *not* take his money. I am no mercenary. I repeat, I am Bailiff to Abbot Champeaux, an officer. I take nothing from Lord Hugh. If you have concerns, raise them with your lord. For my part, I have other business to attend to.'

'You can't leave me here! You have to help me find more wood!'

'Get your own damned wood, you feeble-minded sodo-mite! I've been trying to help you all this long day, but now I've had enough. You were given the money to buy whatever you needed, but you've bought rubbish. Either buy more or make do. Either way, leave me in peace. I have a tournament to organise.'

'Where can I go?' Sachevyll wailed.

'To hell and back – I don't give a shit, so long as it's far from me,' Simon ground out unsympathetically and turned on his heel.

CHAPTER SEVEN

Sachevyll was close to tears as the Bailiff walked away. He could have screamed with frustration, but that wouldn't get things sorted, and that was what Hal Sachevyll was going to do: get this event successfully completed in the manner which Lord Hugh would expect.

But he couldn't achieve anything in this mood. First he must calm down. That was what dear Wymond had told him, that he must calm down. He'd be no use to man nor beast if he didn't, and there was so much to plan, so much to organise still. Hal had every intention of succeeding – with or without the Bailiff's assistance. And afterwards he could point out to the Lord just how unhelpful – indeed obstructive – this nasty fellow Puttock had been. That thought was soothing. It needed to be developed. The idea of shaming the Bailiff before Lord Hugh was most attractive, but Hal hankered after more dramatic detail: perhaps the Bailiff would beg him for forgiveness, and Hal would spurn him, averting his head from the pitiful creature even as Lord Hugh demanded an explanation and apology for his rudeness and lack of respect to Hal.

Feeling much better now, Hal set off towards the tented market and bought himself a pint of good quality red wine. About to sit down, he changed his mind as a boisterous tipsy youth joined him on his bench. Instead Hal took his wine and walked to the riverside, where he sat on a fallen trunk.

Coming from a city (he had been born in London) Sachevyll viewed these rustic villeins with contempt and mistrust. Peasants were all the same. The Bailiff was clearly of the same stock: untutored, no doubt, mean and unpleasant. A man of taste and courtesy would have treated Hal with more respect. After all, he was the leading designer of lists and stands in the country, not some peasant begging alms at a lord's door.

He would have to acquire more wood. The stuff he had bought was not up to the standard, and he'd have to get more. That would cut into his profits, and his master carpenter's, too. Silly Wymond, making the Bailiff angry like that when there was still a chance he might agree to let them have wood from the castle's own stocks or something. That had been their plan – to buy cheaper quality in the expectation that Simon would cave in and give them better material. It had worked before. But Wymond had seen how annoyed Hal was growing. Heyho! Now they had to buy more themselves with the money they had saved from the job. There were few enough perks to jobs like this one, but taking the money and buying fewer planks or beams than necessary, or getting only cheap stuff which wasn't worth half the amount paid, was one way of making profit. It was all accepted and understood, a means by which talent could be rewarded, like the dairyman who carefully warmed cream and took off a few clotted lumps for his own breakfast; except now it looked as though Hal was going to have to use the money he had skimmed from the deal.

Still, if he could find a cheap supplier, he could come out of it all right – and meanwhile make sure that Lord Hugh knew exactly how unpleasant that Bailiff had been.

Hal was still nervous that the project might be late. The job had progressed alarmingly sluggishly. It was his duty to see to the layout and design of the field, but also to ensure that everything happened on time. Of course his budget was nowhere near adequate. If only he had been given more money to play with, he could have worked wonders.

Sipping his wine, Sachevyll allowed himself to daydream, recalling the plans he had formed when Lord Hugh first asked him to help. In his mind it would have been a gorgeous display: red silks forming a canopy over the Lord's own grandstand, with a throne of wood upholstered with crimson velvet and cushions. Sachevyll had thought instantly of the chivalrous stories of Arthur when Lord Hugh suggested that he might like to help. He envisioned his employer dressing as a king, perhaps wearing cloth of gold and an ermine-trimmed robe, while his knights took on the rôles of Arthurian characters, acting out their parts at the Round Table before all joined in a splendid clash of steel.

That Bailiff could be the evil Mordred, he snickered, his eye drawn once more to the stands.

But no. The King had banned all showy tournaments since the alliance formed to destroy his favourite Piers Gaveston in 1312, and it would be tempting fate, let alone the King's patience, to pretend to be Arthur, to wear a crown and show off his knights as men from the legends. The King would turn a blind eye to a simple tournament with few knights and no other magnates, intended purely to exercise steeds and men together in order to ensure their skill for the better defence of the realm, but it would be very different were Lord Hugh to put himself forward as a king – and not just *any* king, but England's greatest. People might consider that Lord Hugh was getting ideas above his station, and if other magnates were invited, King Edward II would be a fool not to wonder whether plots against him were being hatched. It had happened before.

No, the tournament must have the workaday appearance of simple martial practice. It was terrible, of course, for the spectacle was all there, ready, in Hal Sachevyll's mind, but at least he was working on a tournament again, and that was all that really mattered. He loved them, even after the disaster at Exeter so many years ago.

He hadn't been entirely responsible, of course. There was little doubt in his mind that the crowds moving forward had brought about the stand's collapse, and many of the furious people were crushed by the weight of bodies behind them before the wood had given that appalling, groaning crack and shuddered. There was a kind of silence, then. A pause. Hal had stopped and gaped. He had never heard such a sound before. From somewhere a bird called. And then the dust was hurled into the air as the wood gave way and the screams began.

The memory still made him feel queasy. After that he had travelled, providing smaller stages for other lords, going wherever his master had commanded. One always obeyed one's master, Hal reminded himself. Especially when your master was the King himself.

Recollecting that, Hal stood, fastidiously brushing lichen and mud from his hose. His master would want him listening, watching and learning, not sitting back and whining. He drained his cup and returned it to the wine-seller before squaring his shoulders, putting that scene from his mind; he gave a prim sniff and considered his next move. Perhaps he could ask the wine-seller where he might acquire some wood inexpensively.

He was about to do so when he caught sight of Sir John of Crukerne striding through the crowds.

'Oh my God!' he squeaked, and involuntarily ducked behind the wine barrel. He didn't want to be seen by the Butcher of Crukerne. As soon as he could, he scurried away back to Wymond and safety.

Walking past the smugly grinning King Herald, Simon stormed away from the tournament field. He marched quickly, seething with anger at the carpenter and builder. Baldwin walked a little more slowly in his wake, leaving Simon to work off his ire.

It was not until Simon had reached the entrance to the tented field, near the river, that he realised that his friend had lagged behind. He stopped and waited for Baldwin. 'My apologies, that was an unnecessary outburst.'

Baldwin shrugged. 'The carpenter deserved worse for his lack of respect to an official. What of it?'

'I'll explain more when we find a moment's peace,' Simon said, his face hardening.

Following his gaze, Baldwin saw the King Herald approaching, Odo behind him. Odo gave Baldwin a nod of recognition before going to his pavilion, a small tent near the river. He pulled off his garish tabard, marked with the symbols of Lord Hugh's family and lineage, and Baldwin had to restrain a smile when he saw that beneath it, Odo wore a threadbare linen shirt and a pair of faded hose. Finery could conceal utter poverty, he thought.

The King Herald mockingly bowed to Simon, and although Baldwin saw that his shirt and boots were of the first quality, he was sure that Mark Tyler also used his tabard to hide poverty, although in the King Herald's case it was the poorness of his character rather than of his clothing.

Simon barely acknowledged the King Herald, but instead led Baldwin to the castle, avoiding anyone who wanted to speak to him. 'I would have procured a room for you in the castle,' he told him confidentially, 'except I recall how badly you got on with Sir Peregrine last time you met him at Tiverton. He'll be taking the chamber above the gatehouse and will live there while the Lord Hugh is in residence.'

'That dreary, mendacious lob!' Baldwin said without rancour. 'No, I am happier with the cheery company of the field.'

'Like friend Hal, I suppose?'

Baldwin then said, in earnest now: 'Aren't you worried that the stands may not be strong enough? What if one collapses?'

'If they do, it'll be Hal's fault,' Simon said. 'He's creamed off a load of Lord Hugh's money for his own pocket and he's trying to keep it. He can afford the best. Lord Hugh is generous, especially when he's trying to impress his own knights. No, don't worry, old friend. Hal isn't stupid enough to let anyone get hurt at this tournament.'

At Oakhampton Castle, the two men had to walk along the line of the barbican's outer wall to enter its north-facing doorway and then Simon took Baldwin up the long cobbled corridor that ended at the gatehouse itself.

Looking up at the walkways inside the battlements, Baldwin voiced his earlier thoughts. 'Only a brave man or a fool would attempt this to enter the castle.'

It was easy to envisage a group storming this narrow, deadly killing ground and being crushed by missiles raining down from above. The two crossed the bridge and entered the court beyond. The spur on which the castle was built was shaped roughly like a shield, and here at the entrance Baldwin saw they were at the narrow point at the base. Before them a broad yard fanned out with high walls enclosing a number of buildings, while in the background ahead was the looming grey shape of the keep on its high motte. Baldwin had little time to study the place because Simon strode off to their right, to a long, high hall. Soon they were sitting at a table with jugs of ale.

Simon wiped a hand over his face. 'God's bones! I begin to wish I had never agreed to help with this. If I hear one more complaint from that cretin of a carpenter or his girl-friend Hal, I swear I'll reach for my knife and gut them!'

'It is mayhem down there, isn't it?' Baldwin said, comfortable in the knowledge that his servants would have seen to his belongings and that he need do nothing but idle away the day.

Simon grunted nastily, 'I hope you realise you'll be trying to sleep in the midst of that row.'

He had a point. Since the tournament was viewed by townspeople as a cross between a fair and a market, with the money-making potential of a saint's day feast, there was plenty of raucous entertainment. Outside in the fields they could hear stall-keepers and men-at-arms singing lustily, drinking noisily and behaving as badly as young men would. Even here in the castle's hall there was horseplay. Two lads were involved in a drinking bout that involved one placing a funnel in his mouth while his companion filled it with ale. Apparently the drinker intended swallowing faster than his friend could pour. Baldwin was confident that neither would be able to wake him later with singing or gaming. Their only means of disrupting his sleep would be by their snoring . . . or vomiting.

'What is the plan for the event?' Baldwin asked.

Simon drained his cup and refilled it. 'Tomorrow Lord Hugh will arrive with the last of his household. He's planning a quiet night with a vigil in the chapel to pray for God's blessing, and the day after tomorrow will begin with a procession to the church in Oakhampton, after which the games will start. There's to be a *béhourd* for squires and knights in training, and Lord Hugh will want to reward the best of the lads; some will be given their spurs. Then we'll have two days of individual jousting to keep the men busy and the young girls in a state of feverish excitement before no doubt some of them hie to the woods and offer each other insincere vows of eternal fidelity in exchange for a crafty grope.'

'You sound bitter,' Baldwin observed.

'Bitter?' The other man looked up and gave a feeble grin. 'Aye, well, wait until your daughter is a little older. Don't get me on to the subject of Edith.'

'I see.'

'Not yet you don't, but you will! Finally there'll be a grand *mêlée* for all the knights to show their magnificence and prowess.'

'Wonderful!' Baldwin said drily. 'So all those who haven't already been battered to Banbury and back can have their brains mashed on the last day!'

'Oh, it shouldn't be too bad. At least it's to be fought *à plaisance*, not *à outrance*.'

'Thanks to God for that!' Baldwin said with feeling.

'You don't like to face weapons of war?' Simon asked with a grin. 'I've seen you with weapons in your hands before now.'

'I've fought often enough, and I've killed many men as you know,' Baldwin agreed, 'but this is supposed to be a demonstration of valour and chivalry. Sharpened lances and swords have no place here. It is one thing to be deafened from two days of having a mace or sword clattering against your helm, but quite another to have to avoid some enraged cretin trying to slice through your guts with an upwards stab underneath your plate. There are too many risks with weapons *à outrance*. Better that men should fight with blunted swords and joust with a coronal on their lances.'

'Would you prefer to see everyone wearing toughened leather and fighting with whalebone swords?'

'Ha! There's always likely to be one fool who forgets and turns up with a real sword, or someone who loses his temper and grabs a bill. No, for my money I'll take all the protection I can!'

Simon eyed him. 'I forgot you're nearly fifty,' he said with a faint hint of surprise in his voice. There was enough grey in Baldwin's hair and beard, he could see, but somehow he had never before considered how old his friend was. In the six years since they had first met, Baldwin had remained a solid, dependable factor in his life. Now he realised with a slight shock that his companion was an old man.

'I am not quite ready for a winding-sheet yet,' Baldwin said sharply, reading his mind. 'Don't look at me like that.'

'Like what?'

'Like I am about to drop dead at your feet!'

Baldwin was not alone in viewing tournaments with concern.

In the small tent erected for her alongside Sir John's and Squire William's, Alice Lavandar, Sir John de Crukerne's ward, slept badly. She tossed and writhed on her hard mattress, but sleep eluded her although she was exhausted after the journey. Then, at last, she felt herself drifting off.

But not to peace. It was the old dream. She was back in the tournament ground of Exeter, and before her were two knights, both sitting high on their horses in their war-saddles with the enveloping cantles and high pommels, both wearing full battle-armour, with helmets. They lowered the points of their massive lances to her in salute, and she watched as the protective coronals were fitted, the metal crowns which blunted the points. But then, as the two turned and rode off, she saw the coronals falling from their points. She wanted to scream at them to stop, but her voice was gone; she couldn't speak, she could only observe.

The two men cantered to opposite ends of the field, wheeling so that their horses faced each other. There they stood, their mounts breathing out a fine mist from their nostrils, stepping heavily on the grass, eager to hurtle towards each other.

Alice watched with horror, and now, at last, she recognised the heraldic symbols on both kite-shaped shields: one was her long-dead father, the other, her husband Squire Geoffrey.

In the dream, her feet were rooted to the woodwork of the stand; she couldn't move as she became aware of another man on the staging with her. It was Squire William, Sir John de Crukerne's son, and he leered at her as he walked in front of her. Leaning over the rails, he gazed contemplatively at first one man then the other before facing Alice.

In her hand was a white cloth. She knew that dropping it would be the signal for the two men to gallop at each other, but she couldn't, *wouldn't* let it fall. She refused to make them die. She clung to the small square of gauze, but William reached forward and took her hand. Although she desperately tried to clench her fist about the cloth, although she tried to withdraw her hand from William's, she couldn't. It was as if she was bound with invisible cords that prevented any limb or muscle obeying her panicked, desperate will. She could only watch as William grinned, then held the shred of cloth high over his head.

She wanted to promise him anything – swear that she would marry him, swear that she would for ever give up her love for Geoffrey, anything! – but she couldn't; she could only watch with horror as he dangled the cloth over the edge of the stand, and let it fall.

Her eyes were taken by the fluttering cloth as it opened into a regular square, falling gradually to the grass, but then her attention was grabbed by the horses.

The riders saw the cloth at the same time and spurred their mounts. Both leaped forward as if on massive springs. The horses cantered, then galloped, and the pounding hoofbeats were deafening. All she knew was terror as she saw the two charging ever nearer. Then the points of the lances dropped inch by inch until the heavy wooden poles shod with bright steel, uncapped by coronals, were pointing at each other.

There was a crash, a shattering explosion, and a thick smoke rose from the ground to save Alice from the hideous sight. Then it cleared, and she saw that the horses had collided even as the two men were spitted on each other's lance. She could see the four bodies, the horses strangely peaceful, but the two knights thrashing in their agony, and now both had lost their helms and she could see their anguished death throes, as they looked to her for aid.

Sir John appeared and turned her from the hideous sight, and she took his solace gratefully, thinking he was protecting her; but then she was turned to face William once more, and he gripped in either hand the decapitated heads of her father and her lover.

Her own scream woke her. Drenched in sweat, shivering with horror, she leaned over the edge of her mattress and vomited on the grass before collapsing into sobs.

She had to rise. Even as Helewisia, her maid, wiped the sleep from her eyes and gazed uncomprehendingly at her, Alice pulled a shift over her head to cover her nakedness and went to a stool, pouring herself wine with a hand that shook uncontrollably.

'Mistress? Are you sickening?'

'No, it was just a mare, that's all,' Alice said.

The maid nodded and sat back, her eyes flitting about the darkened tent. The small cresset with its tiny flame lit the place dimly but she knew she would be able to see the goblin if he was still there. Mares were nasty creatures that sat on your chest and sent you evil dreams. Not that anyone believed in such things, of course. It was a story for children, she thought as she suspiciously stared at a fold of cloth that could have concealed a small figure.

Alice ignored her. She sat down on her mattress again and held her head in her hands. The nightmare had shown her an appalling scene. Her father was already dead – killed in the tournament many years before at Exeter. Would Geoffrey die as well?

It was an awful thought. She must let him know how much she thought of him, let him know of her hideous dream, so that he could protect himself from danger. Perhaps that was what the dream was for; maybe God was sending her a vision in order that she might save her Geoffrey. At least at a place like this there were conventions. Heralds were known to be safe messengers for lovers; it was looked upon as part of their duty to aid and abet courtly lovers. She didn't like the look of that greasy man Tyler, but the older, skinny fellow, Odo, he looked all right. She could speak to him and see whether she could entrust him with her message.

To save Geoffrey, she would offer herself as a sacrifice, giving herself adulterously to Squire William in order to save Geoffrey's life. The thought made her want to vomit again, but she recalled the picture she had seen in her mind, of Geoffrey with a lance thrust through his belly, his eyes begging for help as he died . . .

If it would save his life she would marry William.

Or kill him.

CHAPTER EIGHT

The law can move at a snail's pace when no one wants to be involved. And no one wanted to report discovering a dead body when the result was that the finder would be *attached*, held in custody, and *amerced* – forced to pay a surety to guarantee attendance at the next court when the justices arrived.

Sitting in a tavern early that morning, Philip sipped his wine thoughtfully. The revulsion he had experienced while killing Benjamin was gone, this second time. Perhaps because the victim was loathsome – certainly he had caused Philip's ruin still more directly even than Benjamin. Or perhaps killing became easier with experience.

It was certainly easy enough when he thought of his wife's crushed and ruined body or his son's and daughter's tiny broken corpses.

In a just world, this victim would have been outlawed as a felon, could have been legally executed by any man. Philip had visited justice upon him. Like Benjamin, he had taken men's money to ensure that others died. Philip was satisfied that condign punishment had been visited upon a murderer, and that reflection pleased him.

He surveyed the field before him. At this time of day there was a gentleness to the general noise. Smoke drifted from a dozen cooking fires – they weren't permitted within the stalled area, but cooks were allowed their own fires for preparing food, and pies were already being heated, fowls roasting, wine and ale was being warmed with hot, sweetened and spiced water. Over all came the odour of freshly baked bread, attacking the nostrils with the fragrant guarantee of repletion. Philip promised himself a loaf, drained his pot and went to seek a hawker.

As he walked, he glanced about him. Someone had surely seen the body by now, he reckoned, but no one had reported it. The camp was peaceful. Men emerged from their tents and scratched in the chilly early morning air, others rose from the ground, shaking the cloaks and blankets which had been their bedding. To his left were horses, and here grooms were already seeing to their masters' mounts, whistling under their breath or chatting idly. No, the body couldn't have been reported yet. If it had, these unruly youths would have been all a-twitter with the news, scampering about to tell everyone of the discovery.

He walked over to the cooks and bought a small capon. With his knife he split it down the middle then into quarters before wrapping three parts in a scrap of linen. He chewed on a thigh while he sought a bread vendor. With a good rye loaf in his hand, he returned to his own pavilion, where he sat on a stool, set his booted feet on a chest and leaned back against his tentpole while he drank wine from his skin.

Soon, he reminded himself, soon there would come a shriek from the tilting field. A man would run in from the woods, and Philip knew perfectly well who that would be.

It would have to be Hal Sachevyll, the sodomite and lover of Wymond.

Baldwin had agreed to meet Simon near the tented field and the knight was waiting patiently when Simon left the barbican and made his way towards him.

'Your face would look well on a stormcloud,' Baldwin commented happily.

'I'd be better pleased if I'd stayed outside the castle, like you did last night,' Simon grunted.

'It was noisy?'

Simon shot him a darkly meaningful glance. 'This castle is too small to house a host of ants. There's no space anywhere. If you want to sleep, you have to share the hall with all the servants and guests – and that odious cretin Hal Sachevyll comes whining and pleading every five minutes for more money or wood or nails or cloth or something similar. Christ's bones, but I only slept a scant hour. No more. There was a knight from Taunton next to me snoring the night away. And when he was done I'd just got to sleep when some drunken oaf tripped over my feet and woke me.'

'I slept well,' Baldwin lied cheerfully, recalling the singing and shouting from tents all about him as revellers celebrated the tournament to come. One was singing the praises of his hero, Sir Walter Basset, the wild man of Cornwall, while another told him he was a fool, that Sir John from Crukerne would be sure to win.

'Wait till you see 'un in the *medley*, mate. That's when you can tell their mettle,' he asserted.

'Nah! I've seen 'em both and my money's on Sir Walter. He's got the speed and the strength, as well as bein' younger by ten year or more. He'll carve his initials in your man's helm.'

'You reckon, Bob Miller? There's something your 'un ain't got – and that's experience. Sir John is skilled, he is. He's killed plenty o' men in his time.'

'Who hasn't? Sir Walter has too. In the joust, as well.'

'So's Sir John. I remember him slaughtering that cocksure fool Godwin of Gidleigh.'

'Godwin? Oh, I remember him. He was shafting Sir John's wife, if the stories are true.'

'Really? You reckon?'

'That's what they say.'

'That's bollocks, that is!' The man spat. 'That were a bad do, that were. Exeter. The whole Tyrel family died, all except the father, Philip. Big man, he was, powerful, bearded, strong, but his family got flattened when the stand fell. Pretty wife, two nippers. Philip himself pulled the boards off them. Poor bugger.'

'Folks moved?'

'Yeah, they were furious because their favourite got killed by Sir John. They all moved forward and the stand collapsed. Several got flattened, like this Tyrel family.'

'That's because John Crukerne is a murderous bastard.'

'Don't you take that attitude wi' me, Bob Miller, or I'll push that quart pot down your throat so far you'll have to drink it out your arse.'

There was a loud crash at this point, which Baldwin suspected, correctly, was due to a man tripping and taking a table with him, but it was closely followed by guffaws of laughter and Baldwin was inclined to the view that the two had settled their differences in the easiest manner, by sharing another pot of ale.

In the end he and his servant Edgar had exchanged a long-suffering look before rising. They had travelled many thousands of miles in each other's company, both having served together as Knights Templar in God's service, and each was used to lack of sleep due to noise. They had whiled away the night playing dice while the arguments outside continued at a muted level, not finishing until a little before dawn.

Simon would usually have noticed the knight's red-rimmed eyes and yawns, but today he was more taken up with his own concerns. 'Lord Hugh arrives today, and God only knows what that gibbering fool Hal Sachevyll has managed to do. He'll complain, of course. At least,' he added, brightening, 'Meg and Edith will arrive as well.'

'I had not realised they would attend,' Baldwin said with genuine pleasure.

'Try to keep them away! I shall be tied up with Sachevyll and others . . . could you look after them?'

'I should be glad to. It is months since I saw either of them.'

'I'm afraid neither of them thought of you when they asked to come here,' Simon said frankly. 'All they had on their minds was seeing lunatic deeds of courage – and the cloths on sale too, of course.'

'You mean that they would not expect to see courage on my part?'

Simon laughed at his mock-offended expression. 'Let's just say, Baldwin, that both know *exactly* what to expect of you.'

'And I have to remain contented with that, do I?' Baldwin said. He glanced over his shoulder on hearing hooves approaching.

'The King Herald, Mark Tyler,' Simon muttered.

'I recognised his chins,' Baldwin agreed affably.

It was true; he recognised Tyler from the day before. As Baldwin watched, the herald rode past Baldwin's own tent. Edgar was outside, and as the herald passed by, he and Baldwin's armour were spattered with mud. Baldwin saw Edgar look at the man's back long and hard, but then he shrugged. Such accidents could happen even when a man took great care. However, that didn't prevent Edgar feeling resentment at the extra work. He bent and set about cleaning Sir Baldwin's shield again.

The herald cantered on, his nose in the air as if he was trying to keep it away from the smell of the common folk all about him. He was a proud man, very self-important. Not a youngster, Baldwin noted: the fellow was almost Baldwin's own age, certainly over forty. Yet for all his apparent haughtiness, his eyes looked anxious, like a man fearful for his future. Interesting, Baldwin thought.

'Bloody Tyler,' fumed Simon at his side. 'He'll be looking for Hal Sachevyll to pester. He'll want confirmation that all is ready.'

'He was there yesterday.'

'I know, but if he sees more of a mess today he'll not be impressed. I should go straight there and find out what that ninny-hammer managed to screw up after I left last night.'

'There is little enough to do here. Let us both go and see.'

They walked slowly, for Simon was unenthusiastic about seeing Sachevyll. He meandered, buying a cup of ale and draining it before continuing. At the gate they saw the herald again. He was staring about him in a peevish manner, as if he had been expecting to be met by someone of rank.

When Simon and Baldwin came nearer he recognised them, snapping rudely, 'Bailiff Puttock, where have you been? How are things progressing? It is crucial that we have the whole field prepared well in advance. Lord Hugh will not want excuses when he arrives.'

'I'm sure that the builder will have it all in hand,' Simon said soothingly. As he looked about him he could see that things were well advanced and suddenly he was conscious of a sense of relief. The show would be a success, a huge success, and he would be well rewarded by Lord Hugh for his efforts.

Mark Tyler met the sights about him with a grimace of discontent. 'That mincing fool Sachevyll, you mean? I'd be surprised if he has everything ready. Never has before, to my knowledge. The silly arse was almost a day late with the final details at Crukerne six years ago. Christ, but we had to scare the idle bugger to get things done!'

Simon was about to speak when they all heard a scream. Hal Sachevyll burst from the stands, his face white, and tripped, falling in the mud and dung. He wailed, scrabbling as if panicked, trying to lever himself up to escape something.

'You seriously believe that cretin can have all ready on time?' the herald asked scathingly. 'Look at him! I daresay he's hit his thumbkin with a hammer – if he was stupid enough to try to use a real tool.'

But his sneers were silenced when Hal screamed out in a piercing voice: 'Help! Help! God help us! *Murder!*'

Baldwin and Simon were almost at his side when he dropped to his hands and knees and vomited onto the grass.

The carpenter was dead. No one could doubt that as soon as they peered inside Wymond's tent out near the hill in the tilting field.

It was a small pavilion with two cheap palliasses on the floor at the rear of the tent. All about was mess. Leather gloves and aprons lay where the carpenter had dropped them, while pots and a small barrel leaked wine. The place reeked of it, quite concealing the other odours until Simon drew near the mattress on which Wymond lay.

Wymond lay face uppermost, his body part-wrapped in a dirty blanket. Simon took one look at the filthy red-brown stains on the palliasse and covering and looked away, his belly rebelling.

'I thought he was asleep. He often overslept if he'd been drinking, and when I woke I could smell all the wine. I just thought I'd leave him to lie in a while. It never occurred to me that he wasn't all right, not until just now when I came in and shouted at him to get up, pulled the blanket from him . . . My God, and I slept here all night! I slept beside his corpse!' Hal broke off and shoved his fist in his mouth. 'Holy Mother Mary, help me!'

Baldwin pushed Hal out of the way and strode in, crouching at the side of the corpse. Gazing about him, he barked, 'This is your tent as well, Hal?'

'Yes, sir,' Hal said. He turned away from the corpse, weeping silently. 'I slept here last night. My Christ! I was on my palliasse and I thought he was fine. He *was* fine! God's bollocks, who could have done this?'

'Calm down and shut up,' Simon snapped. 'How do we know it wasn't *you*!'

'Me?' Hal sobbed. 'How could *I* kill him?'

'Simon,' Baldwin called, 'there is no sign of a weapon, but this man was savagely attacked. His head is broken.'

Simon was silent a moment. 'His hammer?'

'Is not here,' Baldwin said, standing. 'As far as I can see, there's no stab wound. He was killed by having his head viciously smashed – but I can't see clearly in here.' He pointed to three interested men who were loitering nearby. 'Bring him out and place him on the grass.'

The men reluctantly approached and dragged the body out on its palliasse.

'My heavens!' Mark Tyler declared. 'The poor devil.'

Baldwin remained inside for some minutes, crouched to study the trampled grass minutely, seeking any clue as to the murderer.

Outside, Simon's feelings of complacency were gone, replaced by a mixture of anxiety and anger: anxiety because a murder had been committed, and that would be bound to reflect upon him; but he was also angry that someone could murder Wymond when he still had need of the man. God knew the carpenter was a tricky and truculent bastard at the best of times, but that was no excuse for murder.

'Was it *you*, Bailiff? Did you kill him?' Sachevyll demanded, eyes streaming. He was clinging to a guy-rope near the entrance, but now his eyes fixed upon Simon with a dreadful accusation.

Simon felt his jaw sag in disbelief. 'Good God – why should *I* have killed him?'

'You argued with him. You and he just about came to blows, didn't you?' Hal sniffled. 'I know you were cross with him, but he was only tired and irritable. There was no need to *murder* him.'

'I didn't kill him, you moron! The first I knew of his death was when you appeared just now!' Taking a deep breath, Simon tried to speak calmly, aware that others were eyeing him now but it was not easy. He was embarrassed to be the centre of attention. 'You said you slept in there with him? Didn't you notice he was dead?'

'I couldn't hurt my Wymond!'

There was a snigger behind him but Simon ignored it. 'How could someone else have done this, with you asleep a few feet away?'

'We finished our work as the sun was going down, and went together to buy wine and pies. When we returned I was very tired. We had been slaving hard all day and after a quart of wine, I was nearly passing out, so I went to my bed. Wymond wasn't ready to sleep; he said he was going to go and take a piss. That's all I remember – I must have dozed off. When I woke up today before dawn, I thought he was still resting and left him there. That's all. A little while ago, when I realised that he *still* wasn't up, I got riled and came back to give him a piece of my mind.' The fellow began to weep softly again.

Baldwin had come out and stood with Simon. He glanced at the tent, then back towards the market and castle. Hal and Wymond's tent was far from the rest of the camp. There was no one else nearby, for the architect and his carpenter had pitched theirs here to protect their work. From here it was possible that a scream or shout could be missed from the camp – if, say, a man was belted over the head. But it was inconceivable that Hal wouldn't have heard if Wymond had been attacked here, in the tent. 'I can find no weapon in there,' he said.

Hal stuttered. 'What of his hammer?'

Baldwin shook his head. 'He has no hammer here.'

Hal couldn't help himself and glanced again at Wymond's face. It was all but unrecognisable, the jaw broken, one eye-socket smashed and the eye itself red as though it was filled with blood. Simon followed his gaze, winced, and moved away. He could never come to grips with the evidence of brutality to men. Although he had seen enough corpses in his time, and had killed men himself, he felt a familiar writhing in his guts at the sight of this ruined body. He looked away when Baldwin returned to study the corpse again.

Baldwin noticed Simon's expression and smiled to himself. This squeamishness of Simon's was one of his more endearing traits. Baldwin knew no such qualms. He had seen so many deaths in his youth during the Siege of Acre that he had little compunction in pulling bodies about.

'Well?' Simon demanded.

'Beaten to death. Maybe with a rock, or a cudgel, but a hammer would have done it as well.' He was undressing the body as he spoke, and now he gazed at the man's torso. 'He died hours ago. His body is cool to the touch. No stab wounds on chest . . .' he lifted the arms '. . . or flanks . . .' he hauled the body over, a workman helping him '. . . nor on the back. Hello – what's this?' he declared and pounced.

'What?' asked Simon.

'Bramble thorns in his head here, and also on his shirt,' Baldwin explained.

'So what?' asked Mark Tyler impatiently. 'There are brambles all over the place.'

Baldwin barely glanced at him. 'In the tent, for example?'

'Eh?'

'This means Wymond was not killed in the tent. Do you think Hal could have carried this fellow?'

'*Him?* Look how feeble he is!'

'Then Hal is presumably innocent.'

In his relief at this conclusion, Hal Sachevyll was noisily sick again, heaving convulsively. For his own part Simon wanted to do the same; his belly rebelled and he could taste the bile at the back of his throat.

Baldwin turned to Hal. 'And you say you heard nothing?'

'Of course I didn't,' the man said shakily. 'If I had, I'd have called for help.' He closed his eyes and wiped his mouth. 'Oh Christ. Poor Wymond.'

Mark Tyler looked at Baldwin. 'So where's the weapon?'

'Missing,' Baldwin admitted. 'But the murderer could have taken it and hurled it into the woods or the river.' He was gazing at the ground near the tent's entrance as he spoke, and now he frowned and darted forward. 'Ha!'

'What?' Simon asked.

'Blood,' Baldwin said with suppressed excitement. 'Look, there's a large smudge here. It is the imprint of his head, I think. It proves that Wymond was killed outside, not in the tent.'

'So someone knocked him down out here,' Mark Tyler said. He had wandered over to Baldwin's side and was staring down at the mark. 'Perhaps Hal did it and dragged Wymond in.'

'No! No, I was asleep.' Sachevyll looked as if he might vomit again.

Tyler sniggered, unimpressed. 'Anyone could have killed Wymond and carried him in. Or dragged him.'

Simon interrupted. 'Could Hal have dragged him in, Baldwin?'

Baldwin pulled a doubtful expression. 'Sachevyll is not strong enough. And why should he?'

Simon was eyeing the distance from the tent to the market area. 'Wouldn't someone have heard a man being struck? It's only a hundred yards or so. The noise of the blows . . . When a bone breaks it makes a hell of a din.'

'So Wymond probably wasn't killed here, but further away,' Baldwin mused. 'The killer perhaps set the body down here – while he glanced into the tent to see whether Hal was awake?'

Tyler gave an irritable, 'Tchah! Hal was in the tent. Who else could have killed him?'

Baldwin nodded. 'I think we have to arrest him anyway.'

'Oh no!' Tyler exclaimed, his amusement fading like morning mist. 'You're not arresting *him*. Anyone, but not Hal. He's not finished his work yet, and I won't have Lord Hugh's show ruined to satisfy your fanciful whims.'

'If he committed the murder, he'll—' Simon growled, but Tyler cut across him.

'I said *no*, Bailiff. Or you can explain to Lord Hugh why the field isn't ready.'

'He was the man nearest the body; he was definitely the

first finder; he may have had his reasons to kill Wymond,' Baldwin said contemplatively.

'But I *loved* him, I couldn't have hurt him.' Hal fell to his knees, one hand going to Wymond's shattered and bloody face. 'I loved him,' he choked, and covered his own face with his other hand as he mourned the loss of his partner.

CHAPTER NINE

They left him and withdrew a few yards, Baldwin eyeing the crouching man with sympathy, Simon with contempt, and Tyler watching them all warily. He would move heaven and earth if that were necessary to prevent Hal's arrest until after the tournament.

'Are you sure it wasn't him?' Simon asked.

'Simon, really. Was that man lying?'

'Who knows? Damned sodomite. He could have been a wife, squatting there like that. Pathetic!'

Baldwin said nothing. His experiences in Eastern countries had taught him that love between men was not so uncommon. Over here, even the King himself was said to be a sodomite whose lovers had included that madman Gaveston, until his death, and now Hugh Despenser.

'Whoever did this could do it again,' the Bailiff said grimly. 'God forbid, but he could strike again. What can we do?'

'There's no point in worrying – we have to find out *why* Wymond was killed. And why so brutally? Surely a stabbing would have been easier and safer.'

'A madman?' Simon enquired.

Baldwin shot him a look. 'Some madman, to have been able to kill in this way without leaving a clue. No, I believe this was a premeditated murder.'

'A madman, eh, Bailiff ?' Mark Tyler gave a short laugh. 'Is that what you reckon? And only yesterday you almost drew your knife on him yourself.'

Squire William had risen early, making his way to the lists to exercise his horse, and afterwards had remained, drinking with a few other men who hoped to be knighted. It was good to catch up with old friends after such a long time away, and many wanted to ask him about his adventures in battle.

Knighthood, he felt, was given less than its due respect. Probably it was the fault of the kings who had insisted that base-born men should be permitted to join the knighthood – indeed should be *forced* to join if they earned enough money. This distraint was no doubt good for the Treasury, but it meant that men who could scarcely lift an axe with both hands were now being received into the ranks of the knights.

William had no qualms about joining it himself. He knew that he was different; he had been born to the nobility. All his youth he had been educated in weapons, in handling swords and knives, maces, axes and lances. His honour was beyond doubt, for it was his birthright.

Even a knight requires leisure, though, and today William wandered among the tents of knights and tradesmen, standing a while to watch the youths of the town playing with their bows and arrows, wrestling, or gambling on two dogs fighting. Children were stoning chickens, and William paused to watch until one child, angry at a competitor's use of a heavy stone, went to the maimed cock and broke its neck with one easy flick of his wrist. That led to a short flurry of fists as both boys tried to determine whose bird it was, a tussle that was cut short by a large forester who picked up one boy in each huge hand and held them apart with a bemused expression, then clouted them both over the head once he had set them back on the ground.

William grinned at the sight and was about to move away when he saw her.

She was a good height, slim, with slanted green eyes that looked on the brink of laughter. Young, certainly, but with a fiery temperament, he fancied. With her complexion he guessed she must be fair-haired beneath her wimple, and when the sun caught her face she seemed to glow from within. At her side was a thin, scowling man dressed like a servant. He must be her chaperone. William saw the two join the gamblers at the fight, saw them pause to egg on the dogs. The chaperone stayed watching when she wandered a few feet to a stall selling wine. William observed her, feeling the stirrings of excitement.

The young squire never willingly lost an opportunity to prove his worth in the battle of the sexes. He walked slowly towards her, and as he approached and she noticed his intent gaze fixed upon her, he bowed, low and reverent. 'My Lady,' he breathed.

'Sir.'

Her tone was not welcoming, but often a woman would try to conceal her true feelings, he knew. She was younger than he had thought – perhaps not yet fifteen. Probably a virgin. William had enjoyed virgins before, among the peasants on his father's lands, but this girl was no rough and uneducated wench to be easily persuaded to take a tumble with her lord's son. She was so well-dressed and graceful in her movements, she must be the daughter of a wealthy man; that would make taking her maidenhead all the more pleasurable. He would enjoy snatching her from under the eyes of a rich parent or guardian, he considered, smiling wolfishly.

Taking a quick look about him to see that his father was nowhere near, he continued with his attack.

'Lady, I am blinded. Your beauty outshines the sun herself. Your radiance burns me. Your smile could cure a thousand ills and put to flight a legion of devils, for while a perfection such as you exists upon this earth, all ugliness is doomed.'

'Your attention is not wanted,' she stated with calm precision, like a much older woman. 'Please leave me.'

'Never!' he declared, swiftly moving to block her retreat. 'All I offer is my service as a knight. I —

'You? A knight?' she asked in a rush as though she was at once overtaken with enthusiasm, but then she sniffed and said more warily, 'I don't see your arms or sword.'

He grinned. 'I anticipate myself. I shall be dubbed during this festival, and then my arms will be your arms, my sword yours; my heart is yours already.'

As he spoke he realised that they were no longer alone. The servant had approached and stood at his shoulder.

She too had noticed, and now she smiled as she sipped her wine.

The servant said gruffly, 'Are you all right, miss?'

'Yes, thank you, Hugh. I think the good squire is about to leave.'

'I would prefer to wait and talk, Lady.'

'And I would prefer to be alone. So please leave me – otherwise I might have to ask my servant, Hugh here, to keep you from me,' she said.

'I doubt a servant could keep me from you,' William said bravely, but he didn't like the look of the large stick this Hugh carried. It looked well-used.

She frowned. 'You shouldn't judge Hugh by his dress. He is a good fighter – but more to the point, if you were to be seen attacking him while I called for help, you would be condemned for molesting me. And a squire found brawling with a servant while attempting to shame a woman, would hardly be looked upon as chivalrous, would he?'

Defeated, William bowed low to her. 'But my Lady, I shall never attempt to shame you. How could any man look at such loveliness and think of harming it? I shall look to talk to you at the first opportunity,' he smiled. 'I can hardly be expected to see such radiant beauty without wishing to enjoy a smile from it. I look forward to seeing you again soon.'

As soon as he had gone, Edith Puttock, Simon's daughter, gave Hugh a fierce glower. 'So what were you doing while I was being insulted by that arrogant twerp?'

'You didn't look too upset,' Hugh shrugged.

Edith surveyed him irritably. 'That's a bit rich, Hugh. And don't put on that frown for my benefit. It may work with Mother, but it doesn't with me. I know you too well.'

It was true. Hugh had been her devoted servant ever since she was born; when she wanted a companion or playmate it was always to Hugh that she turned. Her father was too often away from their home for her to consider him in the same light, and in any case Simon was always the stern master of the household. Hugh, on the other hand, was always ready and willing to drop his chores and join her in her games.

If anything he was even more hound-like in his treatment of her since he had come back to the Puttock household. For the last year or more he had been living with a woman up near Iddesleigh, with Simon's grudging approval since Hugh had made his oaths at the church door with her. 'More than I did with you, eh?' Simon had said to his wife when Hugh told them. Simon and Margaret, Edith's mother, had made their vows before witnesses in a field during harvest.

For Edith, who was accustomed to Hugh's constant presence, it had been odd to see him go. Living without him for a year had been strange, as if an adored brother had died. Worse, somehow, was the discovery that a woman could not only attract him, but could tempt him away from the household where he had made his home, especially since she already carried a child who was not Hugh's. It intrigued Edith to know what this wife of his was like, but that was not the sort of question she could ask him. The differences in her position and age compared with Hugh's were too great.

Yet some subtle change had taken place. He was less deferential than before, less prepared to accept orders. There was a new independence in his manner.

'I thought you wanted to talk to him.'

'An overdressed popinjay like him?' she demanded scornfully.

'You looked happy enough.'

'Oh, nonsense.'

'You kept sort of smiling at him, like you wanted him to chat.'

'Rubbish!' she declared with some little alarm. It was true that he had a pleasant enough face, square and rugged without the lines, which all too often denoted cruelty, at his forehead. 'I was just being polite.'

'I thought you wanted company, that's all. You're always saying you do,' Hugh reminded her.

'Well . . .' She was torn. There was something about the man which had attracted her. She was still inexperienced in the rules of courtly lovemaking. At home in Lydford she knew all the boys and had kissed a few, but there was little need for professions of love. She wouldn't dream of marrying Bill or Soll or any of the others, for they were all like brothers, but sometimes it was good to sit on top of a hay rick and cuddle a youth, allowing him to kiss her, perhaps, but never going too far, for that was a sin. But this lad with his charm and obvious admiration was different. 'Well, perhaps I wouldn't mind seeing him again,' she amended.

At that moment she heard her mother calling for her. 'But don't tell Mother or Father,' she hissed.

Hugh shook his head slowly. 'I wouldn't.'

'Good. And now I suppose we should see if we can find Father in this madhouse.'

'Why should someone do that to him?' Simon demanded as Baldwin peered down at the naked corpse.

The herald grinned nastily at Simon's pale face. 'Bit of a coincidence, isn't it, Bailiff? Dead within a day of his picking a fight with you.'

'Shut up!' Simon snarled. 'If you haven't anything useful to say, keep quiet.'

'Calm yourself, Bailiff. I was only joking! But never mind. I shall leave you to it. Do you wish me to send for the Coroner?'

Baldwin nodded. 'I suppose so. You will have to send a messenger to Exeter. In the meantime, where were *you* last night?'

Tyler gaped. 'Me?'

'It was as likely to be you as Simon here,' Baldwin said.

'But the Bailiff must have seen me in the hall. We ate our meal there.'

'So you confirm Simon's innocence.'

'He left a little after dark.'

'What did you do then?'

'Me?' Tyler repeated, with a rising note of disbelief.

'Yes – *You* ! What did you do when Simon wasn't there to give you an alibi?' Baldwin pressed him.

Tyler set his jaw. 'I remained in the hall and drank with Odo, another herald, until I slept. All right? Now what did the *Bailiff* do after leaving the hall?'

'I went to my bed in the bailey,' Simon grated. 'And I was seen by the sentry walking from the hall, I expect, so for Christ's sake stop accusing me!'

Tyler curled his lip and did not answer. He turned on his heel and walked away.

Baldwin gave a grunt of relief. 'Cretin!' he said and led the way behind the tent.

There was a steep bank leading down to the river, which flowed swiftly here. Baldwin stood with an arm wrapped about his chest, his chin cupped in his other hand. Hal

Sachevyll wandered slowly after them, looking lost and in a state of shock.

'What is it, Baldwin?' Simon asked. He was breathing more easily now that the shattered corpse was out of sight, but still the sour taste remained at the back of his throat.

'Someone must have persuaded Wymond to meet him. They walked . . . somewhere, and there Wymond was killed, beaten to death, then somehow taken back to the tent and dumped there,' Baldwin mused. 'But surely a fellow like him would be cautious? How was he lured away? What was the murder weapon, and where is it? We have a duty to find it so that the Coroner can confiscate it.'

Simon nodded. Any weapon used to kill was *deodand*, forfeit to the Church in order to expiate the sin of murder. 'Surely it was Wymond's own hammer that was used?'

'Perhaps, but if so, where is it? Was it tossed in here?'

Simon bent and peered at the river. 'Possibly, but with the water flowing so fast it's hard to see.'

'It won't be here,' Baldwin decided. 'Wymond wouldn't have been killed so close to his friend. The hammer was used somewhere else and left there. Why bring it here? Or was it kept as a trophy? This is no ordinary felonious murder. The violence used was brutal – quite extreme. Yet I don't see a madman planning such a killing. The brutality points to a man who sought revenge.'

'Revenge?' Hal squeaked.

'How well did you know him?' Simon asked.

'As well as you can know a companion. Wymond and I have often worked together,' Hal added evasively. He dropped to the ground and wrapped his arms about his thin legs, chin on his knees.

'Was he always so argumentative?' Simon said.

Hal took a shivering intake of breath. 'He was determined to see things done properly, Bailiff. And before you get on your high horse, remember you argued as much with him as the other way about. Just because you're a Bailiff doesn't mean you're better than everyone else.'

Baldwin grinned at Simon's discomfort. 'Enough, Sachevyll. We're trying to make sense of this foul killing, and you should wish to help us.'

'I do.'

'Then answer our questions. He was the sort of man who'd resort to his fists rather than use words, wasn't he?'

'I suppose so.'

'How long have you known him? Please answer properly.'

'A good fifteen years, I would say. No, more. I met him when I was constructing a marvellous scene for King Edward I, back in 1304. It was a great Arthurian pageant, and no expense was spared!' His eyes shone with pride at the recollection.

'You have worked with him ever since?' Simon asked. He had no wish to be sidetracked into the architect's reminiscences.

'Yes. We worked together again when King Edward II took the throne, and joined forces on the tournament at Exeter in 1306. That was where we met Benjamin Dudenay.'

'Who?' Simon queried.

'He helped finance us,' Hal said quickly. 'Then we went to Wallingford.'

Baldwin was interested. 'Wallingford? That was the encounter Piers Gaveston won, wasn't it?'

'Yes. Piers was wonderful! So tall and graceful! All the nobles were jealous, you know. No one would fight with him.'

'He must have been quite a warrior,' Simon said grudgingly. Like Baldwin, he had heard that Gaveston was a sodomite. Unnatural men like him repelled Simon.

Hal grinned slyly. 'He was young. All the nobles felt he was a cuckoo in their midst, that he was going to keep on taking whatever honours or glory he could, so they united against him.'

'How did he win?' Simon asked.

Hal gave a low chuckle. 'It was easy. The only folk Gaveston could trust were the unimportant: squires and knights with no fortune; all the strong, young bucks with nothing to lose and everything to gain. Opposing them were middle-aged men who would tire and wouldn't recover so speedily from buffets. Gaveston and his accomplices ran rings around them.'

'I have often seen the same happen. When a team of youths attack older men, the younger will win. Bear that in mind before gambling here, Simon,' Baldwin said. 'Hal, did Wymond have many enemies?'

'He was apt to fight, but as head carpenter he often had to. Someone has to keep workers at their jobs.'

'He could be over-zealous in his chastisement?'

'Perhaps. Some may think so, but you can't be too careful. Stands collapse when they are badly built.' Hal cast a sidelong look at Simon. 'Or if the timber's shite.'

Baldwin spoke reflectively before Simon could respond. 'I recall Nefyn. Many were hurt there.'

'That's right,' Hal agreed. 'There were so many in the dancing room that the floor collapsed; I fear one of my own stands has fallen before now.'

'Shoddy workmanship, I expect,' Simon said dismissively.

'*No*, Bailiff. It was when Sir John killed Sir Godwin back in the Exeter tournament. As Sir Godwin fell, the crowds were appalled. They all adored him. An extremely popular, courteous knight, he was. Especially among the ladies. In the rush to the front of the stand, people were crushed at the fencing, and then the whole front gave way . . .'

Hal broke off. He could see it all in his mind's eye. The awnings and carpets red with blood; blood ran onto the grass, thick and viscous as oil. It had been terrible, a bloodbath. Hal saw a child, a little boy, whose body was almost cut in half by a large beam of wood. Next to him was a woman, then another, a little girl who looked like an angel, with a halo of blood, and a man . . .

'I still have nightmares about it,' he told them, his voice low and full of horror. 'It was a scene of carnage. Knights, squires and heralds all tried to rescue the trapped people, but it was so difficult in the shifting mass of timber. Men, women and children were killed – eleven when it fell, and more later from their injuries. One family was extinguished, with only the father living, while many children survived orphaned. Lady Alice Lavandar was one: When her mother died, Sir John took her on in penitence. I could never wish to see such a disaster repeated. It was hideous.'

'Sir John took her on, you say?' Baldwin asked. 'Why?'

'Didn't you know? She was Sir Godwin's daughter.'

'No, I didn't know,' Baldwin said.

Sachevyll cried mournfully 'No, I could never wish to witness such a disaster again. Once was enough.'

'And yet the same thing happened in 1316 at Crukerne,' Baldwin said sternly.

'That wasn't my fault. Sir Richard was forced against the stand and his weight, with that of Sir Walter and their horses, was enough to break the stands. Most of the injuries were from the horse's death throes as it thrashed. It was awful, but it was nothing to do with me.'

'You don't think Wymond made any enemies here?' Baldwin asked.

'Other than,' Hal said coldly, brought back to reality with a lurch, 'the Bailiff here, you mean?'

CHAPTER TEN

William was determined to see Edith again. Although she was young, that was no barrier. She was attractive, fresh and desirable. If it hadn't been for that miserable churl hanging around with her, he might have been able to take her off for a walk in the woods.

Not that he was set on a virgin. Inexperienced women ready to be deflowered were common enough, especially in a field of tournament. Christ's blood! A man had to be careful to avoid wenches hot with lust when he'd enjoyed a good run at an opponent, for women would scream and throw themselves at the winner. He remembered the last tournament he had attended, when he was a mere boy. It was hard to move on the grass near the field because of all the successful knights covering the ladies who had given them the glad eye beforehand. Oh, one or two of the women played hard to get, but they were often all the hornier when they grappled beneath the sun.

He had met enough of them during his time as a squire, following his master from one tournament to another, and when his master had his hands full with one, occasionally William was able to help out with the next one in the queue. When he was younger he had been surprised that older women should fancy him, but he made full use of them. If he didn't, others would, and at least with his fair good looks he had his choice of the more attractive ones. He soon learned that those women who were most proud in public would behave more lewdly than the commonest slut, given the right situation, and the right situation so often involved nothing more than a strong lusty youth.

And often the worst, most flagrant women, were those who were married and who should never have been anywhere near the tournaments.

He was musing pleasantly on such matters, recalling especially the wife of a knight from Somerset whose bawdy behaviour had exhausted him for almost an entire week, when he saw the brunette.

She was almost as tall as him, a leggy, full-breasted wench with enormous eyes which gave him a cursory once-over as her glance ranged over the crowds. When her gaze passed over him a second time, and lingered on him a moment longer than was entirely necessary, he instantly decided to try his luck.

It was the thing about a tournament. The women always expected a tumble, he reflected as he stepped along in her wake. Bugger the ideals of courtly love – the main thing was, it gave an excuse to any woman who wanted to fondle another man's body rather than her own husband's.

Of course some gave no thought for their danger, while others positively hankered after a fling with a lad like William because he *represented* danger; a few more simply didn't care what their husbands thought of their affairs. It was as if some women thought that they had the right to emulate the debauched behaviour of Guinevere with Lancelot – but God help those who were found out.

Privately William often found them rather sad even as he tupped them. The idea that supposedly honourable women could behave in such a manner was disgraceful . . . but only a fool would refuse the sweet taste of their lips and bodies or turn down the exquisite pleasure they offered.

And this one was perfection. From the look of her heart-shaped face, she could have been the Madonna Herself. High brow, arched eyebrows and a mouth with a natural pout that gave her a come-hither, wanton look. With lips like hers she could suck the rivets off my helmet, he thought admiringly. Her attraction lay not only in her face: her body looked firm and taut, as sleek and fit as an Arab-bred pony, strong without being unfeminine, while her gait was as proud and smooth as a queen's.

It was strange that her husband allowed her to walk about the place with only a scruffy-looking fellow to protect her. Astonishing. Some men could be incredibly carefree with their women. Well, William wasn't going to let this beautiful filly slip through his grasp without a fair attempt to come to grips.

He caught up with her, bowing with his most appealing smile, a slight twist to one corner, an eyebrow raised. 'My Lady, you eclipse the sun.'

'Go bull your mother!' the man at her side grated. He was shorter than William, heavy-set and strongly-built, but from closer to, an even more villainous-looking fellow. William felt sure that he was only some servant.

After his defeat at Edith's hands, William was not going to accept a second refusal so easily. He gave the man a surprised glance, but he clearly was not wealthy: the cloak he wore was thin and worn, his tunic faded, his shirt threadbare, his hose of the roughest and cheapest fustian. The husband of this woman would surely be clad in similar finery to her own, velvet and rich fur trimming. No, this fellow was only a guard, William considered. Ignoring the servant, he returned to his open admiration of the woman. 'My Lady, I have never beheld such perfection before. May I—'

'Are you deaf, churl? You are asking for trouble – now shut up and clear off!'

William bridled. He drew himself up to his full height and met the man's furious expression, but then he saw the other take a slow pace forward and reach for a small knife at his belt. His own hand moved, but he had scarcely gripped his hilt when he felt the sharp point at his throat.

'If this was anywhere else, I'd have cut your balls off and fed them to you by now. Leave the lady alone, brat,' the man hissed.

'I was not talking to you, but to the lady,' William said, taking a swift backwards step. His blade was out now, and he stood with the knife held low, ready to strike.

'Well, if you want to talk to my wife, you have to talk to *me* first, you misbegotten piece of shit! I don't like little half-grown bastards trying their bollocks with her.'

'My Lord, I am sorry,' William blurted. 'I meant no insult to you or your Lady, but I didn't realise she was married. My compliments to you.'

Sir Walter Basset was not interested in Squire William's apologies. His anger was fanned by the boy's thoughtless behaviour and he gripped his knife, tempted to launch himself upon the squire as William strode away. Just as he was about to chase after the lad, there was a touch at his forearm.

'He's not worth it. Bollocks, you say? Do you think he has any?'

Sir Walter shuddered with the release of tension and thrust his knife back in its sheath. The nearness of violence had thrilled his blood. He loved to fight, loved the rush of energy that flooded his body and filled his soul, but when some little shit like that tried to get his leg over Helen, there was always a harder edge to his rage. Helen was a beautiful woman, one any man would be proud to have dangling on his arm or adorning his bed, but Sir Walter was keenly aware that others envied him and wanted her for themselves. Let them try! He would cut off the prick of any man who poked it too near his woman. Cut it off and feed it to the crows. The whoreson needed a lesson and Sir Walter would be happy to teach him.

'Husband? Shall we return to our tent so I can prove my loyalty?' she chided him gently.

He chuckled gruffly as the boy receded in the distance, swallowed by the crowd. 'You're sure he didn't insult you? If you think he deserves it, I'll make him eat his own liver.'

Helen Basset smiled at her man. 'There is no one but you, husband. That young fool will realise that when he sees you destroying your foe in the tournament.'

'If I see him there, I'll kill him,' Sir Walter swore.

Geoffrey saw Alice from a distance while he was exercising his master's horse, and he reined in, ambling along gently some distance behind her, twirling a switch in his hand.

There was a gleam at her temple: surely a strand of her hair had come astray from her wimple, and it glinted bright gold when the sun streamed between the tree-boughs overhead. She moved with an easy, long-legged gait that he would have recognised from a mile away, or so he told himself, and then he grinned at the inanity of the thought. With *his* eyes, he'd be lucky to see more than a blob at a hundred yards, let alone a mile.

But from this close he could discern her figure, her walk, her tallness . . . and her beauty. For Alice was very beautiful: her eyes were large and as blue as cornflowers on a bright summer's day, her lips were full and soft, tasting faintly of the spices she chewed, her brow was broad and as pale as the rest of her flesh.

And what flesh! His fingers itched to touch her again, to feel her soft skin, to smell her odour, as sweet and heady as a strong wine! She was everything he had hoped, on that day when they had sworn their eternal love and exchanged their vows, and now, seeing her so close, he was on fire to lie with her again.

Alice had the face of an angel, a face that Geoffrey wanted to kiss again and again. The sooner he could announce to the world that they were wed, the better. Ideally at the church door while here in Oakhampton. That would be best, while the tournament was still in progress, with all the Lord Hugh's knights and bannerets in attendance. Of course Geoffrey would have to be knighted first, but he saw no impediment to his securing that honour: he was wealthy enough in his own right, he had the support of his master, Sir Ralph Sturrey, and he was old enough to be granted his spurs. With the inbuilt confidence of a man who could name all his ancestors even before the invasion of King William the Bastard, a man who still owned his grandsire's sword, rusted and chipped as it was, Geoffrey knew he would become a knight of renown.

He *had* to. The thought brought a shiver to his frame. He must deserve his woman's faith in him, true, but there was more to it than that. His recent history as a warrior left much to be desired. If news of his failure of courage was to be bruited about, he would become an object of ridicule, a joke, a nickumpoop. Geoffrey didn't want that, but he should be safe. All those who had witnessed his desertion at the Battle of Boroughbridge were dead.

Not that he doubted for a moment that his wife would remain loyal. She was wedded to him now, before God, and if accusations of cowardice were levelled against him, Alice would support him.

Seeing his wife walking ahead of him brought to his mind the consideration that she was his now, and must acquiesce to his desires. If he demanded that she join him in a lecherous excursion in the long grasses of the meadow, she must comply.

Suddenly the memory of her ivory skin, the warmth of her body as she encompassed him, was so vivid that the recollection was almost painful. There was a clutching at his heart at the picture in his mind of his wife smiling up at him, the grass cushioning her head, cornflowers and poppies dancing in the wind.

It was too much – he *had* to have her again! Spurring his mount, in moments he was behind Alice and he glanced about him warily.

They were almost alone, apart from a man or two ahead. No one was watching; it was the work of a moment. He reached down with his switch and settled it lightly upon her rump, giggling to himself as she spun round, startled, like some light-footed nymph.

'Haha, that got you, my love, didn't it?' he chuckled.

'Who are you? What do you mean by it, sir?'

With a slowly dawning horror, he realised this wasn't Alice. 'My Lady, I offer my sincerest . . .'

'How dare you, sir!' The woman stamped with rage. 'Do I look like a common slut to be thus tickled? Do I act the whore for your pleasure?'

Whoever she might be, she was not Alice, and her fury made her loud. Ahead, the men had turned round to look at her, wondering at her temper. At such a distance Geoffrey could not see their faces, but he was sure he could hear some laughter, along with some rumblings of anger as well. They thought he had given the woman some intolerable insult, which, he could only admit abjectly to himself, he had.

'No, my dear Lady, I give you my most sincere apology. You see, I thought you were someone else whom I know very well. I would never have dreamed of insulting you. I would rather cut off my arm than let it demean you in such a way.'

'It felt like a lewd and intolerable slight.'

'I fear, my Lady, that I *was* lewd, common and irreverent. But I thought . . .' he hesitated only a moment '. . . you were my sister.' He didn't want to admit he had thought she might be his wife.

'Your sister?'

'Lady Cecilia Carew,' he said.

She drew her chin up. 'You thought me brunette? And three inches shorter?' she enquired with a cold sneer.

He felt panic overwhelming him. Two of the men ahead looked as though they were considering protecting this strident young wench, and if he should be slandered as a womaniser, such unchivalrous behaviour could prevent his being dubbed knight.

Opening his mouth to protest his innocence, he found himself incapable of speech. He moved his jaw but no words would come. Face reddening, he bit at his lip.

'Well, sir? Have you nothing to add?'

Frustration, shame and embarrassment took him over. He jerked at the reins and jabbed spurs to his horse's flanks, riding off as quickly as he could, although not fast enough to miss the woman's jeering curses.

He felt the shame colouring his cheeks, flaming them until he was certain that all about could see his embarrassment. When he heard his name called, he was tempted to turn away and avoid whomsoever it might be, but he had ridden into the press entering the next field and couldn't escape. He set his shoulders and turned to face the man.

'Well?'

'Squire Geoffrey? I am called Odo, the Herald. I have been asked to give you a message.'

'From whom?' Geoffrey asked haughtily, but then his relief was profound when the messenger smiled lopsidedly.

'From a Lady Alice, Squire, if you can spare me a moment.'

When Hal had gone, Baldwin threw Simon a frowning glance.

'You realise the significant point?'

'Of course,' Simon grunted. 'There's a curfew. All the hawkers and tradespeople would be gone.'

'So only knights and their servants could be about . . .' Baldwin said thoughtfully. 'We should first seek the killer among *them.*'

Simon was quiet a while, staring back towards the market. This tournament was to have been an enjoyable event for him, a reminder of easier, quieter times. He could remember the *hastiludes* his father had organised, the rushing of destriers, the rattling crash as steel-tipped lances hit shields or armour, the flags flying gaily, the women watching and giving their tokens, promising their bodies to the knights who upheld their honour and unseated their opponents.

The memories were suffused with the warm, comfortable glow that a happy childhood affords. Simon *had* been a happy lad – and the tournaments in his youth had been wonderful affairs during the reign of the good King Edward I.

And now his opportunity to relive those wonderful times, to prove to himself that he could equal his father in managing such a grand affair, was to come to nought – all because of a confounded murderer.

'You want me to make Lord Hugh's most valued feudatories understand that I suspect them of murder?' Simon said.

'That could make your life short and interesting,' Baldwin grinned. 'No. The curfew is never that strong – but it means that strangers may have been noticed. We should ask whom they saw last night. And the watchmen, of course. If someone was wandering around the place, they should have spotted them.'

'It's asking rather a lot to think they'd have seen much in the dark,' Simon grumbled.

'Well, the murder happened in the dark. There cannot have been many people about,' Baldwin said. 'Come along, Simon. We have solved more confusing riddles before now.'

'The Coroner must hold an inquest.'

'By the time he arrives, maybe we shall have discovered the facts for him.'

Simon nodded doubtfully and called a watchman for help to remove the body of Wymond. 'Do you believe Hal?'

Baldwin looked at him. 'Why should I not?'

'It seems odd. If they were so close, why was Hal content to go to bed and fall asleep while his chamber-mate was out? If Hal thought Wymond was only going for a piss, wouldn't he have waited and raised the alarm when his friend didn't return?'

'Perhaps, and yet they had been working so late, is it not possible that Hal was so exhausted he fell asleep as soon as his head hit the hay? They weren't new lovers, were they – keen to get into bed with each other and . . . well, you know what I mean. They were like an old married couple from that point of view.'

Simon scratched his head. 'Hmm, I see your point. And I don't really believe Hal would have murdered Wymond, and there's no way he could have carried him back here.'

'I doubt whether he could overcome Wymond in the first place anyway,' Baldwin agreed. 'No, I think it is more likely to be one of the tournament-folk – someone who . . . what? Wanted to rob? Or was looking for revenge. But why? And how to seek one killer among so many knights and squires?'

'Good God! I don't know,' Simon said despairingly. 'I am supposed to be organising the tournament, not searching for a murderer.'

'Then you must leave it to me, old friend. I will see what I can discover by talking to the participants.'

The watchmen arrived and soon Simon had organised men to carry the body on a stretcher. Taking his leave of Baldwin, he went with them, leading the way on a path which wound up the hill behind the castle and back to the road.

As Simon had intended, few saw his procession, but he knew that soon the gossip would spread about the field and when it did, he would have to be present in person to calm the anxious, or those vengeful fools filled with self-righteous indignation and ale. But first Simon must go to the castle; he wanted a clerk to take down details of the body, the clothing and the purse so that Sir Roger of Gidleigh, the Coroner, would have a full report when he arrived. It was a great relief to Simon that Sir Baldwin was there to help investigate the murder.

CHAPTER ELEVEN

Baldwin walked thoughtfully back to his tent and told Edgar to make sure that all his armour was in good condition, his mail undamaged, his undergarments well padded and comfortable to wear. A knight must always see that his equipment was gleaming, for the knight reflected his Lord's importance. Shabbiness was shameful. And one never knew whether Baldwin would have to put it on at some stage of the tournament. Meanwhile, he would go among the workers at the stands to ask whether any had seen or heard any strange noises during the night; after that, he would consider which knights and servants should be questioned.

He spoke to many with singularly little result until he found a thin, tired-looking man near the main arena, who shook his head in response to Baldwin's enquiries but then looked carefully about him and led the way behind a stand where they could speak without being observed.

'Look, I don't know who killed him or why, but I'll tell you this: that Carpenter fellow was a nasty piece of work, he was. Always handy with his fists when he thought someone was slacking, but he never did much himself. Him and Sachevyll used Lord Hugh's money, but kept back as much as they could, always buying cheap odds and sods. I'd bet Wymond was killed by someone he'd threatened, or beaten up or someone he'd stolen from.'

'He wasn't stabbed. Why smash his head in?'

'One way of making sure the bastard was dead, wasn't it?' The man spat.

'Did he have any friends here?'

'You must be joking. Only Sachevyll. They've been going about together for some years, from what I've heard. Bloody queens! Makes you sick, doesn't it?'

'I don't care about that. What of their work?'

'Sachevyll designed layouts and decoration while Wymond put it all together. All the bigger tournaments, Sachevyll and Wymond were there. To be fair they could be good at their job.'

'When did *you* last see the dead man?'

'Wymond? After we'd knocked off work last night. It was evening time. I saw him talking to someone down near the river behind his tent – a slim fellow, taller than Wymond.'

'You didn't recognise him?'

'No. It was late and I wasn't that interested. I'd seen enough of Wymond for one day. The only reason I was out and about was because I'd left a wineskin and gone back to fetch it. You know what thieving bastards the watchmen are – I didn't want one of them drinking it. The pair of 'em were standing under the trees. Couldn't see the other one's face.'

'But you are sure he was with Wymond?'

'Yes – I'd swear to it.'

'What then?'

'They walked off together.' He snorted disgustedly. 'Going for a shag, for all I know, dirty buggers! Then I left for my bed.'

'What of Hal?'

'He'd gone. I saw him enter his tent. Waiting for Lover-boy.'

As he spoke, Sachevyll himself appeared around the side of the stand and stared at them. He looked gaunt and pinched, and Baldwin felt a pang of sympathy for him: he had lost his lover, perhaps his only friend and also his companion in business. What future could he expect now?

Sachevyll screeched at the workman, 'What are *you* doing? Don't you want to keep your job?' Facing Baldwin, he pleaded: 'Leave them alone, can't you? Holy Mother, send me patience! With Wymond dead, I have enough to do without worrying that you'll stop the men from their work.'

'You should be grateful: he has confirmed your story. You say you had been in business with Wymond for some years?' Baldwin asked as the man hurried away.

'Yes,' Hal Sachevyll sighed. 'God! What of it?'

Baldwin was tempted to ask whether they had embezzled money from Lord Hugh, but Sachevyll would guess that the worker would have tipped him off. It appeared unlikely, but if Sachevyll *had* killed Wymond, he would make short work of the builder. Baldwin held his peace; instead he asked, 'What interests did you have in common?'

'We enjoyed making tournaments, that's all,' Hal Sachevyll snapped.

'Can't you tell me anything that could help me find his killer?'

'I don't *know* anything!' The man was wringing his hands.

'Did you see anyone with him yesterday? Someone you didn't recognise?'

'No! When I saw him it was only to talk about the timbers. Why the men used them to erect the stands baffles me. A complete waste of time. They will all have to come down. Wymond was supposed to be keeping an eye on all that. The wood is useless. As it is, I have been forced to go and buy more, and you'll never guess how much I—'

'I have no wish to know,' Baldwin interrupted smoothly, 'but I am glad to hear that you can guarantee the safety of the stands.'

He left Sachevyll and wandered pensively back to the river near the architect's tent, looking down into the water again, contemplating the tranquil scene. A little further on the river curved back towards the hill on which the castle stood. Baldwin strolled along the bank. There was a thick muddy patch where cattle came to drink at the far bank, and a corresponding mess on his side. It was a pleasant, shaded spot, with the sun dappling the waters, and the river gave a pleasant, gurgling chuckle as it rippled past. Baldwin stood and rested a hip against a low branch, turning back to face the field.

Baldwin considered Wymond perfectly capable of viciousness; he could well have committed some foul act in the past which was deserving of retribution. His appearance went against him, but so did his quick temper. Baldwin, a man who had seen men-at-arms who raped, slaughtered and tortured, saw in Wymond someone who could have been guilty of the same kind of behaviour. Not, he sighed to himself, that that was in any way an excuse for what had happened to Wymond.

How did the murderer actually commit the crime? Where was Wymond caught, where was he bound, where was he hammered to unconsciousness and murdered?

Before him, in between himself and the wooden stands of the *ber frois* was the tent where Wymond had been found. The stands blocked the view to the fairground scene beyond. Right was the sweep of the river, curving around the whole area. Baldwin was sure that someone who wanted to kill a man would have taken the victim to a quiet area so he couldn't be interrupted. His eyes were drawn back to the hill on his left, behind the castle. Up there the trees might smother a little of the noise, a man's screams or shouts – but a killer would surely want somewhere safer, where he couldn't be seen or heard. The hill was too close to the market and stands for that.

A murderer would want a more private place. Perhaps he found it by crossing the river.

The man they were seeking was not some reckless, random killer. And this was no spur-of-the-moment deed. A man with a grudge was the most likely candidate – but *who*?

He turned and stared out over the river. The water looked deep, but then he noticed that a causeway lay just beneath the surface. Ah, well! he thought resignedly, and stepped boldly into it, trying to ignore the water which lapped over the tops of his boots.

Sir Edmund of Gloucester rode his horse at a fast gallop into the tented area, guiding his mount with an automatic tweak of the reins and subtle shift of his weight. The great charger turned, avoiding a small child by inches, and Sir Edmund laughed to see the brat caught up by an outraged mother.

It was forbidden to ride fast in this area, but he didn't care. Not now. There was nothing anyone could do to him that could affect him. After his last English tournament he had been ruined, a knight without horse, without armour, a wandering, lordless knight, a *nothing*, and he would never forget the horror of that time. He had been forced to leave his home and seek fame abroad. Tournaments in France and Germany had helped hone his skills and had given him a focus, and after his successes, he had returned, laden now with plate and gold.

While abroad he had met Andrew. The older man was experienced, a dutiful servant and reliable squire in the *hastilude*. Together the two had slowly built up their fortunes, assisted by the patronage of a powerful banneret at Bordeaux who was a vassal of Thomas of Lancaster, and it was Earl Thomas who had rescued Sir Edmund from his wanderings and gave him back his pride.

He leaped from his mount at the entrance to his tent and stood patting the great horse's neck while he glanced about him superciliously. The people repelled him: dull, stupid folk who had no idea what life was really about. They none of them had a clue about the meaning of chivalry.

Pulling his horse behind him, he walked to the river and let his beast drink. It was the most important rule for any fighting man: the horse always came first. A knight depended upon his mount before any servant, woman or companion.

He passed his horse to a groom and wandered back to his tent, a brightly coloured pavilion with his shield prominently displayed outside. The thick canvas was painted and stained in strips to match the colours of his shield: red and white vertical bars. He had discarded the marks of his Lord.

The thought was bitter. He was constantly aware of it. His master was dead, murdered by the Butcher of Boroughbridge: King Edward II.

Neither he nor any of the other men in Earl Thomas's host had believed that the man who so completely failed at Bannockburn and during the Despenser war last year would actually *fight* Earl Thomas. It had seemed ludicrous to think that so pathetic a King, who preferred swimming and play-acting with peasants to hunting or taking part in honourable pursuits, would dare confront a proven warrior like Earl Thomas. Edward had even banned tournaments; and only a man who was fearful of his own warriors would stop Englishmen from their practice.

When the King rode north with his host, Earl Thomas knew he must protect himself and moved south to block his advance and force a negotiation, but all went wrong. The King avoided direct contact, and instead looped around behind the Earl's forces, threatening to cut him off and forcing the Earl to retreat.

That was the reason for the disaster. During the long march northwards, trying to outmanoeuvre the King's forces, several of Earl Thomas's allies proved their dishonour. They simply faded away as the line of march extended; not only peasants fearing for their lives, either, but magnates like Sir Robert Holland, who rode off with all his retainers, the foresworn coward!

The final disaster came at the river. Sir Andrew Harclay stood on the bridge with only a small force, but they were resolute, a band of veterans from the Scottish wars. Earl

Thomas rode to a ford to take Harclay in flank, while his friends held Harclay at the bridge, but the attacks failed. Harclay had mingled archers with dismounted men-at-arms, and the Earl could make no impression on them. At night the fight was halted, and it was then that Earl Thomas told his companions to ride away if they would save themselves.

Sir Edmund refused to desert his master, but Earl Thomas took his sword and cut the trailing tail from his banner. 'There, Sir Edmund. Now you are a knight banneret.'

'My Lord, I don't have the income to justify . . .'

'Never mind that,' Earl Thomas said, beckoning a clerk. He took a heavy purse and pressed it into the younger man's hand. 'Take this and save yourself. I will grant you a manor near Exeter. Make yourself known to Hugh de Courtenay and he may accept you into his household. If the King is merciful, you may be permitted to remain there.'

'What of you?'

'There is nothing I can do. I am advising all my friends to save themselves,' he said heavily.

'I should remain at your side, my Lord.'

'You should obey my commands, Sir Edmund!' Earl Thomas had snapped, and that was that. A matter of days later, he was executed on the orders of the King, in the most demeaning manner possible for someone who was himself of royal blood.

Sir Edmund had obeyed his last wish, and now he owned a pleasant manor east of Exeter near Honiton, high on a hill from which he could see for miles. It gave him a sense of security knowing that he could see an enemy's approach, for he was convinced that the King himself would want to persecute him for his support of Thomas; if the King did not, then the Despensers would see to his destruction, for in their greed they sought always to ruin their enemies and steal any lands they might for their own enrichment.

That was why Sir Edmund was here, at the tournament. To be safe he needed a new lord, a master who could protect him against the most powerful men in the realm after the King. The alternative was to go into exile again. Lord Hugh was not the wealthiest baron, but he was no threat to the King or Despensers either. If Sir Edmund could join his host, he might be safe. The Despensers had bigger fish to catch.

A tournament offered a unique opportunity to shine before a lord. Other knights had won patronage from new lords after demonstrating their valour and prowess in the tourney, and there was no reason why Sir Edmund shouldn't as well.

His squire, Andrew, was not in the tent. His Welsh archer, Dewi, sat on a stool stropping his long-bladed knife.

'Where's Andrew?' Edmund demanded.

'There's been a dead man found. He's gone to watch.'

'Morbid bugger! Tell him I've gone to the tilt-yard. Men will be practising and it'll be useful to assess their skill.'

He left his archer and made for the tilt-yard, but before he passed through the main field, he suddenly saw a face he recognised.

'Sir John!' he breathed.

Sir John of Crukerne heard his name and glanced about. Seeing Sir Edmund, he stared hard a moment, but then slowly his face broke into a grin. 'Ah! Edmund of Gloucester. I am pleased to see you, Sir Knight. I shall look for your shield, I promise; after all, you will need an opportunity to regain the wealth you lost six years ago!'

With a sudden roar of laughter he slapped his thigh with delight and walked away, leaving Sir Edmund frozen, his face set into a mask of rage and disgust.

Sir John was the man who had ruined him in 1316; the man who had caused Sir Edmund's flight.

The knight was gripped with a loathing that tightened his chest until he found it hard to breathe. He watched, his features twisted, as the tall figure of Sir John marched away, and then his expression changed into one of longing and sadness as he caught sight of Lady Helen Basset.

The woman who had promised herself to him. Before she married Sir Walter.

It was peaceful at the other side of the river. A small stand of trees blocked this part of the stream from the noise and bustle of the stalls nearer the castle, and no one had advanced over the water to this meadow – possibly because they didn't want to get their feet soaked, Baldwin considered as he pulled his boots off and upended them. The squelching had become all too noticeable as he walked in the meadowland.

There were cattle standing in a wary huddle and Baldwin avoided them, walking instead along the bank near the fast-flowing water. The sunlight filtered through the branches to spot the ground and the river was a constant chuckling companion. Even bearing in mind the serious nature of his investigation, he felt his mood lighten.

However, the good weather had one negative aspect: it had been so dry that the soil was dusty and, although he looked for signs that Wymond could have come this way, the ground was too hard to show footprints.

If Wymond *had* come here with another man, was it, as the workman suggested, for sexual favours, Baldwin wondered. What other reason could the killer have given for bringing Wymond to this deserted place? There was no proof that the carpenter had, in fact, come here.

He strolled further along the bank, until he arrived at the far corner of the meadow. The cattle had remained in the middle, regarding him suspiciously. Usually he found them astonishingly inquisitive: only worried animals huddled together. And the scent of blood unsettled them.

There was no obvious sign of a scuffle or murder at the riverside. Baldwin surveyed the view back to the castle. Through the trees he could see the vibrant colours of the pavilions, the darker russets and ochres of the market's tents, but the rowdy noise of Oakhampton's population enjoying themselves was stilled by distance and the trees.

Trees! Baldwin gave an involuntary start. The one thing that Hal and Wymond wanted was *wood*. Could someone have brought him here to show him trees or branches which he could buy or thieve?

The idea caught his fancy. He looked all about him, trying to see where a man might go. It would be better for the killer's security not to kill Wymond too close to the river, for there he would run the risk of lovers wandering at the waterside hearing him. No, if Baldwin were to commit such a crime, he would do so up nearer the treeline above the meadow.

Setting off away from the river, he crossed the field and was soon climbing a reasonably steep incline until he came to the trees.

They rose from what looked like an ancient hedge which had been left to its own devices. Where the straggling branches should have been cut back and new branches threaded in among the others to form a solid barrier against wolves, sheep and cattle, the limbs had been left in place to grow. This place was so badly looked after that many of the bushes had over time grown into trees and now the old line of the hedge could be seen as a row of boughs straggling slightly along the edge of the pasture. Between the trees there was a thick line of smaller bushes and brambles, impenetrable for Baldwin since he was wearing one of his better tunics and he knew what his wife would say were he to attempt to force his way through. Instead he moved slowly along the line until he came to a gap.

Kneeling, he studied the place with a frown. The brambles and young twigs had been pulled aside, dragged into the field as if a cow had pushed her way through – but there were no hoof-prints.

Baldwin had investigated enough crimes to know that there were always little signs, if you knew how to spot them, which would tell you how a man had been killed and by whom; and he never lost this special frisson of excitement as his investigation suddenly took off. He felt much like a harrier which had detected the scent of a fox or rabbit and was circling to find out which direction the quarry had taken before howling to attract the attention of the rest of the pack.

The gap was mucky where the branches had been trodden underfoot, and there must be a spring hereabouts since the soil was extremely damp, but although Baldwin searched for footprints there was nothing to be seen even after a careful study. Where the twigs and stems had been pressed into the mud, they had sprung back, destroying any tracks. Even if there had been a print, the mud was so liquid that it would have been erased, so Baldwin turned his attention to the sides of the opening.

Immediately he could see that the gap was not caused by a large animal. Some of the brambles had lost all their thorns and had the bark stripped away as though hauled from the hedge, not slashed by a sharp billhook or knife. If a man had used a hammerhead to scrape the stems away it would leave a mark a bit like this, he thought, before clambering through the gap into the woods.

A blackbird flew away along the line of the hedge uttering its raucous, chattering call, and there was a rustling from among the leaves not far from him. He stood stock-still and stared until the colours and shades resolved themselves into the figure of a large feral cat which stared unblinkingly back at him before padding off on silent feet.

It was the cat that drew Baldwin's attention to the line in the leaves a few feet to his side. There was a sweep in the litter at the foot of the trees, as if a gigantic snake had made a casual path through the detritus. His breath quickening, Baldwin followed the track, which led a short way among the trees, and he stooped to pick up a heavy hammer. Weighing it in his hand, he glanced back towards the castle. The top of the keep showed above the treetops, but the thick foliage of plants lower on the hill concealed all signs of the pavilions, tents and stalls in the meadow at the castle's feet; the noise of the building of the stands, of the chattering, shouting and laughing people, was all a dim, distant murmur from here.

A hammer was as important to a carpenter as a great sword to a knight. Wymond would have taken this tool with him everywhere. It defined him. Yet it had fallen here.

'So this is where you died, Wymond,' Baldwin murmured, gazing about him. 'And no one heard you, not this far from the camp. But who did this thing – and *why*?'

CHAPTER TWELVE

Simon left the body after he had seen to the official reporting of the wounds before the local jury. It took some time and might well prove pointless, since the Coroner would want to conduct his own inquest in order to record the facts, but at least Simon was content to have confirmed the main details before witnesses. No one could accuse him of not being thorough.

Although Hugh de Courtenay was not due to arrive until later, much of his household was already in the castle. His harbingers had arrived the day before: one yeoman of the chamber, one clerk of the kitchen, a groom of the chamber, a cook, a sumpterman with the clothsack for the bed, servants to look after all the clothing, as well as an usher for the hall.

It was to the clerk of the kitchen, Paul, that Simon turned for recording the wounds and once he had finished, Paul carefully rolled up his parchment and stoppered his inkhorn, secreting all his reeds and knives away in his little scrip before glancing one last time at the body. 'A nasty business,' he said as he left the room. 'But a nasty man. It's no surprise he came to this sort of an end.'

Simon had to agree as he stood staring down at the body. 'Out!' he snarled when someone entered behind him. 'This room is not to be used until—'

'You don't want my help? Fine. I'll say goodbye then.'

Simon whipped his head round and smiled in relief. 'Coroner Roger! It's a delight to see you!'

'Hmm. Sounded like it,' Sir Roger of Gidleigh said, peering down at the body. 'Here I am, visiting a pleasant little tournament in the hope of some relaxation, and what do you do? Present me with a stiff. How did it happen?'

Simon passed him Paul's report and leaned back on a table. 'Well, it's like this,' he began. It didn't take long to tell Sir Roger all he knew, finishing with, 'And the worst of it all is, he was such an unpopular bastard that almost anyone in the town could have wanted to see him die. He even picked a fight with *me* yesterday.'

'You should control your temper, or you may find yourself accused,' Roger joked.

'*I* did. It was him who didn't.'

'Never mind. Have you begun to question people?'

'Baldwin was about to start while I saw to the body.'

'Then let's see if he has enjoyed any success. He can't have done worse than I have recently.'

Simon asked politely, 'How is your good Lady?'

'My wife? She is well.'

His unenthusiastic tone amused Simon. Although he had never met Sir Roger's wife, gossip had it that she ruled her household with a rod of iron.

As they reached the tilt-yard field, Sir Roger glanced at Simon. 'What is it? You look as glum as a whore in a nunnery.'

'Lord Hugh won't be very impressed when he hears there's been a murder. He wanted a quiet tournament. God knows what he'll have to say to me.'

'Quiet, eh?' Sir Roger chuckled. He glanced at the paper on which Paul had noted the injuries, then whistled quietly. 'Well, that's a coincidence. Dudenay, a man who was bludgeoned to death in Exeter recently – his head was beaten savagely, too.'

'The dead man back there – Wymond Carpenter – he used to work with a fellow named Dudenay,' Simon told the Coroner. 'He was their banker. Did you find his murderer?'

'No. I've reached a dead end on that investigation. Naturally the first thing I did was go to his home and look at his books.

'Apparently he was owed money by several people. Squire William and his father Sir John of Crukerne both owed him a fortune; so did Sir Richard Prouse and another man . . . Sir Walter Basset.'

Simon considered. 'Let's ask the other usurers here whether they can help.'

The usurers tended to keep together. Since they could pay well for their privileges, they took seats up close to the entertainments. That was also where they were needed, so that a knight who lost his bout could speedily pawn his goods to pay his ransom.

Simon walked with Sir Roger along the outer line of the tents, past the knights and squires, past the hucksters and on to the edge of the third field. There Simon stood and surveyed the bankers and merchants with a suspicious eye. There were times when a man needed to make use of their services, he knew, but that didn't stop him feeling doubtful about them. It seemed as dishonest a way to make money as he could conceive, lending it out in return for interest. It was deeply immoral; not like a man with an honourable trade, like a glovemaker or saddlemaker or a mercenary man-at-arms.

Near the entrance to the usurers' section was an empty table, and next to it sat a wizened old man with a narrow, hatchet face and a pale shock of fair hair. He sipped from a large mazer of wine while a clerk sat at his side making marks on a long scroll with a reed.

'That's the one to ask,' Sir Roger murmured. 'Always scared and confused. Rarely knows whether he needs a piss or a shit.'

Hiding a smile, Simon followed in his wake as he strode to the trestle. Once before it, the clerk and the old man eyed Sir Roger with respect. The Coroner was familiar to all who traded in Exeter.

'Master . . .?' Simon enquired. The man had a small board with the picture of a star and a cock painted roughly in yellow.

'I am called Alan of Exeter. Do you have a need of some ready cash? I—'

'No,' Sir Roger said flatly. 'We want to know how closely Benjamin Dudenay worked with Wymond the Carpenter. What do you know about them?'

Alan's eyes were suddenly hooded. 'Why should I know anything, Coroner? What business could I have with such as them?'

'Enough, Alan, or I'll tell Lord Hugh about your wine imports.'

The old fellow paled. 'If I could help, I'd be pleased to, sir, but how I can serve you, when I know nothing?'

'You know already that Dudenay is dead. Now Wymond has been murdered and I seek the murderer before someone else is killed.'

Alan fiddled with a reed. 'I can tell you this much: Benjamin used to work closely with Hal and the carpenter. He funded their more magnificent builds, charging interest when the Lords paid for the work, and in return he would get a good profit from the knights who attended. It was easy business for him. It made many of my friends and companions here,' he waved a hand to encompass the other moneylenders in the field, 'very jealous – although not me, of course.'

'Why not you?'

In a reversal of his previous nervousness, Alan playfully tapped the side of his nose. 'Benjamin always made a load of profit from tournaments.'

'I don't follow you.'

'Come, Coroner! Benjamin made his living by lending money to knights and noblemen of all sorts and charging them large sums in interest. And then he also gambled heavily on them, too. He would take bets from anyone. Who would win a tilt, how many courses he would take, whether a rider would be knocked from his horse . . . He was bound to make enemies – he was fleecing men trained in killing and earning money from their misery. Me, I take less interest and never bet. That way I can seem more sympathetic.'

Simon tried to prevent his revulsion from showing in his

voice as he asked, 'Did he share any enemies with Wymond? Could they have been killed by the same man?'

'Perhaps. Hal and Wymond both helped Benjamin. They built the stands, and then they'd help during the jousts by passing lances to fighting knights as well, so they both got good positions to watch everything. As did Benjamin.'

'You think their only shared business venture was tournaments?' Sir Roger asked suddenly.

Alan agreed, but he looked shifty and his smile had gone.

'Not necessarily always in Devon?' Simon pressed him.

'No. Wymond and Hal have travelled all over the country,' Alan agreed reluctantly. He cast about quickly to see that no one else observed them, then hissed, 'Coroner, it doesn't do to enquire too closely into their business.'

'Eh? What do you mean?'

Alan leaned forward. 'Because Benjamin and his friends were *spies*, that's why. They listened to all the conversations between knights and reported the lot back to Despenser.'

'Oh, Christ's bones!' Simon murmured, recalling how he had coldly insulted Hal about his building expertise.

'Yes, Bailiff. I have seen Wymond myself, eavesdropping around knights and squires, then going back to report to Benjamin. What else would he be doing but spying for the King? It's said he was up with Earl Thomas before Boroughbridge. Perhaps someone from the losing side saw them here and took revenge.'

Simon groaned inwardly. The very last thing he wanted was to discover that Wymond was a spy for the King. 'Are you sure?'

'Well, they haven't been here recently. Last time I saw them in these parts was during the tournament at Crukerne – oh, a good few years ago now.'

'How long ago?' Sir Roger insisted.

Alan frowned at the ground. 'I suppose five or six years back – yes, 1316.'

'Have there been any tournaments since then?'

'Coroner, there have been pageants of all sorts since then! I have helped at small tournaments, at markets and at saints' days. All exactly the sort of events where you'd expect to find Hal and Wymond. Yet they weren't there and I know that Hal was seen in France with Despenser the Older.'

'That's all I need,' Simon said glumly. Then a thought struck him. 'How is Hal getting the money together to pay for the show now his banker is dead?'

Alan tapped his nose again. 'He has some good friends, Bailiff. I have always been a loyal vassal of Lord Hugh, and when Hal approached me to help our Lord by advancing money, I was happy to assist. I have already given Hal money to buy more timber. I understand he wasn't happy with the wood supplied.'

'So it will be added to the bill for Lord Hugh?' Simon said. 'You can tell Hal from me that I will be advising Lord Hugh not to pay any more for wood. I know how Hal was trying to save money by risking the use of inferior stuff.'

Soon Simon and Sir Roger had left the old money-lender and were wending their way towards a wine-seller. Both men were more than ready for a refreshing draught.

'What do you think of that, then?' Sir Roger asked.

Simon didn't answer at first. 'What was that about his wine and telling Lord Hugh?'

'Hah! Topsham has to unload all the ships which want to deal with Exeter, but one third of customs are due to Lord Hugh and Alan has been avoiding paying that. He's paid the

City, but if Lord Hugh should find out, Alan would regret his actions.' His expression hardened. 'As to his information . . .'

Simon nodded dismally. 'Yes. What the devil do we do if Benjamin *was* a spy for the King?'

Sir Walter walked to a pie-seller and bought a lark in pastry for his wife, selecting a roasted partridge for himself, washing it down with a cup of strong wine.

Helen had calmed him already. It never took her long. With her ready wit and willing smile, let alone the promise of her superb body under that light tunic, she always made his anger dissolve.

And it was fortunate she did, because although he adored his wife, when the red mist came down over him, the desire to kill was uncontrollable.

Sir Walter was the son of a squire who had died in a fight with outlaws many years before. It was because of the way he had tracked down the murderers that the Earl of Cornwall had knighted him, as a reward for his dedication. Not that Sir Walter had done it to gain recognition. He'd done it because he wasn't going to let them get away with it.

So he had trailed after them for more than ten leagues, on foot, until he found the six in a clearing near the Devon border. And filled with a righteous anger, he had drawn sword and dagger and run into the midst of them.

It was like entering the lists. At first he was cautious and fought with science, aiming his first blow at the largest man. When he went down, Walter had time to smash his fist into the face of a second man before sweeping off the head of a third with a single vicious swipe of his sword. Kicking, hacking, thrusting and butting, he soon found himself beset by four men, but then someone got under his defence and marked his shoulder. That was when the red rage overwhelmed him.

Afterwards, all he could recall was a blur of fury, of intense energy and passion that seared him like demons whipping him on with white-hot metal flails. He shrieked, then hurled himself against them, his blades moving as fast as serpents, his mind cleared of all but the desire to maim, to hack and thrust and stab, to *kill*.

And then it was over. He came to, blood dripping from arms and fingers, from his breast and belly, and about him lay the dismembered bodies of his foes, the men who had killed his father. He had taken a great breath and bellowed to the sky in a long paean of glory and brute delight. He couldn't even feel the pain from his wounds.

That was the first time he had killed in anger, but it was not the last. Since being knighted, he had deliberately sought out battles and tournaments. He loved warfare as others enjoyed their women. The sight of a man spitted on a lance filled him with pure delight. To Walter there could be no greater pleasure than seeing a man demand peace and agreeing to be ransomed. Nothing could equal the glory of winning.

Helen's arm was through his and she gave him a squeeze as if affectionately reminding him of her presence. He smiled down at her. Yes, Helen was a worthwhile mate. She was soothing and sweet, and her lovemaking was reason in itself to want to keep her. And yet even with these attributes, if Sir Walter ever found that she had been disloyal, he would kill her like a rat.

He thought of the pipsqueak squire who had paid court to her, and snorted contemptuously. Then he recalled the face of the knight from Gloucester upon catching sight of her. Sir Edmund – the man from whom Sir Walter had taken her.

'Well, one thing is certain, and that is that I will have to hold a formal inquest into Wymond's death.'

Simon glanced at Sir Roger. The Coroner was staring thoughtfully into his wine bowl. 'So you think there *is* a connection between the two deaths?'

'Benjamin and Wymond? Yes, there can't be much doubt. I started thinking that it was a simple crime, committed by someone determined to avoid repaying his debts, but now it seems that Dudenay was a spy, it is a different matter.'

Simon nodded. 'Yet it could be that the two are unrelated. Or perhaps they died for a different reason.'

'Such as what?'

'I don't know – just as I don't understand why spies should suddenly be killed here. There is nothing to suggest *why*.'

'No doubt we'll learn that in good time,' Sir Roger said. He noticed that Simon was gazing ahead blankly. 'Is something wrong?'

'No, I was just looking at that scruffy devil,' Simon said. 'He seems to be wearing a sword.'

'Gracious God, anyone would think he was the lowliest villein, wouldn't they?'

'Who is he? Is he allowed to carry a weapon at the tournament?'

'That fellow, Bailiff, is Sir Walter Basset. He dresses like a slovenly cur, but don't for God's sake mention the fact to him or gaze lasciviously at his wife, Lady Helen. He has killed men for less, if the stories be true.'

'You expect to see a knight in his finery.'

'Yes. But Sir Walter appears to take a pride in going about dressed worse than the meanest peasant on his lands.'

'It is curious that a man in the wrong dress can appear so utterly different,' Simon shrugged, then put the disreputable-looking knight from his mind.

Soon afterwards the Coroner left him, and went off to make his arrangements for the inquest.

Simon had been about to stroll towards the combat field, intending to see how the works were progressing, when he passed a group of lads leaning nonchalantly against a fence, one sitting astride it as if to gain a better view of the people before him. He was apparently ogling a young woman, puffing out his cheeks in pretended admiration and feigning despair when she tilted her head and turned from him.

'Just look at the arse on that,' one of the boys said, and belched loudly.

Simon gave a wintry smile. Youths were the same the world over. Randy sods! Give them a female to gawp at, and they'd pant like hounds after a bitch. From the wafts of beery breath reaching his nostrils, the four here had been drinking. Simon could remember behaving much the same way when he was younger, especially after drinking. It was good to be distracted for a moment from his anxieties about the murder and the effect it would have on the tournament.

He idly paused to listen.

The lad on the fence gave a low whistle. 'She is beautiful! I saw her before, and I thought then I had never seen such perfection, but now I am certain.'

One of his companions clutched at his breast and turned soulful eyes heavenwards. 'Oh, for a touch of her hand, for a lick of her shoe, for a kiss from her lips, or a fondle of her tits . . .' The others laughed loudly.

'Shut up, you prating cretin,' Simon heard the boy on the fence say. He was only listening with half an ear, because he had just spotted his daughter. He hadn't thought that Edith would be here already! She and her mother must have arrived while he was seeing to Wymond's corpse. Where was Meg? he wondered, peering at the crowd.

'Shut up yourself, William!'

'Look at her legs,' the blond boy said dreamly. 'They are the length of a . . .'

'A good mare's?' his friend on the ground interrupted with glee.

Another broke in; 'It's not the meat on the legs, it's where the legs meet!'

Simon felt his mouth fall slackly open. These ugly, poxed, inane brats weren't ogling a woman! Their target was Edith!

Feeling his blood stir, Simon would have walked away, but then one of the lads at the fence made a filthy sign at Edith, a lewd beckoning, as if he were calling over a whore.

Luckily, Edith didn't see her father, but she saw the youth's signal. She haughtily raised her chin and slipped among the crush of people. Try as he might, Simon could not see where she had gone. He hoped – he prayed – that his servant Hugh was nearby to protect her from the two-legged wolves who were parading themselves about the area.

'Did you see the tits on that?'

It was the boy who had made the sign. Simon walked over to him. Although a part of his brain took careful note of the position of each lad, his rage was fanned by the careless attitude of the fellow who had insulted his daughter. 'Are you talking about the lady who was over there?' he asked coldly.

'Yeah.' The boy was too drunk to sense danger. He sniggered. 'Wouldn't mind stumbling over that in the dark!'

'You'd never find her in the dark, Nick,' said the lad on the fence. 'You're always too bloody pissed.'

'Speak for yourself! *I'd* find her, I'll bet!' The lad was shorter than Simon by a head, a barrel-chested youth of maybe twenty, with thick, short fingers, and a dull expression. Large brown eyes slowly swept around the crowd, seeking a new target. 'Mmm! Sweet, she'd be, like a taste of sugar syrup.'

Simon looked up at the youth on the fence. 'What's your name?'

'Me? I am Squire William, son to Sir John of Crukerne. Why?' William asked and lightly swung down from the fence. 'You have a problem? You aren't a knight, so you can't command us, and you're surely no squire, so what's your difficulty?'

Nick, the barrel-chested youth, circled slowly around Simon. 'I think he's a merchant, Will. Not successful, though. Look at the hose, and that tatty tunic. Surely a mean little peasant man should be punished for speaking insultingly to a group of squires. What should his punishment be, d'you reckon? A ducking in the river?'

Simon ignored him. William appeared to be the ringleader and Simon concentrated on him with a steady, unsmiling stare. 'I am Bailiff Puttock and I'm here to organise the tournament. And I don't like to hear women slandered. Nor would Lord Hugh be pleased to hear that the fairest ladies of his household could be insulted by a mess of youths who had hoped to win the favour of the *collée* from him.'

The gang's expressions altered subtly. They had been expecting to have some fun tweaking the nose of this grim-faced man, but none wanted to risk the wrath of Lord Hugh. Especially since his Bailiff might be able to put in a bad word about them to the heralds, a bad word which could take many years to clear. No one wanted their character stained.

Squire William recovered his aplomb first. He smiled and allowed his head to tilt to the side as he shrugged apologetically. 'Sir, I am deeply sorry if we appeared to be disrespectful, but we were only admiring a woman.'

'She was beautiful,' the one called Nick said unwisely. 'Built like the prettiest wagtail the King himself could afford! To see her wriggle her arse under that tight skirt . . . it was like watching a pair of cats fighting in a sack. Tee hee! You should have seen her figure, sir. Any man would fall in love with her for the opportunity of seeing her remove her skirts and tunic. I'll bet even *you'd* give your soul for the chance of mounting her, Sir Bailiff. Tee, hee!'

Simon hissed, 'Shut your face, you poxed son of a whore and an idiot! She's my daughter! If I see you sniffing about her, I'll cut off your balls and feed them to the pigs. Understand?'

William put a hand on his friend's arm. He was reluctant to back down before any man, even an enraged Bailiff like this one. 'Your language is intemperate.'

'*My* language, you puppy?' Simon roared. 'Your words would offend a Breton pirate! You're no knight, and I can well understand why. A whippersnapper like you doesn't deserve preferment. A Bristol shit-collector'd be more courteous!'

'You are intentionally insulting me, Bailiff. I won't stand for it.'

'You think you can demean a lady and still win your spurs? I'll show you different, you ignorant—'

'Bailiff ! I'm glad to have found you,' came a smooth voice. Simon turned to find himself gazing at the King Herald. 'And you have met the son of Sir John Crukerne, I see. How fortunate. I'm sure you'd both like to continue your . . . *conversation* . . . but I think Lord Hugh would be perturbed if his Bailiff and one of his most valued squires, a young man who could have antici- pated a reward for years of honourable and loyal service to one of Lord Hugh's knights, should become fractious.'

'I'll not apologise to a . . .'

'Neither will I, Bailiff,' William said hurriedly. 'But neither will I brawl vulgarly in the field like a common man – a man who is not of the knightly class. Come, Nick.'

'Leave my daughter alone. If I find you've been trailing around after her, I'll—'

'Bailiff,' William said, eyeing him gravely, 'if I wish to see your daughter, I shall. And there's nothing you can do to stop me.'

'Leave him, Bailiff,' the King Herald advised. 'His father's powerful enough to harm even you. I wouldn't want our lord to be shamed because of a silly quarrel.'

'He's not my lord,' Simon muttered as he shrugged his arm away, but he was relieved that the Herald had been there. He had been close to drawing his knife, and he was sure that it would have been a mistake. There was no point orphaning Edith to protect her honour.

'Thank you,' he added ungraciously.

William gave a faint grin and was about to walk away when a thought struck Simon. 'Wait one moment, Squire. Where were you after dark last night?'

'Me? I left the hall quite late and joined my friends here at a tavern. Why?'

'Which of your friends here will confirm on oath that you were with them?' Simon asked curtly.

'Any of them will, but why?'

'How well did you know Wymond Carpenter?'

'That shite? Well enough to avoid him.'

'What was wrong with him?'

'What is this?'

Simon smiled. 'Answer the question and I'll tell you.'

'You enjoy your mystery, do you, Bailiff ? Very well. The trouble with Wymond is that his work was poor. Piss-poor. In Exeter he caused the deaths of many when the stand he had built collapsed.'

'I believe you owed money to Benajmin Dudenay?'

'What if I did?' The youth was startled at the change of subject.

'For what?'

'I am a *warrior*,' William said with withering contempt. 'I had to join our King's host at Boroughbridge and I needed new mail. I borrowed money from Benjamin to buy it.'

'How much?'

'I don't keep track of such things. Now, if that is all, I have other . . .'

'Were you in Exeter to attend the court this year?'

William glanced at the King Herald and made a show of shrugging. 'I was there with many other *honourable* men.'

'Such as your father.'

'Yes. What is all this about?'

Simon studied the lad pensively without answering. He had no reason to suspect that William could have had a motive to kill Wymond, other than his instinctive dislike for a boy who had leched after his daughter, and he was fair enough to know that his feelings had nothing to do with justice, only with a father's righteous anger.

'Come, Bailiff, explain yourself.'

'Because Dudenay was killed in Exeter and Wymond was murdered last night.'

'It looks as if I cannot be suspected, then, doesn't it?' William said lightly.

'Did you see anyone else about last night after dark?' Simon asked.

'There was that old cripple, Sir Richard,' William said with the brutal callousness of the young and healthy. 'And some new fellow – Sir Edmund, I think his name is. He was walking about the place with his squire.'

Simon watched him arrogantly swagger off to rejoin his friends at a wine-seller's bench.

'What now, Bailiff? A brawl with a pot boy? Or a wench in a tavern?' Mark Tyler asked sarcastically. 'Christ! The way you question people, anyone would think you were determined to take on the Coroner's job for him. Have you a genuine suspect? Or are you insulting people for personal enjoyment?'

Simon wasn't in the mood for his hectoring. 'Have *you* ever used the merchant and usurer Benjamin Dudenay?'

The herald's face suddenly went still. 'I have heard of him.'

173

Simon had seen his expression change. 'Did you owe him money?'

'A little, perhaps.'

'Enough to want to kill him?'

'The only man who seems to have the temper to kill is yourself,' Tyler said neatly, recovering himself. 'Two fights in as many days, Bailiff. Scarcely the sort of record Lord Hugh would expect, is it?'

CHAPTER THIRTEEN

Baldwin carried the hammer with him as he investigated the area, but there seemed nothing more to be found and soon he set off back towards the castle, swinging the murder weapon with a speculative air. It was heavy – weighed at least four pounds. Enough to crush a skull.

When he came to the gap in the hedge, he tried to guess the direction that the killer would have taken to get back to the jousting field. There was no sign of dragging grass, so he assumed that the body had been carried down towards the river.

He was beginning to feel a reluctant admiration for the murderer: a man who could persuade Wymond to walk all the way up here to look at a tree for timber, perhaps proposing a share in the profit; a man who could strike down even so ferocious a foe as Wymond, and drag or carry him back to his own bed and brazenly tuck him in. That spoke of someone with courage, mental resources and physical strength. Wymond was not tall, but he was solid.

Why put him back in his bed? Most people would surely have left the corpse up in the woods to be eaten by wild animals, concealing the evidence. Baldwin was convinced that the deed was done so as to leave a message. But was it for Hal – or someone else? And if so, who?

Baldwin set to wondering how the murderer had returned to the camp. He might have turned right, following the line of the old hedge. Working on this conviction that no sensible man would walk in the open carrying a dead body, Baldwin strolled near the trees, his eyes fixed upon the ground. It took little time to find tracks: boots sunk deep into the ground.

He walked faster now. The trail took him down to the ford where he himself had earlier crossed the river, and he nodded to himself with satisfaction. His guesswork had proved to be accurate.

But now he was unsure what to do. He still carried the hammer, and that would have to be given to the Coroner when he arrived; he could pass it to Simon for safekeeping in the meantime. Baldwin felt a pang at his belly and realised it was time he ate. He walked thoughtfully to the stalls and drank a pint of watered wine. At another stall he bought a pie and munched on it, sitting on a bench with a fresh pint of wine before him while he contemplated the people passing, wondering whether one of them was the killer. It was an unsettling thought.

He found his attention caught by a large knight.

Tall, strong, and with an expression that could melt moorstone, Baldwin thought that the stranger was an ideal suspect. If he was inclined to arresting people on sight based solely on their manner, this man would be the perfect candidate for a cell. Before long the knight looked about him and noticed

Baldwin watching him. Baldwin found himself being surveyed with minute detail. He motioned to the jug of wine and the stranger gave a shrug and joined him.

'Please allow me to serve you, sir,' Baldwin said respectfully.

'I am grateful.'

Both raised their pots and drank. There was a ritual to their slow introductions, for knights meeting at a tournament could well find themselves fighting and perhaps even dying at the other's hand in a few hours.

Baldwin bowed his head and introduced himself. 'Sir Baldwin de Furnshill.'

'I am Sir Edmund of Gloucester. You will be challenging?'

'I fear I am too old to be a *tenant* or *venant*,' Baldwin chuckled. 'No, I am here to watch.'

'I see.' Sir Edmund appeared to lose interest in Baldwin, his attention flying back to the people walking by. He was still furious at Sir John's slighting words to him about winning back his wealth, and confused by the sight of Lady Helen.

'I do not remember seeing you at other tournaments,' Baldwin said, breaking into his thoughts.

'I have been abroad.'

'Ah.' It was not easy to talk to this man, Baldwin considered. He caught sight of Odo and waved a hand in recognition. The herald inclined his head, but hurried on his way.

'Was that Odo?' Sir Edmund asked.

'Yes. You know him?'

'I have met him in Exeter – and France.'

Baldwin saw how his mouth snapped shut after saying that, as though Sir Edmund regretted saying so much, and Baldwin suddenly remembered the herald's tale of his saving a Templar. Sir Edmund was not familiar to him, but it was possible that he had been a Knight Templar. He was old enough.

'I scarcely know Odo. He is Lord Hugh's man and I don't see much of our lord, I am afraid.'

'He is a good man,' Sir Edmund said. 'Have you heard about the murder?'

Baldwin, who had been hoping to bring their conversation round to Wymond, settled back more easily in his seat. 'You mean the carpenter?'

'Yes. Do you know anything about his death?'

'A little,' Baldwin admitted. 'He was found in his own tent.'

'I see. And is anyone suspected?'

'We shall have to wait until the Coroner completes his inquest. Were you up last night?'

'Why do you ask?'

'It seems that the murder happened after the curfew. The only people who should have been about were knights or squires. I merely wondered if you might have seen anyone.'

'No, I didn't. After eating I walked a little to clear my lungs. The room was very smoky and I felt the need for some fresh air. My squire was with me.'

'But you saw no one?'

'No. There were some servants about, but only few.'

'Did you and your squire return to your tent together?'

'No, he came after me. Why? You seem very interested.'

'I am a Keeper of the King's Peace and I like to solve little problems like this.'

'Well, I am afraid I can't help you,' Sir Edmund said, standing abruptly. 'My thanks for the wine, but I must go.'

'Of course,' Baldwin murmured graciously. 'It was pleasant to meet you,' he added as Sir Edmund stalked away.

Seeing a watchman, Baldwin stood and spoke to him. He gave the man the hammer, telling him to take it to Simon in the castle because it might be the murder weapon. Then, before he could buy another drink, he heard his name called. Turning, he saw a tall, slim woman with fair features, holding a swaddled child in her arms.

'Margaret! It *is* good to see you again! And how is young Peterkin?' He tentatively prised a scrap of material away from an ancient-looking face, which blinked and glared at him.

'Careful, don't put your finger too close; he's teething,' Margaret laughed. 'Baldwin, it is good to see you too. Peterkin is fine, he's growing heavier daily and occasionally, just occasionally, he allows me to sleep through the night. How is Jeanne – is she here with you? I hope you are enjoying fatherhood.' She cast a quizzical look up at him. 'Are you quite well? You haven't had bad news?'

'No, I have been considering a murder, that is all,' he laughed. 'Jeanne is fine, if tired, and young Richalda is loud. Good lungs! How is Edith?'

Hugh stood at Margaret's shoulder. Taciturn, narrow-featured, and with the slim build of a moorman, his gaze remained fixed upon the ground, his thin mouth drawn into a prim line. 'Edith's fine,' he said sulkily.

As he spoke, Edith herself appeared from behind him and pushed past him to Baldwin. 'Out of the way, Hugh. Just because you've been enjoying yourself lazing about in the north is no reason to hide me. Hello, Sir Baldwin,' she said, and curtseyed graciously. 'I am well, I thank you.'

He eyed her with amusement. She might only be thirteen or fourteen years old but she already had the carriage of a lady. Like her mother her hair was of fine gold and she had been graced by Margaret Puttock's expression of gentle calmness. Baldwin thought her features would not have looked out of place on an angel, but having heard so many stories of her disruptive behaviour from Simon over the last years, he knew that appearances could be deceptive.

'I hear you're setting the hearts of all the young men about Lydford and Tavistock a-flutter.'

'Me?' she enquired as if startled, her blue eyes widening. 'Oh, I shouldn't think so. They must all think me very dull. A young maid who isn't allowed to visit or ride with her friends or—'

Margaret hurriedly cleared her throat and put a hand in front of her daughter. 'I am sure she is setting as many hearts alight as she could wish, Sir Baldwin. Sadly she has no desire to do so with her own parents.'

'That's not fair!' Edith declared and in a moment her gentle expression became a glower. 'If only you were reasonable, I'd not have to complain and—'

'I am sure the good knight has many other things to consider without listening to your ranting, Edith,' Margaret said tiredly.

'I think he would be more interested to hear how my mother treats me than listen to your tales of sowing seeds and lambing,' Edith said scornfully. 'Your conversation is, I fear, rather dull to educated people, Mother.'

Baldwin glanced away. He couldn't bear the look of hurt and sadness that sprang into Margaret's eyes.

Simon breathed a sigh of relief. It was good to be at a loose end for a few moments. Now, he reckoned, was as good a time as any to find himself a pot of ale and swill the grit from his mouth.

Accordingly he steered his path to the market area. There was a brewer there who was known to him, and he grudgingly passed Simon a quart of ale free. Simon leaned against a post while he drank. It tasted good; very good.

The show had taken weeks to prepare and Simon would be pleased when it was all over. He dreaded telling Lord Hugh about the carpenter's murder, although he was glad that Sir Roger was there to take responsibility for the investigation. Lord Hugh would arrive later that day, but there was nothing Simon could do to make the news any more palatable and he was essentially a pragmatist. If something couldn't be changed, he wouldn't keep fretting about it.

He had come to the conclusion that since the first quart had gone down so well a second might be an improvement, and had turned to ask for another pot, when a large man appeared at his side.

'Are you the Bailiff?'

Simon groaned inwardly, but nodded.

'I am Sir John of Crukerne. My son tells me you questioned him about where he was last night. Well, he was with other squires. All right? There are plenty of people to confirm his alibi.'

'And if I need more, you will pay for extra witnesses, eh?'

'You catch on quickly. I congratulate you.'

Simon smiled thinly as the knight gave him a quick look up and down, but his smile hardened as the knight spun on his heel and made to walk away. 'Sir John?'

Pausing, the knight turned his head. 'What?' he snapped rudely.

The sight of the man's back made Simon's hackles rise. He took a deep breath and stepped forward. 'Sir John, I wouldn't like to think that you could be bribing people to perjure themselves. If I was to think that, I'd have to inform the Coroner.'

Sir John slowly turned to face him.

Simon continued, 'And if I find that your son was not telling the truth, Sir John, I will see to it that he is arrested and questioned. I hope that is equally clear.'

The knight said nothing, merely sniffed and turned away again.

Simon said sharply, 'I'm not finished!'

Sir John turned and gritted his teeth. 'You are trying my patience, Bailiff. You have no jurisdiction over me.'

'This land is Lord Hugh's. I am his representative here.'

'I don't give a shit who you are.'

'I want to know what *you* were doing last night after dark.'

'Me?' Sir John burst out. 'You think I had something to do with Wymond's death?'

Simon held his stare, but then he was disconcerted to see a smile breaking out on the knight's face.

'Well, Bailiff. If you must know, I went to my tent and slept there. Alone.'

'So you have no one to confirm you were there?'

'Yes, I have. My ward, Lady Alice. She was there when I

returned from the meal. She can confirm that I arrived shortly after dark. I bade her a good night.'

Sir Peregrine of Barnstaple rode proudly at his lord's side, sitting easily on his great bay stallion. The weather was fine and dry. He could feel the sun on his dark crimson velvet tunic and the dust rose in choking clouds, tickling his nostrils and throat.

At his side his standard bearer carried his square banner on its long shaft and the sight of the cloth fluttering in the breeze warmed his heart. Barnacles on a yellow background, a play on the link between his family and Barnstaple, always made him happy, but today he felt honoured, for his arms were being displayed beside Lord Hugh's.

His lord was not of a mind to chat and their journey had been quiet, Lord Hugh speaking rarely except during their occasional breaks to rest the horses. Sir Peregrine knew that his master had much on his mind; also, with so many men-at-arms about them, he couldn't talk because a man could never be too certain who might be willing to accept a fee for information about a magnate's thinking – and the King's friends had weighty purses filled with gold for those who helped them. The men were neccessary, because Lord Hugh's household was travelling with him and he had need of protection for the carts with the chests filled with plate ready to be pawned to buy cloth, pay retainers, reward knights who showed particular prowess, and generally impress all who came to see his tournament. A knight needed to display many qualities: courtesy, humility, loyalty, hardiness, a love for the truth, but not least among them was *largesse* – spending freely to show his own disdain for cash.

Not, Sir Peregrine noted, that many knights eschewed money. They couldn't, not when their lives depended upon good armour, good horses and good weapons – none of which came cheaply. They must look to their manors to provide them with enough funds to maintain their lifestyles, yet it was not easy to squeeze the last pennies from reluctant and recalcitrant peasants.

Lord Hugh with his household could devastate an area. They were forever in the saddle travelling from one manor to another, and it took little time for the meagre stores at each point to be consumed. Sir Peregrine was often involved in assessing the stores at different places, especially within Lord Hugh's forts, and knew exactly how much the men needed. It was no surprise that many of the farm peasants looked upon the arrival of the lord and his retinue as a form of purgatory to be endured, rather than a cause for excitement and pleasure.

At least this visit would be different, he reflected, looking about him. Everyone enjoyed watching the spectacle of a tournament and even the townsfolk would be happy with the profits they could make from the visitors to the market.

On entering Oakhampton, people on either side came out from shops and houses to gawp, a few to cheer, knowing that Lord Hugh's household meant increased sales of food and drink, and that the celebration of the tournament would soon begin. Shabby townspeople thronged the streets, while urchins ducked under arms and stood at the roadside to gape at the men-at-arms in their finery, with their caps on their heads, their mail chinking merrily like so many coins as they walked, the badges holding the enamelled insignia of Lord Hugh shining at the horses' harnesses, the leatherwork squeaking and groaning, the weapons gleaming blue or silver, the edges well-honed, the polearms slung over men's shoulders ready to be swung into play. Well might the towns-folk stare. This cavalcade of twenty horsemen, carts, wagons, thirty more men-at-arms on foot and all the supply horses, not to mention the great destriers eagerly skipping and occa-sionally lashing out at each other or at a bystander, was the largest that the town had seen in years.

Sir Peregrine could see that Lord Hugh's mind was not on the hordes waiting upon each side. His thoughts were still on the King and the recent death of Thomas of Lancaster.

The suddenness of Thomas's death had shocked men up and down the country. For the wealthiest man after the King to be dealt with so peremptorily was terrible. A short hear-ing, then justice: he was set upon a mule to be taken to the gallows, but at the last moment his punishment was changed to simple beheading rather than hanging and quartering as a traitor deserved. Wiser counsel had prevailed: his noble blood was acknowledged in his death.

Lord Hugh had been a mover behind the scenes for some years, helping those who sought to obstruct the King's fool-ish spend-thriftiness. Especially when Gaveston was created Earl of Cornwall and given rich estates. It was pathetic to see how the King doted on him. After Gaveston's murder, all those who helped bring him to the block were viewed as trai-tors by the King, Lord Hugh knew that the King eagerly awaited reports of his own treason. As soon as that happened, Lord Hugh de Courtenay would be condemned.

In part it was to distract him that Sir Peregrine had suggested a tournament. Lord Hugh was an enthusiastic supporter of martial arts and his wife eagerly seized upon the idea: she knew her husband needed to relax. However, there was an ulterior motive: if the King should take it into his head to attack the West Country, it would be far better that Lord Hugh's knights should have had practice, and that as many of the youngsters who wanted to win their spurs should do so, receiving spurs and arms from Lord Hugh himself. A man would only rarely consider treachery against the lord who had given him the *collée* to dub him knight.

Sir Peregrine knew King Edward II distrusted him. Last year Sir Peregrine had unsuccessfully advised Lord Hugh to join the Marcher lords standing against the King. For a time the alliance had been successful and the two Despensers, Hugh the Older and his son Hugh the Younger, had left the realm, the father to take up the idle life of an exile, his son to become a pirate thriving on the trade ships which passed along the Kent coast; but now the Despensers were back, and strengthened in pride and arrogance by the removal of their most bitter foe, Thomas of Lancaster.

Hugh Despenser the Younger had a long memory for those who had thwarted his appalling ambition. When Hugh the Younger was not given what he wanted, he imprisoned those who stood in his path – or killed them – and Sir Peregrine of Barnstaple was known to be implacably opposed to him. That was why Sir Peregrine wanted Lord Hugh's men fully prepared for war.

His attention moved on to the strange knight who had appeared in the castle at Tiverton with his squire and archer. They were a very unsettling trio. Wandering knights were common, especially since the Earl of Lancaster's men had been so fearfully cut about and dispersed, but Sir Edmund of Gloucester looked more dangerous than most. It was there in his grim, intelligent features, in his quick, assured movements and curious stillness when he stood silently observing others. He warranted watching. Sir Peregrine didn't trust him, which was why he had sent the man and his companions on ahead with Lord Hugh's harbingers and heralds.

Looking up, Sir Peregrine saw that they were almost at the castle and he looked about him, all senses alert. If someone wanted to harm him or his lord, it would be an ideal place for an ambush, here in the river's cutting before the road took them all up to the castle's barbican. Sir Edmund had an archer with him, Sir Peregrine reminded himself.

He glanced to either side, his tension growing. The townspeople didn't look cheerful; they should have been happy to see their lord, yet there was a pall of anxiety or worse hanging over the place.

As Lord Hugh clattered over the timber bridge to the barbican, Sir Peregrine gazed up at the walls above. A short Welshman with a cruel scar from one ear almost to his nose, one of Sir Peregrine's own men, nodded cheerily from the battlements and Sir Peregrine relaxed a little. If he thought all was safe, Sir Peregrine was content.

Men had been sent on with the harbingers to ensure that the place was prepared for Lord Hugh and the others. All told, Lord Hugh and his household were almost sixty men and that many required a goodly number of barrels of ale and of wine to be prepared, let alone the grain that must be put by for breadmaking. Oats must be stored for the horses, meats bought, the hall cleaned, the yard cleared, tapestries hung to stop the draughts from behind the shutters once the place was closed up for the night, and the portable altars set out.

Oakhampton might be small compared with other castles, but it offered Sir Peregrine a sense of safety as he entered the tunnel to the bailey, and he smiled to see his men at their posts. The main gates opened, and he trotted in behind Lord Hugh, their hooves ringing and striking sparks from the moorstone that paved the courtyard.

CHAPTER FOURTEEN

While the lord and his men ensconced themselves in Oakhampton Castle, Baldwin went with Margaret and Edith to watch some of the pre-tournament displays and to seek Simon.

'I thought he'd be here when we arrived,' Margaret said. She sounded a little disappointed.

'There is much to be organised still,' Baldwin said. He cast her a quick look. 'And someone was murdered here last night so he has extra work.'

The shadows were growing and people lounged at rails watching a succession of hopeful squires exercising their masters' horses through the lists, galloping the great mounts to warm them, turning and charging back again.

There were other entertainments as well. A juggler was sending an endless succession of balls up into the air, while idlers watched and unemotionally chewed pies or slurped from jugs of ale. Boys shot arrows at targets while farther on, a pair of men were circling warily, bare-chested, both holding small riding swords, fighting for God knew what reason – perhaps merely for money. Sometimes fights were staged to resolve arguments, sometimes just for display, but either way these combatants were winning a good reward. Every time the two backed away from each other, spectators threw coins.

It was an unequal battle, for one of the men was taller and had a longer reach, while the other had short arms. The shorter fellow was already wearing a pattern of bloody slashes across his chest while the other had only a couple of cuts on the palm of his left hand where he had defended himself. Baldwin, Margaret and Edith watched the two for some little while, having sent Hugh for a jug of wine, but soon it became obvious who would win and they lost interest. Edith professed a desire to see the weaker man prevail, but it was a forlorn hope; he had no chance, especially a moment later when the taller man ran him through the shoulder.

It was good for Baldwin to forget the murder, if only for a little while. The affair was an issue for Simon, certainly, and the Coroner, but not Baldwin, Keeper of the King's Peace from faraway Crediton. Yet Baldwin was concerned. He couldn't get the idea out of his mind that Wymond's body was left specifically to convey a message to Hal.

He tried to put such thoughts from him as he walked with Margaret, but he was keenly sensitive to the mood of the place. Everyone had heard of Wymond's death by now, and many of the townspeople were gossiping about the murder, but to Baldwin's relief there was little fear. The townspeople were not going to let the death of an unpopular carpenter stop them enjoying themselves.

With Simon busy, Baldwin felt a duty to keep Simon's wife entertained and he was determined to do so with as light a manner as possible. Although Edith was a young woman now, she could forget herself occasionally and fall into childish ways. Seeing a man selling sweetmeats, she ran on ahead and Baldwin took the opportunity of asking Margaret how she was.

'I despair,' Margaret said when the girl was out of earshot, rocking gently to soothe the child in her arms.

'Is she that difficult?' Baldwin asked, smiling inanely as the infant opened his eyes and glowered at the world. Catching sight of Baldwin he frowned and then vomited.

'More than you could imagine,' Margaret sighed as she mopped up. 'She exhausts me. One moment she declares she adores me, the next she shrieks that she loathes me. Naturally I am a saint if I have just given her a treat and an ogre if I've denied her one. At other times she is merely sullen and unhelpful.'

'I presume preventing her riding with her friends makes her sullen?' Baldwin guessed.

'Just so. Last week she wanted to ride to Tavistock – on her own, I ask you! She said she was old enough to be wedded, so she was old enough to ride to see her friends. I soon corrected her.'

Hugh reappeared, scowling ferociously as he barged his way through the crowd, two jugs gripped carefully in one hand, while he held his staff in his clenched fist.

Baldwin nodded towards him. 'It is good to see Hugh back.'

'You think so? The miserable devil!' she giggled. 'But yes, I'm happy he's returned.'

'It has been about a year, hasn't it, that he's been living away? Has he married Constance?'

'So he says.'

'It's hard to imagine a man leaving his wife behind.'

'Servants grow accustomed to leaving their families for long periods.'

'I know. Yet since I married Jeanne, I find it hard to imagine leaving her for weeks at a time. Is Hugh happy with his wife?'

'I think so.' She gave a slow nod in assent.

Baldwin knew that Margaret disapproved of the woman called Constance because of her background. Constance had once been a novice nun, and the thought that Hugh had slept with her offended Margaret, who was highly religious. She could not accept that a woman who had given her vows to God could later take up a new life and a secular husband. Tactfully, Baldwin chose to change the subject. 'Simon must be highly considered if he is asked to organise events such as these. I think your husband may be destined for advancement.'

'You think so?' Margaret responded eagerly. 'He has certainly done very well for himself. When we first met, he was a mere gentleman with land out at Sandford, and now look at him! I feel quite nervous, thinking of the nobles who will be here.'

He gave her a long, pensive look. 'When you have met as many of the breed as I have, you will soon lose any nerves. You will learn to make allowances for them.'

She blinked. 'What *do* you mean?'

'Margaret, most of the truly noble knights are mere vain, primping coxcombs. They have less brain in their heads than they were born with – those that have any at all. Look, there are two there.'

Following his finger, she saw Sir John of Crukerne and his son walking to the combat area where they had seen the two swordsmen. They leaned on the rail, talking. 'What of them?'

'They have the knightly attributes, or so they think. Both, from what I have heard, can handle a horse with great skill; both can wield lance, sword or axe; both have great stamina – but there is more to knighthood than that. They show no courtesy, humility or pity. Many knights like to demonstrate their courtesy by elaborate praise of beautiful women, and many would leave their attentions there, having made their target feel flattered as a lady should after such recognition, but there are some, like that squire,' he jerked his head, 'who would always try to take more. By force, if necessary.'

'And the other?'

'Sir John is no libertine. But a man like him, who has been in many jousts, must have lost much of his sense.'

'You have been in several yourself, I am sure?'

'And haven't you noticed how my brains have been addled?' he asked lightly. 'When you are hit about the head by a madman wielding a sword which weighs at least five pounds, you naturally have to wear a helmet, and for all the padding about your brow and ears, the din is appalling.'

She laughed aloud, but her eyes remained upon the two standing at the bars. The fighters had stopped, the shorter man being helped to a corner, blood streaming from the gash in his shoulder and other stab wounds. The victor, the taller man, was chatting to Sir John, but even as Margaret watched, Sir John turned and met her gaze. Although she tried to look away as if she had not observed him, she saw the knight's sudden wolfish smile and the sight of it made her colour.

Averting her face, she tried to put him from her mind, but she couldn't. That man's open stare had made her feel as though he had undressed and mounted her; if not in reality, she was convinced that he had in his mind. She felt as though she had been raped.

Andrew, Sir Edmund of Gloucester's squire, walked idly to the racks at the edge of the field. This was the starting-point for riders before charging at an opponent, and lances were fitted into their slots, ready for the first challenges.

Lifting one from its rest, he held it at its centre and frowningly gauged its heft and balance. It felt a little top-heavy, but that was normal enough. Squinting along its length he saw that there was a definite curve to it. All the better for the rider who faced it, he thought, for the wood would shatter most spectacularly on impact, making the two riders appear all the more brave for their harsh collision with shards and splinters of wood flying in all directions. The *coronal* was a goodly lump of iron, with four blunt prongs projecting to disperse the force of the lance and protect the opponent. Otherwise a sharp point with the full mass of knight, horse and armour all riding on the tip could puncture even strong armour and pin a man inside his steel coat. Andrew had seen it happen.

He set the lance back in the rest and took up another. This was straight enough, and he gave a grudging nod of approval as he peered along its length, but as he lifted it back to the vertical and thumped the base against the ground, he thought there was a feeling of weakness in it, as if it had a crack in the wood.

Putting the lance back, he eyed the arena. Imagining himself on horseback, he peered hard, searching for any potholes or tussocks which might conceal a molehill. The last thing he wanted was for his mount to stumble or swerve. With a heavy charger travelling at speed, that could end in disaster: the opponent's horse might try to dodge, leading to the lance-point striking at an odd angle, perhaps slipping beneath the plate armour and hitting a vital spot, or the manoeuvre could lead to the horses colliding, killing both each other *and* their riders.

The ground was clear so far as he could see. Reassured, he thrust his hands in his belt and leaned against the rack, idly watching the other squires and knights as they walked about, until suddenly his eye lit upon a slim, fair figure.

He stood, his hand reaching automatically for his knife-hilt. Slowly he walked around behind the rack and watched as the figure approached.

'*Geoffrey!*' His low, hissing voice made the other squire start and gaze about him. 'You cowardly whore's whelp!'

Geoffrey was only a few yards away, and he turned with a baffled expression.

'*Geoffrey!* You *shit!*'

'Eh?' A man was standing near the rack, Geoffrey could see, but at this distance, some twenty feet, he could only make out an imprecise blurred figure. His sight was poor at the best of times, but here, in bright sunlight, it was hard to see who was standing in the relative shade of the trees at the riverbank.

'Forgotten me, have you?' Squire Andrew called. He pulled his knife from its sheath and stalked forward. 'I've wanted to see you again ever since that night. You remember

– the night before we ran into Harclay at the bridge? Only you *wouldn't* remember, would you? You weren't there.'

'I don't know what you mean. Who are you?'

Andrew smiled thinly. There was a subtle note of fear in the other's voice. 'So you *have* forgotten me – that's sad. I was in your company when you were riding with your master at Earl Thomas of Lancaster's side. I remember you perfectly. You were a bold little cock there, weren't you? Offering your advice to all and sundry. Except you weren't quite so brave when you realised that the King was getting near, were you? You went off to seek forage, only you never came back.'

'Of course I didn't!' Geoffrey lied. 'I got cut off by a raiding party. I fought through them and went ahead to return to the Earl's side, only the bridge I had to cross was taken. Harclay and his men were already there. I had no choice.'

'Liar!' Andrew spat. 'You bolted. You rode off as soon as you could; you deserted your master.'

'I would never have deserted him,' Geoffrey declared hotly.

'You're lucky he died with the others on the bridge. Shot down by a random arrow, then crushed beneath a horse. He died there honourably, Geoffrey. Just as you should have done. Except you were too cowardly to risk your neck, weren't you? You had to get away.'

'I had no choice,' Geoffrey said weakly. 'What would you have done?'

'I'd have fought to get back, so I could die with my master,' Andrew said. 'As I did.'

'Well, all I can say is, you can't have been cut off in the same way I was,' Geoffrey said. 'I had no chance.'

'Really?' Andrew asked cynically. 'Don't you recognise me yet?'

Geoffrey stared as Andrew approached him. Then his mouth fell open and he held up a hand as if to ward off evil. 'But you were dead! I saw you fall!'

Andrew smiled mirthlessly. 'You thought so, did you? Well, if I died, I have been brought back to life to see you suffer for your cowardice, you bastard! And you'll suffer soon, believe me. I'll trample your reputation in the mire for running away from the enemy even when your master needed your support. You left him and your Earl to die, just as you left me and the others in the party to die. I shall denounce you.'

Geoffrey retreated a pace as Andrew came closer, his hand reaching for his sword. His palm was slick and he could scarcely grip the hilt, but then a tussock caught his heel and he tumbled down with a squeak. He saw Andrew above him, a long knife in his hand, and he whimpered, snapping his eyes shut, bringing an arm up to protect his face.

There was nothing. No prick of pain, no kick, nothing. He heard a low chuckle of contempt and when he opened his eyes, he saw Andrew's back as the squire marched back to the fields.

It made him want to sob. He couldn't be shamed in front of all the people here. It would be unbearable – he'd never be able to hold his head up in public again. Terrible! Utter social ruin. And what of Alice? She would hardly want a coward for a husband.

The scene came back to him with appalling clarity. He had been at the side of his knight, as he should be, when the little party had been given permission to 'ride out', the technical term which meant seeking plunder with the Earl's permission. Of course he was already anxious because of the stories about the army which the King had brought up against them all. Who wouldn't have been? It was scary knowing that you were committing treason. There was a special punishment for that: slow hanging till nearly dead, then drawing, being gutted while alive, the still-beating heart hauled from the chest before the body was beheaded and hacked into quarters. Hideous!

He slowly climbed to his feet, the bile acrid in his mouth.

When the suggestion that he should seek fodder was made, he hadn't intended running. He was a squire, committed and determined to do his duty by his knight. He and a number of other men had gone. And Andrew had been one of them.

He was dead. Geoffrey had seen him die! How could he have come back from the grave?

Their route had taken them towards some smoke in the distance, thinking that it must be a farm. Farms had food. Except when they arrived, there was a strong force of the King's own men waiting and the little group had been surrounded. Andrew had been one of the first into the medley, shrieking some weird cry, sword on high as he spurred into them. Geoffrey wasn't going to fight – he thought he could ride back and get help, get away from the clattering, clanging battle, but when he looked over his shoulder, he saw that they were already cut off. There was only the one way to safety, and that was ahead.

He had taken a moment to grit his teeth, swallowed his terror, clapped spurs to his mount and lowered his head as his charger leaped forward. There was one place where the fighting was thin. Andrew and others were in a solid mass to his right, but Geoffrey wasn't stupid enough to head for them. The weight of him and his horse could have beaten back the ambushers, but he would have been embroiled in the same dangerous fight and he had no wish to die. Andrew had screamed at him, just the once, and as he thundered through the thin ranks of foot-soldiers, eyes squeezed tight shut against the horrible sight of polearms and axes aimed at him, he had glanced back quickly to see Andrew fall from his horse, dead. Or so it had seemed.

Geoffrey had not stopped galloping until he was convinced he had not been followed, and then he had not known where to go. North lay the Earl's own estates and men, but there were also groups of the King's men who were trying to capture any stragglers. Southwards was the King's host, and yet . . . If he were to go south, he might be able to avoid the King's men, perhaps skirt around them all and make his way homewards. It was a better chance than any other.

Shivering with fear, he had made his choice. He had no desire to die like Andrew and the others, and he had no desire to join the Earl's men if they were all to be slaughtered as they subsequently were.

That was his saving. He had escaped, and later he heard how the King's men stopped Earl Thomas at Boroughbridge, holding him and his men at the bridge and a ford until the King's main host arrived. There was a great killing there, the river running red with the blood of the brave men who contested the passage over that long day.

All Geoffrey knew when he heard of the battle was relief. He might have been there, and if he had, he would have been at the side of his knight Sir Hector, who died on the slick wooden bridge; if Geoffrey had been there, he too would probably have succumbed to an arrow, a bolt or a sword just as his master had. But thank God he had been saved from that doom, emerging unscathed from the danger and without anyone to accuse him of cowardice.

And now a witness had emerged. A witness who could testify to his running from the enemy.

Edith had paid for the sweetmeats before she realised she was free. Her mother was still talking to Sir Baldwin in a low voice some way off, and neither was glancing in her direction, they were too involved in their own conversation. Hugh was watching a man testing a bow. They had moved since she had left them, and that gave her the excuse she needed. She bent her gaze towards where they *had* been – she could easily say she'd thought they'd still be there – and under the cover of a small group of passers-by, she walked back steadily the way she had come, towards the ring where the swordsmen had been.

They were no longer fighting, although their swords were still there lying on a table with other weapons: daggers, long-bladed knives and iron-shod staffs lay with axes and cudgels. She meditatively went to them and felt the edge of one of the swords. The blade was chipped and notched where it had hit the other, and there was a fine sheen like oil on it. When she took her finger from it, she saw that it was blood; there was a red stain on her hand which made her pull a face in disgust. She didn't want to mark her new tunic, so instead she wiped her fingers on the table's edge wondering whether it was the blood of the shorter man. It probably was, she reckoned. The taller man was almost unmarked.

The loser wasn't attractive, but Edith admired his courage in standing against an opponent with so much greater reach. It was silly of him to get into a fight like that, silly but brave, she felt, and she wondered what they could have been fighting over. Perhaps it was foul words, for men so often insulted each other with 'villeinous and blasphemous swearing' according to the local priest, but Edith hoped that there was something more honourable at the heart of their battle. Perhaps it was a fight over a woman.

It was a lovely thought, that two men should fight for one woman's favour. She imagined that they might fight over *her*, and smiled at the idea, hugging herself gleefully as a most unchaste thrill ran though her. That, she decided, would be best: to have two men risk their lives to impress a woman who would then grant her favours to the winner and hold him up, still bloody from his encounter, to everyone's adulation – that would be really good. Everyone would judge her magnificence and beauty by the blood shed to win her.

And it would show her mother and father that she was no longer a child to be commanded at their whims: to 'go there, come here, do as you are told,' she snarled to herself.

That was the trouble: her parents couldn't see she wasn't a baby any more. Standing haughtily near a fence-post, Edith considered the field and the milling people while she brooded on her parents' unreasonable attitude. They seemed to think that she needed to be constantly supervised and protected. It was so *stupid*! If she was left alone, she would be fine. She knew how to protect herself. She certainly didn't need to be locked up at the house like one of her father's prisoners at Lydford Gaol. Not that she was ever locked in, exactly, but it came to the same thing, being told she couldn't go to

Tavistock to see Susan when she wanted. *Susan* could go out more or less when she wanted, but no, Edith had to stay in. She'd told them, if they were worried, they could send Hugh with her to look after her, but although her father had initially said yes, that permission was immediately withdrawn when Simon heard that she had already asked Margaret and Margaret had meanly said no.

It was Mother's jealousy, Edith decided. Margaret couldn't bear the thought that her daughter was more beautiful than her. Pure spite, that's what it was. Well, she'd have to change her mind, that was all. Edith refused to be tied to the house just because of the misguided emotions of her mother. There were times when Edith almost thought she hated her mother.

'Hello, my Lady.'

She glanced up at the sound of the voice, low and respectful, with a hint of passion. 'Good day,' she said coldly. Although she had liked the look of him earlier, she had not forgotten the group standing at the fence, one of them making that disgusting sign to her. This squire was with them, she recalled, sitting úpon the fence.

'I have never before met a woman with such an enchanting smile. You make the sun seem dim.'

She tried unsuccessfully to keep her features neutral. 'I think you're a little over fulsome, sir,' she lied.

'I am not. I was drawn to this place just by the magnetic power of your beauty, which would outshine Helen of Troy or Venus herself. Your smile could cure a man's wounds, your touch would make him invincible, your—'

'Enough! God's blood, sir! After your friend was so crude and unpleasant, too.'

'My friend?' he enquired.

'Your friend, that nasty boy who was with you earlier and made an unpleasant sign to me. And now you try to make me dizzy with your hyperbole. Do you always wait until your companions have insulted a woman and then introduce yourself to her in such terms?'

'Never! May I fall dead if I ever praise another woman!' he swore with well-concealed dishonesty, a hand pounding his breast. 'I have seen you, and I can wish for no other. If a friend of mine annoys you, point him out to me and I shall make him regret his words or deeds. My heart is engaged. Whatever I do from now on, I do in your honour; whatever prowess I display, I do so to demonstrate the magnificence which you yourself possess; any feats of arms I achieve, I achieve solely by the power which your beauty lends to my arm. Everything good I do from now on, I do for love of you.'

Her heart fluttered and she felt a sudden faintness. All thoughts of her parents were gone as she studied his face from beneath lowered eyelashes. Tall, well-formed, with good thighs and ankles, he had the body of an athlete, with strong shoulders and thick biceps. His handsome face was to her very finely moulded, with a small scar over one brow. His eyes exhibited only fervent desire for her. This was the first time a man had expressed such devotion – especially at such short notice – and it was intensely gratifying. Once more she struggled to keep her smile at bay while trying to sound mature and reproachful.

'You think me some easy woman to tempt with your vows just because I am young? I am scarcely of Canonical age, when you must be full five years older.'

'What does age mean to lovers? We are old enough to marry, my love. Would you consider me?'

She held up a hand, seriously startled. There was a definite feeling of attraction to this fellow, but to speak of marriage was one step too far.

'Ah – I have scared her! My love is too strong for her, may God forgive me. I shall leave you, my Lady. If my death would remove the fear I have put into your eyes, I shall seek it instantly.'

'Be quiet a moment!' she scolded. 'Are you always this overblown? I won't speak of marriage. It's ridiculous! If I were to marry a man without asking permission of my father, it would be a man whom I loved, and I can hardly love you. I don't know you.'

'I don't know you, but I love you already,' he countered with a sly grin.

That sudden twist to his mouth made him more normal, reduced his previous words to the level of flirting. She was comfortable with that, and could herself smile. 'Perhaps, but I doubt even after all this whether you'd seriously want to wed quite yet. And I couldn't wed a mere squire, anyway,' she added, glancing away, feigning disinterest. 'My father would hardly be happy to see me thrown away on a nobody.'

'Then tomorrow, when I gain my spurs . . .' he teased.

'You will?' she gasped, then recovered herself. 'Yes, well, I daresay several lads will be knighted.'

'Ah, not so many. I shall be riding in the joust with some others, and when all is done, I shall be taken before the Lord and will accept my spurs and sword from him. And I shall wear the favour of my Lady, if she will permit me?'

She eyed him haughtily and sniffed. 'Oh, you think so? I am not so sure.'

'My Lady, please. A small token, anything. It will spur me on to great feats in your name. Without it, I must surely lose. Perhaps even die for longing.'

'Nonsense,' Edith said.

'How can you doubt me?'

'Easily,' she retorted.

'Let me persuade you, then.'

She peered over his shoulder. 'I have to find my mother.'

'Can I see you later?'

'I suppose we shall see each other at the feast,' she said.

'But how can we meet alone?'

'Well . . .' She was reluctant to deliberately disobey her father, but surely if Simon knew what a pleasant fellow this was, he couldn't object.

'Perhaps if I speak to the heralds, one of them can arrange to bring a message to you,' William said.

'Perhaps,' she agreed noncommittally.

'So may I wear a token of yours?' he asked.

'Don't be ridiculous!' she said, and refused to discuss the matter further, but unaccountably, when they separated, she dropped her neck-scarf apparently without noticing.

CHAPTER FIFTEEN

Baldwin smiled at Margaret while she spoke but he was concerned to hear her words. He had heard from another friend that young girls needed to be whipped more than any hound to be kept in line, but Margaret's complaints brought home to him how unprepared he was for fatherhood. How would he feel in later years, when Richalda brought home some wayward minstrel and proposed to wed him, or perhaps she might decide to marry some gormless peasant boy? Baldwin felt his cods shrivel at the thought.

Leaving Hugh to protect Margaret, he went to seek more wine. It was while waiting to be served that he saw a squire stumbling near the river. The lad appeared to be upset, walking with a clumsy gait like a man who was ill, and Baldwin watched him some little while before setting off after him.

'Who are you?' Geoffrey demanded.

Baldwin was some distance away still and all the squire could see was a large, square-built man trailing after him.

True, his tunic was a plain cream colour unlike Andrew's red hose and shirt under a jack, but Geoffrey was not of a mood to notice details.

'I am Sir Baldwin de Furnshill, Keeper of the King's Peace. Are you all right?'

Geoffrey couldn't meet Baldwin's eye as the knight approached. He looked down at his feet and took a deep breath, then sniffed and walked on. Seeing Squire Andrew here was appalling. Dreadful. If Alice got to hear of his behaviour at Boroughbridge, she would surely throw him over. The shame – to be disgraced before everyone, and just when Geoffrey had thought things were going so well. His messages were being delivered and the responses fired his heart with hope. Alice was happy to repeat her love for him. They would declare their wedding before Lord Hugh as soon as Geoffrey had won his spurs.

'You are a squire?' Baldwin asked gently.

'Yes. To Sir Ralph Sturrey.'

'Sir Ralph? I saw him only a few weeks ago and he had no squire,' Baldwin said mildly. Sir Ralph was an old friend and had bemoaned his lack.

'I joined him only three months ago,' Geoffrey admitted. 'Before that I served Sir Hector Barr, but he fell at Boroughbridge.'

Baldwin considered him a while, then, 'When I was young, squires used to meet in taverns. Does that still happen?'

'Of course it does,' Geoffrey said scathingly. 'Why shouldn't we?'

'I see. Where were you last night after dark?'

'Peter and I went to a tavern near town.'

'What time did you return?'

'I don't know. Late.'

'What of your friend?'

'Peter? He passed out. I left him there.'

'On your way back to the camp, did you see anyone else?'

Geoffrey shook his head, then: 'Oh, there was one man – up near the lance-racks.'

'Who?'

Geoffrey gave a wry grin. 'My eyes are bad. At twenty paces in daylight I find it hard to recognise a man. In the dark I have no chance. All I could see was a shape. Why all the questions, sir knight?'

'Wymond Carpenter was murdered last night.'

Geoffrey curled his lip. 'That vicious bugger?'

'Many people say the same,' Baldwin sighed. 'It seems everyone loathed the fellow.'

Geoffrey was quiet a moment. 'I couldn't swear to it, but it's possible that the man I saw was him.'

'Alone?'

'Well, I did see another shape with him – ach! How can I tell?'

'And there was no one with you when you saw him?'

'You mean you suspect *me*?' Geoffrey stopped and peered up at Baldwin. He would like to be able to speak to someone whom he could trust, and Baldwin's grave features were comforting, but his secret must not be divulged to Sir John. Making a quick decision, he said, 'I am married, Sir Baldwin. Lady Alice is my wife – although we have not announced our wedding. We are waiting until I am knighted. She was with me. Perhaps she recognised the men.'

'I see.'

'But please do not tell anyone. Our marriage was clandestine and there would be trouble if news should be spread.'

'Why?'

'Her family perished when a stand collapsed in Exeter several years ago. Since then she has been the ward of Sir John of Crukerne, and he wants her to wed his son Squire William. He would remove her from this tournament if he realised she had been already married. He'd reject it. You know how much power a man has over a ward.'

'Yes, indeed,' Baldwin considered. This was interesting, but surely it was irrelevant to Wymond's murder. 'But you think she might be able to tell me who this man was at the lances?'

'It's possible.'

'Did you walk her back to her tent afterwards?'

'Of course.'

'So what would Wymond have been doing there at the lances so late at night?' Baldwin wondered. 'And who was the man with him?'

Andrew saw William stoop and collect the scarf. It was typical that the squire should try his luck with the girl. The kid was attractive enough, certainly, but Andrew knew from long association with Squire William that he would seek to storm almost any bastion of feminine defence more as a matter of practice than from any genuine need.

'She fell at your attack?' Andrew said drily.

William started, then gave a shamefaced grin. 'Christ's bones, but you can walk quietly when you have a wish!'

'Guilty conscience?'

'No need for that, Andrew. Some of us only ever behave with the best of intentions.'

'I am sure you're right, but when it comes to women, your intentions have always been murky.'

William gave a fleeting grin, but his attention was fixed on the disappearing Edith. 'She is beautiful.'

'She looked it,' Andrew agreed. 'So were many of your other conquests.'

'I wouldn't put her in the same category.'

'No? You don't mean you're in love? Good God, you're too young for that!'

'Just because you have never married.'

'No, it wasn't possible.'

'Wasn't possible?'

Andrew said nothing and William gave him an interested glance. He had not met Andrew before the Boroughbridge campaign and the thought that a man of some thirty-five years should have found it impossible to marry seemed peculiar. 'You must have found opportunities to marry. Didn't you ever come across a woman whom you desired?'

'My master was strict,' Andrew said shortly.

'Ah, I remember you saying that you were living in France. They can be strange over there,' William said dismissively and returned to a more interesting subject. 'She is a graceful filly, isn't she? I shouldn't go near her, for I promised my father that I wouldn't risk my match to Alice – but she's a tempting morsel.'

'He still wants you to wed Alice?'

'Oh, I shall. I can marry her and use her lands, and she will be delightful to embrace on a dark and chill winter's evening.'

'What if she refuses to marry you?' Andrew asked.

'She can't. There are pressures a guardian can bring to bear on his ward. No, I don't fear that.'

'Then what of this latest one?' Andrew said, jerking a thumb at Edith's back.

'Ah! Well, she is the Bailiff's daughter, and he's annoyed me.'

'So you'll take her in order to get back at him?'

'What better way? Well, other than bulling his wife and pinning the cuckold's horns on him,' William laughed.

'Christ Jesus! Are you sure of this?'

'You can't understand,' William said tolerantly.

Andrew bridled. 'I may be five-and-thirty, but I can remember what it is to desire a woman.'

'What better way to get my revenge on him than by deflowering his daughter? It will be doubly pleasurable for me, and all the more bitter for him.'

'But she will be ruined,' Andrew said more quietly.

'The alternative is a vulgar fight with her father. I'd certainly rather sheath my weapon to the hilt in her than have him thrust his dagger in *me*.'

'At least there is some honour in a fight.'

'True. Standing with comrades to defeat the enemy.'

'If you can trust your comrades,' Andrew said.

'That sounds bitter.'

'It was.'

'Yet your comrades were stout-hearted enough. They attacked many times.'

'Horses and armour are poor protection against a small but determined band of archers protected by men-at-arms,' Andrew agreed.

'It was a good fight,' William said. They had been on

opposite sides during the battle and William had captured Andrew. 'Why are you bitter about your companions?'

'Before Boroughbridge I and a small group of foragers were ambushed and I was knocked from my horse. Several of us were killed, but one, a coward, fled the field.'

'That's disgusting!' William said vehemently.

'And he will be knighted.'

'You'd prevent it?' William asked doubtfully. 'He could challenge you to combat.'

'If he's too scared to risk his life in a fight, I doubt he'd test his skills with me,' Andrew said dismissively.

'Who was it?'

'Geoffrey.'

William gaped. 'No! Christ's blood! He's the man Alice wanted instead of me!'

'If she wants him,' Andrew said, 'she should be quick. He may not be around for much longer. And if he is, I'll make sure he's never knighted.'

'Do so with my pleasure. But if you say he deserted you during the fight at Boroughbridge, you may have to stand in a queue to get to him!'

While Margaret rocked her young boy waiting for Baldwin to return, Hugh absently scratched his head and sucked at a piece of meat stuck in the gap of a broken tooth. It was while he was standing with no particular thought in his mind that he saw Edith talking to William.

Hugh was a lonely man. Raised as a shepherd on the moors, he was used to quiet emptiness with only dogs and lambs to talk to, and until a year before he had felt jealous of other men who had their own women, like his master and Sir

Baldwin. Even Edgar, Sir Baldwin's man, had married after many years of philandering, but Hugh had been convinced no woman could want him. Until recently.

He had left her at her home up near Iddesleigh. The child she had borne was more than nine months old now, and she was over the worst: not only must she cope with the birth of her child, her house was old and more than a little dilapidated. Once it had been a cottar's home, with a vegetable garden at the rear and a shaw to provide all the owner's wants in terms of wood, but the cottar had died and the place then left to rot.

When Constance arrived, she found she must renew thatching, clear weeds from the yard, hack back the overgrown shaw and prepare the soil for planting. That was outside; inside, the hearth must be renewed, furniture replaced, the walls replastered and painted. A woman already far into pregnancy could not achieve much and Hugh had taken on the work, his wiry frame bending and hauling and dragging and painting stolidly, until evening when he returned indoors, undemonstratively eating the bread and pottage she had made for him, before they both went to the only bed in the house.

His admiration for her was forged and tempered in the passionless environment of the convent, but now it grew as he created a place where she could bring up her child. Until winter and the freezing chill, he had not touched her in their bed, lying carefully away from her, but with the snow the two clung together for warmth.

When the boy was born, Hugh was there to help her settle, but he hadn't expected her to grow to love him. The dour, uncommunicative moorman accepted his own love for her

like a responsibility which must be shouldered, never antici-
pating that it could be returned. He was a servant and knew
his position. She had been a nun, and was thus inviolate, but
she had been persuaded into a man's bed, and now bore a
bastard child.

Soon after the birth, when she brought the child to Hugh
and told him that it was named after him, he had felt a curious feeling of hunger, an emptiness that couldn't be filled,
and for a while he held the swaddled child, unable to speak.
Her action had overwhelmed him. He stood contemplating
the baby, whose eyes had opened and fixed Hugh with a serious squint before trying to suckle from his leather jack.

'I'll get back to work,' Hugh had said gruffly, passing the
baby back to his mother, and going out with a light step to
fetch his axe. That afternoon he scarcely managed half the
work he'd intended.

Constance was ever kind and appreciative. A trained infir-
marer, she was used to calming the ill, soothing their pain
with her soft voice, her light touch and warmth of spirit. For
Hugh these qualities were all but unknown in his life. He had
helped her from a desire to assist a mother whom he loved as
one might love the Madonna, a woman seen from afar and
admired for her qualities, but by the time the baby was born
he adored her utterly. Before the end of the spring they were
married.

It had been hard for him to leave her at their home, but his
master owned him, and at least Simon allowed him time to
travel home and see his woman whenever he wanted. It was
better than most servants received.

Today, seeing William talking to Edith he felt torn. The
girl was his own secret treasure: since her childhood, he had

been her closest accomplice and ally, often delaying his duties in order to see her smile, giving himself as a mount when she wanted to pretend to ride, playing hide-and-seek with her or whittling sticks into fantastic shapes while she watched open-mouthed.

That was years ago. Now she was a mature young woman, and sought friends of her own age. It felt like a betrayal, the way that she curled her lip when told to remain with Hugh at the house, but Hugh phlegmatically accepted it. He knew girls of her age would lose interest in childish pursuits and would be keen to move to more mature behaviour. It was natural, even if it was hurtful. And from the look of her, she had found a lad who had a similar interest in her. Not some scruffy churl from a peasants' vill, but a man of better birth than Hugh or even Simon himself: a squire.

He only caught a fleeting glimpse of Edith's face as she left the lad, but Hugh was sure he saw in her features the same joy, the same happiness he had felt himself last year when he first realised he was in love.

That was why he didn't tell his mistress about Squire William. He was not to know that if he had, he might have been able to save himself and his master a great deal of trouble.

Later, as the light was fading, Andrew walked along the road towards the tavern where he had arranged to meet William, when he heard feet behind him. He continued without breaking his step, but his attention was concentrated behind him.

Caution was an essential part of him now. It wasn't an act to impress women, much though frivolous fools like William sometimes assumed it was. Andrew had no need to impress. He was confident in his own abilities. That was enough.

Whoever it was had approached closer now. 'Hey! Don't I know you, Squire?'

'Me, sir?' Andrew demanded and spun around. Then he recognised Odo.

The herald had lost much weight, he thought. His head was hanging lower than it had before, although that light was still there in his eyes, but at his cheeks and forehead were the lines that denoted pain and exhaustion.

For Odo's part, he saw that Andrew had improved no end since their last meeting. 'You have a new master, my friend,' he stated. 'It is clear from your tunic and weapons.'

'Aye. A good man called Edmund.'

'Sir Edmund of Gloucester?' Odo asked.

'You know him?'

'I have heard much about him. He is without a lord, I hear?'

'True. But perhaps he will be fortunate here. I understand Lord Hugh could always use a strong arm.'

'Yes. I am hoping he will want a useful herald with an eye for an enemy's coat-of-arms, too!' Odo said with a chortle.

'A man can grow tired of wandering,' Andrew said, eyeing Odo's worn boots and faded hose.

'And of sitting atop a horse. Yes.'

'What are you doing here?'

'Ah, I seek a man, a squire. I am acting as a go-between, to give messages to him from his beautiful lover.'

'If only I could be so fortunate.'

'Andrew, my friend, you and I are too old by many and many a year to hope to win the heart of a maiden. We must accept bachelorhood and assist those who, younger than we, would seek a wife from the ranks of young maidens here.'

'Godspeed your delivery, then.'

'Ah, but surely a pint or two would speed me still faster on my way,' Odo laughed as he pushed his way into the tavern behind Andrew.

When they both held jugs and could drink their fill (for this tavern had no more pots or cups to offer), Andrew glanced at Odo from the corner of his eye.

'So is this some wealthy young buck who seeks a woman for a night or two?'

'No, no, no!' Odo tutted. 'If that were all, I'd tell him to come here and sample one or two of the wenches. No, he is convinced of his love for this girl. And she declares her love for him.'

'A pretty tale. I suppose neither has enough money to wed? Or are they waiting for a suitable moment to announce their intentions?'

'Hardly that. They have already exchanged their oaths and enjoyed the first proof of love, but clandestinely. The girl is a ward and cannot tell anyone of their marriage until her husband is knighted.'

'A ward?' Andrew shot him a look. 'It's not Lady Alice, the ward of Sir John, is it?'

Odo said nothing, merely sipped contentedly at his jug.

'And her husband?' Andrew frowned, thinking his friend had lied. 'Is it Squire William?'

'No, another local squire.'

'My God! Squire Geoffrey,' Andrew breathed.

CHAPTER SIXTEEN

Today being the first night Lord Hugh was staying at the castle, there was a feast planned, to which all the participants in the tournament were invited. First a service was held in the chapel, while servants and more lowly officials were fed so that later they could serve the guests.

While standing in the yard waiting to enter the hall, Baldwin and Simon had an opportunity to share their experiences with the Coroner. When they were finished, Sir Roger cocked an eye at Baldwin.

'I may be able to give you a little more information. When Benjamin died, it was shortly after he had called in several debts – mainly from knights. I thought Sir John, Sir Walter, or Sir Richard could have been responsible. Or the Squires William or Geoffrey. All these men were in Exeter at the time and attending the court.'

'The murders could be unrelated,' Baldwin said slowly.

'You don't believe that any more than I do.'

Baldwin turned to the Coroner. 'How did the banker get involved? If Lord Hugh was paying for the tournament, what exactly was Benjamin's part in it?'

'Lord Hugh may have ordered the stands to be built, but he'd not entrust too much money to a messenger, nor would he wish to come here early just to keep an eye on the work in progress. No, he would have passed his instructions to Hal and given the architect a budget. How Hal decided to work within that budget was up to him, but Lord Hugh would only have given Hal an advance on the total owed – and Benjamin, who was a party to all this, would be expected to monitor things so that Hal wouldn't go over his budget. Afterwards Lord Hugh would reimburse Benjamin for his share of the expenses and give him a profit as well.'

Simon continued, 'So Benjamin would provide the ready money that Hal needed. And if Hal could construct the whole show for significantly less than Lord Hugh had budgeted, both he and his associates could pocket the difference. Lord Hugh would still pay the full amount to Benjamin as agreed.'

'Which was why Hal was against buying more wood?' Baldwin asked.

'Yes,' Simon said. 'Hal bought in the cheapest stuff he could find so that he could cut costs. If I had to guess, I'd say that he later realised it was much worse than he had anticipated. Hal wouldn't have wanted to have a stand collapse again, so he tried to force me to *give* him fresh timbers, blaming the townspeople for taking advantage of him. They didn't, of course. He paid for cheap stuff and that was what he got. Later he went back and bought better materials when I refused to let him have it for free.'

'So there is no incentive for a murder in that scam,' Baldwin said slowly.

'Unless Lord Hugh wanted to punish Wymond and Benjamin for taking advantage,' Coroner Roger shrugged.

'Lord Hugh wouldn't do that,' Simon responded.

'Why should someone murder Wymond with his own hammer?' Coroner Roger wanted to know.

Baldwin answered, 'I think Wymond always carried his hammer with him. It was as important to him as a sword to a knight – it showed what he was. Where he died was up in the woods – I wondered whether he was lured there with the promise of good, fresh timber. Someone told him where he could get strong wood and save himself having to buy from the town. Then he was struck down and in the dark his killer dropped the hammer and couldn't find it.'

Roger was thoughtful. 'I have held the inquest. As you'd expect, there was nothing much to be learned.'

'No. How can the local jury accuse anyone when there are so many strangers in the town?'

'Usually all too easily, if it means getting rid of a known troublemaker,' Simon grunted cynically.

'I still don't understand why his killer chose to carry him back to the tent and leave his body there,' Coroner Roger said, frowning. 'He could so easily have woken Hal and been discovered.'

'Maybe he didn't know Hal was in there?' Simon suggested.

'Or was it a message?' Baldwin said, musing on the thoughts he'd had earlier.

Coroner Roger gazed at him intently. 'Message?'

'A sign that he must stop doing something? A sign that he could have the same happen to him?' Baldwin guessed.

Simon scuffed a boot in the dust. 'This rumour that he was a spy for the Despensers . . . could someone have learned of this and killed Wymond to stop reports being sent to them?'

'Anything is possible,' Baldwin said heavily. 'But surely then the murderer would have killed Hal as well.'

Roger was grim-faced. 'Perhaps the killer intends doing that. He may have been interrupted last night, or was too tired after Wymond's killing. What if he means to go back tonight?'

'That is what I was thinking,' Baldwin said. 'I do not want to return tomorrow and discover that Hal has died.'

Simon beckoned a watchman. 'Get a man to go to Hal Sachevyll's tent and guard it. Understand? Hal could be in danger from the same murderer who killed Wymond.'

'Spies!' Simon muttered bitterly. 'And murder, all during the first tournament that *I* am responsible for.'

'I am sure you will find it is all resolved quickly,' Baldwin said easily.

'When we cannot even tell who might have been near Wymond's tent last night?' Simon said. He caught sight of a group of knights in their silks and gorgeous robes. 'Hah! Look there. See that man? The one with the beautiful tall wife? He is Sir Walter Basset.'

'Yes, I have met him before,' Baldwin said. 'Not a pleasant man. Rough and too willing to take any comment as an insult. He likes to draw his sword.'

'He's also the tattiest-looking son of a whore I have ever seen,' Simon said. 'I saw him earlier and he could have been a villein from the poorest demesne in the land.'

'It is difficult when you see a man out of his usual – or rather his expected – garb.'

'Yes. He looks well as a knight, but when I saw him with Roger, he had lost all status.'

Coroner Roger agreed, but before he could speak Sir Peregrine joined them. 'So, Sir Baldwin, are you helping with another murder?'

'You have heard about the poor fellow?'

'I knew of him,' Sir Peregrine smiled grimly. 'Lord Hugh used him a few times for similar events.'

'Were you aware that he was a spy?' Simon shot out.

Sir Peregrine's smile broadened. 'Ah, you are speculating that I may have decided that a spy was too dangerous and arranged to have him killed. Is that your concern?'

The Coroner answered. 'We are searching for a murderer, but I for one have no desire to mingle with politics.'

'Then you can rest your mind, Coroner,' Sir Peregrine chuckled. His face grew more grim as he faced Baldwin. 'I assure you that neither I nor Lord Hugh wanted him dead. Yes, Wymond and others spy for the King . . .'

'Benjamin and Hal?' Simon asked.

'Yes. And therein lies my problem. Their deaths could persuade King Edward that my Lord Hugh is guilty of removing the King's own men.'

Baldwin squinted at the ground. 'And of course the King would wonder why you should want to do that. He would assume that Lord Hugh was guilty of some – um – impropriety, to justify killing his enemies. That could be dangerous at a time like this when the whole country is close to war again.'

'I do not deny that,' Sir Peregrine agreed sombrely, but then he flashed a grin. 'More to the point, the King will send new spies to replace those who have died. At least when I knew who the spies were, I could ensure that only the relevant information was given to them. Now . . .' he became introspective. 'Now I have to uncover more, which means endless secrecy and difficulties. Lord Hugh and I were the two men who had least desire to remove Benjamin and Wymond.'

'Do you believe him?' Simon asked Baldwin.

The knight was watching Sir Peregrine as he stalked away to rejoin Lord Hugh. 'Yes,' he said at last. 'I think that was why he came here – to let us know that he was innocent.'

'Do you believe him?' Coroner Roger repeated.

'Against my better judgement,' Baldwin said slowly, 'I rather think I do.'

There was a general move towards the hall for the feast, and as the three men joined the throng, Baldwin saw Odo and Andrew hurry in through the gate together. Seeing Baldwin, the herald joined them.

After introducing Coroner Roger, who had never met Odo, Baldwin asked, 'Odo, were you at Exeter for the court?'

'What court?'

Sir Roger smiled at Baldwin. 'He wasn't there. I'd have seen him.'

'Why do you want to know?' Odo asked.

'First, where were you last night?'

'Me? Here. As herald I am expected to sing and play for the guests. Then I went to my tent. My King Herald, Mark Tyler, wishes me to stay in the camp and ensure that there is no ribaldry. In truth, I think he wants me to learn how uncomfortable being a herald can be, in case I seek to take his job!'

'What of you, Andrew?' Baldwin asked.

'I walked a little. I do not sleep well,' Andrew said coldly.

'You were alone?'

'Of course. And now please excuse me. I have to serve my master.'

Baldwin watched him as he walked away. Then; 'Odo, tell me, what do you know of Sir Edmund?'

'Of Gloucester? A good, strong man, if unlucky in his loyalties and love. He had been going to marry Lady Helen, before she wed Sir Walter Basset of Cornwall. Then he lost all when Sir John captured him at a tourney. With nothing in his pocket, he fled over the sea and earned himself a new fortune.'

'What of Sir John?'

'Ah. He and his son are curious folk,' Odo told him. 'Sir John is no longer a wealthy man. He has lost much through murrain and the famine. He seeks to weld his estates to those of Lady Alice, from what she tells me. I fear that although she is his ward, she may seek to evade Squire William's advances.'

Baldwin understood him. 'So often a ward will not wish to wed the boy she knew as a brother,' he said. 'What of other knights?'

Odo murmured about the other men who were attending the tournament while they all found seats at tables. Then he had to leave them. 'Please ask for me if you need anything more, sir, but I must go now. I have to prepare music to aid your palate.'

Sir Roger stared balefully after him as he walked away. 'Is that man always so cocksure?'

'Who cares? At least he has given us some information to work with,' Baldwin said. 'And now we must see if we can talk to this Alice, the woman who was with Geoffrey when he saw Wymond and another man.' He looked along the table. 'I suppose that is her, seated between Sir John and Squire William.'

Baldwin was able to speak to Lady Alice before too long. After the meal, Squire William walked over to join a group of other squires, and Sir John soon rose from his place to seek the privy.

When both were gone, Baldwin went to Alice's side. 'My Lady, could I speak with you for a moment?'

She was a pretty child, he thought, with large and lustrous eyes, a most appealing and kindly expression, and an aura of calmness that was more mature than seemed quite natural for her years.

'Of course, sir.'

'My name is Sir Baldwin.'

'And you wish to ask me about the night that Wymond died. My husband told me you would want to talk to me.'

'You have spoken to him?'

'There's no need to look so surprised, Sir Baldwin. He passes messages to me through the good herald Odo, and I reply.'

'Then you know that I wish to find the murderer of Wymond. Geoffrey told me that you saw Wymond out near the lances.'

'Yes. And there was a man near him, but he was behind Wymond and not distinct,' she said.

'You didn't recognise him?'

'No. I was concentrating on my husband,' she said simply.

'Of course. Tell me, how did you come to be a ward of Sir John?'

She sighed. 'There was a tournament at Exeter, and my mother and brother went to watch my father's battle as I understand it – you see, I was a tiny toddler at the time. There was a terrible accident and my father fell, struck down by accident. I am told he was popular, as some of these knights can be, and the crowds moved to the front of the stand to shout their anger at the man who had killed him. The stands were not sound enough, and the movement of the people led to the stand collapsing. My mother and baby brother were crushed.'

'I am sorry.'

'I have never known any different, Sir Baldwin,' she said with a spark of defiance. 'I have grown from childhood knowing no parents.'

'So Sir John was your uncle, or perhaps—'

'He is *nothing*!' Her eyes flashed with rage and she was silent. Then she lifted her head proudly. 'You do not understand, Sir Baldwin. That man, Sir John, was the knight who killed my father Sir Godwin. It was his blow that took away my father and my mother and their baby boy. I had no other family and he offered to protect me until I grew to maturity. Yet all the time I think he had his eyes fixed greedily upon my inheritance. He sought to win all that my father had left me.'

'It would be an act of gross cynicism.'

'It is. He hated my father – things he has said prove that. He insists that I should marry his son, and that way he will keep my family's inheritance tied to his own. Well, I decided many years ago that I would never agree – and then I met Geoffrey. I love him. That is why we married.'

'Sir John knows nothing of this?'

'Nor his son. We shall declare our marriage here, as soon as Geoffrey has been knighted and before all the knights and their ladies. Sir John may try to contest the legality of the wedding, but he would find it difficult to separate us if Lord Hugh gives us his blessing.'

Baldwin nodded, considering. He had known that Alice was Sir Godwin's daughter, but only now did her appalling position occur to him in all its horror. However, the investigation was more important than his feelings of sympathy for the girl. Right now Baldwin was confused about one point. He knew that Sir John owed money to Benjamin. If the banker had demanded his money back, Sir John could have decided to kill him – but if Wymond's death was connected with Benjamin's in some way, the implication was that Sir John must also have had a motive to kill the carpenter.

'Tell me,' he asked Alice, 'do you know whether Sir John had any reason to dislike Wymond?'

She looked at him very directly. 'The carpenter helped build a stage for Sir John some six years ago. It collapsed when Sir Walter forced Sir Richard Prouse against it, and Sir John blamed Wymond because the carpenter had used shoddy wood. He was making profit from my guardian by taking money to use the best materials, then buying cheap rubbish and pocketing the difference.'

'Did Sir John have a grudge against Benjamin Dudenay as well as Wymond?'

'Oh yes. He owed him an enormous sum. And that little man, Hal – he hated him as well. He hated the lot of them. Called them every name under the sun.'

'Sir John told me you could confirm that he came back to your tent last night and that he could not thus have murdered Wymond.'

227

She looked at him in surprise. 'He came in and saw that I was well, but that was late, after I had returned from seeing Geoffrey. As a matter of fact, he woke me when he came in.'

Her face was full of innocence, but Baldwin didn't know whether he could believe her or not. Her evidence suggested that Sir John had had enough time to commit a murder. But Baldwin had no idea when Wymond had died. Then a thought struck him. 'You say that you saw a man with Wymond – could it have been Sir John?'

She considered. 'Perhaps. But if it had been him, surely I would have realised?' she added fairly.

Baldwin nodded and soon afterwards left her, to move to the table where Sir Walter sat. The Cornishman was a powerful-looking man, Baldwin thought, with dark eyes that glanced keenly about him. This was no fool, whatever one might assume about such a muscle-bound, oafish-looking fellow. Baldwin introduced himself and Sir Walter was polite in return. It was always safer for a knight to be courteous in case offence might be given.

'It is a pleasure to meet you. I have heard much about you from Lord Hugh,' Baldwin said.

'You know him well?'

'I see him fairly often. I live between his castles of Exeter and Tiverton, so he occasionally visits me.'

'A good lord.'

'Yes. Honourable and generous.'

'Yes.' Sir Walter smiled widely. 'Very generous.'

So Baldwin had guessed correctly. This man was more interested in obtaining a financial reward than in displaying the other aspects of knighthood. It was the modern way, he knew, but he could not help but feel it to be contemptible.

'So shall I meet you in the lists, Sir Baldwin?'

'I fear not, Sir Walter. I am over-ancient for lance-play.'

'True,' Sir Walter said without thinking. He was eyeing the quality of Baldwin's clothing sadly, as though mourning the wealth that he would miss by not being able to capture Baldwin in the ring. 'Still, there'll be others, I suppose.'

'Yes,' Baldwin smiled. 'I am sure you will find enough targets for your lance.'

'I always do,' Sir Walter yawned.

'You have fought often?'

'Enough. I've made my money from tournaments in Europe.'

'It is an expensive pursuit.'

'It can be,' Sir Walter agreed. 'But if you win often enough, the expense is left to the other man.'

'Quite so,' Baldwin said. 'It is the loser who has to travel to the money-lender to have his purse robbed by those such as Benjamin Dudenay.'

'You knew that bastard, did you? He was a godless, poxed shit, that man. Thank Christ he's long dead.'

'Did you know the carpenter who died – Wymond? He was an associate of Benjamin's,' Baldwin said mildly, but his eyes were fixed upon the other man with greater than normal keenness.

Sir Walter met his gaze with a fixed stare. 'You think I killed them? You're mad.'

As he spoke, his wife returned to the table. She walked with an effortless grace which Baldwin considered would suit a queen, as she approached the table where the two men sat. 'My husband? Is all quite well?'

Sir Walter eased his shoulders and appeared to physically relax. He leaned back in his seat and grinned mirthlessly.

'This good knight seeks to accuse me of murdering a peasant. If you want to, Sir Baldwin, carry on. No one would convict me of a crime of that nature. No, I wouldn't worry about an accusation like that.'

As he spoke, he glanced idly about the room, and suddenly Baldwin saw him clench his jaw and glare with real rage. He almost stood as though to go and fight.

Lady Helen put a hand on his arm. 'My husband, please. The fellow is only a boy. He means nothing.'

Baldwin turned to see Squire William with his friends, but although the other lads were enjoying their freedom and Lord Hugh's ale, Squire William appeared to be staring directly at her.

Sir Walter turned and leaned towards Sir Baldwin. 'I didn't kill that pathetic carpenter, nor that thieving arse of a banker, but I'll tell you this: if that little shit ever touches my wife, you can come straight to me when you find his corpse. All right?'

Much later, Hal left the tavern, stumbling along the road in the clear night air.

The atmosphere in there was just awful. Horrid! Smoke-filled from the badly drawing fire, cold from the multiple draughts that sought entry through the shuttered but unglazed windows, loud with the roars of the men-at-arms and their squires as they drank, belched, ate, sang, and quarrelled. One man was stabbed, although his attacker apologised profusely once he had calmed himself. And all this accompanied by the wailing and thumping from the musicians in the little gallery.

Hal swayed gently at the foot of the castle and sniffed back another sob. There was no point in weeping and wailing. Wymond wouldn't have wanted him to be upset; Wymond was too strong and hearty for that, but Hal was desolate without his friend and lover.

They had met many years ago now, building a tournament together, and they had hit it off immediately. Then they met Benjamin, who was not interested in them in the same way, for which Hal was grateful. He couldn't fancy the banker. He had always been attracted to very masculine men like Wymond, and Benjamin's podgy figure was revolting. Not that he'd thought Wymond could possibly want *him*. No, Wymond was the source of some delightful fantasies, but Hal never thought it could go further – until one night he got the carpenter terribly drunk and the two of them fell together as soon as they returned to their rooms. Rough, coarse, occasionally cruel – all described Wymond; and yet he was also curiously vulnerable. The harshness was a show put on to protect him from hurt.

Hal sighed and closed his eyes, feeling the tears approaching once more as the memories flooded back. The tears weren't only for Wymond, but for himself. He didn't know how he could live without his lover.

If he could, he would have admitted his other job, too, but he daren't. All he could achieve was enemies. Nothing more. Lord Hugh's men would be furious if they learned that he, Wymond and the banker had spied for Hugh Despenser.

Hal suddenly wondered whether Wymond's death was the result of his spying.

It was so inexplicable! Hal had gone to bed thinking that his lover would soon follow him. They tended not to share beds while working, because it was too tiring, but both slept in the same room. Hal had thought Wymond was going to return – in fact, he had a feeling he *had* half woken when Wymond had returned – and now he knew that it was the murderer who had woken him.

And the next morning Hal had let him stay in his bed. How did he not realise that something was wrong? How could he have missed the glaring, terrible fact that his lover was dead? True, they never rose together normally, they didn't care to be too obvious about their relationship, but Hal, when he woke and hurried from the tent, should have realised that Wymond was dead.

Hal walked the few paces to the bridge over the tiny stream and sat at its edge. Disconsolate, he had no energy. The prospect of all the years to come, long decades alone, seemed intolerable. That was the curse of his kind: no companionship. If another man with the same simple urges was ever found, he was to be held on to with a fierce grip, for it was so hard to seek out another. At least a man who lost his wife could count upon being able to find a new woman; most would have a son or daughter to remind them of the happiness they had once known, but not Hal. His life was ended as effectively as if he had hanged himself. Whoever had killed his lover had destroyed him too.

He closed his eyes and wept silently. The tears had been with him all day, but only now that he was alone could he indulge in his misery. And he would be alone for the rest of his life.

'Are you all right, master?'

Hal looked up into sympathetic eyes. 'No. I am devastated,' he wept.

'There is a cure for that.'

'Ale, wine, both give oblivion, but I need a stronger cure for my bereavement.'

'I was thinking that the best cure is to talk about it, master. Would you like to tell me your troubles?'

'No. But if you aren't busy, I will buy you a pot of wine and we can talk and you can take my mind from them.'

'Very well, sir,' said Wymond's killer, and he smiled as he helped Hal to his feet.

CHAPTER SEVENTEEN

Just as the skies had promised, the morning of the first day of the tournament was clear and fine when Simon walked from the castle towards the tilting ground, resolutely putting all thought of Wymond and Benjamin from his mind.

He was up before dawn and drank his morning whet of a pint of thin ale at the castle's bar before setting off. As he gathered up watchmen and inspected the field to make sure that all was ready, walking about the *ber frois* and reassuring himself that everything was prepared, he couldn't help but be glad that Coroner Roger was responsible for investigating sudden death. Simon had enough to occupy him already.

He checked that Lord Hugh's seat was safe and hadn't been stolen (stranger things had happened) before peering beneath the stand and making sure all looked sound. It would be dreadful to have Lord Hugh's own stand collapse, not that it was only the fear of poor construction that made him nervous. He was concerned. The sight of Wymond's mutilated body had shocked him and the more he considered it, the more he was sure that a killer who could strike once in so devastating a manner could do so again. That was why Simon had wanted to come and check the area once more. To make sure that there were no more unpleasant surprises lurking for Lord Hugh.

Lord Hugh had listened with frowning disbelief when Simon and Roger spoke to him of Wymond's death, but his first thoughts were for his tournament.

'Whoever it was must be mad,' he concluded after consideration. 'But you must find him, Coroner, Bailiff. If someone could be a danger to other people here, you must stop him.'

'Fine,' Simon muttered to himself. 'Show me who he is and I'll catch the bastard!'

With no clear idea who could have killed Wymond or why, Simon found himself scouting about the stands, glancing beneath all those which did not have solid wooden walls, poking in the bushes lining the field with a stick and generally reassuring himself that no one was lying there dead like Wymond the previous day. He had to keep occupied, keep moving – the alternative was to sit and fester, wondering who and why, and whether another attack would take place.

He had completed a half-circuit of the ground, and was standing at the riverside, morosely contemplating his tunic, hose and boots, all of which were sodden and wrinkled with the dew from the long vegetation, when one of the watchmen gave a muttered curse and called to him.

'What is it?'

'Some drunk. He's puked all over himself,' the watchman called back, kicking at a figure lying supine near the river some yards away.

Simon wrinkled his nose. Even from where he stood he could smell the rancid stench. He ordered another watchman to help and stood back while the drunk was hauled upright and half helped, half dragged away. Simon continued on his rounds reflecting with satisfaction that even drunks hadn't caused too much trouble with this event. Evicting one snoring reveller who had over-indulged the previous night didn't compare with other festivities, when men and women could be found drowned in their own vomit, or in a well, or having tripped and fallen into a stream or river.

There were legions of dead associated with events. Sometimes it was children who, having enjoyed ale or wine with their parents, would fall asleep out of doors and freeze to death. Simon had himself, some years before, seen a boy running about a campsite after too much wine, and fall into a fire. Such deaths were natural, if unpleasant.

There was a loud splash. Simon saw that the two watchmen had hurled their burden into the river. One of the watchmen was walking back, chuckling to himself.

'Is he all right?' Simon asked, jerking his head towards the noise.

'He's smelling a lot better already. He sobered up soon as the water closed over him.'

Simon opened his mouth but the watchman reassured him. 'Don't worry, he's not going to drown. It's only a couple of feet deep there.'

At the bank Simon could see the second watchman standing and laughing. Simon assumed that the drunk was still in the water, hidden by the trees, and nodded to himself. 'Fine. Let's get on, then.'

As they continued their slow progress around the staged area, Simon found it hard to maintain his solemn visage. All was well; very well. The ground was a little damp and muddy, but this was Dartmoor, and the ground was *always* a bit damp and muddy. Flags had been raised and hung heavily, waiting for the first breezes to clear the dew from them, while every wooden surface Simon touched was slick with the damp, but all was as well-prepared as he could hope. Feeling his spirits rising by the moment, he led the way into the tilt-area itself. The sight of the lists was daunting and he was pleased not to have to worry about fighting here, with the local population and strangers from miles around watching to see if he might dishonour himself by incompetence or cowardice.

The space was flanked by the *ber frois*, each of which had strong boards facing the fighting area, all painted with the heraldic symbols of many of the knights who would be fighting here. Lord Hugh's own shield was painted before his seat, at the point where the competing men-at-arms should meet in their headlong clash, for there was no point patronising tournaments if you couldn't enjoy the best view. On the last day all would change, for this would be the day that the two ends would be blocked off, and all knights would compete inside the enclosed ground to fight with whatever came to hand, while *diseurs* and heralds noted who had achieved signal feats. The *mêlée* was always the most popular of the events staged.

However, today's show should be a good sweetener, a taste of the displays to come, for today selected squires would show their skill. Riding to prove their courage in front of their lord would lead to some being knighted – although

Simon knew perfectly well that all the men to be knighted had already been chosen. It would be foolhardy to leave such things to the last minute. Especially since many of them were to be rewarded for their fathers' service or for some praiseworthy deed supporting the Lord's interest.

As the thought came to him, he realised that others were already arriving. Sauntering over the grass were knights and squires. Some heralds were already standing in a small knot and gazing about them as they agreed where each would stand in order to have a clear view of the tilting.

'Where is Hal?' he grumbled to himself, glancing over to the tent where Wymond and he had slept during the building of the tournament. There was no sign of the man, nothing at the tent, nothing in the *ber frois*, but neither was there any sign of the watchman sent to guard him, so Simon told himself resignedly that the silly little sod must have gone to fetch wine or bread.

Philip Tyrel watched them as the stench of vomit gradually faded. It was a relief that the Bailiff had not recognised whom he had caught; a wonderful relief ! Especially with the body lying so close.

When the Bailiff and watchmen appeared from the market, he had realised that he only had the one means of escape. He had pulled the tunic from the body, stiff and chill from cooled puke, and hauled it over his head, then emptied the remaining wine in his skin over his head. He reeked, but he should be safe if he was careful. Quickly he drew ferns and weeds over the corpse and crawled until he was in full view on the grass at the foot of a stand. He was not concealed. Why should he be? He was guilty of nothing so far as anyone knew. No, he was only a drunk who had spent the night snoring in the open air. He was safe enough.

The two watchmen had dragged him to the river and thrown him in, but he was grateful to have been taken away before the Bailiff could see his face. Far better that he should be remembered as a vagrant without features. There were so many others here in a similar condition, it was no surprise that he should have been found there. It was practically a daily occurrence. He sat on his arse in the water and belched, scooping water over his head to make his hair dangle over his features and hide them. That way nobody could swear to him. Wearing this tunic, no one would associate him with his usual finery and in any case no jury would be happy to convict him. Before long the second watchman lost interest in him and gave a yawn before strolling away to rejoin his friend and the Bailiff.

As soon as the guard was gone, Philip stopped making a fool of himself and climbed from the water on the farther bank, shivering. The water came straight from the moors, and was as cold as ice. Walking in the shade of the trees into the field where he had killed the carpenter, he cast about constantly for other people who could be watching him, but everyone was busy breaking their fast: bakers were stoking their little fires, poulterers preparing fowls and songbirds, pastrycooks kneading dough ready for the first spiced pies. All had plenty to do without watching a man dressed in soaking wet garments walking away.

The field curved about the line of the hill and soon he was out of view. Walking up the hillside, he went to a natural gash in the ground, and here he sat down for a moment. He took off the dead man's tunic. There was no need for it now.

Screwing it into a ball, he tossed it away from him. Here, among the long grasses, it could lie hidden until winter. Removing all his own clothes, he set them out to dry on the grass, then lay down patiently to wait.

There was a tingling in his whole body as the sun crept over the trees and its warmth touched him with the softness of a kiss. He felt almost as though he had been rebaptised by his immersion in the river. Gazing up at the clouds floating past so slowly, he could almost believe that God was up there even now, watching him with a smile on His face while He considered Philip's acts.

Three had died. Three! All by his hand, and he felt no remorse. How could he? What, regret the loss of Benjamin the usurer, Wymond the carpenter, and now Hal? Who could regret the passing of such men! They deserved the punishment meted out to them. The guilty had paid for their crimes.

Except one.

He shivered. There was a leaden sensation in his bowels. Why should all the others have been punished, but this last one escape justice?

Closing his eyes, he tried to ignore his qualms. He was at ease here, as the sun warmed him lying among the long grasses; it was hard to bring to his mind the anger and determination necessary to kill. What was the point? Did he truly have justification? He had murdered three, and surely that was enough? This last was not even *involved*. The sole reason for executing him was to make another realise his evil. Make him confront his crime.

Here in the sunlight that scene of carnage seemed so remote, so impossibly distant in time, that his long-planned vengeance appeared almost as foul as the original act. It was as if he had suddenly acquired a sense of proportion which had thrown all his plotting into confusion. It was a terrible possibility – but what if his slaughter made him no better than his enemy?

He felt tears running down both cheeks. With them he could feel his remaining determination seep away like water dripping from a leaking wineskin. His plan had been to kill the murderous bastard's son as a fitting revenge for the loss of his family. That thought, together with the deaths of Hal and Wymond and Benjamin, had driven him. Yet now it seemed absurdly cruel to execute the youth. If anyone, he should kill the father, not the whelp.

Undecided, he lay trying to clear his mind but the thoughts would give him no peace. They chased about his heart: the boy should die, an eye for an eye; the father was guilty, not the boy. He couldn't make a decision. It was impossible.

Sitting up, he felt his clothes. They were dry enough, but his shirt and hose were dreadfully scruffy. He would have to get changed into clean finery for the *béhourd*, but there should be plenty of time. Rising, he walked up the hill in among the trees, then followed the line of the woods eastwards until he was past the castle and on the way to Oakhampton. Here a tree had fallen over the river, and he waited a moment, clawing his hair back from his face and tidying himself, before clambering on to the tree and stepping assuredly along the trunk until he reached the other bank. Once there he turned back towards the castle, a late-night reveller wandering homewards. None of the other travellers on the road took any notice of him.

Philip entered the tented area and was about to go to his own small pavilion when he saw the last man. And he felt the rage, freezing as winter frost, ice its way along his spine, felt the muscles of his back and belly suddenly clench as if he was preparing to strike the mortal blow.

He turned away and entered the pavilion, quickly doffing his clothes and washing his face and hands before selecting a fresh shirt and pulling on his tunic. Soon he was back in the tilt-yard.

His determination had returned. He would kill one more time.

'You have achieved much, Bailiff. Is there any news of the dead man?'

'I thank you, Sir Richard. No, there is nothing yet on Wymond, but the Coroner has hopes.'

There was no need for an introduction to Sir Richard Prouse; everyone knew who he was. His scarred features, with the appalling line of twisted and raw-looking flesh that ran from his temple, close to the milky white and ruined eyeball, down through his ravaged cheekbone to his broken jaw, were instantly recognisable. Seeing him so close, Simon felt his belly lurch. He looked away hurriedly.

'You need not worry about my feelings, Bailiff. I know I am an ogre now, a repellent creature used to scare children when they misbehave. "If you don't behave and do your chores, they'll send Sir Richard Prouse to take you away!" I have heard it often enough.'

Wanting to change the subject, instead Simon found his mouth running on. 'It was in a tournament you got that wound, wasn't it?'

'Yes, Bailiff. I got in front of a dangerous man. I was only twenty-four when this happened.' His eyes clouded and a slight tremble made him lean more heavily on his stick. Hobbling slowly and carefully, for his right leg still dragged, he walked to the stands beneath Lord Hugh's seat and stared about him. 'It was in Crukerne, back in 1316 – another tournament designed by that sodomitic cretin Hal Sachevyll.'

'You are angry with him?'

'How would you feel?' Sir Richard snapped, his voice rising as he spoke. 'The Goddamned fool didn't strengthen the stands. That was how I got this!' He spoke with a bitter, shivering rage, but gradually his fury ebbed. 'Damn him! I was riding in the *mêlée* and became the target of an attack by Sir Walter Basset. The murderous bastard managed to squeeze me up against the stands, where he started beating me about the head with a mace. I was forced up against the wooden barricades, and he was on my left side. It was hard to wield my sword to protect myself, and he was battering me with two or three blows for each one of mine.'

He could recall it perfectly. The mount beneath him kept trying to move away, but was forced against the wooden boardings while Sir Richard felt the heavy ball on its reinforced wooden shaft raining down upon him.

'I was young and resilient, but deafened by the clanging of steel striking my helm. It felt as though my head was being used as the clapper of a giant bell. And there was no let-up to the ringing, hammering torture. Do what I might, I could not stop the assault. Nor could I escape. Some of my anxiety was reflected in my horse, too: pushing forward, then pulling back, trying to release himself from Sir Walter's great destrier, but he was snared. And meanwhile I could feel the energy sapping from my arm. I will not lie – I was panicked.'

It was terrifying, and with the terror came the realisation: he was a failure just like his father; he would be captured and ransomed. A fool who would lose all, who would see his properties mortgaged once more.

'A heavy blow caught my head and glanced onto my right shoulder. Instantly my arm was dead. No sensation whatever. I had no defence. My sword-arm was gone. You know, at that moment I could look into the eyes of the spectators. They were so close, I could see into the throats of the men and women as they roared . . .'

He was quiet a few minutes. 'It was as if time stood still. I saw people shaking their fists, shrieking with blood-lust, longing to see a man die . . . to see *me* die. It was very curious.

'Then another buffet knocked my head and I knew I must get away. My only safety lay in flight. I was desperate and spurred my horse until the blood ran in rivulets, staining the cloth covering.'

He had tried to move, Sir Richard told Simon, but he had no purchase. He barged forward and tried to thrust a path between the boarding and Sir Walter's mount, but the Cornishman wheeled his horse to block them, his mount's rump slamming into the *ber frois*. 'I swear that at that moment I could hear a dreadful creaking,' Sir Richard said quietly. 'It was like a kind of grumbling, as though the barrier and plankings were complaining. That was it, a sort of moaning, like an old man muttering under his breath as the cold weather seized up his ancient joints.

'And then, with a crash, the section nearest me gave way. I was falling, and as I went I felt an explosion of pain in my neck. The mace had struck the weak spot between my shoulders where the mail was feeble from age and rust. I had never worried about it before, but now, with my head bent, the spot was exposed. That blow felled me like an ox under the hammer. And if it wasn't for Hal Sachevyll, that section of barrier wouldn't have collapsed and I wouldn't have fallen.'

'Was it the barrier that did that?'

'You mean, was it the barrier which so ruined my face and looks, Bailiff?' He smiled thinly. 'No. This was a sword. I fell through the barrier, and as I fell a chance blow almost broke my neck. I was not aware of anything else for some time. But as I fell, Sir Edmund of Gloucester came to help me, I thank God. He rode up and fought with Sir Walter to protect me, but Sir Walter was a wild beast at being frustrated in capturing me. He set about Sir Edmund and so belaboured him that Sir Edmund was driven back.

'I knew I'd been seriously injured. My horse was dead, impaled upon a metal spike, but when I saw Sir Walter was fighting someone else, I pulled my helmet off to breathe. God, it was hot! When he returned to me and bellowed at me to yield, I couldn't hear. My head was full of a clamorous row, because of the beating I'd received. When I noticed him, I knew only fear to see him again. I grabbed for my sword, which lay a few feet from me and as I caught hold of it, Sir Walter swung.'

He remembered that blow. It came to him at night, when he was in a deep sleep, the sight of that notched and scratched blade swinging down at him as though time was standing almost still. Then the slamming agony of the blade above his temple and the hideous dragging as it clove through his flesh and skull, tearing and rending its way down, through eye-socket and cheek and on down to his jaw. That was where the blade and the horror ended. At last Sir Richard's mind surrendered and he passed out.

'Have you ever seen a bear enter a ring to be baited?' he asked quietly. 'Sometimes it will look mild, until the dogs begin to snap at it, and then it will defend itself, but without fury. That comes later. At first the bear wants only to protect itself, but then, once a mastiff has got to it and maybe chewed the bastard's leg, that is when the thing becomes enraged and flings its tormentors away or smashes them. Sir Walter became like a bear, may his cods shrivel.

'He brought it down two-handed,' Sir Richard said softly, adding, 'I felt every moment as it passed through my bones and skin.'

'It must have been terrible,' Simon said with an awed hush.

Sir Richard stared over Simon's shoulder as his hand rose to the dreadful scar. A forefinger traced the line of rippling and badly mended flesh, following it from his ruined eye down to his cloven jaw. He looked like a man who lived in a permanent nightmare, a man pursued by his own terrors.

'Terrible, Bailiff? You could not possibly imagine. At the time I thought it was going to kill me. It never sprang to my mind that I would soon wish it had.

'It almost split my head in two. And then Sir Walter, *brave* Sir Walter, would have gone to find another victim, but the people were so furious that they ran forward to attack him.' His good eye hardened. 'They chased him from the field. That bold, proud man fled before the rabble of Crukerne. But gentle, kindly hands came and collected me and took me to a convent where I was gradually healed. Although then I was ruined financially instead by the usurers.'

'Because you had lost?'

'Yes. I was captured by Sir Walter, so I had no escape. He demanded my money since I had yielded to him, and would give no quarter when it came to his cash. What would he care? He had destroyed my life, so he might as well have my money as well. And he had a willing accomplice. Benjamin the Bastard came to me and said that he had settled on my behalf. I demurred, said I hadn't agreed to any funds, but Benjamin had a clerk with him, and they showed me a document I had signed and sealed. It confirmed I had asked him to settle with Sir Walter.'

'And you hadn't?'

'How could I?' Sir Richard demanded sadly, his anger fading as swiftly as it had flared.

'How could I have managed such an agreement while my face was being stitched or when the flesh had caught afire with agony as the fever gripped me? No, Bailiff. I knew nothing of this. Benjamin came to me in the convent while I suffered, pretending to be a friend and counsellor, but in reality he was a thief. And I could not even prove it. All I can say is, the bargain was less costly than my father's.'

'How do you mean?'

'My father Godwin was a knight in the great tournament in Exeter of 1306, but he died when a mace caught his neck. At least I have my life, even if I've lost my leg and my arm,' he said, gesturing with his left arm towards his useless right arm and leg.

'I've heard of that one,' Simon said. 'There was a whole family killed.'

'Yes. So I seem to recall,' Sir Richard frowned. 'Tyrel, that was their name. The father was there. Poor devil saw the stand collapse and tried to rescue his children and wife, but it was no good, of course.'

'Christ Jesus! You mean that he was there and saw his family die?' Simon winced.

'Yes. Poor fellow. Philip Tyrel. I was only young, of course, but I remember him.'

'What was he like?' Simon asked.

'Tyrel? A large man, big-chested and with a great belly, if not very tall. He had a strutting arrogance, and he was always wary of insults. He took his own importance very seriously.'

'He sounds like Tyler,' Simon said half jokingly.

'Hmm. If Tyler wore a beard, I would almost say they were brothers. Certainly not dissimilar.'

'Really?' Simon was interested. 'Did this Tyrel survive?'

'He disappeared soon after the disaster. His heart was broken, I think. Whose wouldn't have been?'

Simon tried to imagine how he would have felt if he had seen his own wife and children killed. 'Have you seen him since then?' he asked absently, and then his head shot up. 'Christ Jesus! You haven't spotted him here, have you?'

'Who, Tyrel? No, I'd have noticed someone like him. Tall, strong, dark of hair and bearded, he wasn't the sort of man you'd miss. No, he's not here. Poor devil has probably died.'

'Yes. Perhaps,' Simon said, unconvinced. 'But if he did return here, it would explain much.'

'His seeking revenge on the men who destroyed his family, you mean?'

'Yes, and all because of money. At least Benjamin won't fleece anyone else now,' Simon said soberly 'He's dead.'

'Yes. The devil's gone, thank God. May he rot in eternal fire. He almost cost me my castle.'

'Do you know how he died?'

'Beaten, I heard. So what? Many a cut-throat will execute a victim with a club.'

'True. Where did you hear of his death?'

'Do you think me guilty of his murder? Oh Bailiff, you should arrest me at once! Do you know, I can't remember who told me about him. Perhaps it was an itinerant carter passing by my castle.'

Simon gave a faint grin in apology. 'I am too used to suspecting everyone.'

'Perhaps you should.'

'Do you think he helped finance the *ber frois* that collapsed at Crukerne?'

Sir Richard gave him an intent stare. There was no shame or fear in his eye, only an increased sharpness. 'You *do* think I killed him? Perhaps I did, Bailiff. But if I did, it was because he funded a cheap piece of work which indirectly led to this damage. That is all. Surely if I wanted revenge, I'd have killed Sir Walter?'

'Perhaps you thought that would be more difficult?'

'Aye. Perhaps I would,' said Sir Richard with a twisted smile, glancing at his feeble leg. He opened his mouth but, as he did so, his expression hardened and a shiver of revulsion made him tremble like a willow in a gale.

Turning, Simon saw that he was staring at the figure of Sir Walter Basset.

CHAPTER EIGHTEEN

Sir John had left his son to go and talk to a couple of armourers. Having settled with them for a new sword and matching dagger, he left the rattle and hammer of their anvils, and strode along their lines to the usurers' discreet section of tents and tables.

It was hard to keep his features under control. Useless swine, the lot of them! All of them of low birth; not one nobleman in the country would want to be accused of moneylending: it was a source of shame. Worse than entering into mercantile ventures.

The pity of it was that men had to make use of them occasionally. He had himself been forced to go to the usurers: for arms, for Pomers – even for sheep, because he'd never have restocked his flocks else. After the famine, his sheep had died almost to a ewe from a murrain that struck down not only his own flocks but also all the others in the country.

He cheered up a little as he recalled the hatred on Sir Edmund's face. It was refreshing to see that a man whom he had beaten so many years before still felt the humiliation of his conquest.

Sir John marched along the money-lenders' tables, his mind on the difficulty of replacing that shit Benjamin. But he had to, somehow. With so much of his property already in pawn, it was going to be much harder to borrow. He could almost believe that Benjamin had warned everyone not to take any debts from him, from the reception he was getting. At least he didn't need to repay his old debts now Benjamin was gone. Widow Dudenay could whistle for it. She could threaten all she wanted, Sir John would never return the money her husband had lent him. He cast a speculative eye towards the arena. *That* was the best way to win more money.

Not that he needed cash for long. Surely his flocks would soon recover, now that he had brought in rams and ewes, and then he could look to redeem the plate and gold he had left in pawn.

However, if he were to find another Sir Edmund, life would become a great deal easier.

The thought was an idle one, but it was enough to bring a beaming smile to his face. Then he caught sight of Sir Baldwin. There was a man he'd like to meet in the *hastilude*. It'd be next to impossible to lose against a pathetic-looking specimen like him. Sir Baldwin was the archetypal farmer-warrior. Just enough money from his manor to justify the retention of his titles and keep him in good clothes, if Sir John's guess was accurate. Probably as bound up with financial troubles as he was himself. Certainly not Sir John's ideal companion. A good, sound man-at-arms was more to his taste; someone with whom he could drink his fill of strong ales or wines, then gamble on a horse or a knight in lance-play, not some straight-faced old bastard like Sir Baldwin. However, any man was better company than no one. And anyone at all was better than his son William at present. He was going about the place like a bear in the pit.

Seeing an attractive woman at Sir Baldwin's side, Sir John's smile grew. At least he had a pleasing decoration. 'Sir Baldwin, how go things in Furnshill?'

'Well, I thank you,' Baldwin answered, fitting a dishonestly welcoming smile to his face.

Margaret hoisted her child higher on her breast as she gave the knight a polite greeting.

'I was just thinking I will have to enter the tournament,' Sir John told Baldwin. 'Take a look at the youngsters here. Any one of them could be thrashed with one hand bound behind me. A man could make a fortune.'

'Surely you aren't thinking only of money, Sir John?' Margaret exclaimed. 'Not when you could win renown for your courage and deeds in the tournament?'

Sir John smiled patronisingly. 'Lady, a man might easily win honours for his prowess, but when all is said and done, a purseful of coins speaks loudest. A knight wins no praise if he never wins at a fight, and the natural accompaniment to success is wealth. Besides,' he added, glancing at the milling squires and servants, 'look at the fools here. Many of them should be grateful for a good lesson taught at the hands of a practised knight.'

'They should be grateful for being beaten about the head?' she enquired, and Baldwin nearly laughed out loud.

'Lady, the lessons learned here on a field with bated weapons will stand many a fellow in good stead upon a field in which the weapons are all sharp. And anyway, there is nothing wrong with a man winning money from his captives.'

'Combatants can die even with bated weapons,' Baldwin observed.

'Of course. How else do you teach a man chivalry if he won't risk his own life?'

'Have you killed many in the lists?' Margaret asked.

'Not many. A few.'

Baldwin looked at him. The lists were supposed to be for practice, not to kill. 'I heard that you fought Sir Richard's father in the lists.'

'Godwin? Yes. He was a popular fellow, but not much good as a fighter. A splinter of steel from his helmet cut his throat while he fought me, and he died.'

'Was that at Exeter?' Baldwin enquired, recalling Hal's words. 'Didn't a stand give way?'

'Yes. Rot the bastards! The crowd was furious to see their darling little Godwin fall! They surged forward in the stands and people at the sides of the *ber frois* moved forward, all howling like wolves. I've never seen a mob like it! And then someone fell, or a rope gave way – I don't know – and a mass of folks tumbled down. Several died.'

'But you escaped.'

'Yes, Sir Baldwin. When those people were turned off the stand like so many felons pushed off a cart, others ran to help them. I managed to get to my horse and leave the field.'

Margaret was smiling in a brittle, insincere manner. 'You must have been terribly upset. To have killed a popular knight and thus cause the death of innocents . . .'

'I was pleased, Lady. *Pleased*! Godwin had cuckolded me!' Sir John burst out. He was suddenly silent, staring away into the distance. 'Godwin was known for it. He was useless as a fighter, but he loved to dally with women. Well, I heard he'd been dallying with mine. She's long dead now, I fear, but then I wouldn't have it! If I'd had the chance, I'd have challenged him formally and killed him in legal combat before God, damn him!'

The rush of words was embarrassing. Baldwin met Margaret's eye. Sir John saw their look and quickly changed the subject.

'It is rare to kill men now. And one shouldn't wish to. Not with the rewards of ransom. In Crukerne in 1316 I captured several.'

'Any we know?' Margaret asked brightly.

'You may know some. One was Sir Edmund – I think he hails from Gloucester. I was not actually a combatant at the time of the *mêlée*, but I was watching from an inn, and disgusted with most of what I saw. Youths who hardly knew how to hold a blade were trying their luck against older, more honourable fellows and beating them through sheer strength of numbers.'

'Isn't that always the way?' Baldwin asked with some surprise.

'I suppose it is sometimes, but it's hardly right, is it? One of the only decent fighters was Sir Walter Basset. Now there was a man who could fight! Stormed from one combat to another, winning horses and armour on all sides. Wonderful work! He pushed Sir Richard Prouse through a wall.'

He smiled at the memory. The sight of the clumsy fool tottering sideways through the wooden stand had been hilarious.

'And this arrogant young puppy Sir Edmund stormed in to attack Sir Walter. Christ! Oh, forgive me, my apologies, my Lady, but what can you say about a fool like that? What did he think he was doing? Sir Walter is trained and experienced, as well as having a very short temper. It was predictable. Sir Edmund tried to fight, but kept being pressed back, his horse suffering as many buffets as Sir Edmund himself, until he had to break and ride off. Sir Walter had the choice of chasing him or returning to his already fallen prey and like a cat he went back to Sir Richard, except now his blood was well and truly up, which is how he came to half kill poor old Prouse.

'I was drinking ale and saw all this. As it happened, my horse was saddled, and I was armoured. I thought, Well, here's an opportunity for some money! I climbed up into the saddle, took a lance, and hurtled off after Sir Edmund. I caught him completely unawares, the damned fool, and in a moment he was out of the saddle and sprawling in the dirt. So, I captured him and took him back to the diseur who confirmed I had won him legally.'

'Did no one try to stop you?' Margaret asked.

'No, the other folks had seen how badly hurt Sir Richard was, so they were all busy fetching leeches and suchlike. No, no one tried to stop me. They were making sure that Sir Walter escaped the mob. So many of the folks grow angry to see a man win his bout; they try to catch the man who stopped their own favourite win. I recall Benjamin was happy to see me – he had a large bet on Sir Edmund losing his armour and I helped him win the gamble.'

'What happened to Sir Richard?' Margaret enquired. 'He didn't die, did he?'

'He lives yet,' Sir John said thoughtfully. The thought of living like that, unable to walk or run, without the use of an arm or the sight in one eye, and with those scars! Terrible! Every fighter's nightmare. 'Better perhaps that he had died,' he said heavily, with the faintest touch of compassion. 'He was badly crushed when the *ber frois* collapsed on him. And not only him. Several people were killed when he fell, especially since his horse was flailing about with its hooves and killed some folks before it, too, died. It's unfair, of course, but some bystanders blamed Sir Walter at the time.'

'Why?'

'Because when Sir Richard fell through the barriers many people were crushed. Most were villeins, though. No one significant.'

Baldwin was frowning. 'Do you know who was responsible for the *ber frois* that collapsed?'

'Of course I do. It was at my manor – I'd arranged it,' Sir John said impatiently. 'The stands were designed by Hal Sachevyll, and constructed by Carpenter Wymond. Who else builds tournaments in Devonshire?'

'Didn't their failure cost you dearly?'

'I don't think that's any of your business.'

'I am surprised that after that, Hal and Wymond were used again,' Margaret said.

'Hal has a good eye for spectacle. He's always in demand.'

'Not recently, surely,' Baldwin murmured. 'While the King has his ban.'

'Hal was with the King himself until recently,' Sir John said. 'I know he was at court until the end of last year. And then I believe he helped Earl Thomas. Before the Earl was executed, of course,' he added with a chuckle.

'They could travel from one side to another so easily?' Baldwin asked.

Sir John grinned. 'Everyone likes to see a tournament. And the King would have liked to know what was happening in his uncle's camp.'

'You think they were spying?' Baldwin shot out.

'At Crukerne, Hal was very friendly with Despenser's allies. What would *you* think?' Sir John laughed and left them.

As soon as he had gone out of earshot, Odo apologetically cleared his throat from behind them. 'Sir Baldwin? Might I have a word?'

'Of course, my friend. What is it?'

Odo shot a look at Margaret, and she smiled graciously and left them, walking a few feet away.

'It's confidential, Sir Baldwin, but I thought you should know. I am taking messages between Squire Geoffrey and Lady Alice. They are married.'

'I had heard that,' Baldwin said loftily. He disliked gossip and had no wish to see their affair becoming common knowledge until they were ready.

'But were you aware that Sir John is heavily in debt and seeks to have Alice marry his son so that he can use her estates to support his own? If he learns she is married to Geoffrey, he could become dangerous.'

'I see,' Baldwin said. He mused a while. 'What of Sir Edmund? What do you know of him?'

'He's a very a good man. Honourable, a renowned fighter on the continent. Why do you ask?'

'He is one of the men who was in Exeter at the time Benjamin Dudenay was murdered. I merely wondered about him.'

'You need have no concerns about him,' Odo said.

'You sound very convinced.'

'Sir Baldwin, I know many knights and squires. I may be less than a competent squire in Mark Tyler's eyes, but I know my job. Sir Edmund is an honourable man.'

'Yes. It is sad, isn't it?' Baldwin said quietly. 'All the squires and knights here should be decent, honourable, chivalrous folk – yet someone is a murderer.'

Seeing Sir Peregrine, Simon bent his steps towards the banneret. Although Baldwin professed an intense dislike for the man, Simon was ambivalent. Sir Peregrine was no more fearsome than many other men he had known. 'Morning, Sir Peregrine.'

'Ah, Bailiff Puttock! I am glad to see you again. How are you this fine morning?'

'It is very clear, isn't it, thanks to God!' Simon agreed fervently. 'I feared normal Dartmoor weather.'

'Aye. Mizzle, drizzle, rain or howling gale. It's rare enough you see sun for more than a few days,' the knight said, his teeth showing briefly. He could never entirely trust the Bailiff, for Simon and Baldwin had once suspected him of murder, but Sir Peregrine was a fair man and he could see that his behaviour had been suspicious, so he tried not to hold a grudge. 'Any news of the murdered man?' he asked quietly.

'Nothing, I fear. There is no clue as to who the killer could be. Perhaps he was a mindless fool who has since run away.'

'Stranger tales have come to my attention before now,' Sir Peregrine nodded. 'But if I were you, I should tell the watchmen to keep a wary eye open. I suppose you have heard that people are joking about Hal and his lover . . . you knew that Wymond and Hal were bed-fellows?'

'Was anyone not aware?'

Sir Peregrine grunted in assent. 'It wasn't exactly a secret, was it? But who cares? The King himself . . .' Caution made him silent a moment. 'The point is, the spectators may become unsettled. When that happens, they are likely to seek a new target for their anger. An English rabble roused is unpleasant. Ah well! Let's just hope.'

They walked on in silence, Simon shooting small glances at the banneret, wondering whether he had his own suspicions – but it wasn't something he could ask Sir Peregrine. Instead he chose an uncontentious topic. 'Are any of your men to join in today?'

'Not mine personally, not in the jousting,' Sir Peregrine said, thinking of the whip-like Squire Andrew. He had been present at the feast last night, serving his master with the calm and unhurried elegance that showed both his breeding and his education. Yet all the while his precision spoke of his deadly skills. Sir Peregrine still had no doubt that the man was a killer, from his toes to his scalp. It was a relief when Andrew left the room. 'There is one I should like to see fighting, though.'

Simon caught his tone but Sir Peregrine declined to comment further. In truth Simon had enough to consider himself. His daughter had been an unholy pest the whole of the previous evening, snapping at Margaret, being sarcastic to him. God's teeth! He could sometimes wish he had never had any children; it was almost an attractive thought. Poor Baldwin had watched her during one of her tantrums with a faraway look in his eye, like a man who was realising that this might be served up to him soon, now he had his own daughter.

For the most part Edith was a well-behaved, responsible child, but just recently she had taken to outbursts whenever she was refused permission to do anything, although Simon had tried to point out to her that it was her very argumentativeness which tended to make him turn her down. Last night it had been a ridiculous demand that she should be allowed to go out to a tavern. Ludicrous in a town like this, with strangers on all sides, cut-purses, horse dealers, fakers and thieves of all measures, but Edith wouldn't listen to reason. Margaret had just asked her where her scarf was, and Edith didn't even seem to hear her, instead asking about going into town. Mad, absolutely mad!

'I can take Hugh to guard me,' she'd stated. 'There's little enough danger.'

'No.'

'Why not?'

'It's not safe.'

'What will you do, fence me in an enclosure where no one can ever come to me?' she'd demanded.

'I will not have my daughter wandering the streets like a slut!'

'You think me no better than a whore?'

Simon had drawn a breath to hold his temper. 'Don't twist my words.'

'That's it, isn't it? You don't trust me. You never have! You think I'd fall into the arms of the nearest smelly groom as soon as I was out of your sight.'

'Edith, please,' Margaret had pleaded. 'Your father is only trying to protect you.'

'*Protect* me?' she'd sneered. 'He's just making sure I'm not violated, that's all. He wants me to remain unsullied by nasty groping servants. Well, I want to see Squire William. Hugh can chaperone me.'

'Squire William? What, the son of Sir John?' Simon gasped, recalling the lewd group at the fence.

'Yes, why? What's wrong with him?'

'You are *not* to see him. Or talk to him,' Simon stated flatly.

Immediately tears of frustration had sprung into her eyes. 'But why? He's—'

'That's enough. I have given you my decision. Don't go near him,' said Simon. His daughter's face twisted a knife in his gut. He hated hurting her, and this news had made her face crumple like screwed-up parchment.

'Father, please!'

He couldn't tell her why. If he did, she would likely choose to disbelieve him, and if not she would be dreadfully hurt by the proof of her own foolishness in trusting William. Better that she should think it was an arbitrary decision from an autocratic father. 'Edith, shut up or I'll send you back with Hugh tomorrow at dawn.'

'But . . .'

'I am not joking. One more word, and you'll be gone.'

It took away any residual pleasure in the tournament. Now he would be glad to be leaving at the end of it all.

But not yet. Margaret had been looking forward to it for weeks, Simon knew. He sighed. If he could, he would leave now. But he couldn't. Margaret had found a wetnurse to look after Peterkin, and she would want to remain and see the whole show.

Soon they heard the chapel bell tolling and Simon and Sir Peregrine parted. Simon wanted to attend the morning Mass to pray for a tournament free of fatal injuries.

Later, that innocent prayer would strike him as ironic.

CHAPTER NINETEEN

In the little tent erected for her beside Sir John's more magnificent pavilion, Alice finished brushing her hair and nodded to her maid to help pin the long tresses into position.

Today, if all went well, should mark the end of her long-confined life. No more listening to Sir John, for as soon as Geoffrey had earned his spurs, he could claim her. Their vows had been exchanged legally, and there was nothing her guardian could do to alter that.

And yet . . .

The dream had repeated itself to her. That vision of blood and gore tore at her like the claws of a wildcat, springing into her mind even during the daytime, striking her dumb with fear. She couldn't bear to think of losing her Geoffrey, for he was the stone foundation upon which her life was built, but the mornings found her progressively more gloomy. Somehow she had the feeling that her dream was a premonition, that she was being given a warning.

Alice winced as the comb pulled, and looked sharply at her maid, but the girl rolled her eyes in apology and Alice couldn't be cross, not today. She sighed and bent her head so that the maid could work more easily.

When could she declaim her love for Geoffrey? Perhaps he would ride to her and demand one of her favours. That was what knights did in the romances – but she and Geoffrey had agreed on silence, so perhaps he wouldn't. Not until he had his spurs. Then he could wear her tokens publicly without fear of Sir John or his horrible son William.

Praying that he would be safe in the lists, Alice closed her eyes fervently.

She was considering how pleasant it would be to tell William that she was already married, when her maid leaned forward. 'Have you heard of the dreadful murder?'

Alice threw her an intrigued look and the maid carried on breathlessly. 'They say that some ordinary churl was found dead near the castle, out on the hill behind, that his head was all broken . . . you know, all smashed.'

'Ugh!' Alice pulled a face squeamishly, but looked back at her maid with interest.

'Someone told me it was an evil witch who wanted his blood or something, but another man said that was rubbish and he was attacked by an outlaw for his purse.'

Alice considered. There was more romantic merit in the ghoulish tale, she felt, and gave a luxurious shudder at the idea of blood-drinking vampires. 'An old witch, hiding up in the woods, probably,' she said.

'Probably, yes, and waiting to steal the heart and lungs of any youth who wanders too close to her haunts, so that she can eat them and make herself look young again . . . Yuk!'

Alice ignored her servant. Her mind was back on her husband and she gazed into the distance in a pleasant daydream. Some time soon she would be able to proclaim her marriage. It was a wonderful thought.

'We must hurry, Dame!'

Alice tutted, but knew she must go through with the pageant. She had been chosen to be 'Dame Courtesy' – the virgin who would open the tournament, the woman who epitomised the virtues of the tournament and chivalry generally. She must lead the procession to Lord Hugh. It made her want to cringe. Especially since she was no virgin and was married!

Oh God, she longed so much for the moment when she might confess her marriage.

Andrew sipped from a pot of wine and eyed the contestants. None struck him as overly fearsome. He had charged against better men in his time. Before long he must return to his master. Sir Edmund would be wanting to prepare himself and watch the early tilts. Looking up, Andrew gauged the position of the sun, then looked down at the shadows. It was growing late.

He drained his cup and left it on the wine-seller's table, then set off to his master's tent. He took the path which meandered through the middle of the camp, because it was the most direct route, but a squealing pig which had been intended for butchery, objected to its early demise and escaped, setting off across the way. It destroyed two tents, snapping the guy ropes, bit a man in the calf, knocked over a table of cloths, and then escaped into the river.

Any diversion was always welcome, especially in the fair-time atmosphere of the tournament. Suddenly Andrew was surrounded by shouting, laughing people who set off in pursuit and although he tried to duck away he was swept along for some distance and missed his master's tent, instead finding himself nearer the castle than he had intended.

A pavilion was open, a servant polishing carefully at a blue riding sword, and Andrew smiled at him. 'Do you mind if I stand here until the tumult has died down?'

'Not at all. You are a squire?'

'Yes. To Sir Edmund of Gloucester.'

'I'm Edgar, servant to Sir Baldwin of Furnshill,' Edgar said. He glanced out at the thick crush of people. 'Would you like some wine?'

Andrew nodded with gratitude, and while Edgar rose to fetch a cup, he looked at the bright blue riding sword, admiring the quality of the script on the blade. Perhaps not as well executed as some he had seen, but still very good. He picked it up. It balanced perfectly in his hand, and he eyed it enviously.

'You like my master's sword?' Edgar asked.

'I've used many, but this feels better than any,' Andrew said feelingly. He set it back down, and then he noticed the other symbol.

The sign of the detested, illegal and heretical group called the Knights Templar.

Clouds appeared overhead while Simon stood before the small altar, and his attention wandered while he observed the sky darkening through the lovely glass windows, feeling relief when the service ended and he could hurry outside. There he was happy to find that although the sky was presently grey and heavily overcast, the clouds showed no promise of rain. True enough, as he snuffed the air, he could smell no hint of damp.

There were many bystanders here to watch the official opening of the tournament. Philip Tyrel stood with his arms folded, standing still as a man-at-arms should and watching while the people milled about. Simon never so much as glanced in his direction. From interest, Philip eyed the Bailiff. Simon Puttock looked a pleasant enough man, someone with whom he would have liked to broach a barrel of ale, to discuss the realm's difficulties now that the Despensers were the arbiters of power. It was a shame that he would never be able to do so.

He was distracted by the trumpets and noise of the knights and squires. A glittering pageant appeared at the castle's gate, led by one startlingly beautiful girl dressed all in virginal white and leading a white mare. Behind her were other girls, all similarly robed in white.

Despite himself, a trace of sadness passed over the killer's face. The last tournament he had seen in Devon had started in much the same way, except then he had been a part of the parade with his woman. And his children had been there too, proud to see their father. It was at just such a tournament as this that they had died, the unwitting victims of other men's greed. They had died for money. He could cry to recall it.

That day had started perfectly bright and clear, not like this. Far from the town's fires, the air was pure, blowing straight from the moors beyond the river. That day had been as gay and lively as this, with flags fluttering in the breeze and women dressed in their best and finest clothes, watching the men lined up, smiling at them flirtatiously or flaunting themselves. Older women contemplated the men with a more speculative gaze, offering bets on which would win his jousts.

Tyrel's reverie was destroyed when he saw Sir John a short way away, the grizzled old bastard standing proudly with his arms folded, his pup at his side. The two looked bored, as if they had seen so many events like this that one more was of little interest to them.

It made Philip set his jaw to see them so arrogant, but he forced himself to relax and not show his tension, for then his revenge against Sir John might somehow be deflected. No, the final blow of his vengeance must be struck as soon as possible – although he had no specific plan as yet. However, it would come.

The first target for punishment, Benjamin, had been waylaid, it was true, but the other two had been carefully enticed from their work: Wymond by the promise of fresh green timbers for a pittance while he worked at making new lances, and Hal by the invitation to drink. The fool knocked back all he could, sobbing about his friend Wymond and condemning the Bailiff for his incompetence. He couldn't handle the strong wine and was grateful for the offer of an arm to steady him back to his tent as it grew dark.

Carrying Wymond down the hill had been backbreaking, but necessary. Otherwise it might have been ages before anyone found his body, and Philip wanted Hal to know that something was happening – and by God, it had worked. Hal had plainly been putting off the evil moment when he had to return to his bed alone. Without Wymond, he was lonely and wanted company.

In fact, Philip had a feeling that Hal knew who he was. When they were in the area before Lord Hugh's *ber frois*, Hal had walked on ahead determinedly, like a man going to the block, careful never to glance behind him at his executioner, as if he knew he would die and wanted to get it over with.

It was as well. Hal had met his eyes a couple of times in the inn earlier, and there was a sort of gratitude in them. At the time, Philip simply put it down to Sachevyll being thankful that he had someone to talk to . . . but now he wasn't so sure. Perhaps Hal had seen something about him, something in his eyes, or something about his face, that revealed the truth. And maybe a man who was fearful of killing himself even when he was certain that there was nothing left for him to live for, would be glad that someone else would do the job for him. Hal was actually thankful for his deliverance.

Tyrel shivered. Surely no man could hate life so much that he would welcome death. Something had made him feel sorry for the fellow and Philip struck swiftly. Hal collapsed and lay with his eyes closed while his breath snorted, and then he was sick, the vomit spewing over his tunic and dripping on to his hose. Philip struck once more and the breathing stopped. He picked up the corpse and made his way to Hal's tent – and only when he was near did he realise that there was a guard near Hal's pavilion. Patiently he settled to wait, while the puke dried on Hal's cooling body. The blasted man was still there next morning when the light came, and then he saw the Bailiff and others approaching. That was when he grabbed Hal's tunic and pulled it on.

The train of thought had distracted him. He watched dully as the procession wound around the castle yard, then Alice approached Lord Hugh with gifts.

If the men were truly in the hands of God, was he justified in exacting his own revenge? He glanced again at Sir John and his son. He saw Squire William smile courteously at Alice, saw him bow honourably, just like a *preux chevalier* and suddenly he was racked with shame. If the lad was decent, he couldn't deserve death!

Simon watched Alice advance towards Lord Hugh. The girl was beautiful, he thought, pale, serene and elegant, and it looked as though the Baron felt the same. He stood with his wife on his arm, smiling graciously at the girl as she passed him the gifts to welcome him to his castle and thank him for the tournament.

When she was done, Lord Hugh's Almoner appeared, ceremoniously holding a large leather money bag and, while the Baron and his lady looked on, money was given to the poor of Oakhampton who had been waiting at the castle's gate. Once they had all been given some money they were directed to the kitchen door where bread and all the leavings from the previous day's meals were set out.

Only when the poor had left the area did Lord Hugh and his wife proceed down the long corridor and out beneath the bailey. Turning right they led the way to the field of combat, with their guests processing along in their train.

Simon took his place behind Lord Hugh and followed him to the field, but he could not help peering about to find Hal. 'Where *is* he?'

Hal was nowhere to be seen. Simon had a shrewd guess that the architect would not willingly miss being around to welcome Lord Hugh to his seat, so his absence came as a surprise.

Lord Hugh apparently felt the same. He looked about him with evident dissatisfaction. It was a matter of courtesy that the builder should appear. Seeing him, Simon could appreciate how much of an honour Hal would have been granted by being here. It seemed strange that a man so committed to show and flamboyance should have missed his moment of glory.

That thought set a worm of unease squirming in Simon's belly but he forced himself to ignore it. There couldn't be anything wrong. He had checked the field himself with two watchmen, and Hal had been guarded all night.

Even so, not until Simon stood at Lord Hugh's side and watched the other stands fill did he feel the concern slip away, together with the weight of the last week's work. He had done his best, and now he could relax. If there were any problems it would be the fault and responsibility of someone else, he thought thankfully. Probably Hal's – and since the fool wasn't here to defend himself, if anything were to happen, he would be bound to be forced to shoulder the full blame.

There was to be less ceremony to this tournament. Often in the past, participants would first compete to earn respect from the overblown praise of their lord. Thank God, Simon thought, there would be none of that nonsense here. Lord Hugh had one aim with this tournament, which was to see to it that all his men had a chance to exercise their skills. On this first day, the competitors would be the squires – especially those who wished to be knighted.

The heralds appeared, riding in on their great mounts, batons of office held by all three of them, the King Herald, Mark Tyler, who was Lord Hugh's own man, and the two others. Simon knew Odo, of course. Like Mark Tyler, Odo seemed to have a high opinion of himself, but then heralds often did. They were little better than actors, to Simon's mind. Invariably overpaid, their duties mostly consisted of playing musical instruments and singing. And every so often they would disappear around the world to seek out new songs, new stories of imagined prowess and overblown pride.

Simon didn't like heralds.

However, today he couldn't help but feel happy to see them. They were proof that the tournament was going off without a hitch, and he couldn't get himself worked up over them. They had their uses, he supposed.

The King Herald edged his horse forward a little. 'My Lord Hugh, my Lady. We are here to begin the tournament held in your names, and I and these heralds have registered the names and arms of all the knights who wish to display their prowess and courage before you. May I beg leave of your lordship to continue?'

Lord Hugh waved a hand with imperous dignity. 'Carry on.'

The King Herald jerked at his horse's reins and turned the mount around. His chest expanded until he resembled a barrel set atop his horse. Opening his mouth, he roared in a voice that could surely have been heard in Oakhampton itself:

'NOW HEAR ME, HEAR ME! The tournament proper will open tomorrow, with individual knights jousting with their lances, each charging together to see who can survive the clash of arms. There will be three courses run by each pair, and afterwards the knights will fight with sword and axe.

The jousting will take three days, but on the last day there shall be a full *mêlée* so that all knights can demonstrate their skills. I and my two heralds shall be *diseurs* and our word will be final unless the Lord himself overrides us.

'The laws are as our great King Edward, our King's father, laid down in his *Statuta Armorum*,' the King Herald continued, glancing at a roll of paper in his hand. 'All men are hereby adjured to hold the King's peace. Only rebated weapons are to be used *à plaisance* and no weapons of war are to be allowed in the ring. Knights are only permitted to have three men to support them. Any knight or baron participating in the tournament who has more than this must tell the excess men to leave the field.' At this point he glowered at the crowds as if daring them to bring in more men.

'Grooms and footmen are not permitted to wear pointed swords, daggers, long knives, clubs or other offensive weapons of any sort. If a knight falls, only his own men may help him up again. Spectators are not *at any time* to interfere! And at any feasts the Lord decides to host, only a knight's personal squire may enter the hall in order to serve his lord. All others must remain outside.'

He went on to dwell at length on the punishments and fines which would inevitably fall on the head of any man who sought to infringe the rules, sternly reading each and staring at particular knights or men-at-arms as he did so. Simon wondered after a while whether each of these men had been guilty at some time of infringing these rules and was being reminded not to repeat the offence. At last the apparently interminable list was done and the King Herald sniffed and cleared his throat.

'But today, to open the celebrations, we have a special *béhourd* to warm us all up. Certain squires shall show their skills and run against each other.'

There were many more details, but Simon's attention had wandered and the words flowed over and past him.

Opposite, he noticed, his wife sat with Baldwin. Edith was between them. Edith looked quite lovely, he thought with a pang. Much as her mother had when he had first met her in her father's farmyard, a slim girl with a lazy smile and laughing eyes. He could remember her as she had been still more clearly whenever he looked at his daughter. Their faces were similar, if Edith's was a little wider, their eyes the same shape, their mouths and chins identical. If he was twenty years younger, he would make the same choice again.

The thought made him give a cynical grin. God help the man who chose Edith as his wife, though.

At that moment, the first pair of squires appeared before the stand and the heralds departed to the ends of the lists, apart from the King Herald, who remained before the Lord to witness the meeting of the two.

At a signal from the King Herald, there was a sudden pounding of hooves, and the two squires, both unrecognisable under mail and their coats-of-arms, charged headlong. Simon felt his heart thunder as if in time to the hoofbeats, which almost, but not quite, drowned out the din of metal clashing against metal. It was like listening to a kitchen in which every pot, pan and plate was being systematically beaten while chains were rattled unceasingly. From here he could see the whole tilt area, and as the two men came together, he almost felt the crash.

One lad's helm was hit by the lance of the other. The lance struck the chin-piece and there was a great crack, then the helm was flying through the air. Simon almost expected to see gouts of blood from the lad's neck where his head had been, but he smiled at his fancy. The helm's lock had sheared, which was the cause of the loud noise, but the boy was all right, although he twisted his head this way and that, as though his neck had been badly wrenched.

Both trotted to the far end of their lists and prepared to take their second run. A squire ran to the middle and picked up the heavy helm. Simon could see it was a modern one designed to protect the wearer from lance or sword – a massy, riveted piece of headgear weighing ten pounds or more. The thought of carrying that on his shoulders made him wince.

Once it was again set upon the lad's head, the King Herald repeated his signal and the two charged. Again the thundering of hooves, sods of earth flying through the air, mud from a puddle, the clatter of metal against metal and then the loud crash of the collision. One lad, the other, was reeling, his shield wearing a great dint where the lance had struck. Men ran to him, but he waved them off and took up a fresh lance. A last mad race, and both struck the other's shield before riding back to the centre to receive the judgement of the King Herald.

'One hit for both on the last ride,' he said while a clerk sitting before Lord Hugh scribbled his record on parchment, 'one course Squire Humphrey won by knocking his opponent's helm from his head, but the next was won by Squire David. I declare that both have matched each other's score.'

There was applause at that, for both were held to have shown exemplary skill. Simon himself was quite impressed with the proud manners of the two. They sat mounted, both with their helms under their arms, both young, neither yet in his twenties, but on the decision being announced, both bowed first to Lord Hugh, and then to each other, before trotting off together, laughing merrily with relief that they hadn't made themselves look foolish.

It was during the fourth joust of the day that Simon noticed the girl who had led the procession. Clearly a little older than his daughter, Alice was watching one of the combatants with an especial attention. Simon followed her gaze and caught a fleeting glimpse of a solemn but well-formed face just as the helm was dropped over his head and left resting there. He took his lance from the squire at his side and trotted regally towards the start point. Simon saw that from his helm trailed a piece of cloth. It looked like a woman's sleeve, and when he glanced back at the girl, he saw her wave, clench both fists and hold them up to her cheeks, standing in an agony of excitement.

'Nothing new in that,' Simon said to himself. He knew perfectly well that tournaments often held a strong erotic charge for women. Many would give tokens to their champions, some would promise to marry their favourites after a particularly good bout. With casual amusement, he glanced over to see how his wife was reacting to the excitement.

Baldwin, he saw, was bored, while Margaret caught his look and smiled, but when he noticed his daughter, he groaned. She was biting at her bottom lip with every appearance of fearful expectation, staring at the other squire.

Simon shrugged. At least she was setting her sights high enough, he thought, but then the signal was given and the two pelted down the alleyway, aiming at each other. There was a ringing *clang!* as they met, and then the two were apart once more. Simon watched the one his daughter had picked and credited her with a good choice. The lad had ridden well and survived the first charge.

It was only after the second charge that Simon noticed the token at the lad's belt. And as he recognised the scrap of cloth he gazed back at his daughter, realising why she had been so argumentative last night. He was dumbfounded.

Geoffrey was aghast. The noise, the horrible sense of being trapped in his metal skin, the fear of an accident, all conspired to petrify him.

He need only survive this third bout to win his spurs, he told himself, trying to boost his courage. As soon as he had completed the three, he could claim his wife before his lord. Then his life would change, for the better – provided that bastard Andrew didn't denounce him as a coward.

To his right as he sat upon his mount, he could see Andrew. The squire stood arms akimbo, then went to the rack and selected a lance. With a mock-respectful bow, he passed it to Geoffrey. The latter knew what Andrew thought of him: Geoffrey was a coward, a weakly man who would run from a real fight. Andrew had seen him run from the battle before Boroughbridge, a traitor, leaving his companions to die.

The horse moved beneath him as he took up the lance, hefting it in his hand. What if Andrew taunted him – or worse, challenged him to a fresh bout? Geoffrey wasn't sure he could bear to be forced back into the saddle again soon after fighting with William.

William was busy selecting a fresh lance himself. Geoffrey watched him shortsightedly. It was bad enough facing

William. If he must face Andrew in a challenge to the death, he would surely die. Andrew was a killing squire, a man with experience of fighting in many battles; it would be suicide to face him.

Then, as the two squires prepared to move off, Geoffrey realised that there was only one way to show that Andrew's accusation was false. With a sudden resolve he couched his lance, determined to prove that he was no coward. He would ride his mount *directly at William's*, not flinching, forcing the other youth to move from his path.

CHAPTER TWENTY

William reined in at the end of the field and rammed his vizor upwards to snatch a breath of air.

It was hot here. Damn hot. The sun was directly above and dust was rising up and clogging his nostrils. When he looked back through the lists, he could see a fine haze as of a thin fog which showed where his horse had taken him. The mount was his father's destrier, Pomers, and now the great beast pranced beneath him, eager to return.

In the space he saw men grabbing at the bits and pieces of the shattered lances and hurling them out of the way, so that they mightn't turn a hoof and break a horse's leg. William didn't care. He simply flung away the stub of lance in his hand and gestured impatiently for a fresh one.

Geoffrey had learned something about fighting, damn him. He was keeping a firm seat in his saddle and aiming his lance-point accurately. Not like he used to be. Useless, he had been, leaning back and letting his point waver all over the place. Now he sat rigidly and let his point find its mark. It was hard to avoid it.

William swore under his breath. He had thought that this bout would be easy, just a swift clash of arms and then he would overcome Geoffrey and be pronounced the winner. In that way he would discredit Geoffrey and justify his marriage to Alice, proving his value by force of arms. Yet the bastard had not succumbed. It was frustrating. Even now Geoffrey was taking a fresh lance from a squire at his side. William saw that it was Andrew. Geoffrey was reluctant to take the lance from him. Probably thought the other man would stab him when his defence was down, William sneered.

He contemplated the lists, wondering how to gain an advantage. Somehow he must show his superiority over Geoffrey, yet it was hard to see how he could achieve it. He absently stroked the token which Edith had dropped and which he had stuffed into his belt. In his heavy gauntlet he couldn't feel it, and the fact depressed him.

A squire was at his side with a fresh lance. William took it, holding it vertically and squinting up along its length. There was a bend in it and William snapped that he wanted a straight one. A curve made for a good display as it meant the lance would shatter gratifyingly into shards and splinters, but William wanted a good, solid strike, and for that he needed a straight lance. Soon the fellow was back and William hefted the new weapon critically. It was as straight as he could hope, but there was a curious feel to it. He rejected it and snatched at the third given to him. It was good.

He released the vizor and it fell down heavily. Immediately his breath became stertorous in his ears, and the world was barred by the grille in front of his eyes. Leaning forward he could see the lists ahead and the King Herald. There was the signal! William slammed his heels back into Pomers's flanks and felt the surge of power beneath him as the mount angrily leaped forward.

The jolting acceleration made him feel he would fall from the back of his saddle, but the immense cantle supported him. Reckless now, he kicked again at the horse, urging the beast on, and Pomers responded. The rattling and squeaking of complaining metal and leather grew into a raucous din that deafened. Dust rose and filled his helmet, making his nose tickle and itch. He had to blink away the dirt from streaming eyes.

His opponent was close. He could see Geoffrey's shape lumbering towards him. William drew his lips back from his teeth in a snarl of defiance and allowed the point of the lance to begin its fall from the vertical.

It was a fine calculation. Too early and the point would fall below the aiming-point; too late and the lance would miss the mark and slip past the enemy's shoulder while William absorbed the full weight of Geoffrey's own point. Unbalanced, William would have to fall and he had no intention of making himself look a fool before all these people.

His horse was a stable base beneath him. He was assured of Pomers's gait. The lance-tip fell gradually even as he caught sight of the approaching lance-point dropping slowly to point at him. It didn't make him flinch. The thing was irrelevant. All that mattered was getting his own lance to hit well. He shifted his grip so that the butt was jammed under his armpit and took a deep breath.

An explosion of noise; a slamming thud against his left shoulder; a rattling clamour of metal; a sharp view of a horse's nostrils, then he was past. His arm was all right, he reckoned. Just hit hard. His shield was probably wrecked, but that was how it went in the tilt. Those were his first thoughts before he realised that something was wrong. He wasn't settled properly in his saddle. Slowly he could feel himself sliding sideways.

Hauling upon Pomers's reins, he tried to regain his seat but it was too late. With a despairing wail he felt himself slip from the saddle and, through the grille of the helmet, saw the ground rushing up to meet him.

Alice could feel her heart pounding as she saw her man spur his mount into the attack. It was terrifying, truly scary, but awesome too, and exciting. Seeing her husband preparing to risk his all like this made her want to scream with pride, especially when she saw that Geoffrey was wearing her token. It streamed out from his helmet like a feather, an ethereal statement of ownership: she owned him, he owned her. She could hardly dare watch as the two men spurred their mounts on, accelerating in a deadly, lunatic gallop towards each other.

She couldn't watch. As if some premonition warned her, she closed her eyes and covered them, praying as the lances lowered and the two men aimed their weapons at each other.

A sudden silence in the crowds, as if all were holding their breath. Then the appalling din of the collision.

It was like an anvil being struck with a large, flat-headed hammer, then a thousand horseshoes hurled onto a sheet of steel. A sigh went up from some people in the audience, while from others there was a hoarse cry of cruel delight.

And opening her eyes she saw that her husband was fallen. Even as she felt the disappointment grip at her throat, Alice realised that something was very wrong. Usually a man would struggle to regain his feet, would roll to clamber to his hands and knees preparatory to levering himself upwards. That was what William was doing, raising himself upwards and tugging at his vizor.

But Geoffrey remained lying on his back, and her fists rose to her mouth as if to smother a scream.

A herald was cantering towards his body. It was the man Odo. Alice had met him earlier during the procession, but now her attention only registered him in passing. She was staring in horror and terror at her man.

Odo rode to Geoffrey and swung down from his mount with both feet out of the stirrups. He landed before the horse had fully halted, and darted to Geoffrey's side. All men-at-arms knew that the first thing to do was to let the poor fellow breathe.

The helmet was a complicated one and it took some time to work loose the hinged clips. Then he lifted away the vizor and was about to begin to pat Geoffrey's face and try to waken him, when he stopped. Beneath the neck of Geoffrey's tunic there was a blossoming crimson stain. 'Jesus!' Odo muttered in shock. Then, 'Someone find a priest and a physician. Quickly!'

In the distance he thought he heard a woman wailing, but he had no time to concern himself over the feelings of a girl. He busied himself with the squire's armour, ignoring the slow movement towards him from the stands. There was nothing new in a crowd wanting to see the dead victim of a bout.

*   *   *

Edith smothered her cry as she saw William fall. Her heart *literally* stopped. She was *literally* frozen with horror. She'd never felt like this before. It was *terrible*. She couldn't believe it. Her William, poor William was *dead*.

Without further thought, she darted from the *ber frois* and ran through the loungers who stood contemplating the scene. 'Oh, William,' she cried.

He knelt dazedly, his vizor open, but bent after the impact. It must have been hard for him to focus, from the way he peered about him. 'My head . . . Is he all right?'

'I don't know. Oh William, I was so scared you had been killed,' Edith said and burst into tears, dropping to her knees at his side to the delight of the throng about them.

William spat blood. When he hit the ground the jolt had slammed his jaw closed and a tooth had snapped. He wanted to rinse his mouth. 'You didn't bring any wine, did you?' he asked plaintively.

Odo gestured for the other heralds to help and pushed men back. 'Give him space. Do you want to kill him? Give him space!'

The muttering groups of men withdrew unwillingly and Odo was pleased to see Mark Tyler leading a dark-clothed physician towards him.

'How is he?' the physician asked.

'I don't know. He looks dreadful and he snores like a sleeping man. There's blood here and . . .'

Odo withdrew as the physician crouched and began his examination. A hand caught at his shoulder.

'Sir, will he die?'

'Lady Alice, I do not know,' he replied heavily. 'He took a bad fall.'

'He can't die. He *mustn't*!' Alice declared, distraught.

'Your husband is in God's hands,' Odo told her compassionately.

'Geoffrey!' Alice wailed, and fainted.

Odo caught her, but as he looked about him, he saw only the shocked expression on Squire William's face.

Edith had seen her father's eye on her as she wept at the side of her lover. There was no concealing her feelings and she hadn't even considered his, but now she was worried that he would have something to say about her rushing to William's side. Probably quite a lot, she feared.

Even though she was convinced he was being unreasonable about William, she hated upsetting him; she loved him too much to see him sad. The trouble was, he didn't seem to realise she was a woman now, not some baby. Christ Jesus! Edith was old enough to wed and bear children. How much *more* proof did he need?

Margaret and Baldwin were approaching her now. Edith had waited while William was given some wine, then helped away. Geoffrey had been removed from his armour and carried off on a stretcher, and now Edith stood in a thinning crowd desperately trying to avoid glancing in her father's direction. She knew what she would see in his eyes: angry confusion at her behaviour, and hurt.

Baldwin would make a good father, she thought. Solemn, true, but understanding. He had been around the world, seen cities, met strange foreign people; when he was young he had joined the last Crusade, Simon told her once. He was old, she thought critically. Someone so ancient was practically in the grave, although she could understand why Jeanne found him attractive. He had something about him, especially with that scar on his cheek. It added a sort of hint of danger.

Even as the word sprang into her mind she recalled the terror she had felt on seeing her champion on the grass. Ah, it was such a relief when he moved. If he had been killed, she would have died too. At the least she must have swooned, overcome with emotion like that other girl. And Edith's love for her dead champion would have become common knowledge, and men and women all over Europe would have heard about her fidelity, and minstrels would have sung about her and her William.

It was a lovely thought, and made her quite light-headed. If she could be sure that she would die on his death, she must surely be in love. It was consoling – and sustaining.

Inspired by this to a spirit of rebellion, she met her mother's eye boldly, but when she saw Margaret's sad expression, she felt her resolve melting. She hated hurting her mother. Sometimes she did so when her temper flared, but she always regretted it even when she couldn't bring herself to apologise.

Margaret merely said, 'Do you love him?'

Edith felt her composure crack like glass. 'Of course I do, Mother.'

'Then,' Margaret sighed, 'if you are sure, we shall have to convince your father.'

Sir Edmund had left his pavilion with a distinct sense of grievance. His mail had gained a faint dusting of rust where it had been insufficiently oiled and there was a rip in his tunic that had not been mended. Both should have been dealt with by his squire, but Andrew was nowhere to be seen. Usually Sir Edmund would not mind, but today he was tense after seeing Lady Helen Basset last night.

She was as beautiful as ever, he reflected. The thought that she had married that brutish man of hers was enough to make him want to puke; the idea that he would be pawing at her body after she left Edmund made him shudder with jealousy and disgust. Andrew had led her away, protecting her from unwanted attention, and now Edmund desperately wanted to speak to Andrew, to hear what he thought of her attitude, but he was nowhere to be seen. Where in hell's name had he got to! Andrew was a good man generally, an experienced fighter and loyal servant, but recently he had become quite lax. Sir Edmund wasn't sure why, but thought it was since they had come down here to Devon after Boroughbridge. In fact, now he thought about it, it was ever since Andrew had met Odo the Herald at the feast. Afterwards Sir Edmund often saw Andrew eyeing the herald with many a sidelong glance.

Sir Edmund had met Andrew in Béarn at a tournament, shortly after Sir Edmund had fled England to seek his fortune. Being beaten by Sir John had ruined him and he needed to win some tournaments and accumulate some money. With neither horse nor resources, he found himself watching other knights fighting in the lists, unable to participate. He had no armour, no squire, nothing.

It was there that he also met Sir Roland de le Puy, a cheery old man who saw his gloom and offered to loan his own horse and armour. Unable to believe his fortune, Sir Edmund accepted with alacrity. But he needed a squire, a man in whom he could trust to protect him. He found Andrew – and after that, the two had travelled widely through France and the English King's territories, visiting all the tournaments. Within a year they had won for themselves more than forty Knights Bachelor and one Count. The ransoms made them wealthy and led to their being noticed by others. Soon they had a new lord, a vassal of Earl Thomas, and when they returned to England it was only natural that they should in their turn become vassals to him.

Ever since, even after the disaster at Boroughbridge, Andrew had been a perfect servant, but recently he had grown slack, as though losing interest. Sir Edmund hoped he had not become over-religious. It happened sometimes that a man who had lived too long in the secular world could seek to hide himself in a convent. Sir Edmund knew that well enough himself – but he hoped Andrew wasn't heading that way. A good squire was hard to find. Still, the fellow would have to be told to mend his ways. Sir Edmund could not tolerate having his own schedule dictated by his squire's. Sir Edmund left his archer oiling his armour, muttering rebelliously, and strode purposefully towards the jousting.

Entering the field, he had to stand back while a pair of galloping men-at-arms shot past, great clods of mud and grass thrown up by their mounts as the riders whooped and cheered them on. Sir Edmund cast an eye over his light velvet tunic to make sure no dirt had been flung upon him, then carried on to the stands in the middle of the field.

As another pair of opposing riders hurtled towards each other, he looked over the field for his man. He was not at either end where the racks stood filled with lances. At each were huddles of squires waiting to pass fresh ones to their friends. There was a lot of laughing and joking in the fairday atmosphere but Sir Edmund's face was not softened by the sounds of other people's enjoyment. He had seen Sir John.

The last time they had met in a tournament was when Sir Edmund had been unfairly captured. Sir John had not been a part of the *mêlée* but he had joined in for profit. And as a result, more people had died. Sir Edmund could have saved some if he had been able to keep Sir Walter off Sir Richard. He had seen the hooves flailing, had seen the bodies.

He was at the side of the stand now, and a trembling in the ground made him halt. Any man who had fought in a battle would recognise that brutal drumming: warhorses. Over his shoulder he could see the first one approaching, gradually building up speed, lance held point high, so that the unwieldy weapon was balanced vertically. That was the trouble with lances, as Sir Edmund knew. The things were long and heavy, impossible to hold on target from a bouncing saddle, so they could only be lowered at the last moment.

This fellow was experienced. His point was still up as his horse cantered on, although it had dropped halfway to the horizontal by the time he entered the enclosed fighting area. Once there, it kept falling until the rear end slipped beneath his armpit and the whole massy pole was pointing at his enemy. Sir Edmund held his breath, waiting for the inevitable crash of metal on metal, and sure enough there it was, a terrible hammer stroke that almost seemed to explode inside his ear drums. Then the audience were clapping, one or two drunks roaring their approval, and a riderless horse cantered past Sir Edmund, stirrups flying. A mounted herald overtook it and snatched at the reins to hold it before it could enter the tented area and cause havoc.

Meanwhile, Sir Edmund could see that in the lists heralds and squires were running to the assistance of the fallen man. There were enough people there. One more would just get in the way, Sir Edmund thought philosophically.

Where *was* Andrew? He cast a careful look over all the spectators, but the squire was not there. He walked along between the stands to the other end, but there was no sign of him there either. This was growing slightly worrying. Andrew could have gone to visit the town, but he usually asked permission, as he should, before leaving his master. Besides, Andrew was a keen martial artist and would not miss an opportunity to watch fighting.

There was laughter and giggling from the riverbank. Sir Edmund wondered whether Andrew could have found a woman, and headed towards the sound. There was thick gorse lining the bank except at the ford which Baldwin had used, but in a clearing Sir Edmund glimpsed a young woman with her man, a youth little more than a boy. He left them and continued along the bank, listening to the soothing noise of the water. The jousting appeared to have ended for a space.

A flash of blue gleamed to his right and he turned in time to see a kingfisher dart up to a branch, a streak of silver gripped in its beak. Sir Edmund admired the silken beauty of the creature, thinking that he should catch and kill one, and use the feathers for decoration on his hat. Idly he wondered how he could trap one. Probably easiest would be to pay some peasant to spread birdlime on branches along this stretch of river.

It was while he mused on the feasibility of capturing and killing the bird that he noticed the rooks squabbling. His attention was caught by the pair as they hopped down and pecked among the tall fronds of ferns that lined the bank farther away. At first he watched without interest, but then a grim conviction began to form in Sir Edmund's mind and he slowly made his way to them,

The sight that met his eyes when he pulled the foliage aside and first saw the blindly staring face was in some ways a relief.

At least it wasn't Andrew, he thought with a sigh.

CHAPTER TWENTY-ONE

Simon squatted before the body. After the shock of seeing his daughter with Squire William, it was another shock to see Sachevyll's ruined body.

Seeing the damage done by the birds' pecking, he winced uncomfortably. At least the body was fresh, thank Christ, and hadn't started to reek, but it was still revolting to see how the birds had gone straight for the man's eyes. Simon pulled a face and sent a watchman to find Sir Baldwin and the Coroner.

Sir Peregrine was first on the scene and he stopped, staring down with an expression more of anger than shock. 'What the hell is happening here? Good God, is everyone gone mad?'

'So it seems,' Simon said.

'Who would want to do this?'

'I don't know. I hardly knew the fellow. In fact, he was an unholy pest, and I daresay there are several other people who'd say the same.'

Baldwin and Roger arrived together, shoving people from their path as they hurried to them.

Coroner Roger peered over Baldwin's shoulder. 'Who is it? Oh, in the name of the Virgin! Sachevyll!'

'Simon', Sir Peregrine said, 'was just saying he never had much time for the poor fellow.'

'I said *many* people didn't,' Simon protested.

'Be easy, Bailiff,' Sir Peregrine said, with his hands up in surrender. 'I didn't accuse you of anything. Be easy.'

'I just don't like dead bodies before my midday meal,' Simon grunted. He took a couple of paces back while Sir Baldwin approached the body.

'Just like the other two,' Baldwin muttered to himself. He surveyed Hal's corpse before snapping, 'Who found him?'

'Me – Sir Edmund of Gloucester.'

Baldwin nodded. Hal had been beaten about the head. Blood had seeped from the thick clots congealing at his temple and across his nose. Baldwin turned to Sir Edmund and found himself looking up into a dark, almost saturnine face. 'He was lying here as he is now?'

'My squire is missing. I was looking for him. I saw rooks fighting here and saw him. I haven't touched him.'

'Did you know him?' Sir Roger asked. His voice was harsher now as he assumed his responsibility as Coroner for the King.

'Only by sight.'

'Where from? Here?'

'No, I didn't see him here in Oakhampton. I last saw him in a small tournament in the north, where he helped make the grounds. That's what he was known for. He was an expert on the pageantry of tournaments and often got recommended to different lords whenever they were thinking of holding their own events.'

'Did he have any enemies?' Baldwin asked Sir Edmund.

The knight shook his head. 'How should I know? I never spoke to him – he was merely someone who was often about, and I saw his stages several times in the last three years.'

'We know who wanted him dead, don't we?' Mark Tyler said. He had approached the men while they spoke in quiet tones. 'It was you, Bailiff, wasn't it? You hated poor old Hal, didn't you – purely because he accused you of killing Wymond. And maybe he was right! Did you have to silence him because he knew you were truly guilty of his oldest friend's death?'

Margaret and Edith returned to the stand where they had watched the disaster so that Simon would know where to find them. Edith wanted to go after William, but Margaret pointed out with acid sweetness that running to him now while her father was absent was not the way to endear herself or her lover to him.

Such sarcasm was foreign to Margaret, but she was exhausted from weeks of broken sleep, waking to the mewling of her youngest child, stirring and fitting him to her breast as quietly as she could, so as not to wake Simon at her side. To learn of Edith's love for this boy Squire William was a great disappointment. Margaret had hoped that she could trust her daughter, but in a few hours Edith had found this fellow and declared her adoration.

Although Edith didn't want to, Margaret insisted that they should go back to the stand. As she pointed out, Simon would expect to find them there when he finished whatever it was he had been called away to. Baldwin had been asked to join him a short while later. For some reason, Margaret felt a strange anxiety in her heart, a weakly fluttering, as though a butterfly was trapped beneath her ribs.

'Please, God, don't let it be another murder,' she murmured fervently. There had been too many deaths already.

Standing and watching the other competitors was at least a diversion from her fears. Several riders tilted at each other and soon Margaret could set her mind to trying to work out the best way, first, to persuade Edith out of her infatuation, or, second, to ensure that Simon grew to accept her decision should Edith prove to be obdurate.

'Mistress, I think we should go,' Hugh muttered, watching a messenger scurrying to speak to Lord Hugh at the stand. He had come from the river bank, from the place to which Simon had been called, and Hugh was worried. Margaret was surprised, but gradually she became aware of a subtle alteration in the noise of the crowds about them. The roar of partisan support for one competitor or another had dwindled to a mutter, and angry faces were turned in their direction; they were watching *her*. Then she felt the blood chill in her veins when she caught someone saying loudly, 'There's been another murder.'

Hearing a nearby voice hissing, 'That's his wife, too, that stuck-up bitch over there,' the skin on her back crawled. The malicious whispering continued. Wherever she cast her glance, all went silent as men caught her eye, but all the time she heard conversations continuing out of earshot, and she could feel a sick tingling in her belly: the beginnings of fear.

Like many others, she had seen crowds turn wild before now. Simon was only too happy to point out that the English are an unruly lot – the worst, he usually added with a perverse pride, being the Devonians. They were ever-disputatious, determined and hardy in a fight. Perhaps it came from having to defend their lands from two sea-coasts, or maybe it was true as the stories said, that the Devonshire men were the last ancestors of the men of Troy. Certainly their behaviour when drunk or roiled was vicious to the point of madness. They would hold their ground against the King's own host if they were roused.

She caught Hugh's eye. He nodded, clasping his stout staff more strongly, and then turned and forced his way through the people towards the gate. One man stood in his path, but Hugh shifted his grip on the staff and glowered, saying, 'She's got nothing to do with any murder; she's only a man's wife, all right?' and the fellow stood aside.

Margaret had grabbed Edith's hand, and now she held on to it for dear life. Hugh, she saw, had made it to the gate that led to the steps at the back, and then she was almost there herself. She thrust Edith forward, and was about to follow when she stumbled, a loose plank or board tripping her. Instantly Hugh was with her, his staff held one-handed, but ready.

'Don't worry, Hugh,' she gasped as he shoved a hand through her armpit and quickly pulled her upright. 'I am fine, honestly. My own clumsiness, that's all.'

Hugh nodded, but his eyes were on the other men in the stand. One or two were openly curling their lips. He saw one man bite his thumb in contempt, and Hugh felt his jaw clench even as he turned the end of his staff in the fellow's direction, but then Margaret was gently pushing him back towards the exit and they made their way through the gap in the wall and down the stairs.

It was only when they reached the bottom and could stare about them that Margaret felt the clutching of terrible fear. 'Hugh! Where did Edith go?'

Baldwin could have laughed at Simon's face if the matter were not so serious. Simon gaped, staring at Mark Tyler while the latter eyed him back severely. The herald was pompous, certainly, a fool in many ways, but in this case Baldwin wondered whether he was an accurate gauge as to the feelings of the mob.

Sometimes it was hard for Baldwin to appreciate the level of anger and resentment that the public could feel. He had spent so many years abroad, studying the martial arts and living the ascetic existence of a warrior monk in Paris and other centres of learning, that he occasionally found it difficult to understand how his own compatriots thought or felt about matters.

This was a perfect example. He had known Simon for some six years; the most honourable officer he had met, a man of integrity and decency, and yet a fool was accusing him of murder.

'You did it, didn't you?' Mark repeated.

To Baldwin's astonishment he saw that others nearby had heard the accusation and were running off to spread the rumours; even now men were setting their features into hard masks, as if preparing themselves for a lynching.

'Wait, Tyler!' Baldwin declared loudly, raising a hand. 'There will be no accusations. Not here. And it is insane to suggest that the good Bailiff could have killed Hal Sachevyll. He had no reason to kill the builder.'

'Hal accused him of murder; I think he battered Hal to shut him up.'

'There is nothing to suggest that Simon was guilty of killing Hal, just as there was nothing to suggest that Simon hurt Wymond. No one saw him hurting them, no one heard him . . .' Baldwin glanced back at the body wonderingly. 'Why should he have been thrust among the vegetation?'

Sir Roger said, 'I wonder none of us saw him here this morning when we searched the grounds.'

'It was concealed well enough,' Baldwin said pensively.

'The Bailiff concealed the body,' Mark Tyler said.

Simon ignored the man. The first shock of being accused was wearing off and now his mind was racing. 'It must have been the drunk we found here, Baldwin! He must have been feigning drunkenness to distract us.'

'What drunk?' Baldwin demanded.

'Some fellow . . . the watchmen and I found him out here. We thought he was in a stupor, but it's easy to pretend to be hammered. He could have killed Hal, thrown him down here and then . . .'

Mark Tyler pulled a face. 'A nice story, Bailiff. Coroner, this man murdered Hal and Wymond before him. I demand that he be arrested.'

'When do you suggest he killed Hal, exactly?' Sir Roger asked mildly. 'I doubt he has had five minutes to himself since this tournament began. Anyone could have pushed the body here.'

'I would never have seen it, had there not been those two rooks fighting over it,' Sir Edmund put in.

'Yes, we would still be wondering where on earth Hal had

got to,' Baldwin murmured. 'What of this feckless squire of yours? Has he often gone missing like this?'

'I am here, Sir Baldwin.' Baldwin found himself confronted by Andrew.

'And where the devil have you been?' Sir Edmund asked crossly.

'I was talking to an old friend. Odo, the herald.'

Tyler looked like a man who had bitten into a lemon. 'I suppose you *are* old friends?'

'We met at tournaments in France. Yes, I have known Odo for many years.'

'I suppose men abroad can't be too fussy about their friends.'

Andrew looked at him with a slight smile at his mouth. 'Do you mean to insult me, King Herald? Because if you do, I should be delighted to stand against you in a battle.'

Baldwin grinned to himself as he noticed Mark Tyler's sudden embarrassment. The King Herald stammered, 'I didn't intend any insult . . .'

Baldwin said, 'Did you know this man Hal?'

Andrew cast a dismissive look down at the body. 'Yes. I saw him in the north. I was at Boroughbridge and was taken by Squire William. Hal was in the King's entourage up there. I assumed he was a spy, for he had been helping Earl Thomas beforehand. Or perhaps he was able to change allegiance very quickly.'

'What of Dudenay?'

'Who?'

'A banker in Exeter.'

Andrew shrugged. 'I avoid such men. I have no interest in such fellows.'

'This is a waste of time. It was Puttock killed the man,' Tyler spat. 'Have him arrested!'

Baldwin eyed him coldly. 'It is impossible that Simon could have done this. Bailiff Puttock slept in the castle last night and the gates were locked.'

'I don't care what you say!' Tyler declared hotly. 'It's obvious to me that the Bailiff held a grudge against these two, Wymond and Hal Sachevyll, and I accuse him of murder. If no one else will appeal him, I shall.'

'Oh, this is insane!' Simon snapped. His temper was wearing thin. 'How the hell could I have got here and done for the poor bastard? I was in the castle, as Baldwin said. And it's hardly likely, is it, you cretin, that I'd get rid of the architect? Anyway, I told a man to guard him.'

'And perhaps paid him to kill poor Hal for you? There's no end of scum would murder for a suitable fee,' Tyler said scathingly.

'We must speak to the watchman,' Baldwin agreed calmly, although his fingers itched to pick up the contentious herald and dump him in the river.

Tyler turned to the Coroner again. 'I saw Wymond arguing with him – both were very angry. If Bailiff Puttock had drawn his sword then, I suppose it could have been justified as defence or a hot-blooded killing – but he didn't! No, he clearly set about to kill both men with malice, planning their deaths in a peculiarly evil manner.'

Sir Roger smiled thinly. 'I don't doubt your conviction, but I don't believe Bailiff Puttock to be guilty. It's rubbish. Now, Sir Baldwin, why don't we look over the body and see what we can discern?'

Nothing loath, Baldwin crouched at Hal's side and

studied his ruined skull. From the look of the wounds it seemed that he had been struck many times with a blunt weapon, possibly a staff or a simple cudgel. A sword or metal implement would have left gashes with defined edges, but Hal's head showed the typical signs of a bludgeoning. Not far away was a large stack of logs and boughs coppiced from the woods behind the castle, and Baldwin was confident that one would have blood and gore staining it.

Roger untied the man's belt and undressed him while Baldwin peered over his shoulder. There were no stab marks on Hal's pale chest and thighs, but when Roger tugged him over, Baldwin saw that high on Hal's back, a little below his neck, was a large lump.

At last he stood, grunting as his knee objected once more. His joints were becoming ever more fractious, he considered. 'If I had to guess, I would say that this man was lured here, or perhaps followed here, and then struck down from behind. This blow here,' he pointed to a deep gash, 'was probably the first. I believe that Hal was knocked unconscious and then beaten to death.'

'How can you tell that?' Tyler asked scathingly. 'He's a mass of blood and pus. You can't tell which blow was given first. It's impossible.'

'I cannot be certain, it is true,' Baldwin admitted. 'But the blow at his back is low, as if the murderer missed Hal's head because he was trying to attack him in the dark. Consider: a man stalks Hal and delivers the first blow from behind. Hal falls, wondering what hit him. Obviously he would cry out. This would not have disabled him, only hurt a lot. Afterwards come a number of fresh blows, and these are rained down upon him with great violence and indiscrimination . . .'

'How can you tell?' Sir Peregrine asked.

'This one hit his ear and took off a flap of skin, the weapon struck with such force. There are so many wounds, it could only have been done by someone who didn't want to see Hal get up again. The killer must have been driven by rage or hatred, which could explain the large number of wounds.'

It was a point which hadn't been missed by Tyler. 'So a coward struck him down from behind and then beat the life out of him as he lay helpless on the ground. The action of a real hero! I hope you are proud, Bailiff.'

'Why should Simon do that?' Coroner Roger asked patiently.

'Simon didn't,' Baldwin said shortly. He was about to speak again when he became aware that the crowd about them had visibly grown. They were at the centre of a thickening ring of spectators. Baldwin had not realised that news of Tyler's suspicions about Simon had spread so quickly.

Sir Roger was under no such illusions. Like Margaret, he had witnessed how peasants could swiftly turn violent, and now he glowered about him as voices muttered angrily. He looked for men-at-arms, but they were back at the stands, protecting Lord Hugh.

When Baldwin saw his ferocious expression he realised Sir Roger's concern. Lifting his hands over his head, Baldwin called out in a clear voice: 'The body of Hal Sachevyll has been found here. Does any man know of anyone who had reason to want Hal dead?'

'The Bailiff! Arrest *him* if you want the killer,' came a voice.

'Rubbish!' another snapped, and Baldwin heard Sir Roger give a short sigh of relief as Odo the herald appeared, shouldering his way through the press. 'Complete and utter balls! Only the illegitimate son of a Breton pirate could believe that sort of shite! This Bailiff is known to be fair and incorruptible. If he needs to draw a weapon, he fights face-to-face. No knife in the back from Bailiff Puttock!'

His loud voice had held the audience quiet, but as he reached the group about the body, Baldwin saw that he had not arrived alone. As he turned and faced the crowd, men-at-arms in Sir Peregrine's livery appeared, all holding long polearms. Under their silent, threatening gaze, the people began to shuffle. It was one thing to intimidate a few men by strength of numbers, but quite another to risk fighting trained men. Muttering, the crowd began to thin.

'Thank you, Odo,' Sir Roger said as the people dispersed and Mark Tyler strode away angrily. 'Could you arrange for a jury to be gathered and for a guard to be placed upon this body until we have fully recorded all injuries?'

'Of course, Sir Roger,' and Odo glanced about, reassuring himself that the crowd was dispersing, before returning to his duties. Sir Peregrine went with him.

Simon did not notice him leave. He stood with a feeling of bewilderment. Never before had he been accused of any serious crime. Once or twice men had inferred that he had taken bribes when they disliked his decisions, but never had anyone dared to suggest he could have been guilty of murder! The accusation had struck him like a shot from the King's artillery. He was utterly stunned now he realised the enormity of the herald's words; he couldn't even trust his voice.

It was not anger. In an instant Tyler had hit Simon in a place he had always thought himself secure: in his pride. Simon valued his reputation for honesty, and the fact that a fellow official who was working for Lord Hugh could suggest such a thing had rocked him. When Hal accused him of killing Wymond, that was one thing: the architect had just lost a close friend and was lashing out at the first man he could – Simon hardly looked upon that as personal – but this, from Mark Tyler, was a studied insult. It showed Simon that he was vulnerable to attack, that accusations, unreasonable and unfair could be set against him.

And the accusation had not been withdrawn, he noted. If Tyler chose to continue to declare Simon's guilt, the Bailiff would be hard-pressed to defend himself. Tyler was powerful enough, since he would likely have the ear of Lord Hugh.

Simon grimly set his shoulders. No matter who made unreasonable accusations against him, he would continue to perform his duty to the best of his ability. And that was all.

It was as he came to this resolution that a young urchin appeared in front of him. 'Bailiff?'

'Yes? What is it?' Simon barked.

'A message,' he said, holding out his grubby hand.

Simon pressed a small coin into it. The lad studied it, then nodded to himself. 'It's from your wife. She says your daughter has gone missing.'

CHAPTER TWENTY-TWO

Baldwin and Simon hurriedly left Sir Roger with the body and set off to the stands. There they saw Sir Peregrine waiting for them.

'Sir Peregrine, we have to go. Simon's daughter has disappeared and—' Baldwin began, but Sir Peregrine shook his head and looked at Simon apologetically.

'Bailiff, I'm sorry, but these murders are causing a very great deal of alarm as you can imagine, and people are making all sorts of wild allegations.'

'We agree,' Baldwin said. 'We must investigate this latest killing with great urgency. Two murders and we still have no idea who could have committed them, nor why! We must do all we can to find the culprit. After all, a man who has committed two murders may well commit another. We are fortunate that the Coroner is here.'

'Quite right!' shouted Mark Tyler.

Simon groaned as the King Herald appeared. 'What now, Tyler? Why don't you return to your duties here?'

The herald gave him a sour grin. 'That's just what you'd like, isn't it, Bailiff ? Get rid of me so that your guilt can never be proved.'

'That's bollocks, as you well know!' Simon flushed.

'Really? Then you won't mind proving your innocence in front of the jury, will you?'

'There is no need for that,' Baldwin said sharply. 'No one seriously believes that Simon is guilty.'

'That's not strictly true,' said Sir Peregrine. 'Mark Tyler has come to me to officially declare his belief that the good Bailiff here *is* guilty.' He glanced at Baldwin apologetically, then turned his attention back to Simon. 'I have no desire to be involved, quite frankly, but I have little choice. Lord Hugh has no options either.'

Mark Tyler smirked as Sir Peregrine outlined the position. It was enough for Tyler to have accused this Bailiff, without having to worry about the consequences. He was content with the reflection that he himself had been able to point it out. That would surely weigh heavily in his favour in Lord Hugh's mind.

The tournaments were continuing, with squires testing their courage in the yard. From duty Lord Hugh remained on his seat, toying with a large mazer of wine, while all about him the stands erupted in cheering or booing as one after another of the contestants tumbled to the ground, for these were the younger squires, the ones with least skill and expertise. It would be many a long month before they had the ability or the strength to challenge a real warrior, but at least they were getting their knocks and being winded, which was always a good experience for a man.

Mark Tyler noted the scene with only a part of his brain. Most of his attention was focused on Odo, the man brought in by Sir Peregrine, he felt sure, to replace him. Devious, lying churl that he was! He'd inveigled his way into Lord Hugh's household like a slug, slithering in and leaving his slime over all that he touched. Well, he'd better watch out. Mark was too fly for him; he wasn't going to give up his place at his lord's side for anyone. No, this odious Odo must get his comeuppance. Mark was no fool and he'd see to the arse.

Odo had finished monitoring the latest joust and there was a short pause in the events while Lord Hugh left the stand to take a piss against one of the grandstand's stanchions. While he was gone, Odo trotted on his pony towards the huddle of men, his expression bemused. 'What's happening?' he asked.

'I have accused the Bailiff of murder,' Mark told him haughtily.

Odo glanced at Mark with an expression of surprise. 'But the Bailiff is needed by Lord Hugh.'

Mark stiffened. 'The man is a killer! Would you have him next to your own lord?'

'I've killed no one here,' Simon sputtered angrily. He would have liked to continue, but Odo cut him off.

'There is no need to worry, Bailiff. I am sure that Mark has merely made an error. Isn't that right, Mark?'

'I've made no . . .'

'Lord Hugh was *very specific* just now that he wishes the Bailiff back at his side as soon as possible.'

Mark stared at Odo. There was unsheathed steel in the other herald's voice, a conviction and firmly threatening tone. Mark turned to Sir Peregrine and would have appealed to his better judgement, except he caught sight of a wink from Sir Peregrine to Odo: the two were in league! Mark felt his guts lurch, but then he managed to reply with hauteur. 'Of course. We can't have a murderer *arrested*, can we?'

'Lord Hugh was sure you would retract your allegation,' Odo said, with emphasis. 'He is convinced that the good Bailiff is innocent.'

'Then of course I withdraw,' Mark agreed tightly. 'If my lord tells me so, it must be true.'

He couldn't wait and listen to their chatter; he had to get away. Being beaten like that by a man so new to the trade he could scarcely call out the colours of Lord Hugh's own host was a proof, if he had needed it, that Lord Hugh's patronage was gone. The writing was on the wall; Mark could see that. He had known for some little time that Sir Peregrine was disatisfied with him, but he hadn't realised just how low was the esteem in which the banneret held him. It was a shock that Peregrine would side with a new herald and a Bailiff who was not even of Lord Hugh's household in order to get rid of *him*, Mark Tyler, King Herald.

The Bailiff had been a thorn in his side from the moment they had first met. Big-headed shit! He thought he knew how to set out a tournament, how to lay out horse-lines, how to site stands, where to put lance-rests and equipment. As a mere Bailiff, Mark considered that Simon had managed reasonably well – but that didn't alter his opinion that the Bailiff was a cocky old fool with little idea of how to perform the simplest task. And he had quarrelled with both Hal *and* Wymond. He was the obvious suspect! Mark had to wonder why on earth Lord Hugh should bother to protect him.

Then Mark recalled the disaster at Crukerne where folks had died, mainly because Hal and Wymond had scrimped on the timber. The stand had collapsed when that fool of a knight, Sir Richard Prouse, fell upon it, and spectators were crushed beneath his mount. Hal and Wymond had promised to erect suitable stands and then thieved Sir John's money for their own purposes. That horrible accident had enraged Lord Hugh himself, for he had friends in the stands who could have been wounded.

Well, sod them! If Mark couldn't accuse the Bailiff himself, he knew how to spread gossip.

Arriving at a wineseller, Mark sank a large pot. 'It was the Bailiff.'

'Eh?' The wine-seller gazed at him blankly, already more than half-drunk himself.

'That Bailiff killed Hal and Wymond,' Mark said. 'Probably thought Lord Hugh would reward him. After all, Lord Hugh hated the two sodomites.'

The wine-seller nodded knowingly, but Mark was sure he hadn't taken it in. No matter. He could see another man listening intently, from a table in the corner. Mark knew the rumour would be all over the place by dark.

There was little or no satisfaction in it. Mark knew his position was gone. His thoughts became more and more gloomy. It was obvious that Sir Peregrine wanted him out of the way; that Odo coveted his position for himself. No one would support Mark. All were keen to see the back of him.

Perhaps he should leave. Go to France, to the south where it was warm, or to Bavaria. There were good opportunities for an experienced herald there, so he had heard. New tournaments were being arranged there all the time, with all the great families lining up to display their finery and bash the living daylights out of each other. A herald could pick up a patron with ease, if he had a good tongue and could sing new songs, and the English ones that filled much of Mark's repertoire should be new enough for any Swabian or Bavarian count.

He squinted up at the sun as a wave of sadness washed over him. It was all very well talking about going to visit new countries, but Mark was happy here in Devon. The thought of packing his few belongings and traipsing over to Europe held no appeal.

Yet it could become necessary. If Sir Peregrine and Odo had their way, he would soon be forced from his position. And the Bailiff, too, wanted him gone. He was playing the same game as Sir Peregrine and Odo.

He purchased more wine and gazed glumly into the depths of the liquid. The trouble was, if they were all to gang up against him, he was powerless. The worm Odo must feel that he as good as had Mark's job already.

Well, he *hadn't*! The herald squared his shoulders. He would see off any man who tried to get him thrown from his master's household.

Any man at all, he thought, as a picture of Odo appeared unbidden in his mind.

When Simon saw Edith, he felt an overwhelming relief that she was all right, but that was quickly washed away when he saw with whom she walked.

It was among the food stalls that he sighted her. He and Baldwin had hurried that way as soon as they had spoken to Margaret. The tearful woman was standing at the rear of the stand while Hugh glowered at the world, wanting to seek Edith but unwilling to leave his mistress. Margaret was consumed with dread for what might have happened to her daughter.

'You were right to stay with Meg,' Simon said when he'd heard the story. As he spoke he was jostled by a burly fellow, who looked the Bailiff up and down insolently before carrying on his way. If Simon had been less concerned about his daughter, he would have demanded an apology, but as it was, he let the incident pass. 'Did either of you see where she went?'

'Couldn't,' Hugh mumbled. He was prone to sulkily muttering towards the ground when he wasn't sure of his actions, and today his black countenance showed his concern. 'Had to help the mistress from the stand.'

'Was it bad in there?' Baldwin asked.

'Everyone looked at us,' Margaret sobbed. 'Someone said Simon had been responsible for a murder – that he killed the designer.'

'News travels fast,' Baldwin commented. He looked up to find himself being stared at by a man. Catching Baldwin's eye, the stranger gave a brief shake of his head and a grimace, then walked away.

It made Baldwin frown, and then he began to watch others about the place. With a chill he saw that many people in the immediate area were eyeing Simon, one or two fingering their belts as though they regretted the fact that their knives had been left behind in accordance with the ordinance against carrying weapons to a tournament. Men became tribal in their support of their own champions against others, and fights were all too common at such events, but never before had Baldwin felt so deeply grateful to the dead King Edward I for his far-sighted restrictions on the carrying of weapons among the public. Only knights and squires could walk armed.

'She could be anywhere, Simon,' Margaret declared tearfully.

'We'll find her, Meg,' he said reassuringly.

'Of course we shall,' Baldwin soothed. 'But there is no point in waiting here, Margaret. You should return to the castle and we will contact you there. After all, she may have returned there already.'

Simon gazed about him. 'You think so? What if Edith should return here? Wouldn't it be best for Meg to wait and—'

'If she was to return here, she would surely have done so already. No! Far better that Margaret should wait in the castle,' Baldwin said firmly, and Hugh nodded.

Simon was willing to be persuaded. 'If you're sure. Take her back, Hugh, and Baldwin and I'll look for Edith. Silly imbecile!' he added as the other two disappeared in the direction of the castle's entrance. 'Where could she have run to?'

Baldwin rested his hand on his friend's shoulder. He could hear the anxiety in Simon's voice, and no words were necessary. 'Come!'

They walked from the stands to the river, and while Simon stayed on the northern bank, Baldwin crossed at his ford and checked the farther side. He found three men with their women concealed in the long grasses, and each time he hoped that one of them would be Edith – and each time he dreaded it. In the event he could not find her, and none of the boys or girls there could help. No one had seen her.

Disappointed, Baldwin continued on his way while Simon kept pace on the other bank. It was as they passed by the line of stalls run by the armourers that Simon suddenly gave a hoarse cry. Glancing towards him, Baldwin saw the direction of his gaze and, following it, found Edith. 'Thank God,' he breathed, for although he had not voiced his fear, he had been worried that she might have been captured by an errant lad or a drunk, and perhaps raped or worse. Seeing her chattering delightedly with the well-formed and good-looking man at her side, at least he could be sure that she was unharmed. If she had submitted to the fellow, it was not unwillingly. He eyed the water but decided against trying to cross it here. It was flowing too quickly for his taste, and instead he hurried back to the ford.

'Edith! Where in God's name have you been? Your mother has been worrying herself frantic!' Simon had just about had enough – of everything!

The girl broke away from her lover and joined him. 'I left the *ber frois*, Father, as Mother told me, and then she didn't come out,' Edith said coolly. 'Then some men came over and would have molested me.'

Simon studied his daughter. She looked calm, if ratty at being accosted like this, but there was no trace of guilt on her countenance; no flush of shame. He was about to thank the lad at her side when he saw that from his belt the squire carried a woman's token, and at the same moment he recognised Edith's neck-scarf.

'Father, Squire William rescued me,' she said. 'Even with his wounds, he came to protect me.'

'Yes, very good,' Simon said coldly. 'And now I shall take you to your mother so that she can see you're well. She was petrified; didn't know where you had got to or whether you'd been captured by some felon.'

'I shall come along shortly,' Edith said distantly.

'You will come now!'

'I can look after her, Bailiff,' William said.

'I thank you, but I can protect her well enough,' Simon said with poisonous gratitude.

William's face coloured. 'I think you should trust the man who has saved her already.'

'Do you? I think I should *not* trust the boy she has been seeing behind her parents' backs.'

'I haven't,' Edith declared hotly.

'No? You mean that he found that token lying in the road?' Simon exclaimed angrily, pointing at William's belt. 'Don't lie to me, Edith!'

'Bailiff, there's no need to raise your voice,' William said.

'I shall speak to my own daughter as I wish, and I would be grateful if you would not interrupt.'

'Father, William simply happened to be there and saved me from the peasants behind the *ber frois*. I don't see why you can't be thankful that . . .'

'Some puppy took you away from your mother? Or that he met you clandestinely and has been carrying your token? Or that in order to conceal it from your parents, you chose to *lie* to me?'

Edith froze at his furious outburst. 'I didn't lie to you.'

'No, you were careful to deceive us more subtly, weren't you?'

'Bailiff,' William tried again, but Simon made a gesture with his hand.

Approaching them, Baldwin saw Simon step forward. He saw him reach for Edith, but at the same time William retreated a pace, his hand whipping to the long-bladed dagger that hung at his belt.

313

Roaring, '*No!*' Baldwin sprang forward the remaining thirty yards. Simon, he saw, jumped back as the blade danced in the sunlight; he heard Edith give a short shriek, her hand going to her mouth, while William took her shoulder and pulled her towards him. Simon made as if to reach for his daughter, but William's knife was already there and Simon almost grazed his forearm on the wicked steel.

Baldwin darted to William's side, and the boy saw his movement and shot a glance at him. As Baldwin saw William's eyes take him in, he kept going until he was almost behind the lad. Simon made a grab for his daughter and William's attention was diverted. He turned to face Simon and instantly Baldwin was in close, one foot lashing out to catch William behind the knees. The youth's legs collapsed and he fell like an arrow plummeting into water, his wrist gripped in Baldwin's hand. Simon took Edith's arm and pulled her away.

William reached for his knife, which he had dropped, but Baldwin stepped upon it and put a hand on the lad's shoulder. 'Enough!' he cried heartily. 'There is no blood spilt, no harm done. I think we should forget that this ever happened.'

He held William's gaze as he spoke, and although his tone was genial and pleasant, there was nothing amiable in his face. William could see cold contempt there, and glittering anger in his brown eyes.

'I'd give a shilling on the Bailiff,' one voice called. Another drily observed, 'You think so? I'd give the boy my shilling. The Bailiff needed a friend to beat one boy.'

'There will be no more fighting,' Baldwin stated. 'No, and if you want to see fighting, go and watch the jousts. That is where the action is. The squire here won't fight with the Bailiff, after all. The Bailiff can't be seen to be squabbling with a squire, and no squire who expects to be dubbed knight would want his honour stained by picking a quarrel with the father of his maid, would he?' Baldwin smiled, still staring, unblinking, at William. 'Not unless he wanted his lord to stop his promotion. A squire who fights Lord Hugh's Bailiff can scarcely expect him to be impressed. Lord Hugh is more likely to refuse to knight a man who insults his officers like that.'

Squire William nodded in good part. 'You are right, Sir Baldwin, and I am impressed with your skills. I'd like to pit myself against you in the tournament.'

'I fear my own days as a jouster are far gone,' Baldwin said untruthfully. If he never had to joust again, he would be content.

'Perhaps we could test our relative prowess?'

'There would be little merit in a fight between a youth full in his prime and an old fool like me,' Baldwin countered politely. 'I am sure your better training and the strength of your youth would show.'

He bent and offered William his hand. The squire grunted with pain and winced as he clambered to his feet. Baldwin motioned towards the knife. 'Do not leave it or it might rust,' he said.

'Bailiff, my Lady Edith,' William said, and gave them his courtliest bow. 'I look forward to meeting you again soon. Sir Baldwin, good day.'

Baldwin watched him go with a small smile. 'I used to be much like that,' he said.

'Thank God you've learned to be more respectful to your betters,' Simon grated.

'He was perfectly respectful until you insulted him!' Edith burst out. 'Why did you have to be so rude to me?'

'You deliberately misled me and your mother,' Simon rasped. 'Don't now try to blame us for your own failings.'

'I did not lie,' she equivocated.

'When we asked you about your neck-scarf, you changed the subject, didn't you?'

'That has nothing to do with . . .'

'Come back now. I can't trust you alone.'

She stamped her foot with a quick fury. 'You can't expect me to leave the field just because *you* want to go to the castle! I won't!'

Simon stepped closer, and the light of battle was in his eye. 'You can come back with me willingly or not, but by God's cods, you are coming back right now. I will not leave your mother thinking you could be in danger, no matter how badly you behave.'

Edith drew in a breath, meeting his angry stare with a gaze quite as unflinching. 'I won't.'

'Then I'll carry you.'

'You wouldn't dare!'

Baldwin groaned. 'May I interrupt? Edith, I think you should assume your father will dare do exactly that, so please do not tempt him. And Simon, Edith is prepared to fight you, so may I suggest that Edith comes back with me? If you would care to follow, Simon? There is no need to create even more of a spectacle than we already have, is there?'

His suggestion was followed, to Baldwin's gratification, although some of his pleasure was dulled as he led the way to the castle when he heard a voice declare:

'Wot, won't there be a fight, then? I was going to bet tuppence on the squire.'

CHAPTER TWENTY-THREE

Philip Tyrel contemplated the field as the last of the squires handed his reins to a friend and dropped from the saddle with relief. It was a long way down, sitting up there, with the high seating position inches above the mount's back. Once there, leaning back into the cantle that surrounded a man's body, curving around his kidneys, one realised how far it was to fall.

He had witnessed the tilt between William and Geoffrey, but he had seen many such collisions in the lists – some fatal and others in which, miraculously, both seemed unhurt – and now his interest was taken by the direction in which William was going, back towards the pavilions.

The lad was nothing to him. Nothing at all . . . he was the bait, the lure to the father, that was all. And yet in some ways, he was the embodiment of the crime.

It was strange. At first Philip had not expected to get further than Benjamin, but then when he arrived here at this tournament, he realised that he could make Hal Sachevyll and Wymond Carpenter pay for their part in the crime. Now there remained only the last of the four, the man whose greed had directly led to the deaths. The man who had ended Philip's marriage by seeing to it that his beloved wife was killed. And his two young children.

It was a curious fact that William happened to be around the same age as his children would have been now, had they lived; it almost made the next stage feel like a divine form of retribution, as if God Himself had willed that Sir John should pay for his offence with the blood of his own son.

He followed William to the tents with a feeling of calmness and ease. All of a sudden, his pain and grief were eradicated. He felt better each morning when he awoke, soothed by the death of the men who had ruined his life. Their destruction was balm to his soul.

This boy was different, though. He was not directly responsible for anything. He was merely the tool of vengeance. Nothing more.

While Philip watched, William ducked into his tent and the murderer heard his father's rumbling tones. Philip dared not approach too close, but from the other side of the lane between the tents, he could hear Sir John enquire after his son.

'I know a knock like that can shake a man.'

'I'm fine. I lost a tooth, got some bruises but that's all.'

'How about Geoffrey?'

'What do I care? The fool lost.'

'And a fortunate thing. He may die and leave you a safe tilt at the girl.'

'She will do as you tell her.'

'You think so? Did you hear what she said? That she was already married to Geoffrey?'

'Deny it. You are her guardian and you never gave her permission. A clandestine marriage cannot be proved. Anyway, if she is married, she will soon be a widow.'

There was a pause, then, 'Don't you care if she has lost her virginity?' Sir John's tone expressed disbelief.

'Father, I have slept with many women. Few of them were virgins. Why should I care if this one is or is not?'

'You should treat things more seriously! This woman is to be your wife – what if she's poxed, eh? If she's been incontinent in lust, what then? She may give birth to half-wits or lepers. Do you want a leper for a son? And what if she's over-sexed? She may search about for other men.'

'Oh, if she's experienced, she'll be more enjoyable.'

Philip could almost hear Sir John forcing the angry response down. 'You enjoy taunting me. So be it. But it's your future we're discussing.'

That was the start of a list of recriminations for William's loose lifestyle. Sir John remonstrated with his son, reminding him of the sacred nature of knighthood. It made Philip smile. That an avaricious, murdering swine like Sir John of Crukerne should try to instil honour and decency in his son was laughable. What of his own failings? Were they to be eradicated with absolution on his deathbed? Philip couldn't help but grimace as he walked away. There was no need to remain. He knew where he must go.

With a hand resting at his knife-hilt, he strolled to the castle and waited outside the chapel, leaning negligently at the wall. It wasn't long before he saw the burly figure of

William, freshly dressed in clean tunic and hose, walking with his father to the chapel.

He hated Sir John. Once again, Philip was struck with the conviction that there was something wrong about executing the lad. He was so young, so full of life, and now he was about to be made a knight, an honourable and chivalrous position for a man entering adulthood.

Philip watched as the two men halted near the door, Sir John instructing his son with a pointing finger, Squire William listening with a serious frown before nodding.

The two looked like a picture of the courtly ideal. Sir John, tall, grizzled, powerful and experienced, his son slimmer, a little shorter, but handsome with his perfect features and hair moving in the wind. He could have been a saint if looks were all, and the sight of the two of them talking in a low undertone, clearly in accord, gave the killer a pang. Tears threatened his eyes, blurring his vision, and he groaned quietly. A passing servant gave him a curious look, but he waved his hand and the fellow carried on his way.

It was that scene: the two men so content in each other's company. Their happiness was almost tangible, like an enveloping halo that protected them from the world and suffering. The bond which forged the love of a father for his son and a son for his father was so powerful that no man should destroy it, Philip thought. No man had the right. It was foul to contemplate it.

But what of his own little boy, destroyed by Sir John's greed? Sir John had wrecked many other lives. Wasn't it justice to see him pay for his crimes? He deserved to be punished – and yet by taking the action he planned, Philip would punish the son as well as the guilty man.

Wiping at his eyes, he glanced back at the two men. Squire William stepped forward and the murderer could see his face distinctly. Calm, unworried, handsome and haughty, aware of his rank and the coming celebration in his honour, it was the face of a lad any man could be proud of. Philip himself would have been pleased if his own son had grown like this.

The two men nodded to the murderer standing by the chapel, and then entered, and as they walked in, William's voice carried on the clear evening air.

'I know, Father. As far as I am concerned, as soon as I have taken Mass and been dubbed knight, I will become renewed – reborn. I intend to take my vows seriously. Before God, I promise you that I shall uphold the knightly virtues of courtesy, honour and prowess. What is chivalry, if a knight behaves no better than a drunken churl? No, a knight should be beyond reproach, should be clean-living and uphold the law. I certainly intend to be exemplary. You'll be proud of me, and so will Alice. As you wish, I shall marry her.'

The killer closed his eyes while his heart pounded and his resolve fell from him like filth sloughed away in the rain. With those words Squire William had saved his life. Philip couldn't kill a lad who professed such integrity. If he was serious about upholding the law and behaving as a perfect husband, he was so far removed from his father as to be inviolate. Philip couldn't kill someone like that. It would be a genuine crime.

No, his wife and children must be satisfied with the revenge he had already exacted. Surely three dead men was sufficient.

His heart was heavy; he was not sure that he was doing the right thing. He gazed up at the heavens, praying for an answer, but there was none.

'Sir? Sir? Are you all right?'

Opening his eyes, he found himself staring into the morose features of Hugh, Simon's servant.

'Could you fetch me a jug of wine?' he asked shakily.

It was a slow service, William thought. Slow and dull. He must kneel devoutly for God was watching, if the priest could be believed – not that this fool cleric seemed to have much idea – but in Christ's name, it was hard. All his muscles complained, his back was aching from his tumble, and his head hurt abominably. It was the normal result of a tilt, but that was no comfort.

Yet over it all, William was aware of a thrilling eagerness. It was a curious sensation, this. A sort of glow emanated from his belly and warmed his heart at the thought that he would soon become a knight as he had always wanted. A knight, a full chivalrous member of Lord Hugh's host!

The service done, William avoided his father's company. Sir John was too serious and besides, William needed a drink to soothe the bruises and strains from his fall. William left Sir John at the church door and went to join his friends. Nick had already drunk a fair amount, but he'd made himself sick and now he was ready for more. William was a little wary, thinking that he'd do well to keep his head and avoid too much wine or ale, but he was thirsty and the prospect of a quart of Lord Hugh's ale proved too tempting.

They walked to the buttery and stood at the bar. It was hellishly hot in there, with the heat from candles and oil-lamps adding to the fug and odour of sweat from the servants who had worked all day in the sun on Lord Hugh's lands. The warmth made the faces of the serving-boys glisten and run with moisture, and it wasn't long before William felt the same.

At the bar, the group of young men ordered their drinks from a sweating pot-boy and took them outside to sit at a bench. Girls walked past and were leered at or respectfully acknowledged, depending upon their status. Serving wenches suffered if they approached too close to Nick, for his tunic stank of vomit, and he grabbed any who passed by.

'You should bathe and change your clothes,' William said as another girl screwed up her face in disgust and ran from Nick.

'What's the point? I'm going to drink a lot more before I collapse tonight. *Sir* Nick I become today. A knight! Hah! Give me two years and I'll be a banneret, just you see,' he said, trying to focus seriously on his friend.

William laughed. The ale made him glad to be alive. 'And I'll be Sir William. Here's to the knights of Oakhampton, eh?'

They all raised their jugs and pots, and soon after Nick stared into his jug and grumbled that he needed a refill. His face was pale and gleamed in the light of the torches in the court, and William was unpleasantly persuaded that he was about to be sick.

Nick glanced about him. 'Hey, you! Come here.'

Simon's servant Hugh heard the summons but chose to ignore the beckoning finger.

'I said come here, churl! Don't disobey a knight unless you want to feel my boot up your backside,' Nick growled, but even as Hugh hesitated, Nick bent over and spewed.

'That's better,' he gasped, wiping his mouth.

'You are revolting,' William said with disdain. 'Look at you. It's no wonder you've no prospect of marriage.'

323

'You think so? I could take any woman I wanted,' Nick belched. 'You! Fetch us more wine.'

'I'm fetching wine for my master,' Hugh mumbled, scowling at the ground.

William grinned. 'Which woman could you take, then?'

'Me? Well, none will be available tonight, but tomorrow . . . well, how about I take that little wriggle-arse from you? The one we saw in the crowds – with the angry father.' He sniggered at the memory of Simon's furious face.

'Little Edith? Ah, I don't know. I fear she prefers the subtle charms of a clean-living fellow like me.'

'Bollocks! She'd rattle me happily enough.'

'I'd wager a shilling you'd not take her with her permission,' William said.

'A shilling? It'll make it all the more worthwhile.'

'Only after I've had her, though. And then I'll have to become chaste for my wife.'

'Poor Alice,' Nick laughed. 'She doesn't realise what she'll miss in marrying you.' He reached for his jug, recalled that it was empty and glowered around. 'Where's that poxy servant gone?'

William stood. 'I'll fetch more ale.'

It was still crowded in there. Servants who were finished with their day's service in Lord Hugh's fields or members of his household seeking their daily ration, all stood more or less patiently waiting to be served.

Hugh was leaving with three jugs of wine on a tray as William entered. The squire grinned. Right – 'I'll take those.'

'You can't. They're for my master.'

'Too bad. Go and get more for him. These will do for me.'

'No.'

William drew himself up. 'You do realise who you're talking to, don't you? I am a knight. So let go of that tray! If you want more wine, get it from the bar.'

'Why don't you fetch your own drinks?'

'What is your name, fellow?'

'Hugh.'

'Well, Hugh. *You* go and get more wine from the bar. Because if you try to keep these, I'll see you regret it.'

'Something wrong, Will?'

Nick had thrust his face in through the door and was staring aggressively at Hugh.

'No, it's all fine,' William said, taking the tray from Hugh's reluctant hands.

Lady Helen Basset was late and she could already hear her husband's remonstration, feel the harsh slap of his hand on her face, on her rump. He would be furious.

This time, for the first time, he would be justified. He must never know what she had been doing. Day-dreaming about the man she had once promised to marry, long before she had met Walter, wondering what Sir Edmund would have been like as a husband. A part of her quickened to see him, but as soon as he spoke, she realised he was too soft for her. Not a real, vibrant man like Sir Walter. No, she had made a better choice. All she felt for Edmund was a tolerant sympathy, like a sister might feel for a brother.

It was last night that she had gone to meet him – the first time they had been together since that terrible day when he had been captured and ransomed by Sir John. Helen had been close to refusing to go, she was so petrified that her husband might find out – but then she told herself that since she was only going to ease the spirit of a man who had once been her lover, it was a matter of simple duty.

Squire Andrew had spoken to her so respectfully, so persuasively, on his master's behalf. Later, she had sneaked away with him, the squire cautiously scouting ahead, making sure that the coast was clear so her reputation couldn't suffer, and checking all the time that they were not being followed. At the river he went ahead and sought a quiet place and then left, soon after sending Sir Edmund to her. He remained on guard just out of earshot, to prevent anyone approaching.

Sir Edmund had changed so much since that fateful afternoon six years ago at Crukerne, when his future was devastated in the tournament. After Sir John had captured him, he was ruined, completely. He couldn't even afford a jug of wine. Sir John had taken everything – even the horse, which Sir Edmund had borrowed from a friend.

Helen was thrilled by his history: his escape to foreign lands, his apparent salvation when he found himself vassal to Earl Thomas, and finally his return to the West Country in search of a new master.

'I thought you would wait for me,' he told her.

'How could I?' she protested. 'I had no idea where you had gone, nor for how long.'

'So you wed the man who ruined me?'

His bitter tone had stung. 'What would you have had me do? Wait for a man who might have been dead?'

'No, my Lady, of course not.'

They had walked in silence then, she trying to think of something that would placate without patronising, while he scowled up at the castle.

'I must return,' she had said nervously at last. 'My husband . . .'

'Oh, the hell with him! What of *me*?'

'Edmund – I married Walter. I loved you, but that was a long time ago.'

'So you do not love me any more, Helen?' he had said with despair in his voice.

There was nothing she could do to ease Sir Edmund's envy; he must grow accustomed to the fact that he could not possess her – but against her better judgement she had agreed to meet him again later, after tonight's feast.

Helen hurried up the tunnel towards the castle's main entrance and stood a moment to settle her breathing. Fitting a serene, innocent expression to her face, she made her way to the hall's entrance.

Sir Walter's violence could terrify her, but it was thrilling as well. Most of the time he was a courteous, pleasing husband. He lived to satisfy her, with frequent assertions of his love for her, his utter and undying delight in her. His lovemaking was rough, but she found that satisfying, more so than she would some polite, insipid youth who might roll on to her and roll off with a calm murmur of gratitude. She wouldn't want that. She wanted a man with fire in his belly and loins.

Sometimes though, it was hard, when his jealousy came to the fore. And he detested to be kept waiting.

'My Lady, you are alone?'

'I am going to meet my husband.'

Squire William was feeling good after the wine. Following on top of the ale, it hit his empty stomach like a flame, filling him with the sense that he was all-powerful and irresistible.

Alice would soon change her mind about marrying him once she saw him in his knightly finery, he thought optimistically. As for Edith Puttock, he'd be able to rattle her as soon as he got her alone. Her languishing expression when he was knocked from his horse told him that. She'd also let him bull her just to tweak the nose of her father. The Bailiff would be very angry indeed when he heard. His fury would be over-whelming, William thought contentedly. Edith might need protestations of undying love to get her to lift her skirts for him, but if it was necessary, William could promise marriage. If she made problems later, it would be his word against hers. And who would believe a sulky girl's claims against the word of a knight?

As the night grew more chill his friends had moved into the buttery itself; he had left them there while he came out here to empty his bladder against the hall's wall. It was while he was adjusting his hose that the woman had approached. It was only the second time he'd seen her but, as before, the sight of her fired his blood. She was beauti-ful, he thought, drunkenly certain that she couldn't refuse him.

'You must give me a kiss, Lady, before I let you pass.'

'Sir, you are pestering me.'

'I only want a kiss, Lady. No one would ever know.'

'Leave me,' she snarled. 'I don't have time to play with children.'

'Me – a child?' William gasped. He'd teach the cow a lesson. His arms grabbed her before she could run or cry out. Ignoring the guards who meandered along the battlements, William pulled her towards him and sought her lips.

'Leave me!' she gasped.

'Child, am I? Have a feel of this!' he demanded, taking her hand and pulling it towards his hose. 'I've got a better prick than your husband, I'll wager!'

His arm was around her waist, his other hand slipping down to her buttocks, then up to her waist and breast. There was nothing she could do to prevent him. He held her too firmly.

'Get off me, you drunken bastard!' she managed.

'Not until you kiss me,' William leered.

Hugh appeared in the doorway and quickly crossed to them. 'Lady, are you all right?'

It was enough to break William's concentration. Helen pulled away, then snapped her knee up to his groin, feeling the softness as her knee connected. His breath left his body in a short gasp and his hands were off her. She walked past him, head high, and gave Hugh a coin. 'Thank you,' she said quietly.

'No, Lady,' Hugh said, glowering at the wheezing figure of William. 'Thank *you*. That sight was payment enough.'

Glancing back haughtily at the moaning William, she sniffed and entered the hall.

She didn't recognise Andrew in the doorway. She just pushed past him.

CHAPTER TWENTY-FOUR

The feast was intended to celebrate the magnificence of the tournament's opening and give people a taste for the events to come, but Alice sat there, waiting for it to begin, her appetite nonexistent. The choicest meats would taste of nothing; mere ashes would have been as good. The wine was like vinegar, the smoke stung her eyes, and the raucous enjoyment of the other men in the place was all but intolerable. She felt sick with worry about her man, terrified that he might die, appalled to have seen his near-fatal fall from the horse.

Odo had ensured that Alice's maid and two gentlewomen had attended to her after her collapse. All Alice could remember was waking and hoping it had all been a nightmare. She prayed that the vision of Geoffrey being hurled from his horse by the evil lance in William's hand was but a dream, a hideous scene sent by a Mare to terrify her.

But as soon as she awoke, Alice found herself staring into the compassionate eyes of a female attendant – and realised that it had been no dream. Her husband was lying at death's door, and she could do nothing to help. Rising, she learned that Geoffrey had been taken to a chamber near the castle's hall and she hurried there, ignoring the servants who tried to bar her way and prevent her from entering. 'He is my husband!' she declared, with tears in her eyes.

The physician and priest could give her no positive response. 'If he is to heal, it is in God's hands,' the priest said, trying to soothe her, but in his eyes she could see the terrible truth. Geoffrey wouldn't live; she was sure of it.

Now, at the feast, her mind was trying to come to grips with this new terror. Without Geoffrey, she was entirely alone. Her sole support and protection was dying and there was nothing she could do. She had sat at his side, gripping his hand, directing his face to the altar and crucifix and begging him to pray for his safety while she too pleaded with God, but there was no response. The hand remained quiescent in hers, the breathing so shallow and quiet that several times already she thought he had died.

What could she do? If he died, she was entirely at the mercy of Sir John. Marriage to William. The very thought brought a sob to her throat and a feeling of nausea, and now she was expected to join in a feast!

It was while she was considering this that she saw William himself swaggering towards her.

He was drunk – that was obvious. His face was flushed, his manner truculent. Christ, how she detested the haughty youth! He saw her and gave a hawkish grin. 'Ready to marry at last?'

'I am already married.'

'Ah, but you'll soon be a widow,' he said dismissively, and belched. 'At least I can offer you security. So long as you're good for breeding, that's the main thing.'

She felt her face blanch. 'You think I would wed you? I should rather die.'

'You'll have little choice, my Lady,' he sneered.

'I am married already. I am the wife of Geoffrey.'

'If you want to remain known as the wife of the Coward of Boroughbridge, fine. You may not like me much, my Lady, but at least I'm no deserter.'

'You dare to slander a man because he's unwell?' she spat. '*That* is cowardice of the worst sort. You are contemptible.'

'Perhaps,' he agreed easily. 'But I'm also alive, vigorous and soon to be wealthy when I have married you.'

'I will *never* marry you!' she screamed, standing.

The room fell silent, and William realised too late that everyone was listening to their conversation. He gave a nervous smile to the watching men and women and tried to walk away before Alice could embarrass him further.

'I will never marry you,' she repeated, then fell sobbing back on her bench. The men at either side pulled away a little, unwilling to become involved in the woman's problem. That could only lead to trouble with their own wives, were they to challenge Alice's tormenter.

She had no one. No one. Except . . .

Except her messenger.

It was a few moments later that Baldwin entered the hall with his servant. There was a tense atmosphere, he thought, glancing about him, despite all the finery.

Alice swept from the place as he walked inside; behind her Baldwin saw William, chatting to some of his friends. The din they were making did not please Baldwin, who thought that youths should learn to control their drinking. He deliberately chose a seat at a more peaceful table.

Simon and his family had not yet arrived, he saw. Nor had Lord Hugh. Baldwin stopped a servant and took a cup of wine, sipping idly while his attention ranged over the guests already gathered for this important meal, hoping to spot a friendly face, but not even Coroner Roger had appeared.

At last he saw a man he recognised. Andrew, Sir Edmund's squire, walked towards him with a set expression. 'Sir Baldwin, may I speak to you a moment?'

'Of course.'

'Outside, perhaps – where it is quiet?'

Baldwin raised his eyebrows, but assented and followed the man out to the court, accompanied by his own man Edgar.

'Sir, I must first apologise. I have seen your sword. *Seen the cross.*'

Baldwin pursed his lips, but said nothing, gazing fixedly at Andrew. Templars were heretics and outlaws; any who didn't confess and join another Order were to be punished. It hadn't occurred to Sir Baldwin that he could run too much of a risk of discovery here in Devon, but now someone had seen the evidence of his 'guilt'. 'So?' he grated.

'Sir, that is how I know you can be trusted. I was a Templar myself – a sergeant. I wanted to warn you about Squire William.' He told Baldwin what had happened out in the yard and how Hugh had prevented the molestation of Lady Helen.

'Thank you for the information, but what do you expect me to do about this?' Baldwin protested. 'It is nothing to do with me.'

'It was the Bailiff I wanted to warn, Sir Baldwin. It is said that his daughter is enamoured of Squire William, that she might intend to marry him. Many heard the Bailiff and his daughter arguing about Squire William – yet only just now, Squire William told Lady Alice that *she* must wed him. He is playing with the Bailiff's daughter. He will seduce her and toss her aside. That is the measure of the man.'

'You are sure of this?'

'Sir, if you doubt me, ask anyone in this company – or speak to the Bailiff's man. He saw it all.'

'I am grateful to you,' Baldwin said, but in fact he was reluctant to become involved in the family of any man, even his best friend. Simon would be sure to resent his interference, quite rightly. 'Why do you not go straight to the Bailiff yourself?'

'He would be more likely to listen to you, Sir Baldwin.' Andrew looked earnestly at him. 'Sir, I know all the squires. They are young – I am older. I could not be made knight, not with my meagre lands, so I remain a squire, but I think I understand chivalry even so. If William is prepared to molest Lady Helen, is prepared to swear that he will marry Lady Alice, then how honourable can his intentions be towards the Bailiff's daughter? He would ruin that young woman, merely to satisfy his own momentary lust.'

Baldwin looked at Edgar. The servant nodded and Baldwin grunted. 'Very well. I suppose I shall have to look into it.'

'You will speak to the Bailiff tonight?'

'No. I shall consider what action to take and when I have decided, I shall see to it that young Edith is safe from whatever danger. Precipitate action tonight might not be wise. No. I shall have to think carefully.'

'I thank you, Sir Baldwin.'

Baldwin watched the squire bow and return to the hall. 'What do you make of that, Edgar?'

'I think that he would prefer to see knights and squires behaving decently.'

'Then he wishes for bloody miracles,' Baldwin said. 'Come! I believe there is to be a meal shortly. Let us eat.'

He walked to the door, and was about to step inside when he caught a glimpse of white. Off near the chapel door he saw Alice, her head bowed, talking to Odo. The herald looked magnificent in his tabard, the gold wires and purple silks catching the torchlight and glittering with each breath of wind, but Baldwin's keen glance took in Alice's miserable expression; she had a look of near-despair.

'Yet how should she look while she waits to hear from the physician about her husband?' he mused.

There was no comfort he could offer her. He left her with Odo and strode indoors, taking his seat at Simon's side.

Odo was saddened to see the look on Alice's face. She looked like a young girl who has become separated from her parents, bewildered and overwhelmed.

He followed her out to the yard, and was pleased to see how her face eased ever so slightly to come across a friend and ally.

'How is Geoffrey?' she asked.

'Last I saw, he was no better, I fear, my Lady,' he said gently.

'Oh, God! How can You do this? Why take his life when there are so many others who deserve death?' she demanded, clenching her fists impotently at the stars.

'Lady, it isn't for us to say who deserves life and who doesn't.'

'Don't chide me, Odo. My husband lies dying and his killer wants me to marry him.'

'Refuse him.'

'I am ward to his father.'

'Perhaps he would make a good husband,' Odo ventured tentatively.

'William? Never!' she spat. 'I need Geoffrey. If he dies, I shall have no other husband. God, that this should have happened! Tomorrow, once he was knighted, he was going to declare our marriage. One day more and I would have been safe. Now I can't even declare my love, for Lord Hugh must listen to Sir John if he denies me. Sir John is a *man*,' she added with vitriolic emphasis that quite unnerved Odo.

Then she realised how her words might have upset him. 'My friend, I am sorry. I didn't mean to cause you any concern. You have been a good and loyal accomplice to my husband and I.'

'I am a herald and wish only to serve honourable men and their wives.'

'Thank you. I only wish you could serve us now.'

Those words rang in his ears now as he watched the knight-ing of William and five of his friends.

All had bathed in scented water and eaten liquorice to cleanse their breath, before visiting the chapel to confess their sins ready for this ceremony.

Now they stood arrayed before Lord Hugh in fine clothes, all of which held deep symbolic importance, for Lord Hugh wanted all to witness that he sought to ensure that knights dubbed by him would recognise their responsibilities. As a herald Odo could note each stage and its importance.

The selection of clothing came first. The six wore white robes to remined them of the cleanliness of their bodies; crimson cloaks because they must shed their blood when God commanded it; stockings as brown as the earth in which they would be buried, to remind them to prepare for their own deaths.

Servants bound pure white belts about their waists to show that they must exercise restraint and chastity. Then there was a short delay and a few moments later a line of squires entered the hall with pillows in their hands. On the pillows were their new spurs, all gleaming gold in the candle-light. They flashed and shone as they were fixed to the boots of the waiting men, each of them looking a little awed as the significance of the moment caught at their imagination.

More squires moved forward now, with the swords. They went to the respective owners and tied the belts about their waists. As all knew, the sword was the most important symbol of all: the two edges showed that justice and loyalty should always go together, that a knight must always protect a poor or weakly man from a bully, while the cross of the quillons showed that all served Christ.

It was at this moment that Lord Hugh moved forward. His sword was sheathed at his side and he stood a moment contemplating the six. When the room had fallen absolutely silent, Lord Hugh stepped up to the men and struck each on the shoulder with his clenched fist. Each bowed his head while the blow was given, and when they looked up again, each truly did appear to have been reborn. Pride and the knowledge of the honour done to them shone in their eyes.

Odo nodded to himself. All were knights. Each had been dubbed. It was a day none of them would ever forget.

Nor would the others, he decided as he took in the faces around him. Most of the audience was composed of families or friends of the new knights, with one or two women watching, thrilled, as their betrothed men became marriageable. Among the remaining squires he saw boredom, amusement and yes, some envy, but little else until he came to Andrew's face and saw the naked hatred there as the older squire stared straight at William.

That was enough to depress Odo. What had begun as a powerful display of chivalry and honour had been spoiled by that expression on Andrew's face, but just as he thought that, any remaining pleasure was shattered as the physician entered the hall and peered about the place.

As he approached Alice, she began to shake her head in frantic denial, and gave a shriek of horror.

The next morning, Simon was in a filthy temper after a poor night's sleep. Although Lord Hugh had celebrated the knighting of so many youths along with everyone else, the discovery of the second body had made him thoughtful, while whenever Simon caught the eye of the King Herald, the man's manner left no ambiguity about his opinion of the Bailiff.

As if that was not sufficient, he also had the matter of his daughter's deception and apparent love affair with the insolent, overbearing heir of Sir John of Crukerne. It was not a match Simon could sanction, not after the way that Edith and William had deceived him. Edith's behaviour had hurt him – although William's was no surprise. He was his father's son.

Edith might not be quite the apple of Simon's eye as once she had been, but she was still his daughter, and Simon was convinced that a father-in-law like Sir John would make her life miserable. Also there was another factor to be measured: Simon had always felt that a man's son often grew to be like his father, and he had a fear that, should Edith marry William, the latter would, in years to come, be more rough, more casually violent and cruel. Especially when given a focus for his bile – the daughter of a Bailiff. Simon could almost hear the scorn in his voice: 'And your father was little better than a peasant, was he? No wonder you don't know how to behave among the nobility!' In his mind's eye he could see Edith weeping herself to sleep after he had taken her roughly and unkindly, too filled with wine to care about her feelings.

Simon was certain that she would have a miserable time of it should she wed the boy, but that didn't stop her proudly declaring her love for him. The Bailiff only prayed that she hadn't been stupid enough to spread her legs for him.

He walked out of the castle and down to the tented area, and here he saw Baldwin. The knight was resting on a low stool with a cup in his hand, while to his side sat a very hungover-looking Coroner Roger. 'Wine, Simon?' Baldwin said heartily. 'I hear it takes away sour tastes from too much food the night before.'

'A jug would be better,' Simon said, noticing how Roger winced and swallowed on hearing wine mentioned. 'Ale for you, Coroner?'

'Bailiff, you are a cruel and vicious man. Has anyone told you that before?'

Baldwin jerked his head to his servant, but it was unnecessary. Edgar had already marched into the tent to fetch the men their drink.

'How is Margaret this fine morning?' he enquired once Simon had taken his ease on the trestle table holding Baldwin's armour.

'She's all right – if you ignore her tiredness and annoyance at Edith's attitude.'

'So there has been no truce?'

'Truce be buggered! There'll be no peace until I take a belt to her backside. Even Hugh has given up. He left Edith to my tender care last evening. Usually he would guard her to her chamber, but not in her present mood!'

Baldwin shrugged. Sometimes young creatures had to be punished, but he wasn't sure that a beating would achieve much in Edith's case. 'What of the murders? Is there anything new?' he asked, trying to delay the moment when he would have to impart the unpalatable information Squire Andrew had given to him about William's behaviour and intentions.

'Christ's bones! I am baffled,' Simon grunted into his jug. 'What do you think?'

Baldwin glanced up at his servant's face. 'You've heard the gossips talk, Edgar. What do they say?'

Edgar spoke reluctantly. 'Many here still seem to believe that the Bailiff killed the two men, because they heard the King Herald accuse him; and there is a belief that Lord Hugh only protected him because Lord Hugh *himself* told you to kill them, sir.'

'Me! *Me!*' Simon exclaimed. 'Why should I agree to murder that pair of galloping sodomites?'

Edgar coughed. 'They say you were paid exceedingly well, Bailiff.'

'But that is ridiculous! Why should Lord Hugh want to punish them? Has anyone an explanation for that?'

'They say that the collapse of the stands reflects badly upon him personally. Even the failure at Crukerne, which was paid for by Sir John, enraged Lord Hugh because he had guests of his own in the stand. And any man who insults or steals from Lord Hugh's vassal is stealing from Lord Hugh himself. He is proud of his status.'

'You see how these things get about?' Baldwin grumbled. 'We must solve the matter as swiftly as possible – not only as a matter of justice to the two dead men, but also to wipe the dirt from your name, old friend.'

'I have paid a fellow to ask questions at the taverns and alehouses, and one innkeeper says he saw Hal in his inn, drinking with another man. He didn't get a good look at the man that Hal was with, but the pair of 'em left late at night. Where could they have gone?' Coroner Roger asked, adding thoughtfully, 'We haven't yet spoken to the watchman who guarded Hal's tent.'

'A good point, Coroner,' Baldwin said. 'What facts do we have? We know the killer must be fit and healthy. Anyone who could carry Wymond down from the hill and back inside his tent must have a certain amount of strength.'

'Wonderful! So almost anyone among all the contestants here could be the man,' Simon said sarcastically. '*And* the servants, *and* most of the local farmers – *and* many of the townspeople. That makes our task *so* much easier.'

'Simon, calm yourself. We shall prove your innocence,' Baldwin said seriously.

'I'm sorry. I've never felt like this before,' Simon muttered, passing a hand over his brow. He felt fractious and peppery from lack of sleep and a surfeit of worry.

Baldwin said patiently, 'Let us just whittle the possible culprits down a little, shall we? We know that Hal and Wymond could have been at the site at any hour of the day or night. Who else could have been there? At night there is a nominal curfew, and no one but Lord Hugh's men should be in the area.'

'So?' Simon demanded.

'The watchmen may have seen someone. Surely if there was a stranger about, they'd know.'

'And what if they didn't?' Coroner Roger scoffed.

'We have a number of possible motives for these murders,' Baldwin said slowly. 'We know that the three were thought of as spies, which would have made them enemies; we know that people reckon Lord Hugh could have wanted them dead . . .'

'That's rubbish!' Simon protested.

'Possibly,' Baldwin agreed, 'but we have to consider it nonetheless. Then there is the point that these men have all in their time been involved with building stands which have collapsed.'

'What of it?' Coroner Roger said.

'I cannot stop myself from returning to the idea that there could be a desire for revenge, and that it is *that* which is causing these murders.'

Odo saw them leave Baldwin's tent and was tempted to join them, but decided against it. He had passed a cold, lonely night, wishing that he had a warm, comforting woman in his bed with him.

When he had told Baldwin that he needed only a tune, his ready wit, some poetry and a purse of money, he hadn't counted on having all four thwarted by a malicious King Herald. Most of the *diseurs* were living up at the castle, but not Odo. Mark had set him to stay in the field in his inadequate tent, keeping an eye on the people to stop fights while Mark himself took full advantage of Lord Hugh's hospitality and wine.

No, Odo had woken up, shivering and lonely. He wouldn't be good company for anyone. Besides, Simon and Baldwin had the appearance of men who were about to perform an unpleasant duty – especially since they were joined by the Coroner – and Odo was happy to leave them to it. He already had enough on his mind from the previous night.

Poor Alice had been overwhelmed when she heard of Geoffrey's death. She had fallen to the floor and had to be carried out and taken to a chamber in the bailey, which had necessarily dampened the festivities. People whispered that she would be unlikely to survive her young husband's death by many days. Odo, who had acted as the couple's go-between, was upset to see such beauty devastated by so great a sorrow.

Still, the sun was already warm, even this early, and he had bought a pot of warmed wine and a hot pastry to break his fast. To Odo there was nothing more delightful than a good breakfast, with the knowledge that the day held little in the way of work. After all, no one in their right mind could call the job of *diseur* strenuous.

It was pleasant here near the river. The water rushing past was noisy but comforting. Even at night it was soothing, although Odo would have preferred to sleep at the castle, which he would have done, had it not been for that fool, King Herald.

'Talk of the devil,' Odo murmured to himself as a shadow fell over his open tent-flap.

'Still eating?' Mark Tyler snapped. 'You've got work to get on with.'

'I am just finishing my meal,' Odo said calmly.

'Didn't you eat enough last night?'

'No, I didn't have time. As you well know.' Odo had been ordered by Mark to play music to Lord Hugh and his guests, and when he had finished there was practically no food left. Another of Tyler's little jokes. Mark himself had retired early.

'Oh, I was thinking that perhaps you didn't sleep well, and *that* gave you an appetite!'

Odo smiled. 'It was very quiet here, King Herald. All the knights and their squires were tired and slept soundly, and so did I. Any noise was drowned by that lovely river. It smothers even the loudest snores.'

As he had expected, a tremor of annoyance passed over Tyler's face on hearing this, and with a stern command to finish his food and get to the field ready for the day's jousting, Tyler whirled around and – well, if he had been a woman, Odo would have said he flounced off. Tyler wanted Odo to sleep badly. That was why he had installed him here, in the midst of the squires and knights.

Mark Tyler had instinctively disliked Odo from the first moment they had met. He had let his eyes run slowly down the other herald's tabard, taking in the rich cloth before sneeringly asking how long he had been a herald, as if its freshness was proof of his incompetence. His words to Odo had been insulting, sly digs at his background and training. Mark Tyler had been in the Courtenay service for many long years, whereas Odo had learned his trade in the King's continental lands, wandering from one lord to another.

Yet for all Mark's apparent contempt for Odo, his fear of him was almost palpable. He was petrified that he could lose his position, and saw Odo as the threat that could topple him from his perch.

This privately amused Odo. He had not taken any interest in Mark's position when he first arrived. He was happier wandering, as so many heralds and *diseurs* did, learning new songs, new tunes, and constantly looking out for deeds to record, new coats-of-arms to memorise. Every so often he would hear of a tournament and ride to it, offering his services to the lord who was patronising the event. He would remain there a while, partaking of the lord's generosity, but always happy to be moving on again.

Mark's antipathy towards him had made him react, and once having sensed the possibility of taking over the post of King Herald, he was tempted. Lord Hugh looked after his men, and those in his household lacked nothing: good food, new suits of clothing each year, quantities of wine or ale each day . . . and wherever the Lord stayed, warm rooms and even palliasses. As King Herald, Odo could even expect a decent *bed* on occasion. The prospect was appealing.

Of course Mark Tyler would have to leave first, but that was no problem. From the little that Odo had heard from Sir Peregrine, the knight banneret clearly considered the King Herald to be incompetent and thought Mark Tyler should be replaced. He had said as much only yesterday. When Simon and Baldwin had rushed away to seek Edith, Sir Peregrine had muttered to Odo, 'That cretin Tyler will have to go. He's a liability – useless and an embarrassment. After your efforts, I'll be happy to drop a good word in Lord Hugh's ear for you.'

'That is very kind of you,' he had replied, 'but I am content.'

'Content to wander for the rest of your life? Don't be a fool. Here you'd have an easy life, and with your singing and playing, you'd please Lord Hugh. Take my advice: when you're asked, accept the post with gratitude.'

Odo stood and stretched. His future was all very well, but right now he was a mere herald set to control knights and squires during their jousting and here, in the tented area afterwards, he was a watchman responsible for preventing fights escalating into pitched battles.

Setting his mazer on a small table, he left his tent, nodding to a servant at the tent opposite and making for the fighting area.

Everyone was awake now and the noise was all-but deafening. Hawkers bellowed their wares, girls cried out about the quality of their bread or fruits, dogs barked and horses whinnied. As he progressed towards the jousting field, Odo could hear the snarling from a ring in which two dogs fought, the hoarse calls of cocks fighting, men cursing and swearing, cart-wheels creaking and groaning under the weight of cloth or food. And all about was the chatter of people discussing the coming events.

No, he corrected himself. Not all were discussing the events: several were talking about the murders.

It had been odd to see the Bailiff turn pale and then redden yesterday when Mark had accused him of murder. True, Bailiff Puttock *had* threatened the two dead men – but only in the same way that others could have done. In fact, even as Mark Tyler accused Simon of murder, Odo had thought that of the two men, the red, porcine features of the King Herald looked infinitely more likely to be those of a murderer than the tall and pleasant-featured Bailiff. Odo wondered whether Sir Peregrine had also thought that. In any case, it was plain that Lord Hugh did not intend to have his hired Bailiff accused during his tournament. He had stepped in sharply enough when Odo had pointed at the confrontation.

Odo would be interested to know why Lord Hugh was so keen to protect Simon. But it was probably for no special reason.

He carried on to the stands and stood with arms akimbo, considering the watchmen as they strolled about the place, thrusting their heavy staffs into the longer grasses in a lacklustre manner. They might have been told to look about for possible assassins or dead bodies, but their every movement showed that they would prefer to be in their rooms with jugs of ale.

Yes, it would be interesting to be a member of Lord Hugh's household, he reckoned. And as this reflection occurred to him, he caught sight of a slim, frail-looking figure walking along the riverbank. 'Thank God,' he breathed with real pleasure. 'I'm glad you've recovered a little, Lady Alice.'

CHAPTER TWENTY-FIVE

Edith had been determined to give her parents the slip for at least one hour in the day to see her squire, and yet it proved almost impossible. Even Hugh, who had been her ally in her last attempts to see William, had grown reticent, mumbling about how angry her father, his master, would be if Hugh were to help her.

After breaking their fast, Simon had hurried away, his face set into an anxious mask, and Margaret had chewed fretfully at her lip as she watched him leave the hall. Edith knew that her parents were both concerned after Simon had been accused, but it was too stupid as far as she was concerned. No one could seriously believe that her father might have had anything to do with the murders; Lord Hugh himself had squashed the rumours, telling everyone that Simon was guiltless. In her youth and innocence, Edith found it impossible to believe that a man so plainly honourable could be a serious suspect.

Margaret had seen men accused on less evidence and hanged. She knew, from what Simon and Baldwin had let slip over the years, that it was easy enough for a vindictive or foolish man to persuade a gullible jury to condemn an innocent man and, having felt the waves of hatred at the *ber frois* yesterday, she had no wish to see her husband set before a local jury or the county's grand jury. He had enough enemies among the families of those whom he had sent to the gallows who would be happy to pay others to perjure themselves or bribe a jury to find him guilty.

'If only we could leave here now,' she said.

'Mother, it'll all be fine,' Edith said dispassionately.

'Don't be a fool, Edith. You were there yesterday – you must see your father's in danger,' Margaret snapped.

'He'll be safe. Lord Hugh won't want to embarrass the Abbot of Tavistock.'

Margaret bit back a sharp rejoinder. 'The Abbot is a long way away.'

'Don't be angry with me, Mother.'

'How can I not be angry after the way you deceived your father and me?'

'I didn't deceive you, I just—'

'You deliberately concealed your behaviour with that youth.'

'He's not a "youth", he's a knight. Wouldn't you like me to marry the son of a nobleman? He'll inherit his father's manor some day.'

Margaret felt a headache begin to throb dully behind her temples. 'Edith, I don't want to argue with you. You are not to see that boy again yet. I need time to bring your father round to agree to let you see him. Then you can decide whether you seriously want to marry him.'

'Very well, Mother,' Edith said meekly. 'I love him. I could tell that when I saw him fall from his horse, but I won't see him secretly if you don't want me to. Still, I'd like to watch the jousting. There can't be any harm in that.'

'I suppose not,' Margaret said wearily as a figure appeared in the doorway.

It was Sir Peregrine and he peered about the room as he walked inside.

'Good day,' Margaret said. When he stepped into the shaft of light from the hall's window, she saw how exhausted he was. His face was lined and pale. 'Are you well?'

'Just tired,' he said, smiling. 'While there is a murderer about, I serve my lord by keeping guard outside his door. I didn't sleep.'

'I'm sure my father and Sir Baldwin will catch the man soon,' Edith said.

'I hope you are right. I've seen enough death with Hal and Wymond. And it's not good for Lord Hugh to have these things going on at his tournament.'

'I wouldn't like to have to pull about dead bodies like theirs,' Edith said, curling her lip.

Sir Peregrine gave her a dry but indulgent smile. 'I'm not surprised.' It was true. She was a lovely young thing, and it would have been unthinkable to Sir Peregrine, who had no children, that such a fragile beauty should attend an inquest. Especially one with two such hideously ruined bodies. 'You are suited to love and life,' he added quietly, 'not to mayhem and murder.' He bade them a good morning and hastened away.

She tossed her head spiritedly. 'Love?'

'Edith!' her mother said warningly.

'Oh, I can't even talk to other men, now, Mother?'

'Not if you are going to be rude, no.'

'Rude? I see no—'

'Enough! Edith, you will remain here in the castle until you learn to be civil.'

Edith gaped at the injustice. 'What? But then I'm miss all the jousting . . . You can't mean it?'

'I do mean it. You will remain here until you learn to be polite. I can't trust you, not even when you are with me and Hugh. You proved that when you went off with that boy yesterday.'

'Very well, Mother,' Edith said, and bowed her head. 'I shall go and walk on the walls, then. At least I can see a little from there.'

She turned and was about to leave the room when she heard her mother command Hugh to accompany her. 'Don't you trust me?' she flashed out.

'No.'

After asking another watchman near the castle's gate, Baldwin, Simon and Coroner Roger were given directions to find a man called Fletcher, the watchman set to protect Hal on the night of his murder. He was sitting at a bench nursing a jug of ale.

Coroner Roger stood squarely before him. 'Are you Fletcher?' On seeing the man nod, he continued, 'And were you the man sent to guard Hal Sachevyll's tent the night before last?'

Baldwin watched as Fletcher set his mug down with a sigh and inclined his head again. The watchman was a lean, rangy man, probably in his late forties, from the look of him. His hair was bleached white from long days in the open, and his eyes had the dark intensity of a Celt, but he was a shrivelled man, worn and broken by too many disasters. He had the same appearance of desperation in his eyes that Baldwin had seen in the faces of peasants during the famine.

Giving the Coroner a significant look, Baldwin was pleased to see Roger shrug and allow Baldwin to continue. Unsure how best to proceed, Baldwin took a seat beside the man, contemplating the dusty, baked soil at his feet. 'You were chosen to protect Hal – why was that? There were many other watchmen about.'

'It is because I live alone. The other men about here have wives and children to return to at night, but my family is dead.'

'I am sorry. The famine?'

'No, sir. I was working in my lord's fields when my house caught fire. The thatch. My family was inside and they perished. I could hear them.' He shivered, his eyes focused on something far away.

Baldwin was silent a moment. The thought of losing a family in such a way was hideous. 'So you are often selected for duties like this?'

'Yes, sir.'

'Did you see anyone that night?'

'No, sir. I went there as soon as I was ordered. I had nothing better to do. I don't sleep well. I . . . I can hear my wife's screams when I dream, and I prefer not to. So when I was called, I rose immediately. I was there outside his tent a little after nightfall.'

'And there was no one near?'

'No. I saw the girl, Alice, but no one else. In fact, I was surprised that there was no sign of Hal himself. I assumed he must be asleep, for there was no sound from his tent, and when I scratched at a guy rope, there was no response. I just thought he was dead to the world, exhausted by all his work.'

'What time did you leave?'

'It was daylight. I was very tired by then.'

'I can imagine. After staying up all night.'

Fletcher turned his gaze upon Baldwin. 'I haven't slept properly for two years or more, Sir Baldwin. It's nothing new.'

Simon interrupted with some impatience. 'Your life is sad, no doubt, man, but we need to know who was out and about that night. There was someone lying in the grass next morning pretending to be pissed out of his mind. Did you see him?'

'No.'

'*Think!* There must have been something,' Simon pressed him irascibly. 'In Christ's name, you must have seen or heard *somebody*!'

Baldwin glanced at his friend. Simon sounded as though he was close to the end of his tether. The last two days, especially with that fat fool Tyler accusing him of murder, had taken their toll. Now the Bailiff was out of patience, and his attitude was putting Fletcher on edge.

'Fletcher, look at me,' Baldwin said softly, holding up a hand to silence Simon. 'Now, think back. When you were standing there outside the tent, was there any noise, any disturbance at all?'

Fletcher sipped at his ale thoughtfully, then he remembered: 'Yes, there *was* something. I reckoned it was a badger or a fox – the buggers are all over the place at night. But it stopped and I thought it must have gone.'

'Where was this?'

'In the bushes near the river.'

'You know where Hal was found?' Baldwin asked.

'Yes – and it would have been about there.'

Simon would have spoken but Baldwin shot him a look, then said, 'It strikes you as strange now, does it? Why?'

'I heard something in there, rustling, but it stopped.'

Coroner Roger couldn't hold himself back. 'That's not unusual. Noises happen all night.'

'Yes, Sir Roger,' Baldwin explained mildly, 'but a fox or badger would have made more noise in running away again as soon as it smelled a man.'

'That's right.' Fletcher was frowning now. 'It never ran.'

'That's because our murderer saw no need to. He wanted to dump his body – but you prevented him,' Baldwin said.

'Why'd he want to put Hal back in the tent?' Simon demanded. 'You thought Wymond was there as a message – perhaps to Hal. Well, it looks like you could have been right, but why leave Hal there?'

'It would show that the two murders were connected,' Baldwin hazarded. 'Perhaps there was a message in that?'

Coroner Roger frowned at him. 'You mean this killer could be planning to murder again?'

Baldwin was silent a moment. When he spoke he had been thinking aloud, he hadn't considered the consequences of his words – but now he slowly moved his head in agreement. 'I am afraid so,' he said heavily.

'And that means there may be another body out there waiting for us,' the Coroner grunted. 'Jesus! What a disaster!'

Baldwin turned back to the watchman. He spoke soothingly. 'You see how important all this is? Fletcher, you said that you saw Alice. Where was she, and how late was this?'

'It was at the darkest hour. I saw her walking among the trees at the bank of the river.'

'Was this before or after the rustling?'

'Oh, some time before.'

'Then we can ignore her,' Baldwin said. 'If she was seen by you, she would have seen you as well. A murderer wouldn't bring a body to a place where a witness stood. It is only people you saw *after* the rustling with whom we need concern ourselves.'

'The drunk in the field wasn't a woman, either,' Simon said.

'The drunk could have been an innocent,' Baldwin said. 'We do not know for sure that he was involved.'

'The only man I saw was late,' Fletcher said, frowning. 'It was as dawn was breaking and the camp was coming alive. All the folks were waking and I saw the squire.'

'Which?' Baldwin asked.

'The one with that knight from Gloucester. Sir Edmund.'

'Squire Andrew?' Simon said.

'That's the one. He had been in the trees and as the light came I saw him walking back from the stands. He'd been there a while, I reckon.'

They asked more questions but Fletcher either wouldn't or couldn't help them, and soon he rose, saying he had duties. Baldwin waved him away.

'This is mad!' Coroner Roger declared. 'We hear that the man was likely in the bushes with his dead victim, and now we hear that another man was walking about the place.'

'Andrew, yes,' Baldwin said. He was watching Fletcher as he walked away. 'What was the girl doing out at that time of night?'

'And this Andrew,' Simon pointed out.

'Yes,' Baldwin agreed. Fletcher was swallowed up by the crowds, but Baldwin remained staring after him a while. The watchman's story had touched him. Fletcher's life had lost meaning and sense, that was clear, and yet he continued to perform his duties like any honourable vassal. Baldwin wasn't sure that he would have been able to carry on so stoically if he had heard his own wife and daughter dying in a fire. The thought was enough to make him feel faintly queasy.

Andrew had been near the stands. Why? Then another thought struck him and he drew in his breath sharply.

'What, Sir Baldwin?' the Coroner asked.

'We have heard of the stands collapsing during a tournament. What if a man saw his family die there? Wouldn't he want revenge against those who killed them?'

'Perhaps. You suggested that earlier.'

'It would be justification for killing the men who profited by using rotten wood. There were three of them: the banker, Benjamin, the carpenter, Wymond, and the architect, Hal.'

'I see what you mean.'

'No – I must be wrong,' Baldwin said. 'If Hal's body was going to be put into the tent as a message, surely the killer sought another victim?'

'If he wanted to leave a message. But the placement could have been merely symbolic, to show that the killer had murdered again for a purpose, for revenge,' Coroner Roger said.

Just then they heard the scream and all three men rose simultaneously. 'What in God's name . . .' Coroner Roger began.

Simon had paled. 'God's bones! Please, not another murder!'

*   *   *

'Come on, Hugh! Just a quick wander down into the arena. It can't hurt.'

'Your mother said no. She said to stay here in the castle.'

'That's so unfair! Why should she tell me what I can and can't do? I'm not a silly little girl.'

'Stamping your feet won't make me change my mind. Your mother gave me orders and I won't disobey her. Especially after the look of those men in the *ber frois*. It's too dangerous.'

'That was *yesterday*!' she said scathingly. 'Just because that man was found dead. We'll be all right today. They've had time to sleep on it.'

'You think an English mob forgets after one night's sleep?'

'Hugh, don't be sarcastic! No, but most of them don't know who I am anyway. It won't matter to them having a young girl walking in their midst.'

'Mistress Edith, if only one of them takes it into his head that you are the daughter of the Bailiff, you could be in danger. It's not right.'

'I want to see my friend. He's just been knighted – *knighted*! Can you understand what that means to me? I want to congratulate him.'

'When Master Simon says so.'

'I love him, Hugh.'

'You only think you do.'

'Don't patronise me!'

'Eh?'

'I love him as surely as you love your wife.'

'That's different!'

'You can deny it as hotly as you wish, Hugh, but I do.'

357

'How can you tell?'

'By the beating of my heart; by the lightheadedness when I see him; by the certainty that the sun is brighter when he is near; by the sense that I am languishing every moment that I am not with him.'

'You've got poetic.'

'I *feel* poetic at the thought of him. Is it so wrong that I should love him? He would be a good husband, Hugh, a knight.'

'Yes, well, I've known knights.'

'But William is different. He's strong and kindly and generous and honourable and courteous and . . .'

'That's what you think.'

'Don't be so short, Hugh. I still love you, too – I always will. You were my closest friend when I was young, but I am an adult now.'

'Not what your mother says.'

'She's a crabbed old woman and jealous of me!'

'You think so?'

'Of course she is. She's forgotten what it's like to be in love.'

'She loves your father.'

'Oh, that's different. That's old love. It's not young and fresh and full of life like mine. She's too old to appreciate my sort of love. I feel I should burn if my love were to touch me, Hugh. Do you think my mother feels that when Father touches *her*? Of course not! I would burst into flames if William should come too close to me, though. The sight of him makes me tremble from head to foot. The thought of kissing him is . . . is . . .'

'Your mother said no,' Hugh said flatly.

They were standing on the wall above the chapel, Edith leaning out to try to catch a glimpse of the jousting field, but failing, Hugh standing, glowering, nearby. His voice, usually so full of sullenness, was today filled with melancholy to Edith's ear. Somehow she was sure that he was the unwilling servant of Margaret's wishes. He himself had found love late in his life and detested being gaoler to his favourite charge.

She sighed once more, giving up on the view (it was impossible to see through the trees and round the hill to the stands) and fixing him with her doleful expression. 'So I am to be restrained by you?'

'I can't ignore my Lady Margaret's instructions,' he said shiftily.

Edith screwed up all her determination, bringing to mind her favourite pony, who had been killed three months ago when he fell in a rabbit hole and broke his leg. Simon had taken one look and had fetched a huge axe, taking off the pony's head with one blow. The memory of the gout of blood brought a genuine tear to her eyes. Speaking huskily, she said, 'So that is that, then.'

He nodded glumly, but turned away to avoid catching her eye as the tears began to fall.

Instantly she whirled around and pelted across the wall to the door. Before Hugh fully appreciated what she was doing, she was through it, had hauled it shut, laughing quietly, and fled down the stairs to the main yard. There was no one to stop her, and while the dismayed Hugh watched from above, she ran to the gates and out.

CHAPTER TWENTY-SIX

At the castle's foot where the tented camp lay, knights were standing and swinging arms encased in bright steel, ensuring that their armour allowed full movement.

Edith had to slow her steps at the sight. It looked as though there were hundreds of men there, the knights in armour, their chainmail showing beneath their *gypons*, and plates of armour of all sizes and colours gleaming in the sun. Some were grim, grey metals, but others were bright peacock-blue or silver; some even had dazzling, swirling patterns.

She recovered herself and hurried on along the road, lifting her skirts as she heard Hugh shout from the castle's gate.

Filled with elation, knowing that she would be in severe trouble when the reckoning came, yet rashly not caring, she darted between men, women and animals. One old wife cursed her loudly, but a man called, 'Shut up, you old whore. She's a lady, and don't forget it!'

The thought that she would see her man was overwhelming. Edith had never felt like this before about anyone, but the way William smiled at her made her knees go wobbly; the way his nose moved as he laughed made her want to kiss it. And his lips were a temptation in their own right. She longed for him to put his arms about her again, as he had yesterday after he rescued her at the stands. Not that it was much of a rescue, really. Some fellow had made a coarse comment as she came down the steps, and William had told him sharply to be quiet. Then they had walked and chatted, through the long grasses at the other side of the river. That was all. All innocent.

Not that Edith wanted that state of affairs to continue. She was done with innocence.

She had passed almost all the way through the market now, and came up against the gate to the jousting field. Risking a quick glance over her shoulder, she saw Hugh hurrying red-faced towards her. With a small squeak of alarm at his speed, she took off towards the river, hoping to evade him.

There was a line of trees at the river's edge, and she must avoid the thicker bushes of gorse and bramble which lay beneath, for they would catch at her and slow her down (and make a mess of her clothes, which she could ill afford moments before seeing her lover). She saw a gap in the bushes and pelted towards it, even as she heard a man call out, asking whether she was in danger. Another voice took up the cry and as Edith jumped over a small bank and landed on the shingle, she realised that Hugh was being accused of trying to molest her. Peeping up over a tuft of grass, she saw him arguing with a group of belligerent-looking squires.

Edith had no wish to see Hugh in trouble, but this was her chance to escape. She had but two choices: go to Hugh's aid, in which case he would no doubt take her straight back to the castle and her mother, or disappear from this place as quickly as possible.

She made her choice. The river gave her an escape, but she must be careful and avoid getting her feet wet. If she were to turn westwards, she would follow the loop of the river around the back of the jousting field away from most prying eyes, but surely that was the direction Hugh would expect her to take. No, she would go eastwards, back towards the market area.

Resolved, she lifted her skirts and went to the water's edge. She removed her shoes and stepped reluctantly into the water. 'Oh!' It felt freezing. A few short feet away there was a small island in the midst of the river, and she made for it, then crossed to the other side, where she put on her shoes once more and hurried from tree to tree, feeling more and more like a felon avoiding the reeve's men.

She had gone a matter of twenty yards when she came across a lad scowling over his shoulder at her. His shirt up over his naked buttocks, he was kneeling between the plump thighs of a grinning girl whose skirts were thrown up over her breast.

'Oh – I . . . I'm sorry,' she said, flushing bright crimson.

'Haven't you seen a man and woman together before?' the youth demanded scathingly.

Edith left them to their rutting, circling around them in a wide sweep, averting her eyes, but aware of a warm feeling of jealousy. She wanted to be the one lying there on her back, getting leaves and brambles in her hair and clothing, while William knelt above her.

The thought held her spellbound, and she felt the familiar tremble of desire in her belly. Realising she had come far enough, she looked at the riverbank once more. There was a thick mess of brambles, but a short distance from her was a gap. She pulled her skirts closer to her legs and trod carefully between the thorns, then stepped down into the shingle. Removing her shoes, she warily crossed the river and stood slipping them on again before raising her eyes to the riverbank.

And screamed.

Simon had a premonition of disaster as the shrill cry broke out. He turned and his eyes met Baldwin's, and then he was moving towards the river as fast as his legs would take him, closely followed by Baldwin and Coroner Roger.

Edith's scream had come from near the horse-lines, at the riverbank where the pavilion field met the market, and many squires and archers who were not needed by their knights, as well as several knights who would not be jousting for some time, were also hurrying to see what was going on. Simon saw several faces he recognised, including Sir John, Odo the Herald, the King Herald Mark Tyler, and Sir Peregrine.

Simon forced his way to the front of the crowds as the screams came with redoubled force, and then he saw her: Edith, her mouth wide with horror, her hands clenched at her sides as she stood, petrified, uttering scream after scream.

His heart felt as though it would burst to see her so desolate – but he was also filled with dread. Whatever could have so terrified his daughter like this? Perhaps Hugh was hurt – or Margaret?

He ran to her side, pulling her stiff body to him, murmuring soothing noises, patting her head and rocking her slightly from side to side. He felt her head gradually sink into the angle between his shoulder and neck, until he could sense that she was relaxing, and could gently turn her away from the awful sight that had so shocked her.

Baldwin was already at the body, and he gave Simon a look of sympathy. Simon couldn't understand what it meant, but then he saw the bloody face of Squire William lying among the grasses and brambles.

'Dead?' he mouthed, although the question was unnecessary.

Baldwin nodded without speaking. The Coroner was already standing over the corpse while bystanders shuffled and glared at Simon suspiciously.

'Who is it this time?' Mark Tyler demanded, swaggering over with his thumbs in his belt. 'Another carpenter? Or is it someone more . . .' He broke off as he took in the face. 'Gracious God in heaven, Sir William of Crukerne!'

Sir John had followed in the King Herald's wake and now he stood dumbly staring down at his dead son. He gave a single choking sob, sinking to his knees, his features twisting in despair and desolation.

Baldwin put a hand to his shoulder, but the knight shrugged it away. 'Who did this?'

Nobody answered him. Coroner Roger cleared his throat, then bellowed, 'Back, you whoresons! Stand back, in Christ's name! Jesus, God and Holy Mother Mary, if you don't give me room I'll have Lord Hugh find space for you in his worst dungeons. Back, you misbegotten sons of a worm-infested mongrel!'

He stood a while staring down and Simon could see that he was reluctant to get between Sir John and the corpse. 'Sir John, you recognise this boy?'

'It's my son,' the man said dully.

'I know who killed him!'

'Who was that?' Sir Roger called, scanning the crowd which stood so thickly at the bankside. 'Who can tell us who the murderer was?'

Simon too was staring at the figures on the bank. Edith was quivering and sobbing in his arms, and he was trying to pull her away from the scene when the voice called out again.

'It was the Bailiff! He was arguing with the lad yester' even, because young William fancied his daughter. That's who killed your boy – it was Bailiff Puttock!'

Sir John slowly turned to face Simon. 'Is this true?'

Edith suddenly went rigid in his arms. She pulled away, her eyes staring into his with an expression of revulsion. 'Did you, Father?' she said brokenly. 'Did you kill him to keep him from me?'

Simon felt his heart shrivel within him at her accusation. 'By Christ's bones, by the life I hope to win in heaven: NO!' he declared, but even as he said the words he heard Tyler's snide voice.

'I said he was the murderer, didn't I? I accused him only yesterday, because he murdered Hal and Wymond. Now he's slaughtered this honourable lad as well. Is there no end to his lust for blood?'

Sir John stood and walked to Simon. Baldwin automatically stepped between them. 'Sir John, this is only an unsubstantiated accusation, nothing more. I do not believe it, and you shouldn't either.'

365

'Bailiff, I accuse you of the murder of my son and I demand trial by battle to prove your guilt or innocence.'

'Trial by . . .' Simon stuttered. 'But I've done nothing. I can't fight you, a knight!'

'Name your champion, Bailiff. I challenge you to trial by battle, and if I kill him and win, you will hang. I swear it!'

Margaret sent Hugh to fetch them wine, but then sat with Edith cradled in her lap, sobbing. She had given her son to Petronilla and now rocked her daughter as she listened to the men talking.

Sir Roger was shaking with emotion. 'Bailiff, you can't accept the challenge. It would be insane. The man's a killer, he's often killed his foe. Prove your innocence in court, it's much safer.'

'He challenged me before all those people,' Simon said dully. 'Even my own daughter thinks I am guilty. If I refuse, many will assume I *did* do it, that I don't dare to throw my fate into God's hands, that I prefer to bribe officials, jurors and lawyers to find for me.'

'Let people believe what they want,' Baldwin said earnestly. 'Do not risk yourself in this way.'

Simon met his eye a moment, but then looked back to Edith and his wife. 'Meg, I am so sorry. I should never have come here. It was a matter of pride. Stupid pride. I thought that if my father could organise tournaments, I could do it as well. I never thought I'd be risking everything.'

'It wasn't your fault, Simon,' Baldwin said.

A servant thrust his head through the doorway. 'Bailiff? Oh, good.'

Behind him was the herald Odo and Sir Peregrine, both with grim features as they entered. Simon wasn't interested in their sympathy. All he wanted at this moment was some private moments with his wife and daughter, to try to soothe them and persuade Edith he was innocent.

Baldwin said to the Coroner, 'Have you completed the study of the body?'

'Yes, and I am afraid that there is nothing to show who could have killed the fellow. He was stabbed twice in the back, then his throat was cut. Blood everywhere.'

'So he died there,' Baldwin noted. 'And was not beaten to death like Benjamin and the others. Is there any suggestion that someone other than the Bailiff might have been responsible?'

'Only Simon has been accused.'

Simon nodded. 'Everyone thinks I did it, don't they? Even my own daughter.'

Baldwin frowned. 'Never mind what everyone thinks, Simon. You did not kill the lad, so we must show you are innocent.'

'If you think so,' Simon said wearily. He walked to his wife and dropped onto the bench at her side, putting a hand on Edith's back. 'But how I can prove that? I know nothing about the boy.'

'Then we shall have to find out about him, won't we?' Coroner Roger declared.

Odo cleared his throat. 'I think I might be able to help a little, Sir Roger. I knew the lad. He was in the host at Boroughbridge, serving under Harclay. He captured Andrew, squire to Sir Edmund of Gloucester.'

'Is Andrew the kind of man to take offence?' Baldwin asked, recalling that the watchman had seen him the night Hal died.

'I would say not,' Odo said firmly. 'He always struck me as honourable.'

'Did Squire – sorry – Sir William have enemies?'

'I only know of one. Geoffrey, who died last night. Geoffrey had married Alice Lavandar and would have declared their matrimony after being knighted.'

'Ah, but William had intended marrying her.'

'Yes.'

'Except since Geoffrey is dead, he can hardly be the murderer,' Baldwin said. He sighed and closed his eyes. He had a headache. It was painful to see Simon and his family suffering like this. If he could, he was determined to prove who was the real murderer.

'I daresay this was the random act of an evil man,' Sir Roger said with distaste. 'You often find murderers are like that. How else can you explain their behaviour? Murdering an architect and carpenter, and a banker, and now this fellow – it's madness.'

'Perhaps,' Baldwin said, his attention fixed on the dejected figure of Simon. 'However, I have usually found that there was an understandable explanation for any murder when I sought it.' He faced Odo again. 'What else can you tell me about this fellow?'

'I am not sure I know much more.'

'You mix with the squires, don't you? Heralds always do. You must know their secrets.'

'Perhaps a few,' Odo said easily, allowing himself a small smile. 'But I confess I have no idea who could have killed Sir William. He appeared to have many friends.'

Coroner Roger clapped his hands together. 'It is plain enough that I must discover first where William went last night. What did he do and whom did he see? Once we know that, we can begin to form an impression as to who could have done this foul thing.'

Odo gestured to Simon. 'What of you? If you were with other people . . .'

'I was exhausted after the strain of the last weeks,' Simon said. 'I went to my bed early.'

'Oh,' Sir Roger sighed.

Baldwin nodded. 'If I may make a suggestion, Sir Roger, why don't you speak to the other squires and get an idea from them as to whether there could be any other people with a grudge against Sir William.'

The Coroner nodded and was about to leave the room when another herald appeared in the doorway, peering in nervously. 'Bailiff? I have been sent by Sir John of Crukerne – he asks whether you have chosen your champion yet.'

Baldwin glowered and stated loudly, 'The Bailiff will refute this ridiculous accusation in court. There is no question of his being foolish enough to respond to a grieving parent's very natural misery.'

'If the Bailiff will not give Sir John satisfaction to resolve this matter speedily,' the herald said hesitantly, 'Sir John says he will assume the guilt and cowardice of the Bailiff. He will come and whip the Bailiff over the whole length of the tilt-yard.'

'Tell Sir John that he can do no such thing and that should he attempt it, he would be arrested,' Baldwin grated.

'Tell him that the Coroner will have him arrested if he so much as thinks of it,' Roger blustered furiously.

'Sir,' the herald turned to Baldwin, 'I fear Sir John is determined, and the mood of the crowd is growing ugly.

There are too many who are prepared to declare the Bailiff guilty, and there is a clamouring for his blood. If he doesn't accept the challenge, hotheads could demand the Bailiff's head.'

Baldwin glanced at the Coroner.

Sir Roger set his jaw. 'I'll go and reason with the miserable churls. I'll have no lynchings here.'

'No!' Simon declared. 'Damn the bastard, but I'll find me a champion. I'll not have any man declaring me a coward. I will venture God's judgement because as I stand here, I swear I am innocent.'

'Who will you employ as champion, Bailiff? You can't fight him yourself,' Coroner Roger asked.

Simon looked at him. 'Who could I ask?'

Baldwin sighed. 'I shall fight for you, Simon. God help us both!'

Simon gave his farewell to Meg and tried to kiss his daughter, but Edith buried her face in her mother's neck and wouldn't look at him. 'Look after them, Hugh,' he said stiffly as he withdrew his hand from his daughter's back.

'I will, sir.'

'Simon – Baldwin, be careful, won't you?' Meg suddenly cried out. 'No, Baldwin, you can't go like this. Wait!' She deposited her daughter on the bench and ran from the room, returning a few minutes later with a scarf which she thrust into Baldwin's hands. 'Wear this, my dear old friend, as a token.' She reached up and kissed him, resting her warm palm for a moment against his cheek.

He took her hand. His features were stern and composed, but he managed to give her a gentle smile as he gazed into her weeping eyes. 'I will wear it, Lady, and I will bring your husband back to you, safe and unharmed, I swear. For as God is my witness, I reject the accusations against him,' he added in a louder voice, gazing sternly at the herald.

Odo was still in the room, standing near to Sir Peregrine. 'Sir Baldwin, I entirely agree with you that the good Bailiff is innocent – but how can one prove another man was guilty?'

'Herald, I do not know,' Baldwin said. 'All I can ask is that Coroner Roger questions all those he can, and if you could help him, I would be most grateful.'

'I shall help in any way I may,' Odo said sincerely.

'And as soon as this mess is sorted out, I'll have that dog's turd Tyler out of my Lord's household,' Sir Peregrine said savagely. 'I'll not have his vicious tongue spreading villeinous rumours like this again. Cretin!'

Simon nodded in gratitude, but he could find no words as he walked from the hall behind Baldwin.

CHAPTER TWENTY-SEVEN

The Bailiff's thoughts were disjointed as he wandered along the castle's corridor towards the entrance and out into the sunlight. The sun was high now and the air was still, so Simon could feel the heat scorching his bare arms. One moment he was seeing his daughter screaming in horror, the next he saw Sir John's pale, shocked features as he took in the sight of his murdered son. And now Sir John intended to kill Baldwin in order to prove Simon's guilt.

Simon felt himself jostled but ignored it. His mind was too set on other matters. He allowed his head to droop, disconsolate.

'Stand up straight!' Baldwin muttered at his side. 'Don't walk like a felon. Remind them who you are.'

'I don't know . . . I . . .'

'Simon!' Baldwin turned and eyed him with glittering eyes. 'You are innocent. If you look like this, everyone will want to convict you out of hand even if I win. Would you like

Edith to go through the rest of her life accusing you? Then stand straight and look these bastard sons of whores in the eyes.'

'I don't think I can,' Simon confessed.

Baldwin grabbed his shoulder. 'Then think of this! If *you* didn't kill the lad, the murderer is out there, in that crowd. If *you* don't care about being accused, that's one thing, but you might see the guilty man and meet his eye. When you do, you may just see something there that makes you recognise his guilt. You may recognise the stare of the murderer!'

Simon gaped. He had been so entirely bound up in his own misery that the fact that *another* man was guilty had slipped from his mind. Now he felt a return of his anger, and with the resentment of being forced to endure the punishment that another man deserved, a flame of rage consumed him. He gritted his teeth. 'I shall watch all the men.'

'Good,' Baldwin said, 'because I need your support, Simon.' He looked up at the castle, at the flags hanging limply from the poles. 'God knows, I need all the help I can get,' he murmured almost to himself. 'It is many years since my last joust.'

Simon felt as though a rock had materialised in his belly. 'When did you last fight like this?'

'Me?' Baldwin considered. 'About 1306 I practised with friends in the lists in Paris.'

'1306? That's sixteen years ago!'

'Your arithmetic does you credit.'

'Baldwin, Sir John has fought in all the tournaments he could. This is madness – you'll be killed. Can't I find another man to challenge him?'

'I don't think so. Not now, Simon. This is a judicial fight and I accepted his challenge.'

Simon looked at him despairingly.

'Do not fear for me. The matter is in God's hands, old friend. And I shall fight confidently, knowing that the cause is just.'

They had arrived at his own pavilion and in the doorway Edgar stood waiting. 'Sir, I have all your arms ready.'

'How did you know?' Baldwin asked.

'There is a certain amount of chatter in the crowds, sir.'

Baldwin entered. On the table was all his armour and clothing. He touched the heavy quilted fustian of his *aketon* and sighed. He had not expected to be forced to ride in a joust and fight to the death once more. It was a daunting prospect after so long a period.

'Sir?' Edgar brought him a mazer of wine.

'Thank you,' Baldwin said, drinking deeply and gesturing to Simon.

Edgar passed Simon the jug, having refilled the mazer. 'Sir Baldwin, would you like to be dressed?'

'Yes. And make sure every buckle and thong is secure. I don't want to shed armour like an outlaw running from the Hue and Cry!'

Baldwin stood while Edgar pulled the thick *aketon* over his head. The padded cloth was designed to soften blows. When Baldwin was happy with it, Edgar lifted the *hauberk* of fine, linked mail, slipping it over Baldwin's head. It covered the knight's arms and reached almost to his knees. Then came the pair of plates, the leather coat with plates of steel riveted to the inside, that was buckled at the back. Baldwin stood while Edgar saw to the fastenings, before buckling the gutter-shaped plates to Baldwin's arms.

Swinging his arms, Baldwin tried to get used to the restricted movement. Although the armour was very heavy, he could move his arms without difficulty. Over the top of this Edgar draped a long, clean white tunic with Sir Baldwin's arms marked out on the breast, his coat armour, and finally Baldwin's recent acquisition, a skull-cap of steel which rose to a sharp point to deflect axe or sword blows, with a loose, padded tippet of mail which hung to his shoulders. Hinged to the front to cover his face was a vizor, which he lifted away while Edgar pulled on bags of mail to protect his hands, then the heavy gauntlet, the *main de fer* or fist of iron, which would protect his left hand as it gripped the reins.

The dressing took longer than Simon had expected, and he sat on a stool while Edgar carefully checked each strap and thong, lifting an arm to bind the steel plates, tugging cloth into place. Baldwin lowered his head to help Edgar settle the tippet of steel links, stepped into the mailed foot-gear, pensively swivelled and bent to check the fit.

Simon could do nothing. The dreadful enormity of the occasion lent an especial solemnity to the process. He sat with drawn features, picking at a loose thread on his hose, praying for Baldwin's safety, wishing there were something he could do.

'Couldn't I borrow some armour and fight with you? Or take your place?'

Edgar glanced at him but said nothing. Somehow his expression was a more definite rejection than Baldwin's quiet, 'No, Simon. You would die in minutes in the *hastilude*. Lance-play is too dangerous for people who haven't practised the art. In any case, Lord Hugh would never permit you to joust. You are not chivalrous.'

Simon could do no more. He sat sunk in gloom. His friend would enter the lists on his behalf, putting his life in God's hands in order that Simon could clear his name. It gave the Bailiff a terrible feeling of guilt. It should be *him* being covered in steel and reaching for the long, two-handed axe with the blade notched from use, muttering that it should be sharpened before he could use it in anger.

At last Edgar knelt and bound a heavy war-belt with enamelled pieces about Baldwin's hips and lifted the front of Sir Baldwin's tunic up and tucked it into the belt to keep it from tripping him. Then he slid Sir Baldwin's great warsword into the scabbard and stood back. Baldwin met his gaze and nodded, then glanced down at his encased body.

'Christ help me! If I manage to move in this lot it'll be a miracle.'

Odo and the Coroner had not waited, but as soon as Baldwin and Simon left the hall, they hurried down to the place where the body had been discovered with a small force of Sir Peregrine's men-at-arms.

'Did you enquire of all the men whether they had heard anything?' Odo asked the Coroner.

Sir Roger looked up at the sun, assessing the time. 'Yes, I had all the men from here as a jury, and took down all their names, but none of them admitted to knowing anything.'

Odo grunted. He hopped down onto the shingle beach below where the body had been found and peered about him, hoping that there might be something, anything, which could give a clue as to who was responsible. Standing upright, he stood on tiptoe to look over the bushes towards the pavilions. Suddenly he gasped, 'Coroner, the man who killed Sir William wouldn't have carried him all the way here. He'd have made too much noise walking on the shingle, wouldn't he?'

'I don't know. The river makes a hell of a din. It'd cover the noise of a man walking about down here.'

Odo glanced up- and downriver. 'Then think of this: would you cross the water here, with slime and slippery stones underfoot, if you were carrying a heavy dead body?'

'Couldn't he have come along the bank?'

'But the beach is very short; it runs out up there and below as well, where the water has cut into the banks. If the murderer carried William here, he'd have to have got his feet wet.'

'True. So you think he was murdered here?'

'Yes.' Odo looked at the ground. 'If that's true, though, why didn't anyone notice? It's very close to the tents.'

'It's rare enough that a man dies without making a sound,' Sir Roger agreed, 'but here, with the water rushing past and the noise from people singing and dancing, drunks snoring, and others screwing, or dreaming that they were, it's hardly surprising no one heard anything.'

Odo nodded, but then sprang lightly onto the bank and gazed about him. To left and right the river curved around the field, enclosing the tents. Pavilions and rougher tents lay all about, while to his right, some forty yards away, were the lines where the horses stood. Most were in paddocks and fields at the opposite bank of the river, but some of the more expensive mounts had been installed nearer their owners' tents. Two bored-looking grooms idled about, brushing and rubbing down the horses which would be used later that day.

His attention returned to the pavilions. 'Surely someone should have heard something? Shouldn't we speak to all the people who slept here last night?'

Before Sir Roger could answer, a young messenger came hurrying. 'Odo? The King Herald asks that you attend to the jousting.'

'Tell him I'll be along shortly.'

'The King Herald was insistent.'

Odo swore softly. 'I'll be along as soon as I can.'

The lad looked worried. 'You should. The Lord Hugh is in a foul mood; he's furious that Simon the Bailiff must suffer trial by battle.'

Baldwin and Simon stood before the small portable altar in Lord Hugh's chapel.

Like so many smaller places of worship, it had no glass in the windows, and while the priest intoned his prayers and sang his psalms, noises wafted up to them from the tented field at the foot of the castle's hill: voices raised in dispute; a shrieking, bawdy laugh from a woman; sudden rattling as a cart rumbled past.

It made Simon feel curiously detached. Here he was, his life at risk, and yet outside all was continuing as normal. People were living their lives naturally, while in this little church, he and his friend were preparing for their deaths.

The priest broke bread and tipped a little wine into their mouths, uttering the soothing Latin words which Simon remembered so distinctly from his youth as a student in the Canonical church at Crediton. Simon had witnessed many deaths in his life, from those who died of disease or hunger during the famine, to seeing those whom he had captured dangling by their necks. Never before had he wondered about the different ways of dying. Would it be very painful, or would it be a sharp crack and instant peace until he found himself – where? Reviewing his life he was aware of several occasions when he had not behaved as God would have liked.

His despondency grew. It was a relief when the service ended and he and Baldwin could walk away, leaving the priest mumbling his way through some final prayers. Baldwin stopped a moment and gazed back at the man, then strode out.

'What is it?' Simon asked.

'The bastard is being as quick as possible so he can come and watch the fight,' Baldwin said.

He walked out into the sunshine and the two were blinded. It was some little while before they noticed Margaret and Edith. Margaret gave Baldwin a curtsey.

'Sir Baldwin, my dear, dear friend, my prayers will go with you. Please be careful, be valiant, and come back safely. Simon, be strong. Have faith.'

Her voice had grown softer and softer and now it tailed off altogether while her eyes closed as if to shut off the flood that threatened.

Simon felt his heart lurch and he went to her, hugging her and kissing her brow. 'Be strong, Meg. I can't be if you're not.'

'Father!' Edith cried. 'I didn't mean it when I said I blamed you. Please be careful! Sir Baldwin, look after him, won't you?'

The knight gave her a sombre look, taking in the over-bright eyes, the thin trickling of tears, the drawn, pale visage.

'Edith, your father is innocent, and while there is a God in Heaven, I cannot lose trial by combat on his behalf.'

It was pleasing to see her demeanour alter, as an expression of relief and gratitude slowly suffused her features. She sniffed and then reached up and kissed him full on the lips before walking to her father and kissing him too.

Ridiculously, Baldwin felt a thrill run through his body. It was as if a liquid fire had filled him, converting his occasionally melancholic humour to a sanguine one. As he and Simon walked from the castle, he felt more alive than he had for many years. This was responsibility, he thought: when a friend's life hung in the balance. As did his own, he knew, for Sir John would kill him if he could. The combat would be to the death.

The two men walked silently along the path to the jousting field. All about them, people pointed and fell quiet. Baldwin ignored them. It was important to keep his mind clear, he knew. That was one of the things he had learned while fighting with the Templars: a man should empty his mind and enter the lists calmly. All fighters knew that a cool head was the first essential if you wished to win. And Baldwin had every intention of winning. That was why he refused to let himself think of his own wife and daughter. Distractions were dangerous.

He prayed as he entered the field. There was a corridor of other knights and squires leading to the area before Lord Hugh's stand, and although some called out his name, Baldwin didn't hear.

Simon often found his beliefs difficult to comprehend, he knew, but to Baldwin it was very simple. He knew that God was the heavenly creator, and that He would listen to the prayers of any man who called out in need. The fact that Baldwin thought the Church a milch cow for the Pope and that while the Pope lived at Avignon under the direct control of the French King he would be flawed and open to corruption, did not affect his own belief in God. The Templars had been destroyed by the greed of the French King, who saw them as an easy means to wealth. Now there were other forms of corruption appearing, with pardoners selling their scraps of paper to promise full remission of sins, provided that the money was right, and priests buying their own advancement.

But whether or not the Catholic Church was falling into corruption, Baldwin knew that God would protect His faithful followers, and although Baldwin had endured a crisis of confidence after the destruction of the Templars, wondering why God did not save His most loyal army, he had come to realise that probably not all the Templars were honourable.

It was only as he approached the main stand that he became aware of his surroundings. He saw Edgar with his destrier and walked to the horse, pulling at the girth straps, patting the creature's neck as he checked the positioning of the bridle, feeling the saddle and making sure it was firm and the wooden frame had not been damaged.

Satisfied, he stood and waited, breathing easily. It was odd, but standing here, before all these fascinated people, he could appreciate the scene. Somehow there was more clarity to the air, for when he looked along the valley and to the hill at the opposite bank, it looked nearer than before, as if the very hills were edging closer to witness the fight. Flowers appeared brighter, more colourful; birds sang with more crystalline purity, making their songs achingly beautiful, while the gurgle and chuckle of the water was a constant but ever-changing backdrop which served to highlight the relative silence all about.

High overhead a lark sang and his attention rose to where the bird soared trilling with a liquid purity. When his gaze returned to earth, he found himself staring at Sir John.

Simon stirred. 'Baldwin, I . . .'

'There is nothing to say,' he murmured curtly. At this time above all others he must concentrate, must focus all his energy, and yet he was preoccupied. Glimpsing the pain in Simon's eyes, he relented. 'Friend, we know you are innocent.'

'Yes.'

'Then put your faith in God,' Baldwin said and turned to face Lord Hugh.

Sir John joined him, his face set, his tilting helm in the crook of his arm, and his face showing his torment.

'Sir John of Crukerne and Sir Baldwin of Furnshill, you have come here today to try your case before these witnesses,' Mark Tyler said.

Baldwin glanced at him. The King Herald seemed nervous and was not using the normal words for the oaths.

Tyler continued, 'This case has been brought by the death of Squire William of Crukerne who was most feloniously killed last night. Sir John accuses Bailiff Puttock of the killing and Sir Baldwin rejects that accusation. Thus we are here today to try the matter in trial of combat. Sir John, do you swear before God that you believe Bailiff Puttock to be guilty?'

'I do so swear.'

'Sir Baldwin, do you swear before God that Bailiff Puttock is innocent of this crime?'

'I do so swear.'

'Then may God show us who is right.'

'Wait!'

Tyler had been about to leave, but Lord Hugh stood and stared down at the men below him.

'Gentlemen, would it not be better for this to be delayed? Perhaps an answer can be found without the need for bloodshed. It would surely be better than to lose either one of you, or both.'

Sir John set his jaw. 'I have no fear of death, my Lord. My cause is just and my son demands vengeance. I will brook no delay.'

'Sir Baldwin?'

'I fear I can hardly back down, my Lord, when a false accuser maintains the guilt of an innocent man.'

Lord Hugh shook his head disappointedly and Baldwin realised the cause for his reluctance: with the present dangerous state of the realm, no lord would wish to lose one of his best fighters. Better that he should win a delay in order that the affair could be ironed out behind closed doors.

But it was not to be, and Baldwin secretly thought that Lord Hugh looked half pleased when the two combatants refused to back down. Like so many others there, he would enjoy witnessing a fight to the death. It was a more interesting spectacle than a joust *à plaisance*, where the danger was accidental.

Baldwin was glad to see that at least Sir Roger did not appear content to see the fight go ahead. He sat frowning at Lord Hugh's side, for it was the Coroner's duty to witness fatal encounters.

Mark Tyler was speaking again. 'Gentlemen, you will take a pass with lances and if one of you is unhorsed, you can continue on foot. This fight is to the death, but if one submits, his cause is lost. Do you both understand?'

Perfectly well, Baldwin thought, studying Sir John's face. He will kill me as soon as he has an opportunity.

Without a second look, Baldwin made the sign of the cross. Then he slowly drew his sword free, a great long weapon he had bought many years before in Paris, with a grey-brown sheen to the notched blade. Baldwin lifted it before him, bowed his head to the cross-symbol of the hilt and guards, and kissed it before replacing it in the scabbard. Abruptly turning on his heel, he went to his horse and Edgar.

CHAPTER TWENTY-EIGHT

Sir Edmund was already on horseback. 'I trust you will accept my assistance, Sir Baldwin?'

Baldwin looked over his shoulder towards the thickset Sir John, who was talking to another knight. 'Who is that?'

'Sir Walter Basset. He will second Sir John.'

'Then I should be glad of your assistance,' Baldwin said.

He walked to the mounting block, a series of steps built at the side of a *ber frois*, and climbed inelegantly on to his horse.

The beast knew something was in the air. He was skittish, prancing excitedly. It was all Baldwin could do to keep the brute steady while he gathered his weapons. The chain of his great axe was set about his neck, his lance was passed to him, and he sat waiting for his opponent. He rested the lance on his foot, feeling the weight. Long and unwieldy as a weapon, it was nonetheless hideously effective when used by a trained man.

Sir John, he saw, had purchased the new armour. He had one large breastplate of dark steel and a great steel pot of a helm which was chained to it. At his side was a massive mace armed with vicious spikes in the metal head. He was already on his horse, a lance gripped rigidly. Seeing Baldwin was ready, he jerked Pomers's reins and rode back to the starting point.

Baldwin nodded to Edgar and checked the straps of his shield before knocking the vizor down. With the lance gripped in his fist, he trotted back to his own starting position near the river.

His mind was clear now. He knew he must fight with a cold precision. His strength was surely no match for Sir John's, nor his speed. His stamina might be his only advantage. If Baldwin was to win this bout, he would have to fight cleverly. Brute strength was on Sir John's side, but Baldwin should be able to counter that with deviousness; Sir John would be well-used to surviving against younger lads, for his successes in tournaments were well known, so he must be skilled at dealing with those who were considerably faster than him, people who had swifter reactions, yet Baldwin must somehow overcome him. It was an interesting conundrum, considered in a detached and rational manner, but even as Baldwin surveyed his enemy he saw Sir John's legs move. Glancing to the main stand, Baldwin saw that the King Herald had given the signal and almost without realising it, he raked his spurs along his horse's flanks and was moving.

There was no time for fear or alarm. He must weld his body and mind to the workings of his horse. The crash of lances was nothing unless mount, knight and lance-point were united and wielded as a single weapon.

His destrier was a well-bred animal with fire in his blood and fighting in his nature. Already he was moving at a canter, and Baldwin held his lance up, balancing the weight cautiously, waiting for the moment to slip the butt beneath his armpit. Then his horse was galloping and Sir John was nearer, his lance all but disappearing as it pointed to Baldwin's face. He allowed his own point to fall until he felt it should be pointing in the right direction, but with the thundering of hooves, the jerking motion and the tiny slits through which he must breathe and see, it was hard to know what was happening.

A sparkle of metal; a flash, and a hideous lurch, then the pain of a hammer-blow at his breast and simultaneously his right arm was slammed back. The two together almost dismounted him. There was a crack from his saddle, a ringing clatter from his left arm, and then he was struggling with his vizor to see what had happened as his mount carried him to the far end of the field.

His lance was wrecked, one third snapped away. He grabbed another, weighing it in his hand. Something felt wrong with it, with the balance, but he had no time to consider it.

He looked back to see that Sir John was still in the saddle, and as Baldwin watched, Sir John wheeled his horse and charged again. Baldwin had to pull his horse's head right about and spur him on, and then the rattling motion began again. Almost too late Baldwin remembered to knock his vizor down again.

This time the blow was less central and he felt the lance skitter away to his left, the point striking his plates, the shaft foiled by his shield. His own lance shuddered and jerked, but he was sure that Sir John didn't fall. There was a short blur of dust and gleaming metal and they were past again.

Baldwin lifted his lance and hefted it in his hand. It felt easier now, as if his arm was becoming accustomed to the weight and balance after all these years. He was sure that he had connected with Sir John. The applause he could hear over his own panting breath seemed to show that someone had achieved something. Baldwin saw the dust rise from Sir John's horse's hooves and felt his lips pull away from his teeth in a snarl. He kicked twice, hard, and felt the explosive power of his horse as its huge hindquarters thrust forwards, jolting Baldwin back against the cantle. He slipped the lance under his armpit, aiming the bright point at Sir John, but then he realised something was wrong. The point was gone; his lance had only a splintered stump where there should have been a steel tip. His belly lurched, he felt the clammy grip of fear clutch at his heart, but he was committed now. There was nothing he could do but put his faith in God.

'Jesus, Mary, and Saint George,' he murmured, but then he felt the terrible blow at his chest and heard an enormous rending. His own lance was still more than a foot from Sir John, it was snapped off so short, but Baldwin barely had time to register that before he felt himself slipping. He felt his horse give one more lurch at full speed, and then his backside was shifting over the horse's rump. Suddenly he was in mid-air.

A moment, only a moment, of peace mixed with terror, and then his feet snagged on the ground. His knees came up. There was a sharp crack as his knees rose to strike his chin; his jaw crunched as his teeth met and he felt an incisor break off cleanly. Blood filled his mouth and he had to lift his vizor to spit out shards.

He was dazed. He knew that. Sitting on his rump in the dirt, his ears ringing, he couldn't move for a moment. He couldn't believe that he had truly fallen like this, but he was on his arse on the ground. He looked up and saw people laughing and clapping, urging on Sir John as he reined in at the far end of the lists, saw him trot forward, knowing his victory was all but complete. Baldwin had to shake his head to clear it, but already dust had blown into his eyes and he was temporarily blinded. Beneath him he saw the broken remains of his saddle. He was still sitting in it. The thing had disintegrated under the force of the blow.

A determination not to die in so foolish a manner gripped him. He rolled away from his saddle and got on to all fours, pushing himself upwards even as he felt the earth begin to vibrate.

He pulled at his shield. It was no use to him and he let it fall, then snapped his vizor shut. Grabbing his axe, he held it in both hands and stood resolutely, waiting for Sir John.

It was easy to see what was in Sir John's mind. A knight would usually meet his opponent with equal weapons, dismounting when his enemy was unhorsed, so that each could fight with equal opportunity, but Sir John was fighting for justice for his dead son. There was no place for chivalry and sentiment. He spurred his horse on, his lance pointing at Baldwin.

Baldwin could have run, but to do so would mean death. An experienced knight like Sir John couldn't miss a stumbling man encumbered by armour, and with the full mass of horse, man and metal concentrated on the hardened steel tip of his lance, Baldwin would be spitted like a hog over a fire.

Instead, Baldwin stood stock-still until the last moment, the sweat trickling uncomfortably down his brow and his back, tickling beneath the thick padding of his coat. Sir John was approaching at the gallop, his lance high, balanced against the horse's motion, and as he drew closer, he allowed the point to fall until Baldwin could see it aiming at his belly. It moved up and down, coming closer at a terrible speed, and when he could bear it no longer, he moved.

It was neither nimble nor swift, but as he dodged sideways he simultaneously swung his axe at the lance. He felt a solid, numbing buffet on his left arm as the lance caught him a glancing blow, then the axe came alive, almost leaping from his hand, and he knew he had almost taken the head of the lance from its shaft – but the point was reinforced with bars of steel that ran along the shaft itself. It could still kill him.

Keeping Sir John in view, he clenched and relaxed his left hand, panting as he tried to force the tension away. He had to remain alert and swift on his feet now he was on the ground. An idea struck him and he retreated to stand before the remains of his saddle, some few feet from it.

After a moment he felt the pounding of the hoofbeats through his feet; he gripped his axe firmly in both hands, waiting. Again he forced himself to confront the swift-running mount whose flanks were flecked with blood where the spurs had pricked, whose mouth foamed, whose eyes rolled madly. Baldwin felt a shudder run through his body, a shiver of fear, but also of a cold, enraged exhilaration. When he felt sure he would feel the crushing spike of the lance pierce his armour and chest, he shrieked in defiance and sought to spring away; his armour slowed him. Even as he straightened his legs to leap from the horse's path, he felt rather than heard the *clang!* as the lance-tip caught the right side of his chest and became entangled in his belt, which snapped, but there was instantly a second thump higher up his chest and he was thrown back with the force as his sword and dagger fell to the ground.

Rolling away, sweat blinded him. He opened his eyes but had to close them instantly as the salt stung and burned. All he could hear was the whistle and roar of his breath in the confines of his metal mask, all he could feel was the shooting of knives along his side and the dull, monotonous ache at his back where he had fallen on a painful projection within his suit. Gradually his hearing returned, his senses assaulting him afresh even as he tasted blood from his smashed tooth. Keeping hold of his axe, he heard a rising wave of noise from the spectators. Confused, he cautiously raised his vizor.

Sir John's horse had not seen the saddle until the last moment. The wooden frame was broken, but as the destrier tried to avoid it, he stumbled on to the heavy cantle at the rear of the seat, and it was enough to turn his hoof. With a vicious crack like a stone smiting a castle wall, the massive horse had fallen and rolled on to his back, his legs flailing in the air, one shattered foreleg waving obscenely and spraying blood over the field.

Baldwin coughed, winded. He slowly clambered to his feet and spat out more blood before waiting patiently.

Sir John was standing at the side of his mount as if disbelieving that such a disaster could have befallen him, but then he appeared to waken anew to full rage and bloodlust.

Grabbing at his mace, he took it up in both hands and lumbered towards Baldwin, the ugly ball gleaming over his head. Baldwin just had time to pull his vizor down again before the first buffet smashed over his helmet. He moved away, his axe up and held at an angle to deflect the foul weapon, but the heavy head scraped down the axe and slammed against his left hand, crushing it against the shaft. Baldwin gritted his teeth and tried to swing the axe low, to threaten Sir John's legs, but the other knight stopped the attempt with contemptuous ease, reversing his movement to swing the mace at Baldwin's left side.

Pain took Baldwin over. It was like an explosion in his chest, a rapidly flowering agony that rose all the way to his head and made him feel as if his eyes would burst from their sockets. Before he could recover, the mace crashed against his head again, the steel of his heavy helm deafening him. Disorientated, he fell back, his axe flailing before him.

'God!' he cried. 'Holy Father, Holy Mother, save me!'

The axe caught Sir John a glancing thump on his head, striking sparks from his helm but the knight scarcely seemed to notice. He came on. Baldwin had enough energy to swing again with all his remaining might, but although he connected with Sir John's helmet, it didn't distract the man. The mace rose and fell onto Baldwin's head, bouncing from the steel and hitting his left shoulder.

It was agony. A spike had slipped between the links of his mail tippet and Baldwin was sure that he could feel it crush and puncture his shoulder. His entire left arm was dead; there was no strength in it to cling to his axe, and the heavy weapon was a dead weight in his right hand. The mace rose again; he lifted the axe one-handedly and caught its shaft, halting its downwards sweep, and a twist of his wrist deflected its momentum so that it turned in towards Sir John's own leg. A roar, more of anger than of pain, told him that the heavy mace head had caught Sir John's thigh.

Stumbling, all but blinded, his nostrils clogged with the dust, panting with the heat, the pain washing all over his left side, Baldwin staggered to break the engagement. Facing Sir John again, he was shocked to see that the knight was almost upon him once more. Baldwin lifted the axe but Sir John's mace caught it and his two-handed swing took the axe from Baldwin's hand, wrenching it from his grasp, snapping the chain that held it to him, and sending it spinning away even as Sir John's forward rush took him past Baldwin, who suddenly saw his sword and belt lying nearby. He reached down to it, the act of gripping the hilt sending a stab of white-hot pain up his forearm, but he gritted his teeth and hauled it free.

Exhausted with pain and the heat, Baldwin lifted his vizor a last time. If he was to die, he would die with air in his lungs. He rested the point of his sword on the ground while he panted, watching Sir John take a fresh hold of his mace. The knight gave a roar of defiance, lifting the spiked ball high overhead, and began a shambling run towards Baldwin.

He was about to swing it down when Baldwin recalled Odo's words: '*À l'estoc!*'

Baldwin felt a small thrill of energy override his pain. It was tiny, just enough to bring a moment of concentration, but that split second was adequate. As if time stood still, he saw that where Sir John's breast steel met the back-plate, there was a gap beneath the armpit. The sight galvanised Baldwin. His sword was low still as he raised the point. As Sir John ran at him, Baldwin side-stepped and thrust it sharply upwards. He almost ignored the crash as the mace-head rang from the crown of his helmet.

The sword sheared through the thin leather and mail which protected Sir John's underarm, and passed through into the soft flesh, the blade burying itself in the bone. Sir John gave a roar of pain, his fury making him try to spin to bring the mace down again, but the act made the blade twist within his chest. Baldwin stepped back, tugging his sword free and eyeing his opponent with cold intensity.

Sir John grabbed at his vizor and pulled it open, breathing stertorously, groaning heavily with each exhalation. He gave a low, hacking cough and spat blood before swinging his arm slowly, contemplating Baldwin. Reaching down, he picked up Baldwin's axe, holding it loosely in his left hand while he swung his mace in his right. Silently he stalked towards Baldwin, both weapons ready.

Baldwin surveyed him with a dispassionate calculation. His vizor open, he felt more free, as if the protection the helmet gave him was actually a constriction that prevented his defence. He clenched and unclenched his left hand, pins and needles making the whole arm tingle while he sought an opportunity. Even as Sir John had screamed in pain, Baldwin had felt his own faculties return to him and now he watched warily as his opponent knocked his vizor down again and came closer.

The axe swung, Baldwin ducked away from it, but then the mace was aimed at his face. Baldwin evaded that too, just in time to see his axe sweeping back to cut at his knees. He thrust the sword blade in the path of the axe and raised it immediately to knock the mace aside as it aimed for his head. Sir John shrieked at him.

But Sir John's attack had produced a fine spray of blood from beneath his arm as he lifted the axe once more. Baldwin knew Sir John was dying, that it was only a matter of time. But the huge man wouldn't give up. Baldwin dodged from under the axe and as he did so he saw the mace lift again.

Quickly, Baldwin shifted his position, lurching forward on exhausted feet to close with Sir John. He clubbed Sir John's mace hand away, and stepped to his side. Sir John tried to slam his helmet into Baldwin's face, then brought the axe to play again, but he was too late. Pushing the point of his sword into the gap between the plates of steel under Sir John's armpit, Baldwin thrust with all his strength, now using both hands to force the point of the blade deep into Sir John's chest, through his lungs, and twisting, grimacing as he butchered the still-living body.

Sir John coughed, choked, and Baldwin could hear the rattling from within his throat as blood dribbled from his mouth and nostrils, but Baldwin could take no risks. He jerked the blade from one side to another, feeling the edge grating on bones.

It was enough. Baldwin felt Sir John sag and had to kick him to free his sword. He tugged it out with difficulty, and was about to try another blow when Sir John fell to his knees, then on to his face, the vizor closing as he dropped.

'Air! Air!'

Baldwin felt a wave of revulsion wash over him. Sympathy for the dying man made him drop his sword and help Sir John on to his back. He fumbled at the knight's helmet, trying to release the heavy metal, but his fingers were dulled after trading blows and it took time. When he did, Baldwin was confronted by a mask of blood. Sir John's mouth foamed with a bloody froth; his nostrils ran with blood; his every breath produced a fine spray of blood.

'Mercy! Mercy!' came, the hoarse, gurgling cry.

Baldwin had seen wounded men often enough in his life. Sir John was slowly drowning in his own blood. Leaving him would be an act of cruelty. No physician could save him.

'Sir Baldwin, I beg,' Sir John choked, a stream of bright blood flooding from his mouth and staining the grass at his head. 'End this!'

Before the seconds could arrive, Baldwin drew Sir John's own *misericorde* and pushed the point through Sir John's eye.

Simon stood in the great stand near Roger, and stared as Baldwin slowly bent and retrieved his sword. He moved like an old man, exhausted from the short but intense battle. Then he straightened and hesitated before walking over to where the shards of the lances lay scattered. He stooped and picked up broken slivers of wood up to two feet long and appeared to be studying them.

Roger gave Simon a delighted thump on the back, but Simon's attention was fixed on the knight. As if he had been a participant in the fight, he was aware of a bone-deep lethargy as though he himself had aged twenty years in the last hour.

Others in the stands and all about did not feel the same fatigue. There were roars of applause as those who had gambled upon Baldwin's success celebrated their victory; a larger number had wagered on Sir John and these men and women rolled their eyes and muttered contemptuously about the dead man's incompetence as they filed away, seeking wine merchants with whose help they intended forgetting their unprofitable speculation.

Simon heard the King Herald bellow the success of his cause and the Divine Judgement, but his mind couldn't take it all in. He found he was shaking, suddenly enfeebled. He had to grip the handrail to support himself.

Out in the field he saw Sir Edmund and Edgar at Baldwin's side. With an affectionate and gentle care, Edgar took the sword from Baldwin and passed it to Sir Edmund before looping Baldwin's arm over his neck and helping him from the field. The sight made Simon realise that his friend was wounded and instantly his torpor fell away. He dashed from the *ber frois* and down the stairs until he found the trio.

Baldwin gave him a weak grin. 'You should be in church giving thanks!'

'I'll go there as soon as I know you're all right.'

'I am fine.'

'Really?' Simon asked.

He stepped forward and took Baldwin's left arm to help lead him away, but the hissing intake of breath made him pause. 'Right, Edgar, you take him up to the castle and tell Meg to prepare a bed in the castle's lodgings. I'll go and call a physician.'

'Oh, in God's name, Simon! There's no need for that. No, I'll go back to my tent and sleep there.'

'I think you need a physician.'

Baldwin was about to argue when another wave of pain washed over his left side. 'Tell him to see me at my tent. But before that, go and look at the lance. I think I know why Hal and Wymond made so much money from jousting. I'll explain later. For now, Edgar, by Saint Paul, take me to the tent.'

Simon stood feeling oddly small and insignificant as the trio made its way towards the pavilions, Edgar supporting the slack figure of Baldwin, his head dangling like that of a hanged corpse.

'You!' Simon shouted at an urchin. 'Fetch the castle's physician and send him to Sir Baldwin's tent. At once!'

Simon was torn. There were many things to be done, but he was aware that the investigation must continue, even if Baldwin was unwell for days. Wonderingly he walked to the tilt-area and studied the shards of wood.

It was because he was there that he didn't see Andrew as he joined Baldwin's little group. 'Sir Baldwin? Could I talk with you a moment?' The squire asked.

Edgar stepped forward. 'My master is very tired, sir. He cannot talk to you now.'

'It is about the lances, Sir Baldwin,' Andrew continued urgently, ignoring Edgar.

Baldwin closed his eyes. 'Later, please. Or tell some one else. I am too worn out.'

'It must be you, Sir Baldwin. Because of your sword, I know I can trust you.' The squire had lowered his voice.

'My sword?' Baldwin echoed dully.

'Yes. The Templar cross.'

Baldwin leaned more heavily on Edgar and paused to spit out a mouthful of blood. He was on fire with pain all over, and his ears still rang with the battle. He could barely speak, for the aftermath of the duel had left him all atremble. 'Very well,' he said slowly. 'Come to my tent and speak to me there.'

CHAPTER TWENTY-NINE

Odo dropped from his mount and patted the mare's neck as he watched Baldwin being helped from the field.

'A good fight, by God!' Coroner Roger said at his side.

'Yes! I'm glad *I* didn't have to ride against Sir John. He was a terrifying opponent.'

'Yes. And now he and his son are dead,' Coroner Roger said heavily. 'Come, we should speak to the Bailiff.'

They met Simon as he was picking up a large piece of wood.

'What is it?' Coroner Roger asked.

'Baldwin told me to look at this. I can't see why.'

Odo glanced over a timber splinter. 'This is odd,' he said. 'Look, the wood here was cut.'

Simon took it from him and examined it. 'Why, yes. Someone has drawn a narrow saw through it – why should they do that?'

'To guarantee the winner,' Odo said grimly. 'I've seen it done in France. A slight saw cut through the lance weakens it so that it shatters as it hits a man without knocking him down. Sometimes men will gamble heavily on a man's victory in the lists, and they'll pay to ensure that the right man wins.'

'But how could they guarantee that the right man would get the damaged lance?'

'By having an accomplice waiting at the lance-rack and giving the damaged lance to the man they wished to lose,' Odo said.

'It's always a squire who passes the lances,' said Coroner Roger.

Simon finished his thought for him. 'And William used to help in the lists! So there *is* a connection between him and the other three.'

'Who would have wanted them to die, though?' Coroner Roger mused.

Simon felt as though he had a new lease of life. 'First let's go back to where the body was found,' he said, setting off towards the camp.

'We spoke to all the men about there, but no one saw or heard anything last night,' Roger said.

Odo recalled his last thought before he was called back to witness Baldwin's fight. 'We spoke to the knights and squires, but there was one group we didn't question: the grooms. If someone was to go that way and pet his horse, no one would think anything of it, would they? And from there it would be a short walk to the river to murder Sir William.'

Simon caught his breath. 'Of course!' It would be the perfect excuse, he thought. Nobody would question a man-at-arms who went to ensure that his horse was settled for the night. Unconsciously, his pace increased as he neared the horse-lines.

Odo hurried too. This development had confused him. It made no sense for Sir William to have been murdered.

The great destriers and several riding-horses of quality were hobbled or tethered near the water up by the castle's bailey. Odo looked about him. Simon did not hesitate but walked straight to a skinny youth clad in a faded and scratched leather jerkin. Odo found himself staring at one of the lad's eyes because he had a terrible cast in the other. Afterwards he could remember nothing else about him.

'Were you here last night?' Simon asked.

'Yes, sir. I didn't go to my bed until very late.'

'Were you alone?'

'Some of the time, when my mates were eating. We all sleep here, so I was never really alone.'

'Did you hear anyone near the river?'

'Not really,' the youth said, but there was a dryness to his tone that caught Simon's attention. He was holding something back: he hadn't been asked the right question and wouldn't willingly volunteer anything to someone in authority.

Simon had dealt with types like him before. 'Did you, or did you not, see or hear anyone there?' he demanded.

'There were some people walking up there.'

'Who?'

'A girl and a man.'

'Who was the girl?'

The lad shrugged. 'How should I know?'

Simon suddenly sprang forward. He reached out and grabbed his jerkin.

Odo moved forward. 'Bailiff, I think . . .'

'Silence, Herald! Baldwin nearly died saving my skin just now, and I don't have the patience to listen to this fool playing games. Did you hear that, groom? Don't try to be clever with me because I don't understand, and when I don't understand I get irritable. Like this,' he said, tightening his grip. 'All right? If you don't begin to help I'll choke the life from you. Is that clear enough?'

The youth could hardly speak, but simply nodded.

'Good. Because I want to know all *you* know about the people moving about last night, near where Sir William's body was found today,' Simon said, releasing his grip a little.

The lad spoke hurriedly. 'The girl was Lady Helen. She is wife to Sir Walter Basset. There was a man with her. Andrew – Sir Edmund's squire.'

'What? Together?'

'Well . . .'

'Tell us what you saw, you damned whore's kitling.'

'That's all. I saw the two of them walking out to the river together. I thought nothing of it.'

'This was after dark?'

'Yes. Will you take your hands away now?'

'Not yet. What of Sir William? When did you see him?'

'I didn't say I did. Ouch!'

'No, you didn't. *I* did. Did you see him before or after the others?'

'He walked up here a little before them – if it was him. I saw him at the other side of the river, then I saw the girl with Andrew.'

'What then?'

'Yes, what then?'

And Simon turned and found himself staring into the congested face of Sir Walter Basset.

'It was awful, Roger. Probably the most embarrassing situation I've ever talked myself into,' Simon admitted the next morning.

They were sitting in the hall. It was the first opportunity they had found to discuss the murders and Coroner Roger shared the same rickety bench as Simon. When either man moved, both had to grab at the wood. 'Sir Walter forced the groom to admit that Andrew had come away from there shortly afterwards, and then after a long pause, Lady Helen left the place, closely followed by Sir Edmund.'

'It was not your fault,' Roger said. He eyed his jug of wine sourly. 'So what have we learned?'

'Little enough. We know that many people over the years could have wanted to see Hal and Wymond dead. It's trying to see who could have wanted them dead *now* that's the problem.'

Margaret sat at the other side of the room, feeding her baby. 'What of the girl?' she reminded them.

'Which girl?' Coroner Roger asked.

'The wife of that squire who was killed in the lists.'

'Alice? What of her?'

'It's just that I don't understand her. She was desperately keen to escape from her guardian, to marry Geoffrey.'

'Yes. She would have done anything to avoid marrying Sir William,' Roger said. 'You don't mean . . .?'

Simon stared at his cup. 'That she killed William to prevent him from marrying her? Why should she have killed the others?'

'Maybe someone else killed the others,' put in Sir Baldwin.

'Baldwin, are you well enough to be up?' Margaret demanded, surveying him anxiously. Her gratitude to this man would never end, she knew.

'Do not fuss. I shall be perfectly well, if a little sore,' Baldwin smiled. Then he said thoughtfully: 'Look at the wounds on Hal and Wymond – and, from what you've said, Benjamin too. All were beaten severely with some sort of blunt instrument. And now we have William *stabbed*. It is a different approach. Then again, a club is definitely a man's weapon, whereas a small knife could be a woman's – perhaps striking in defence rather than in any desire to kill.'

'You seriously expect us to think that a young woman like Lady Alice could commit murder upon a fellow like William?' Coroner Roger scoffed. 'His throat was cut.'

Baldwin reached over to pour himself a cup of wine. He said nothing for a moment or two. Then, 'Margaret, what do you think?'

'If I was her, and my lover had been slaughtered in the field, I would be near to insane, knowing that the man who had killed him was now determined to claim me for his wife and claim my family's lands for his own. Yes, I could easily kill someone who did that.'

Simon spoke quietly. 'And how much more hatred would she feel, knowing that her guardian killed her own father in the tilt-yard?'

'Yes,' Baldwin said. 'I have the unpleasant conviction that she would be capable of it. And, so far as we know, she may have had the opportunity to do it, too.'

'What of the others, though – the men beaten to death?' Coroner Roger wanted to know. 'I am more concerned about three rather than resolving one.'

'A fair comment,' Baldwin said, rising. Instantly he winced and had to reach out to the wall to steady himself. He waved off offers of support. 'I am fine. Just very sore. Come, shall we seek the girl?'

Margaret was left on her own as the three walked slowly, in deference to Baldwin's wounds, out to the castle's court. All knew that the ward of Sir John should be at the chapel with the bodies of her guardian and his son, but when they entered, bowing and kneeling, crossing themselves, and making their way to the altar, they saw that the two hearses covering Sir William and his father were attended only by a poor man. Lady Alice had not been there, he whispered.

Baldwin led the way to the encampment. At Sir John's tent they found a man packing clothing. 'Where is your lady?' Baldwin asked.

'Alice? She's not ours. She's gone to help Geoffrey's men.'

'She won't come back here, she says,' a maid somewhat breathlessly assured them.

'You are?' Coroner Roger enquired.

'Helewisia. I was her maid, but now my master's dead – well . . . I don't know who is my master now. I'm going back with Sir John's body.'

'Why don't you stay with your lady?' Baldwin asked. 'Surely *she* is the one to whom you owe your loyalty?'

Helewisia smiled knowingly. 'I don't think she'd want me with her. I was only ever the servant of her guardian. Sir John never trusted her too much. That was why he had me installed with her. Not that it did him much good,' she added sadly. 'She fooled us all.'

'In what way?' Baldwin said.

'She got herself married to Geoffrey, for a start.'

'Did you ever hear her talk about Hal and Wymond?'

'Occasionally. She hated them.'

Baldwin shot Simon a look. 'Why?'

'Because she blamed them for the death of her mother and baby brother. They were in a stand which collapsed while they watched a fight – and the fight was between Sir John and her father, Sir Godwin. She blamed them and cursed them. Regularly.'

'Where is she now?' Coroner Roger demanded.

'Up at Geoffrey's tent, if she hasn't already left.'

'That foolish gossip couldn't find her own arse with both hands,' Coroner Roger said coarsely as he hurried along the tents. 'It's obvious this wench has nursed a hatred of these men for years – and took her chance for revenge when the whole lot were together.'

Baldwin said nothing. His mind was moving along a different course. 'What of Benjamin?'

'What of him? She was probably in Exeter with Sir John and killed him there.'

'Did his wounds look like the sort to be inflicted by a woman?'

'He was struck a number of times by a cudgel or something.'

'Swung with force?'

'Yes.'

Baldwin nodded. They were at the tent now, a plain and simple campaigning pavilion. Outside was a pair of carts, on to which boxes and barrels were being loaded. Soon Lady Alice appeared in the doorway.

'Gentlemen – you wish to speak to me?'

'Lady Alice, I suspect you to be the murderer of Benjamin Dudenay, Hal Sachevyll, Wymond Carpenter and Sir William of Crukerne,' Coroner Roger rasped. 'What have you to say to that?'

She had paled and now she grasped at a tent-pole as she stared. 'Me? But why should *I* do such a thing?'

'To avenge your father, Sir Godwin,' Sir Roger said. 'We know he died at the hand of Sir John . . .'

'Yes. That's partly why I wouldn't wed his son.'

'And the stand in which your mother died was built by Hal and Wymond. You wanted revenge on them.'

'No! I had nothing to do with them.'

'And their banker, Benjamin Dudenay, took profit from their building work, so you killed him too.'

'No! This is all quite mad!'

'And finally, you stabbed Sir William. Probably because he was trying to force his favours upon you and you protected yourself?' Coroner Roger asked hopefully. He would be happy to allow her an argument of self-defence in that case.

'This is rubbish! Of course I didn't! I wouldn't know how to kill a man!'

Baldwin watched as Coroner Roger hectored her. Her hand was at her throat as if to fend off an attack, but her eyes were wide and alarmed. Every so often her gaze wandered over the men before her, as if seeking a protector. Suddenly Baldwin was struck with her expression. It was that of a hunted beast. He realised that in a few short days she had lost not only her husband, whom she had thought would be her protector, but also her legal guardian, no matter how much she distrusted him. She had no family, no one to whom she could turn.

'Lady,' he said. 'Our apologies.'

'What do you mean?' the Coroner asked.

'Look at her! To bludgeon a man to death – that is not the act of a well-bred lady such as Lady Alice here,' Baldwin said.

'What of a stabbing? She detested Sir William, she saw him out near the river, and she thrust her dagger in under his ribs.'

'What would be the purpose?' Baldwin said. 'She knew that other men here had heard her husband tell them that he was married to her. Sir William could not demand her hand if she was to refuse him. Even after Geoffrey's death, she could have pleaded her widowhood and escaped him that way.

'Then who committed these murders?'

'There was one other person who lost his father in Exeter,' Baldwin said slowly. 'He watched his father die in front of him, at the hand of Sir John, and then he later suffered from Hal and Wymond's work. He fell through the wall of a stand during a fight. Then while he fought for his life, a man tried to help him, but that man was driven off by Sir John again. This person was left badly disfigured and penniless. He hated and loathed the man who had done so much harm to himself and to his family.'

Coroner Roger gazed at him intently but said nothing. Simon was nodding his head thoughtfully.

Alice broke the silence. 'Do you mean Sir Richard Prouse?'

'Yes. Your half-brother, the knight who was so cruelly scarred after his battle with Sir Walter.'

'Where did you hear he was Alice's half-brother?' Coroner Roger asked.

'Simon told us that Sir Richard mentioned seeing his father die in the tilt. Then Alice said the same, but told us that her mother and brother also died there. Not that many knights die in tournaments – especially those with the name of Godwin.'

'And you think Richard could have killed all these fellows?' Coroner Roger said wonderingly.

'He has a bad leg,' Baldwin said, 'but that wouldn't stop him swinging a heavy hammer.'

'It would prevent him carrying a body as heavy as Wymond's back from the far hill,' Simon said sensibly. 'I don't see him being able to kill *and* bring the bodies back.' There was something else wrong, but he wasn't sure what. 'I don't believe he is guilty.'

'Perhaps you are right,' Baldwin said. 'But let us go and speak to him again.'

'What of me?' Alice said.

Roger glanced at her. 'You are free, my Lady. I am sorry that I accused you in error, but you should not leave Oakhampton until these matters are resolved. I may need to speak to you again!'

'Thank you,' she said, but her face still looked haunted as the men left her.

CHAPTER THIRTY

Sir Richard's tent was a poor, green-stained linen thing that looked as though it had lasted longer than it should. Inside, Baldwin found the knight sipping at a large cup of wine. He waved a jug expansively. 'Sir Baldwin! Excellent! And Bailiff Puttock, please come in and celebrate with me. I am drinking your health, really, Sir Baldwin, so it is only fair that you should be here to share in the wine.'

Baldwin felt a slight tremor as of the early onset of nausea but he swallowed it. The pall of the battle of the previous day had not left him yet. The death of Sir John gave him no satisfaction, for in some ways it seemed unnecessary – but then he had to remind himself that it was *entirely* necessary. Sir John had challenged Simon and called Baldwin to fight. Baldwin had to kill him. It was God's will.

He took the proffered cup and sipped as Sir Richard held his own aloft.

'Here's to the bold Sir Baldwin, who defeated Sir John, the killer of my father.' He drank deeply and with gusto. 'Sir Baldwin, thank you for finally avenging my father – something I couldn't do myself.'

'Are you sure you couldn't?' Baldwin said.

Sir Richard smiled uncomprehendingly. 'I don't understand.'

'Did you murder Hal and Wymond and Benjamin as well as Sir William?' Coroner Roger barked.

'Me?' There was surprise on the ruined face, but Baldwin was sure that there was a faint amused smile as well. 'How could I have done that?'

Baldwin reached forward and topped up his cup. There was silence as he filled it. Then he set the jug down again. 'This is ridiculous. We have three dead because of their part in building stands. Another man has died – Sir William – and *his* father perished because he tested himself in battle before God. How many more will die in this tourney?'

'Are you accusing me?' Sir Richard said.

'Do you have an alibi for any of the evenings when these men died?' Coroner Roger asked.

'Of course I do. I was here.'

'Who was with you? Who will confirm that?'

'Not many like to share their evenings with a cripple who looks like this,' Sir Richard said sadly. He stood and limped towards a wine barrel. Setting the jug on the floor, he turned the tap. His right hand remained in his belt.

Simon looked at Baldwin, who caught his glance and nodded. 'How could a man pick up a corpse with only one arm? And yet sometimes a man with one arm will be as strong as another with two.'

'And how do I show you to be wrong?' Sir Richard enquired. 'If I demonstrate that I cannot even pick up a sack of grain, you will simply say that I was deliberately trying to conceal my strength.'

Simon shook his head. 'I am sorry to have troubled you, Sir Richard. We thought we had the perfect suspect, but you are not the right man.'

Sir Roger was about to protest that he was not so convinced, when the mournful bell began to toll in the castle.

'What in God's name?' he burst out.

Baldwin stood, wine slopping unnoticed from his cup. 'Good God, not another death!' He stared miserably at Simon. 'Will there never be an end to all this?' He felt he could endure no more.

Sir Roger was already out of the tent and haring up the well-trodden track to the castle.

'Who now?' Simon said. He, too, had had more than enough.

'Perhaps the murderer has murdered himself,' Sir Richard said, settling himself comfortably on his chair. 'But in the meantime, Sir Baldwin, I shall sit here in contemplation and drink your health again. Godspeed!'

Two new corpses were already outside the chapel by the time Simon and Baldwin appeared. Margaret was in the doorway to the hall and Simon and Baldwin went to her side. When he looked up, Simon saw Lord Hugh standing on the path that gave up to the keep. He appeared to be listening carefully.

'Was your master the kind of man to commit suicide?' Coroner Roger said to the first witness, Sir Walter's bottler, beckoning a clerk to take notes.

'No, sir. He would have rejected such a dishonourable way out. However, he had just learned about his wife.'

'What of her?'

'He believed she had taken a lover. That she was adulterous.'

'Lady Helen?' Coroner Roger said doubtfully, and looked at Simon.'

Simon stepped forward. 'Yesterday, while I investigated the death of Sir William, I questioned a groom. He told me that Lady Helen had been walking with Sir Edmund. Sir Walter overheard us. He may have jumped to the wrong conclusion.'

'I see. Is Sir Edmund here?' Coroner Roger asked the assembled jury.

'I am here,' said Sir Edmund. For once his manner was subdued. He looked to be in a state of shock.

'What do you have to say about this?' Coroner Roger demanded, waving at the two bodies on the ground before him.

'I know nothing of it.'

'Were you involved in adulterous congress with this man's wife?'

'No, I was not.'

'You didn't decide that if she wouldn't allow you to seduce her, no other man would enjoy her? You didn't kill her, and then slaughter her husband?'

'No, I did not! As God is my witness, I would never have harmed a hair of her head. I loved her. I was engaged to be married to Lady Helen when I lost a bout against Sir Walter and Sir John six years ago. Afterwards I was forced to flee and attempt to rebuild my fortunes. While I was abroad, she lost faith in me, thinking I would not return, and wedded Sir

Walter. I met her to try to persuade her to join me, but she wouldn't. She insisted that she had legally given her vows to this monster and wouldn't consider breaking them.'

Baldwin could see that his bloodshot eyes were fixed upon the woman now lying naked upon a cloak. The cruel sword-thrusts in her breast and flank showed all the more distinctly on her pale flesh. Next to her, the body of her husband was almost an anti-climax. The single broad puncture just under his ribs, where the sword blade had entered and pushed up through his lungs and heart, had ended his life as effectively as all the blows rained upon his wife. Baldwin had seen other men throw themselves upon their swords after losing a battle. He had never, so far as he could recollect, seen such a wound when murder had been committed.

Coroner Roger scowled at Sir Edmund. 'You deny murdering them?'

'I told you: I could never have harmed a hair of her head. I loved her more than I love myself.'

'Yet you were prepared to risk her honour by persuading her to leave her husband?'

'No. By persuading her to return to her real husband. Me.'

'It's too late to talk her round now,' Coroner Roger said, dragging a cloak over the dead woman's face. 'Your behaviour has been deplorable. This sort of hankering after another man's wife may be acceptable in France and other such places, but in this country it's not what we expect.'

Sir Edmund said nothing, staring as though transfixed by the sight of Lady Helen's corpse.

Baldwin cleared his throat. 'Surely, Coroner, the wounds are consistent with the husband killing his wife and then committing suicide?'

'Yes,' the Coroner grudgingly agreed. 'But what of the others?'

Baldwin drew his brows together before speaking. 'We know that Sir Walter owed money to Benjamin Dudenay. I think he might have become enraged with Benjamin and his accomplices.'

'Accomplices? What do you mean?'

'We have been told,' Baldwin said, speaking slowly so that the clerk could keep up as he took his notes, 'that Benjamin collaborated with the others in building their stands and tournaments. He provided the money, Hal the vision, and Wymond the building skills. In return, we have heard, Benjamin was often accorded the best positions for his money-lending stall. Most people thought it was so that unhorsed knights would go to him first – but I think that there was another reason.'

'Are you sure you are well, Sir Baldwin?' Lord Hugh called enquiringly. 'You had a severe fall yesterday.'

'I am fine, I thank you, my Lord,' Baldwin said irritably, continuing, 'The other reason was this: that Benjamin also arranged bets on the outcome of the courses. To know which man he would back, he wanted a good view of the course.'

'Nothing wrong with that,' Coroner Roger said.

'No. What was wrong was that Wymond and Hal had damaged some contestants' lances. They arranged the betting so that Benjamin could win almost every time.'

'How?' Coroner Roger grated. His face was growing darker with anger.

'Simple. When I arrived here, I noticed that Wymond was at the lances. Others we have spoken to saw him there. The night he died, he was there again. Why? I wondered.

Yesterday I was in the tilt, riding against Sir John. My first lance was fine, but the second felt odd, as though there was a weakness in it. I could do nothing about it, for then I was in the tilt, but that impression stayed with me.

'After the tilt, I found parts of my lance. It had been sawn through a short distance from the point. Whenever it touched a shield, it must shiver to pieces. That was what Benjamin was looking for. I think that Wymond used to mark certain lances so that Benjamin knew that the holder was at a disadvantage. He could find his mark, but the lance would break. Then his opponent's lance could unseat *him*. Benjamin would take bets and win.'

'But you say Wymond was at the lances even after Benjamin was dead?'

'Yes. Wymond was a devious character and a greedy one. I think he decided he'd not let an opportunity to make some money pass him by. He was going to run some bets for himself. He died before he could.'

'So at least that is ended.'

'Provided Mark Tyler is not allowed to continue,' Baldwin said.

'Explain!'

In answer, Baldwin looked over the crowds. He saw Tyler towards the back, slowly edging away. 'Tyler, come here.'

The King Herald reluctantly obeyed the command. There were too many people for him to be able to escape to safety. He walked stiff-backed to the front of the crowd and stood gazing about him with an air of superiority. 'Well?'

'Why did you command the pages and squires at the lance-rests to give me a lance with a red-painted mark at the handgrip?'

'Who says I did?'

'I do,' said Andrew, stepping forward. 'I was there at the rests and heard the order.'

'It was only that I thought the lances were straighter and more fair,' Tyler said quickly.

'Did you place bets on who would win the fight yesterday?' Baldwin guessed.

'I had no bets!'

'You ordered that I should be given a damaged lance. That could have been an act of murder.'

'I didn't think . . .' Tyler looked away, then past Baldwin to the Coroner. 'It has nothing to do with this. I will not answer any more questions.'

Baldwin eyed him with a sadness. 'The worst thing is that I couldn't understand before why Tyler here was so keen on accusing Simon and protecting Hal and Wymond. Now it is clear: Tyler was making money with them. How else could the position of Benjamin's stand be confirmed? Tyler confirmed it. Why? So that his own profits could be guaranteed. At every stage Tyler sought to ensure his own profit.'

'That's a lie!'

Coroner Roger nodded, then slowly and disdainfully turned his back on the herald. Facing Baldwin, he asked, 'What would this have to do with Sir Walter?'

'How would an honourable man feel if he has lost bets and later learns that it was entirely due to a usurer's double-dealing? Probably Sir Walter learned that Benjamin had won money by giving him damaged lances. Perhaps Benjamin bet against him himself and thus caused many of his debts? Either way, how would Sir Walter be likely to react? Naturally he killed first Benjamin, then Wymond and Hal.'

'And Sir William?'

Baldwin was silent, but at this point Andrew spoke up. 'I can answer that, Coroner. I knew Sir William. He tried to molest this woman Lady Helen in this very courtyard shortly after she had been seeing my master, Sir Edmund. No doubt she told her husband of her shame and horror at being so horribly grasped, and that was why he killed Sir William.'

'Do you have any witness to this?' Coroner Roger asked.

'Yes, Sir Roger. That servant there.'

Reluctantly Hugh nodded as Andrew pointed him out. 'Mmm. I saw it.'

'Was it a shameful ambush as Andrew implies?'

'That Sir William, he grappled with Lady Helen, told her to kiss him. Wouldn't leave her alone. I went to help her, 'cos she was a lady, and then she kneed him in the cods. That stopped him.'

'I see.' Coroner Roger passed a hand over his eyes. 'So it sounds as though the man had reason to want to murder them all. And he finished his rampage by slaughtering himself and his wife.'

At Baldwin's side, Simon had listened with astonishment. He had thought that there was nothing which could surprise him about the events at this tournament, but now he heard his own servant talk, he realised how little he had actually seen. Glancing away from the scene, he saw that Lord Hugh and Sir Peregrine were talking quietly. Sir Peregrine soon walked down the slope to the Coroner's side. Sir Roger looked at him irritably, then down at Sir Walter's body as the banneret muttered in his ear, and Simon saw the Coroner's eyes rise to meet Lord Hugh's wooden stare.

'I find that Sir Walter killed Benjamin Dudenay, Wymond Carpenter, Hal Sachevyll and Sir William of Crukerne before killing his wife and himself.'

While the Coroner declared his findings and began to itemise the taxes that would be levied upon the local people for harbouring the killer and seeing the King's Peace broken, Baldwin watched Lord Hugh up on the slope. He was aware of Simon behind him, but didn't move.

'Lord Hugh wants no more discussion or deliberation,' Simon said.

'No. He wants the whole affair ended. And Christ save the poor devil who tries to find out more – or who accidentally forces Lord Hugh to consider the murders again.'

'Why has he done this, do you think? Just because of the shame of seeing his tournament ruined?'

Baldwin sighed. 'Politics, that is why. Lord Hugh cannot afford to leave the King with the impression that his spies died because of their spying. No, Lord Hugh does not know why they died, but this explanation is convenient. The Coroner has recorded that Sir Walter killed them because of their gambling which stole some of his wealth. That suits Lord Hugh.'

His mood appeared gloomy – and oddly, Simon had the impression that he was holding something back. Possibly it was just because of the bruising from his fight. 'How are you feeling?'

'Battered, but all right apart from that,' Baldwin said shortly. He glanced about the courtyard. Seeing Sir Edmund, he said, 'Come with me a moment, Simon.'

Sir Edmund was still kneeling at Lady Helen's side, but as

419

Simon and Baldwin approached, he had got to his feet and was beginning to turn away.

'May we speak to you, Sir Edmund?' Baldwin called.

'If you must.' The knight's face was ravaged with grief and regret.

'I was sorry to hear of your love for the lady,' Baldwin said quietly 'It must have been a terrible shock to find that she had married while you were away.'

'What business is that of yours?' said Sir Edmund, passing a hand over his eyes.

'Sir Edmund, be easy,' Baldwin told him. 'I do not wish to offend.'

'Then be more careful with your words!'

'Naturally you are unhappy.'

'How would you feel? The only woman I ever loved is dead.'

'It is natural to be sad. It must have been an appalling shock.'

'She told me she had married Sir Walter and she wouldn't break her vows. I don't think she loved me any more!'

'You met her here, didn't you?'

'It was not easy, but yes, we met a couple of times. I persuaded her to meet me. First on the night that Hal was killed, and then on the night that Sir William died. I used Andrew as my emissary, and he looked after her, made sure no one else saw her with me.'

'How did you arrange that?'

'Easily enough. We waited until the bulk of the men in the hall were drunk, when the noise from the musicians and dancers had grown loud. Then we could wander in the dark outside.'

'Didn't Sir Walter notice his wife's absence?' Baldwin asked with surprise. Sir Walter had not seemed the sort of man to be tolerant of a wife's nocturnal meanderings.

'He drank heavily. She left him when he was largely pissed, but she said he always remained at table while other knights stayed. He wouldn't get up in case others thought him weak with wine. She could judge how much more he would drink and made sure she was in the tent before he returned from the hall.'

Baldwin nodded. 'Andrew brought her to you.'

'Yes. Both nights.'

'To ensure your privacy?'

'I didn't want some scruffy churl turning up and interrupting us.'

'Like her husband?' Baldwin said wryly.

After a moment Sir Edmund burst out, 'I could have made her happy – I could! That braggart, that swaggering swine, was no good for her. How could he be? She was constantly on her guard. She couldn't love *him*. Jesu! A filthy moron like him? Whereas I would have wrestled a dragon barehanded to prove my love for her. What more could a knight do? Yet I have lost her, this time for ever. Now *I* am lost.'

'There is always hope, my friend,' Baldwin said compassionately. 'I lost a lord when I was younger, and thought my life was over, but now I have a wife and child and a new lord. There is always hope.'

'Perhaps for you.'

'And for Andrew.'

'Yes, for him too.'

Baldwin paused. 'Did Andrew tell you about Squire William's attack on Lady Helen?'

'No. If I had heard, that young man would have regretted his foul impertinence.'

Simon was peering at him in concentration. 'Sir Edmund, on the night William died, what of him? Did you see him?'

'He walked off after the singer. That was the last I saw of him.'

'Odo the Herald, you mean?' Baldwin asked, surprised.

'Him, yes.'

'What then?'

'I returned to the hall. If I am honest, I'd have liked to have met Sir Walter so I could kill him and win her back. But I didn't.'

'And William?'

'I expect he was up here at the castle with Odo. If you want to confirm it, ask your own servant, Bailiff, he was there too. *I* could not have killed Sir William.'

Simon nodded. He would trust Hugh's word. 'Did you see anything else?'

'One thing. I saw Odo return to the hall a while later. I know it was not long after, for I had only just grabbed a pot of wine from the bar. In that time Odo came back in.'

'A herald could walk about the field with ease,' Simon noted, looking at Baldwin.

Baldwin nodded. 'And if he needed to conceal himself, all he need do would be to pull off his tabard and pull on a scruffy tunic. Do you remember saying you thought Sir Walter was a villein because he was dressed in so shabby a manner? Well, Odo could hide his identity swiftly.'

'Why should he wish to kill, though?' Simon asked. 'What was his motive?'

Baldwin turned to Sir Edmund again. 'You said you first met Odo in Europe?'

'Yes. He was there as herald at various places. I learned to trust him.'

'I recall you told me you met him again in Exeter. Was that while the King's Justices held their court?'

'Yes. It was good to see a familiar face down here. He was delivering the first of the invitations to this tournament. I met him in a tavern and asked him to ensure that I was invited here.'

'I see. When you first met abroad, did he say why he had left England?'

'He wanted to forget a terrible experience, he said. In fact, he said he almost had. He joked about it. Said that when he left England he had been a great portly fellow, but with every pound in weight he lost, he felt as if he was shedding memories as well.'

'And when did you meet him?'

'When?' The knight thought for a moment. 'Before I met Andrew, I suppose, so it would have been during my first year abroad. Yes, it must have been 1317.'

'And he had himself only recently arrived just then?'

Sir Edmund drew his brows together. 'I don't know who told you that. I recall him saying he'd been there for some years already. Yes – that was why he spoke about his weight. He said that it was dropping each year while he lived in France.'

'I thank you for your help,' Baldwin said and walked with Simon back to the hall's doorway with a faint smile of understanding illuminating his features.

*   *   *

Lord Hugh was back in his stand at the lists with Sir Peregrine at his side when Baldwin and Simon arrived at the foot of the stage. Neither the Lord nor the banneret looked at them.

It was fine. Baldwin could wait. The rumbling warned him of another encounter, and he looked up in time to see two knights meet. There was a shattering of lances, and the two rode apart, each waving their broken weapons.

Baldwin sometimes wished life could be as simple. You chose a course and charged, and the stronger man would win. That was how life should be, he thought. And yet it so often wasn't, for politics always got in the way. Politics soured everything and politicians were the lowest slugs Baldwin could think of.

And one of the lowest, he privately maintained, was Sir Peregrine of Barnstaple. He almost groaned aloud when the latter caught his eye and started towards him. Baldwin was suddenly struck with a sense of irresolution. He knew what he should do, he should ignore Sir Peregrine, but right now he was tired of fighting and mendaciousness. It was tempting to simply leave.

'Sir Baldwin. You look like a man who has a desire to speak to someone?'

'I wanted a word with Lord Hugh.'

'Yes, I thought you did,' Sir Peregrine said.

'It is about the dead spies,' Baldwin began tiredly.

'And you think he'll want to hear about them?'

'I am not sure. Perhaps he already knew what they were doing.'

'Oh, he knew. I told you: that's why they were here.'

Simon nodded. 'They were here so that Lord Hugh could keep an eye on them.'

Sir Peregrine led them out of earshot of the stands. 'We've known for some time that the King had spies in our household and we guessed who they were when Benjamin tried to bribe a groom – fortunately loyal to us – to report to him. It was but a short leap to see that his friends were probably helpers too. So then we identified Hal and Wymond.'

'So Lord Hugh had them brought here to have them assassinated?' Simon asked hotly.

'No, Simon,' Baldwin said. 'That wasn't in his interests. Now that the trio are dead, the King will send more. If the others had survived, Lord Hugh could have carried on feeding them with the information he wanted the King to hear. Edward learned only that which was good for Lord Hugh.'

'And good for the King,' Sir Peregrine said imperturbably. 'Naturally Lord Hugh and I want only what's in the King's interests.'

'Whereas now the King will send more people and you won't know who they are.'

'It doesn't worry us. We have nothing to hide from our monarch,' said Sir Peregrine silkily.

'I do not blame Lord Hugh for stopping the enquiry into Sir Walter's death,' said Baldwin. 'It could have been embarrassing, having the motives of a man who had killed the King's own spies investigated.'

'Of course there was no indication that anyone else could have destroyed Hal or Wymond,' Sir Peregrine countered.

'No, but Lord Hugh must have suspected someone else, someone who was on his side,' Baldwin said and glanced up at the impassive-faced baron above him. 'Lord Hugh made his decision and acted upon it. He obviously believes someone else killed the three, and has chosen to protect the man.

If he had not, the King would have wondered why his spies should have died while under Lord Hugh's protection. When an easier solution was offered by Sir Roger, suggesting that Sir Walter was the guilty man, Lord Hugh grasped it with both hands.'

Sir Peregrine smiled but made no comment. He walked back to the stand. At the stairs, he turned again and faced Baldwin. 'You know, I didn't touch them – for the simple reason that you have already mentioned: I wanted to know who the enemies were in my camp. Now I'll have to start all over again.'

'Did you owe money to Benjamin as well, Sir Peregrine?' Baldwin rasped.

The man laughed aloud. 'I owe no one money. I serve my lord and all my wants are supplied by him. No, I have no interest in money.' He turned and climbed aloft to rejoin his master.

'Do you think he did it?' Simon said.

'Him?' Baldwin appeared surprised that Simon should have asked. 'No! As he said, he stood to gain nothing. The man who did it was one who had every reason to go through with his crimes.'

'Odo?'

'Yes. All the knights and squires would have been dressed in their richest clothing. They would have stood out wherever they went, but Odo? He would only have to change one garment – and even you would mistake him. The drunk you saw on the day we found Sachevyll's body – could that have been Odo?'

'Surely I couldn't mistake him,' Simon said doubtfully.

'You managed to mistake Sir Walter when he walked with his wife. If Odo was out of his uniform it would be easy to think him a mere churl.'

'It's not proof, though. A knight could doff his tunic.'

'We know that Sir Edmund said Odo reappeared shortly after, leaving with William following him. That is what made me wonder. Who else could have changed so swiftly? These murders surely happened quickly – yet all the knights are wearing their finery. They have on their best shirts, cloaks, coats. Even if one of them discarded his clean, best outer garments, surely a watchman would see the clean linen of a shirt, or the shine of silk? Yet Odo has only cheap shirts and hose. He would fit in with the tattiest fair-goer.'

'You have more evidence, don't you?'

Baldwin gave a dry chuckle. 'Yes. Andrew used to be a Templar. I spoke to him after the *hastilude*.'

'Oh,' Simon said doubtfully. He knew of Baldwin's past. 'You're sure you're not being swayed by the words of a comrade-in-arms?'

'No, Simon. I never knew Andrew in the Order. But I do know that I can trust the word of a man who served in the Templars.'

'He was there at the river with his master and Lady Helen?'

'Yes, on the night when Sir William died and the night before. More: Andrew knows no reason why Sir Edmund should wish to harm Hal or Wymond. And one last thing, we still do not know who could have harmed Benjamin. You recall Coroner Roger telling us that there was a court, and that the knights were all there?'

'Yes.'

'Andrew saw Odo there, at Exeter. To my shame I never considered the herald as a possible culprit, but now I know that he was there when Benjamin was murdered.'

'Why should he want to kill Dudenay?'

'It's no secret that the banker was in business with Wymond and Hal, is it? Tyrel would have known who funded the stands and stood to make money from the use of shoddy materials, just as he would have known who built them and who designed them.'

'Who is this Tyrel? Does Odo have another name?' Simon shot his friend a puzzled glance.

Baldwin gave a quiet smile. 'Let us talk to him. I shall explain then.'

Baldwin walked along the line of the stand and at the first opportunity, he gestured to Odo. The herald trotted over to them.

'So it was Odo all along,' Simon breathed. Yet he had liked the man – still did.

'You are wrong, Simon,' Baldwin said forcefully as Odo dropped from his horse and tethered it to the stand. 'Our friend the herald has no reason to want to hurt anyone. Odo is an honourable servant of Lord Hugh. Calm, decent and a good *diseur*. He simply could not commit murder.'

Simon burst out with frustration, 'Then, by Saint Paul, who the hell did?'

CHAPTER THIRTY-ONE

Odo was tired of the continual deception. His head ached as though it did in reality contain the thoughts of two souls. Noticing the two grim-faced men walking towards him, he set his jaw, but without truculence. It would almost be a relief to confess at last. 'Do you mean to accuse me?' he said immediately.

Baldwin studied his pale and drawn features for a while. 'No, my friend,' he said gently. 'I wish you to hear a story – and please do not comment until I am done. It is a long tale, but a good one for a herald to consider. It may have merit and deserve to be retold.'

'What is this tale?'

Baldwin considered the ground at his feet, then put his arms behind his back and strolled slowly away from the crowds and any others who might overhear. Odo was grateful. It could have been embarrassing for him if someone like Tyler was to eavesdrop. He was so taken up in his reflections that he hardly heard Baldwin begin to talk.

'In 1306 there was a great tournament at Exeter. It was a marvellous show, with people coming from all about. Many of those who came to watch would normally have led quite workaday lives, and seeing the pageantry and excess would be an occasion of great excitement. Among those present was a merchant who had decided to bring his young family to watch. A certain Master Tyrel.'

'Yes. And a stand collapsed while Sir Richard's mother watched her husband fight with Sir John,' Simon said officiously, breaking the flow of Baldwin's story.

'No. Lady Alice's mother watched *her* husband fight and die.'

'But Sir Richard told me . . .' Simon frowned. 'You mean Sir Richard was illegitimate?'

'Yes. Sir Godwin was a cheery fellow, very keen on exercising his skills in courtly love. You recall Sir John accused him of cuckolding him? He was not without reason. But be that as it may, the stand collapsed and many died. In particular, one family perished called Tyrel. A mother, daughter, son – but not the father.

'He was a large, bearded man – strong and powerful. And when the stand collapsed, I imagine that he tore his great sinews as he tried to free his loved ones. Tried to save them. He probably has a faint humped back even now. Not that he could achieve much. They, along with others, were all dead.

'So he lost his mind. He left England and sought death, in whatever way he could find it. He travelled widely and learned songs, and because of them he became a herald. Lords are always looking out for a man who can recognise arms and who can sing or play instruments. Someone who was also an educated man who had skills as a merchant would be a godsend.'

'But since he was no longer Tyrel the family man, he became Odo the herald,' Simon breathed.

Odo dropped his head. All the protestations that he had intended to use to assert his innocence were stifled. He was sick of lies and inventions. If Sir Baldwin wished to accuse him, he would accept God's fate.

But Baldwin looked at Simon pointedly. 'No, no. I am sure that this man Tyrel remains in France – if he is still alive, of course, which I strongly doubt. I was simply telling you the background to the events here. The Coroner has made his conclusion. There is no point in having him alter it, is there?'

Odo shot him a stunned look. If he had suddenly been struck by a bowl of pottage he could not have been more surprised. 'I . . .' He snapped his mouth closed again, deciding to obey Baldwin's instruction and listen.

Simon growled, 'You mean you'd let him go free? He's murdered four people!'

'Odo the herald has killed no one, Simon,' Baldwin said. 'Odo has no interest in something that happened so long ago. But if Tyrel were to come back and avenge his family, I would not condemn him – would you? If someone had killed Margaret and Edith and the baby in front of you, Simon, would you rest? Ever? Or would you seek out the murderer and execute him?'

Simon considered. In his mind he could see his wife, Meg, laughing in the sun with their children, a competent and beautiful mother; he could see her in bed, writhing against him as they made love; he could see his daughter running happily, giggling, through the long grasses of a meadow. Then he was silent a long while, thinking. At last he cast a look back towards the stands, seeking his wife's face in the crowd. 'I think I am glad that Odo is not related to Tyrel,' he said gruffly.

'So am I,' Baldwin said, his voice hard. 'I hate to think what *I* would do if I were in his position. Bludgeoning men to death in payment for crushing his family to death so long ago seems strangely kind compared to what I would have done . . . What do you think, Odo?'

'Me, sir?'

'What do you think has happened to this Tyrel? Is he alive and nursing his desire for revenge – or is he now dead at last?'

Odo felt a heaviness leave him. It was as if sixteen years of bitterness and torment had sloughed from his shoulders. Suddenly he felt lighter, *free*. 'Sir Baldwin, I think Tyrel is dead. I think he died recently and will never return.'

'May he rest in peace.'

The next day was the finale of the tournament – a massive *mêlée* in which all the knights not already too wounded to take part, rode into the fighting area and fought to a standstill through a sweltering sunny day.

Simon watched unimpressed as knights and senior squires traded blows in a rising mist of dust. Every so often there would be a louder ringing sound as a hollow piece of steel was struck, and then the noise was deafening, but he could see that Baldwin was as bored as he was. It was tedious after the excitement of the last days. The only man worth watching was Squire Andrew, who darted about with flashing weapons like a man half his age.

When he looked at his daughter, he could see that she was uninterested, too. Since the death of her lover, Edith had been overcome with mourning, and she had no desire to witness another brawl.

'Simon?' Baldwin whispered in his ear. 'Could I borrow Hugh for a minute or two?'

'Yes, of course. And try to send him back in a better frame of mind. If Edith's pissed off, Hugh thinks his world has fallen apart.'

Baldwin grinned. 'I'll do my best.'

He stood at the back of the stand while Hugh came down the steps, and then Baldwin led the way out to the river. He sat on a fallen tree-trunk and motioned to Hugh to sit. There was a jug of ale and one of watered wine waiting and Baldwin passed Hugh the ale.

'The murderer was not Sir Walter, Hugh. Sir Walter was a lunatic who decided to kill himself because he was consumed by jealousy, but he had no need to kill Sir William.'

'Maybe he heard what I saw – Sir William with his wife?' Hugh tried hopefully.

'Do you think so?' Baldwin asked pointedly.

Hugh stared morosely at the ground and said nothing.

Eyeing him, Baldwin took a deep swig of wine and swilled it about his mouth. 'The man who killed William was more likely someone who wanted to protect somebody. Now who could that be? I consider it from this way. If someone was to threaten to hurt my daughter, I would stop them. If they tried to molest or rape her, I would kill them and I would have no compunction whatsoever about doing so. Any father who would *not* kill to protect his daughter would be no father. And if I was not there, Edgar would do so in my place, and I would protect him in the courts and elsewhere if he was put to trial because he would be looking after my family as my servant should. Any servant who loves his master would do the same.'

Hugh looked up. For once he met Baldwin's gaze. 'You know?'

'That the fellow threatened to ruin Edith, threatened to make her unmarriageable, and you heard it? Yes. I think you sought to protect her the only way you knew.'

'Not only that. I saw him pawing that Lady Helen, too. I thought of my wife. *She* was messed about by her man. If I hadn't been there, what might have become of her? I couldn't let that happen to Edith, oh no – but here he was, making her go all wobbly over him while he was planning to marry one woman and then trying it on with another.'

'I understand,' Baldwin nodded. 'It was as I thought.'

Hugh sank his head lower. 'What will you do?'

'Me? There have been enough deaths already, Hugh. I shall do nothing.'

'You mean it, sir?'

'Finish your ale, Master Hugh. You are a good, loyal servant. My own concern is, should I tell Simon? You risked your life for his daughter. He would be grateful.'

Hugh considered. 'Be best if you didn't, I reckon. He'd have to keep it from Edith. She'd be terrible upset to find out. Probably hate me, too. My master, he's not good at keeping secrets from her.'

'Then I shall not tell him.'

They sat companionably for a while. Soon Hugh gruffly announced that he should return to his work and drained his jug. He gave a grunt of gratitude, opened his mouth as if he had more to say, but then thought better of it and shook his head.

Baldwin watched him slouch away, then put his hands behind his head and stared down at the water.

He was sad that the tournament had been so dismal an event for Simon; he would have wished that his friend could look back on it with pride, but that was impossible. At least he could keep the truth about Sir William's death secret. It would be unfair to expect Simon to conceal it from his daughter, and revealing the facts could only result in great upset for everyone.

If it was him in Simon's position, he wondered, would he have preferred to know? He had a daughter now, a young child who would perhaps grow to be as difficult a teenager as Edith. Would he want to be secured from the truth about Edgar, should Edgar kill a man to protect her?

There were times when ignorance was preferable to knowledge, he decided.

From the tilt-area there came a raucous shout and a clattering of iron. A man had been thrust from his horse. Baldwin glanced back. It was tempting to return and witness the end of the displays, but he was overcome with a lassitude that prevented his rising.

No, he thought. The *hastilude* was for younger men. It was no place for an old knight like him.

Perhaps his own time was past. Younger fellows like Sir William seemed to hold little regard for the female sex. They bragged about their conquests (whether real or imagined), they boasted and insulted women to their face. Women of all ages and classes – even ladies – were violated to satisfy their lusts. Was this a country in which to raise a young daughter?

Could his own little girl be raped before she was yet twenty by some callow fool like William?

Perhaps, he allowed.

But not while he or his own servant Edgar had breath in their bodies.

Sir Baldwin rode along the deeply rutted roadway from Crediton to Cadbury with a feeling of growing pleasure. As they came to the top of the hill before his home, he left his men with the carts and clapped spurs to his mount, cantering down the hillside, then turning off the road to gallop along the meadows.

The sun was high overhead and it was a pleasure to feel the warmth on his back as the wind whistled in his ears. His horse cantered sure-footedly down through the long grasses, and Baldwin could see all about him that nothing had changed. His peasants worked in the fields, amid long rows of crops, while others watched geese or lambs in meadows.

Somehow Baldwin felt that the scene should have changed. So much had happened since his departure to go to the jousting, so many deaths, that Baldwin thought his own home might have been altered.

When he left Lord Hugh, Baldwin had seen much that he could be glad about. After admitting to his offences with the lances, Mark Tyler had departed to travel over Europe, leaving Odo as the new King Herald in Lord Hugh's household. Baldwin was sure that the quiet, contemplative herald would be a better man than Tyler at the job. Also, just before leaving Oakhampton, Baldwin had watched as Lord Hugh sought to replenish his forces, making good the loss of Sir John and his son. Baldwin had spoken to Sir Peregrine about the matter, and had been pleased to witness both Sir Edmund and Andrew kneeling before Lord Hugh and holding up their hands, palms together, while he placed his own about them and took their oaths of service. Sir Edmund was safe for now, and Squire Andrew was created Sir Andrew, a knight in his own right, with a small manor granted to him.

Baldwin was pleased for Andrew. The squire had lived in fear and obscurity for too long: Pope Clement V and the French King Philip IV were both dead now, but together had seen to the destruction of the Knights Templar purely to satisfy their own greed. But even after death both had long arms, and their legacy remained. After the absurd accusations of sodomy and cannibalism, to be known as a Templar was still to risk imprisonment or worse.

That was the cause of Andrew's suspicion of strangers, the reason why he avoided those whom he did not know. He was in constant fear of his life.

It was good to see that he was at last brought back into the fold, that he could become a knight within Lord Hugh's host. Baldwin was convinced that he would prove to be a worthwhile servant. Certainly his fighting skills were beyond reproach – he had not forgotten the techniques learned with the Templars.

And Baldwin was glad to see that Andrew had been gently, almost shyly, paying court to Alice. She was still terribly affected by Geoffrey's death, but she appeared to take some comfort in Andrew's obvious sympathy and compassion, and Baldwin hoped she might soon get over the loss of her husband and pay attention to Andrew – once a suitable period of mourning had passed, of course.

But then Baldwin smiled. He could never believe that a Templar could make a bad husband, friend or ally. To him, all Templars were perfect.

He was almost at the door, and reined in to slow his horse. All about him, birds called and trilled, there was the noise of animals from the yards, pastures and from the stables behind the house. Barking showed that his hounds and guard-dogs had heard his approach. Baldwin smiled to himself as the door opened to display a wary eye. An older servant had been instructed to protect Lady Jeanne with his life and Baldwin was pleased to see that the fellow obeyed so well.

And then Jeanne herself came bursting from the house.

Baldwin swung himself from his saddle and grasped her, kissing her and feeling once more that he was the luckiest man on earth to have been able to marry her.

Yet he was still aware of the sense that something was different. *He* felt different. His house, his home, might be unchanged to the naked eye, but there was something that was profoundly altered.

He realised what it was as his daughter began a loud crying from inside the house. That shrill mewling made Jeanne wince but it only made him smile and grip her in a tight embrace.

Suddenly he realised that he was coming home not only to a wife, but to a family.

His family. And he would protect it as selflessly as ever Odo had.

Sir Edmund sat before the fire at Oakhampton Castle and drained his cup.

He was grateful to Lord Hugh for taking him on, although he knew it was a matter of simple necessity. Lord Hugh needed all the loyal vassals he could gain in these uncertain times. War was near, if the rumours were true. Many magnates were appalled at the execution of Earl Thomas after Boroughbridge, and still more horrified by the encroaching greed of the Despensers.

Yet his life felt empty. Warfare and chivalry were not enough. He craved the companionship of a woman.

It was hard to believe that she was gone. All through the years he had thought that he might somehow be able to win her back. After the disaster at the hands of Sir John he had thought that she would wait for him, but she hadn't. And then he had learned that she had married that oaf. The murderous bastard.

Reaching for the jug, Sir Edmund poured a fresh cup of wine and sipped.

Sir Walter had been an evil brute – and yet he must have had some feelings for his wife. He didn't go and murder her straight after hearing the Bailiff question the groom, but instead he walked to a tavern and sat drinking in melancholy mood. Andrew had asked about the town afterwards and spoke to the host of the inn where Sir Walter drank. It appeared that the knight had remained there until long after dusk.

Of course Sir Edmund knew what had happened afterwards. Lady Helen returned to her tent to find her husband in a furious temper, inflamed with wine. He accused her of infidelity, then rushed at her and slaughtered her in a frenzy.

Sir Edmund flinched as he recalled the sound of the sword striking her body. He had been standing outside, having just bidden her farewell, and was feeling lost, wondering how he could live knowing that his Helen was married to another man, that she did not love him any more, when he heard the hissed curse and screams, the damp slap of sword cleaving flesh. When he realised what it meant, and without pausing to draw his own sword, he rushed inside, concerned only for Helen.

His beautiful Helen lay slumped, dead on her bed – and without a moment's hestitation, Edmund snatched the sword from Sir Walter and thrust it up deep into the man's chest. Sir Walter fell and, sobbing harshly, Sir Edmund dropped to Helen's side, kissing her, trying to bring her back, but she was gone. He stayed there until the middle of the night, but as her body cooled, Squire Andrew found him and persuaded him to leave that slaughterhouse. There was no point calling attention to the bodies: that could have led to suspicion falling on Sir Edmund. They left the tent, Sir Edmund walking dazedly with his despair, back to their own pavilion, only realising when they arrived that Sir Edmund was splattered all over with Helen's blood. It was Andrew who gently washed his master's face and hands, tearing off the hideously stained tunic and setting it aside to be burned.

Yet even as Andrew rinsed away her blood with the chill water of the river, Sir Edmund had seen with his mind's eye not the corpse of his lover, but the curious dullness in the eyes of Sir Walter as Edmund shoved the blade into his chest. It was as though Sir Walter was already in Hell, as if he was grateful for the final blow.

Perhaps he truly had loved her in his own way.

Michael Jecks

Master of the Medieval Murder Mystery

Discover more about the exciting world of the Knights Templar at

www.MichaelJecks.com

Sign up for the newsletter to keep up to date with latest developments

Connect with Michael Jecks on Facebook

www.facebook.com/Michael.Jecks.author

Michael Jecks
Templar's Acre

The Holy Land, 1291.

A war has been raging across these lands for decades. The forces of the Crusaders have been pushed back again and again by the Muslims and now just one city remains in Crusader control. That one city stands between the past and the future. One city which must be defended at all costs. That city is Acre.

Into this battle where men will fight to the death to defend their city comes a young boy. Green and scared, he has never seen battle before. But he is on the run from a dark past and he has no choice but to stay. And to stay means to fight. That boy is Baldwin de Furnshill.

This is the story of the siege of Acre, and of the moment Baldwin first charged into battle.

This is just the beginning. The rest is history.

Hardback ISBN 978-0-85720-517-9
Ebook ISBN 978-0-85720-520-9